Just off the Great North Road

by

Hugh Chare

Publication Data

Just off the Great North Road © Copyright Hugh B. Chare 2008

Book and Cover design by Hugh B. Chare.
ISBN: 978-0-9824184-2-0

 Kilihune Books

The James Martin series
African Encounter
Across the Zambezi
Just off the Great North Road
Well, there you go!
Back to Africa
The Sagitta Mishap
Flight 5 to Johannesburg

Marieke Englebrecht mysteries
Death in the Mopane
Revenge after twenty years

Other books
The journal of Jan Englebrecht
British Spy in the Bushveld
Federica

Preface

This novel is set in the early 1970s, in the period shortly following the independence of most of the previous colonial territories in Africa. Attitudes of some of the people of that era were often extreme and would today be regarded as distasteful, abhorrent and bigoted. Racial slurs and ethnic terms of that era have been retained for the sake of authenticity, but should in no way be regarded as reflecting the opinions and views of the author.

As Zimbabwe had not yet achieved full self-determination, the names of towns and cities used under the Rhodesian regime have been retained. Similarly, place names in South Africa have been kept as they were in that period.

This is a work of fiction. Names, characters, businesses and incidents are fictional except for obvious references to historical figures or events. Any resemblance in the featured characters to actual persons, living or dead, is purely coincidental.

My thanks to all those who patiently answered my questions, including Jim Davies, British Airways Archive & Museum, Gert Victor, Spoornet, Eurika Deminey, Transnet Heritage Library, Ian MacGregor, Met Office Archives, Simon Wenham, Salters Steamers, Vladimir Bessarabov, United Nations, map section, Professor Jamie Monson, Carleton University, Patricia Collado, Kodak, David Lang, Bucyrus International, Paul Chare and Andrew Coates.

Contents

Rooibos and Marie biscuits

"James, what do I need to take to wear in the UK?" Katrina asked.

"Well, it's late September, or will be when we get there, so something warm as well as your normal clothes," he replied.

"Go over the plan again, please?" she asked.

"Tomorrow we fly from Ndola to Lusaka, then to Blantyre, then on to Jo'burg and finally to Cape Town. We spend almost two weeks with your folks in Calitzdorp, then we take the train from Beaufort West to Jo'burg, then fly to London. We spend about two weeks with my folks in Cores End, then fly home through Lusaka to Ndola," James replied, doing his travel agent bit.

"And, Attie is taking us to Ndola and looking after the house while we're gone?" she asked, seeking confirmation.

"Yes, he should be here shortly to see if there's anything we've forgotten to do before we go. He'll be in plenty of time tomorrow to take us to the airport at Ndola," James confirmed.

"I'm nervous about meeting your folks, James; do you think they'll like me? Do you think your mother will have forgiven you for not marrying an English girl?" she asked.

"Who knows? Who cares? Who could not like you?" he asked in return.

James and Katrina Martin were preparing to take their first long leave in September of 1972 after James had worked a three-year contract on a copper mine on the Zambian Copperbelt. He had signed on for a contract extension, so they were now due a holiday. There had been some aggravation because the mine management had at first baulked about giving him two tickets, because he had married Katrina in the first year of his contract in Zambia, and they argued that, because she had not been part of his original outbound travel, she was not due a leave passage. James had argued, and they had backed down and agreed, making it part of his new contract.

Attie arrived and went through with them what needed to be done for the next month. There was nothing of great consequence. One of the benefits of mine housing was that most household-related expenses were deducted directly from one's pay, so no rent to remember to pay. Attie promised to return on the morrow and deliver them to the airport in Ndola in time to catch the plane.

Katrina then talked to Gibson, their houseboy and gave him his pay for the month and his leave allowance. Gibson would be staying some of the time while Attie was in the house, and then he would be taking a trip with his family to visit relatives. He was most concerned that they would actually be coming back and wanted to know exactly the day and time that they would be arriving. Katrina reassured him and gave him a calendar with the days marked so that he knew where they would be for the entire month.

Katrina had obtained British Citizenship by virtue of her marriage to James. That had been a relatively simple process. They had gone to Lusaka with a copy of their marriage certificate, registered their marriage with the Brits and filled out the paperwork to get citizenship for Katrina. They had gone again, this time to swear fealty to Elizabeth Regina and get the paper. The British High Commission had then issued a passport the next day. Getting around on a British passport was much simpler than trying to deal with the difficulties raised with a South African passport. James had also made sure that his work permit extension covered Katrina so that they could both return. As for money, exchange control restrictions limited the amount of money they could take out of the country, but James felt that they had enough. He had been due three months' leave, but had cashed in two months' worth to give them more spending money in the UK.

The following day, Attie came to collect them. They said goodbye to Gibson and promised to bring him something back from England. Once at the Ndola airport, they checked in and were told that they had to change planes in Lusaka and Blantyre, something they already knew! The flight to Lusaka was a quick thirty minutes, and to Blantyre another hour. There, the layover was not too long before they caught the next flight to Johannesburg. Once in the Jan Smuts airport, they had to deal with customs and immigration. Katrina, as South African born was admitted indefinitely, and James was given a temporary residence permit for a month, more than enough time for their visit.

Unfortunately, South African Airways was not as organised as it could have been, and the flight to Cape Town was delayed. Instead of leaving at three as scheduled, the flight did not get away until five, which put them into Cape Town closer to seven in the evening. Koos and Sussana Englebrecht, Katrina's parents, were there to meet them; in fact, they had been there for a while, as South African had not bothered to let anyone know that the flight was delayed. Koos had decided, as they were so late, that he did not want to drive to Calitzdorp that night, so had booked them into a hotel.

The big topic of conversation over dinner was the killing of the Israeli athletes at the Munich Olympics by the Black September group. Sussana was more worried that the reaction to the events could cause difficulties for travel for Katrina and James. As they would be flying to London, albeit via Nairobi, James did not think that there would be any impact, but it was wise to be aware and alert. The bigger problem over time was going to be the Israeli reaction to the events and what kind of retribution they would exact. They were not known for turning the other cheek, and further bloodshed could be expected as time passed.

The following day, they drove to Calitzdorp. James had wondered if they would take part of the route he had been on three years earlier, through George and then inland through Willowmore, bypassing Oudtshoorn. Koos chose, instead, to go via Worcester, Touws River and Lainsburg. From Worcester to Touws River, Koos drove them through the Hex River valley, and James was amazed at the extent of the grape vineyards that they passed along the way. Koos told him that much of what he saw was grapes for the table and not for making wine, unlike his own vines, which were specifically for wine.

Touws River was a good place to take a lunch break. It was just about the halfway mark on the trip, and a large enough town to offer a choice of eating places. After lunch, they went on to Lainsburg, where they left the main road and made their way through the mountains towards Calitzdorp. Koos told James that they had a choice of routes: to go via Ladismith or cross the Seweweekspoort pass through the Swartberge. James opted for the latter and was rewarded with a spectacular trip over the mountain pass. Koos was busy pointing out landmarks and mountain peaks when James heard a name that intrigued him.

"Did you just say Mount Ararat?" he asked.

"*Ja*, it's one of the peaks at the extreme western end of the Outeniekwa range," replied Koos.

"But, isn't Mount Ararat in modern-day Turkey?"

"*Ja*, but that didn't stop the old *trekkers* from giving it the same name. Most of them only had one book, and that was their version of the Bible," elaborated Koos.

Before they actually got into the town of Calitzdorp, Koos turned off the road and took a small side track that led to their estate. James was not actually sure what to call it. It was not a farm in his sense of the word, no animals or crops, except for grapes and some other fruit trees and a kitchen garden. He supposed that he should probably call it a vineyard, but it seemed much more. The main house was of the Cape Dutch style that he had seen many times on the trip from Cape Town, and the other buildings matched, except for one modern-looking barn.

There were no packs of dogs to meet them, unlike their farm in Zambia, where James had first met the Englebrechts, only one Ridgeback cross who came out to meet the car and see who everybody was.

"We'll have to get our own bags," commented Koos. "This place is different to Zambia. I haven't found any *kaffirs* that I really like yet, so I have only the farm hands and one maid who travels in most days."

"*Partykeer wens ek dat ons nie verhuis het nie!*" said Sussana. "*Die Regering is skynbaar vasberad om ons lewe moeilik te maak, nie net vir ons nie, maar ook vir die Kaffirs.*"

"*Ons sal aanpas,*" said Koos. "*Alles sal reg kom.*"

"*Is dit so sleg?*" asked Katrina.

"*Nie regtig nie,*" her mother replied. "*Meestal is dit anders en ons het dit moeilik gevind om aan al die verdomde Regerings se veranderings aan te pas.*"

"Well, the place looks nice enough," commented James, who had been trying to follow this exchange with only very limited success and who never actually worked out what they had been saying. "Can you make a living here?"

"*Ag* man, yes" replied Koos. "We're actually doing well, but it is only hard work. I never did so much myself in my whole life."

"That's because you won't hire more people," commented Sussana.

"No, why should I?" asked Koos. "I haven't found many yet that I feel I can trust. I picked up only those who were already associated with the place and we manage; although, there are times when we have to pick the grapes that we could use more help."

James took the bags into the house, and Sussana showed him where he and Katrina were staying. The room was nice, large and airy with a vaulted ceiling that exposed the rafters. The view from the window was of the mountains to the west across the Gamka River.

"Man, I'll bet this place could only get cold in the winter," commented Katrina as she followed James into the room. "No wonder there is a fireplace."

"Do you really think so?" asked James.

"*Ja,* didn't you say that you saw snow when you first arrived?"

"True, and I suppose that wasn't so far from here," admitted James.

There was a gentle knock on the door. Katrina answered, "*Kom.*"

Sussana opened the door and asked, "*Sal jy tee of koffie neem?*"

"*Tee, asseblief,*" answered Katrina.

"Okay, *drie minute,*" promised Sussana, closing the door again.

"So, we get tea in three minutes, right?" asked James.

"Right, *kom ons ry ou man,*" Katrina said as she pulled him out of the room.

Tea was served on the *stoep* with some flattish-looking biscuits. James tasted it and it was different.

"What kind of tea is this?" he asked.

5

"It's *rooibos*, you never had *rooibos*?" asked Katrina.

"No, never. What kind of tea is it?"

"No, man, it's not really tea," explained Sussana. "It comes from the *rooibos*, which grows around here."

"*Rooibos*, let's see, red bush?"

"Right," agreed Katrina. "I grew up drinking this at boarding school."

"And the biscuits?" asked James.

"Marie biscuits, *kyk man*, it says on them, Marie," commented Katrina.

"I suppose you grew up on these as well?"

"Everyone in South Africa knows Marie biscuits, and you must have seen them sometimes in Zambia," said Sussana. "Lots of people drink *rooibos* tea with Marie biscuits, particularly around here."

"Tomorrow we'll show you around the farm," promised Koos. "Then later we'll have a *braai* and you can meet the other members of the family who live in the Cape."

Sunrise does not come too early in Calitzdorp in September, not until around six-thirty, and even then, on the valley floor where they were, it was a while before they actually saw the sun. However, judging by the sounds coming from the yard, there was already activity on the farm. Sussana came to be sure they were awake and brought coffee. She told them that Koos was waiting to take them for a quick tour before breakfast.

"Perhaps you should put some clothes on," commented Katrina.

"So, should you don't you think?" replied James.

"Wear something that you don't mind getting a little grubby," she suggested.

"Why?"

"Who knows what Daddy might ask us to do," commented Katrina.

"We could be recruited to prune grape vines or muck out chickens."

"What are you going to wear?" James asked.

"I think jeans and a pullover."

"Good idea, what about shoes?"

"Wear your *takkies*," she suggested. "At least we can wash them."

Koos was waiting for them on the *stoep* and set off immediately they arrived. They walked out into the lines of grape vines, which had begun

6

to bud. Koos told them that he had pruned the vines in the winter and that he would pinch out some of the growth that spring to give him better yields in the grape bunches in the autumn. James was relieved that, at this stage of the process, there was not too much to do, except knock down weeds that were beginning to sprout around the vines. The vines were planted in what looked to James like raised beaches left by old water levels from the river. The river had carved quite a deep winding valley into the mountains over the millennia, and farming followed the water. Koos identified the peak opposite as Swartrug and told James that to the north of them were the mountains, the Groot Swartberge, some of which were over 6,000 feet. To the east of the farm were two much smaller peaks, Wynandskop and Duiwelskop, only in the 1,500-foot range. James presumed that Wynand and Duiwel were probably people at one time in history who had been there and even, perhaps, settled there. Katrina asked her dad where the sheep were.

"*Ja* man, we have them pastured south of the town on a different plot," he replied. "I have a couple of Hottentots looking after them. They get one a month for rations if they keep the flock safe from predators."

Later that day, Koos started to get ready for his *braai*. He and James filled the halved forty-four-gallon drums with the wood they would use and started the fires. Katrina had been co-opted by her mother to help with food preparation, and it seemed to her that there would be enough to feed half of Calitzdorp, let alone the family.

The first to arrive was introduced to James as *Oom* Frikkie; he was a cousin to Koos and lived in Lemoenshoek, on the way to Swellendam. Although he knew Koos and Sussana, he had met Katrina only occasionally, and she did not really remember him at all. He had brought his wife, Bettie and another cousin, Hansie. It seemed to James that as the afternoon wore on, he was being introduced to more farmers than he had ever met in his life. They were all genuinely friendly, but for the most part, spoke very limited or broken English and Katrina was called upon to translate. Katrina knew or had heard of most of them, but there were a few that were new even to her. The notorious brother from South West Africa had not been able to come, so the family group was spared the turmoil of trying to decide how to deal with his black wife.

As the evening wore on, it was apparent that the visitors were going to stay for a while. James was finding it tiring trying to understand the conversations that were now mostly being carried on in Afrikaans. Also, because just about all the people there were farmers, they had little in common with James and Katrina, and they found it difficult to identify with the type of life that one led on the copper mine. For their part, James and Katrina were lost after the first few sentences about crops, livestock, diseases and rainfall. Eventually, Katrina leaned close to James and whispered in his ear and suggested that they excuse themselves on the grounds of being tired and take off to bed.

"*Ekskuus ons*," she said to the general crowd. "*Ons is baie moeg, ons gaan na bed.*"

"*Wat'n jammerte*," commented her mother. "But I expect that you are both tired from the trip and need a break. *Goeienag.*"

"I thought we would never get out of there," Katrina commented to James when they were in their room. "My relatives are nice but a little hard-going sometimes."

"Do you think they were offended because we left?" he asked.

"No, man, it's fine. They understand and are probably a little relieved because now they don't have to try and speak English with you."

"How do you manage to keep up now that you rarely use Afrikaans?" James asked.

"It comes back quickly enough. I think when you have spoken it most of your early life, it is ingrained there somewhere!"

"What are we going to do tomorrow?"

"I think we are going to Oudtshoorn," Katrina replied. "Maybe we'll see some ostrich farms."

"So, how tired are you?" asked James.

"Not that tired," laughed Katrina. "And stop changing the subject!"

"Why, ostriches are not as interesting as the bird that's here!" he commented.

"Watch who you are calling a bird!" she warned.

8

"Maybe I'll get some ostrich feathers tomorrow, and you can do a fan dance for me?"

"What makes you think I would do a fan dance?"

"I don't know; it just seems like a romantic notion."

"Okay, suppose I did, what are you going to do?"

"Sweep you off your feet and pluck all the feathers off!" he boasted.

"So, are you going to get the feathers or not?" she asked.

"I don't know. Do you think they actually have large enough feathers these days, and they aren't all just turned into feather dusters?"

"Well, feather dusters won't cover much, so knowing you, it'll be a short dance," she laughed.

At seven the following morning, there was a knock on the door. Katrina answered, "*Kom.*"

Sussana opened the door and asked, "*Sal jy tee of koffie neem?*"

"*Koffie asseblief,*" Katrina replied.

"Okay, *drie minute,*" promised Sussana.

"Is it always three minutes for coffee or tea?" asked James when Sussana had gone.

"Probably," replied Katrina. "Okay, James time for you to get up, come on, lazy bones!"

"Why, I was just lying here admiring the view?" he said.

"What view?"

"You, you have great legs, you know?"

"You always say that!"

"Well, it's true, I'm probably more of a leg kind of bloke than one that goes for boobs," he added.

"Just focus on getting dressed for now, maybe later we'll get back to the subject of legs and boobs," Katrina promised.

After breakfast, Koos asked them if they wanted to go to Oudtshoorn by the main road or by one of the back roads. Katrina suggested the back road on the way out and the main road to return. So, Koos took them into Calitzdorp and turned north following the Nelsrivier past the Calitzdorp dam and on up into the hills. It was slow going as the road twisted and turned with the change in altitude and the stream crossings. It seemed to James that everywhere there was a chance of permanent water, there was a small farm with orchards and vineyards. Most of the farms had Afrikaans names, and he asked Koos where the black Africans lived and worked. Koos pointed out small dwellings here and there and told James that it was a perennial problem, because land ownership was in the hands of the settlers, if settlers was the right word for a people who had been there a hundred years or more. Because of the land ownership, housing and farming for the black Africans were a problem and would continue to be one. Many of the farms provided some housing, and some even provided the opportunity to participate in the crops and the harvests.

Oudtshoorn, when they reached it, was much larger than Calitzdorp. It had really boomed in the late Victorian era with the fashion of ostrich feathers in hats. Fortunes had been made and probably lost on feathers. Now the market was ostrich skin for purses, suitcases and shoes. Some places even served ostrich meat, and for those who thought that they could eat lots, there was always the challenge of eating an ostrich egg. Something James declined when he learnt that one ostrich egg was about the equivalent of twenty-four hen's eggs. Katrina was reluctant to buy things like a carved ostrich egg for themselves as they would have to carry it to England and back, but did suggest to James that they get one for his family. James lashed out and bought an ostrich skin handbag for Alex, his sister, and a small wallet for William, his brother.

The drive back to Calitzdorp via the main road was much quicker. The road followed the railway for most of the way, or perhaps the railway followed the road. Back in Calitzdorp, Koos suggested that they stop at one of the Hanepoort tasting rooms.
"You mentioned Hanepoort before," commented James to Katrina. "What exactly is it?"
"The South African version of Port," she replied. "Calitzdorp is the Port capital of South Africa."
"Is it drinkable?" James asked. "Is it any good?"
"*Baie goed*," commented Koos.
"Yes," said Katrina, laughing. "It's really good, even the cheap wino stuff with the screw caps."

By the time they went home, it was Sussana who drove because the rest of them were tipsy and she wanted to get home in one piece. Koos was right, James thought, Hanepoort was good stuff. He had purchased some for his father and some for themselves to take home, even if it meant lugging them to England and back.

"*Sal jy tee of koffie neem?*" came the call at seven Monday morning.
"*Koffie asseblief,*" answered James.
"Okay, *drie minute.*"
"What is it today?" James asked Katrina.
"George," she replied.
"Ah, yes," he said. "I remember driving through on my way north three years ago."
"What did we do yesterday?" she asked. "Where did the day go?"
"As I remember, we got up late with a *babelas,*" commented James. "Probably from all that Hanepoort we drank on Saturday."
"Man, my head only hurt for a while there," Katrina added. "But then, if I recall, you got frisky and the day turned out not so badly after all!"
"God, I love you, you know?" said James. "I never get tired of being with you or just looking at you."
"I know you love me," she said. "You tell me every night before we go to sleep."
"Well, if we're going to George today, maybe you should stop stretching like that and put some clothes on, or we won't make it out of here," commented James.
"Okay, okay, *ek gaan my net gou aantrek,*" Katrina promised. She then did get up and get dressed, as promised and chivvied James along to do the same.

After their trip to George, James and Katrina spent a couple of days helping Koos with his vines and other tasks around the farm. Then Sussana stepped in and insisted that they take a day for themselves to just explore the countryside around the farm and Calitzdorp. James borrowed Koos's Land Rover and they set off, packed lunch in hand, up the trail north of the farm. They followed the Gamka River until the trail ran out, and then there were just the remnants of old tracks. With the Land Rover in low range and four-wheel drive, they bumped their way up the riverbank until the banks became too steep and the Land Rover was in danger of rolling over. Then they parked and walked. After about an hour's walking, they came to a valley that crossed the river valley, and there was even a road there, or at least a track. James consulted the map that Koos had provided them and found that it was Gamkaskloof, or locally known as *Die Hell*. Koos had told them about the valley. The road was only built in the 60s; before that, access had been by foot or horseback. The track to the east eventually led to the Stormberg Pass and then to Prince Albert. To the west, it ended high in the mountains.

On the return trip, James spotted something moving on the slopes above them. He pointed it out to Katrina, and she was quick to identify kudu.

"How do you know it's kudu?" he asked.

"Well, look at the size, the horns, the colour. What do you think the others are that are over there?" she asked, pointing to the opposite slope.

"They're small, almost sort of mountain goat-ish, I don't know. What are they?"

"Klipspringer," Katrina announced. "Maybe we should sit quietly here for a while and see what else is around."

"Great! I'm hungry too. What did your mom give us to eat?" asked James.

"I don't know, have a look and see."

"What are those other animals on the rocks opposite, the little ones that look like big guinea pigs?" asked James after he had dug out sandwiches and beers and handed them out.

"Dassies, rock hyrax. Can you also see the *bobbejane* up on the rocks over there?" Katrina asked.

"Wow, there's all kinds of things here, baboons, antelope and those dassie chaps. Do you think there are any predators?"

"Sure, probably leopards, maybe jackals and eagles for sure," Katrina thought.

"Did you feel rain?" asked Katrina.

"Yes, what do you think?" James asked.

"I think if it rains hard, the river will come up fast, so we should get higher up the bank and get back to the *bakkie* quickly."

"Good thinking. I think we left it high enough away from the water," commented James. "But we have several side streams to cross on the way home, and they could also flash flood. We should *hamba checha*."

They did indeed go quickly and found their Land Rover safe and sound, and started on their way back. A couple of the side streams had come up, and when they waded the Land Rover through the water, it came in the bottom of the doors and soaked the floor. However, they had started out quickly enough that they made it to the road before the river and stream levels had come up too high to be fordable.

Over dinner, they recounted their adventures, and Koos then told them some other news. Apparently, a few days earlier, there had been a discovery made in the Cango caves. There was now a whole new section of the cave complex to explore. He doubted that the new section would be open to the public, but the old section was still worth a visit. Koos told them that the caves had been used by the San much earlier, but after the San were pushed out by invading Europeans and Bantu peoples, they had essentially been lost until the rediscovery. He promised to take them the next day to the caves to at least see the wonders of the parts that had been open for a while and that were lit with electricity. James found a reference to the caves in a guidebook and learnt that they were dolomite caves replete with stalagmites and stalactites. There were also speculations that other cave complexes existed in the mountains.

The Cango caves were everything that the guidebooks promised and more. There were spectacular formations in the caves, and the lights had been placed to the best advantage to highlight features. Katrina was not that keen about wandering around underground, but to James, it was no particular worry. He did wonder about water after heavy rains, and the guide that was in the cave with them assured them that they had that covered and if there was any danger, they would leave. The guide was looking forward to getting into the new complex that had just been discovered and had some free days set aside for exploration.

Saturday and Sunday were taken up with a winery tour and another family get-together, this time to say goodbye. The time seemed to have raced by, and now they were getting ready for the next stage of their journey to London. The family had wanted to load them down with gifts, food and wine. They were unable to turn any of it away, so instead made a pact with Koos and Sussana to take what they could not. Koos waxed philosophical over dinner and told Katrina to go wherever James was and told James to look after Katrina. He told them that he realised that it might be a while before they were able to visit again, but that the important thing was to be and stay together.

After dinner, they started to pack because the following day they were leaving for Beaufort West to catch the train.
"What should I wear?" asked Katrina.
"Something comfortable to travel in," commented James. "I presume the train will be comfortable enough, so leave things handy for the plane trip on Tuesday."
"What about this?" she asked, modelling a brief bikini.
"Looks fine to me," James agreed. "What else do you plan to wear?"
"Oh, I don't know, maybe this and this," she said, waving blue jeans and a sweater at him.
"Looks great, what about a bra?"
"Maybe I'll skip the bra, I'll see."
"How about a kiss?" he asked.
"Come here," she commanded. As she kissed James, he pulled down her bikini pants and ran his hands over her buttocks and lower back. She responded by undoing his trousers and working them off. Both naked, they worked their way over to the bed, and Katrina fell backwards onto the bed with James on top of her. She lifted her legs and locked them around James's back, and pulled him into her.
"So, *my ou man*?" she asked. "Are you always going to be this randy?"
"Probably," he replied. "After all, it's hard not to get a hard on around you."
"Oh, that's only pheromones and chemistry," she commented.
"Maybe, but it works every time!"

Jumbo

"Are you ready?" asked James.

"Yes, yes," Katrina replied. "We're only going to Beaufort West, it's not that far!"

"Yes, but we don't want to miss the train."

"I know, I know, when does the plane leave tomorrow?"

"In the late afternoon, early evening, so if the train is on time, there'll be no problem getting to the airport in time."

"Well, come on then. *Kom ons ry,*" Katrina said, grabbing James's hand and pulling him out of the bedroom.

"What about the *katundu?*" asked James. "Don't you think we should take it with us?"

"Man, you can only worry," she said. "Why don't you let Gibson get it?"

"Because, *Suikerbossie*, Gibson is in Zambia and we're here!"

"*Ag* man, I hate it when you're right!" Katrina admitted. "Here, give me a bag; you take the rest."

Koos took the bags from them and loaded them into the back of the vanette. Much to Katrina's surprise, her mother was ready. In her experience, her mother was always the last to be ready, which was why her father usually lied about the time they needed to be ready, to give himself at least half an hour's leeway.

At Beaufort West, Koos checked on the train, and it was due to arrive right on time. The railways liked to run their premier train well, and the Blue Train had a reputation to maintain. The main reason for the stop at Beaufort West was to change engines. Electric traction stopped there, and it was necessary to switch to diesels. What they had not realised was that the train was new. South African Railways had finally replaced the old rolling stock with two completely new trains.

When the train pulled into the station, they looked for the appropriate carriage with the berth they had reserved. An attendant helped them to their berth and stowed their bags for them. James and Katrina said their final goodbyes to Koos and Sussana, and the doors closed as the train started to pull away. Sussana was shedding tears, but as Katrina had previously told James, her dad never cried when she left, but she did think that once she was well out of the way, then he would shed his tears. James suspected that that would be true on this occasion as well.

With the train on its way, it was time for dinner. They made their way through the train towards the dining car, which was still open, despite the late hour, but clearly, most of the other passengers had already eaten and gone. The menu was impressive, appetisers, soup, fish, a choice of meat dishes, dessert, cheese and biscuits and coffee. There was also a list of suitable South African wines. The waiter brought each course that they ordered in turn and, perhaps because they were one of only three tables still occupied, was happy to stay and talk about the train. The whole train was new, only put into service earlier in the month. The old trains were now being refurbished to be used on another route. With the new carriages had also come the switch from steam to diesel on this section of the route, something that James regretted because he would have liked to have seen the steam engines.

Back in their compartment, James checked out the amenities. The windows were a kind of double construction with a remotely operated blind between the glass panes. There were controls for all sorts of things on a wall panel. Their compartment was labelled semi-luxury and had its own shower. The beds had been made up while they were at dinner, and chocolates set out on the pillows.
"Which bed do you want?" asked James.
"Let's try this one," indicated Katrina, pointing to one.
"I'm going to take a quick shower," said James.
"Why don't I go first, then you can follow?" suggested Katrina.
"Okay, I'll be waiting."
When James came back into the main compartment after his shower, Katrina pulled him over to the bed.
"We've never done it on a train," she commented.
"Well, perhaps we need to fix that," James suggested. "What do you think?"
"Just come here!" Katrina commanded.

At about seven in the morning, there was a knock and the attendant announced that coffee was just outside the door. James untangled himself from Katrina, got up, wrapped himself in a towel and opened the door a little. He peered out, saw the coffee and then opened the door enough to retrieve the tray. The attendant had left it and obviously gone back to the dining car to collect other trays.

"Coffee?" he asked Katrina.

"*Ja, asseblief,*" she replied. "Can you see my brookies anywhere?"

"They're right here," indicated James.

"Can you get my bag down and get me some clean ones?" she asked.

"Anything else?" he asked.

"No, I'll get up and sort out what I'm going to wear today."

Washed and dressed, and with suitcases repacked, they went along to the dining car for breakfast. The menu was almost as complete and impressive as the dinner menu. Both of them skipped several of the offered courses and settled for a light breakfast. They had lunch yet to come, just before the train reached Johannesburg and then dinner on the plane. They were not going to starve. They had missed Kimberley in the night, left the Cape and were now in the Transvaal, approaching Bloemhof, just skipping along the northern edge of the Free State.

When they returned to their compartment, the beds had been remade into couches and the bedding removed. For the balance of the trip, they sat and watched the scenery change as they approached Johannesburg. Gone were the expanses of the Karoo and the northern Cape, now they were into more friendly-looking farmlands and less friendly-looking industrialisation. Lunch, they hurried over wanting to be back and ready for their arrival in Johannesburg. They were now anxiously anticipating the next step of the journey, the flight to London.

Johannesburg station was huge, with a mix of long-distance trains and local commuter traffic, unlike the Kitwe station, which had only long-distance freight and mixed-traffic trains. Katrina helped James get the suitcases down and hailed a taxi. The station had been arranged such that motor transport was available immediately upon leaving the train, so they did not have to lug their bags up and down stairs. Although there were motorways in and around Johannesburg, the route to Jan Smuts was a regular street, which meant a slow trip.

At Jan Smuts, they found the BOAC counter for the flight, number BA24 to London, stopping in Nairobi. They had plenty of time, so were among the earliest to check in.

"Tickets and passports, please?" asked the check-in agent.

"Here you are," replied James, handing over the documents.

The agent looked through the tickets, pulled out the relevant coupons and quickly glanced at the passports.

"Is this all your luggage?" the agent then asked.

"Yes," replied James, who then placed the suitcases on the scale.

"Where would you like to sit?" asked the agent.

"I have no idea," replied James. "Do you have any suggestions?"

"Well, on the Boeing 747 Jumbo, the economy class is 3-4-2, but at row 52 it changes to 2-4-1," the agent said. "If I were you, I would take row 52, seats B and C, because there are only two and the space to your left is actually used for a storage bin, so you can put some of your stuff to the side instead of overhead, or under your feet."

"That sounds just great," commented Katrina. "Thanks so much."

"*Nie te danke nie*", the agent said. "*Hier is hy kaartjies en paspoorts en boarding cards.*"

"*Dankie, tot siens,*" replied Katrina.

As they walked away, James asked Katrina why the agent had switched to Afrikaans. Katrina said that she thought it was probably her accent and her maiden name in her passport.

They had enough time before the plane was due to board to get themselves a snack and something to drink, and also to wander around the departure area a bit and look at the few shops that were there. When the flight was called, they made their way to the departure gate and, eventually, on board.

"Look at the size of this thing," commented James.

"It's huge, isn't it?" agreed Katrina. "How does it ever get off the ground?"

"Did you see the stairs, back there?" he asked.

"Where do they go?" wondered Katrina.

"I don't know, maybe first class, maybe a lounge, I've no idea," James admitted.

"Yes, but look at the size, it's huge compared to those little things we came down from Ndola on, even the one to Cape Town was small compared to this," she said.

"No wonder they call it a jumbo!" he said.

When everyone was on board and seated, the crew went through their safety briefings and demonstrations, and they were on their way. From their seats, they had a view out of the window and could see the terminal buildings lit up for the night. The plane lumbered down the runway; it was so big that it truly was hard to tell how fast it was actually going. They took off and made the appropriate twists and turns over the lights of Johannesburg to get them headed towards Nairobi, some four and a half hours away.

Dinner was served between Johannesburg and Nairobi, not quite up to the standard of the Blue Train, but adequate. Occasionally, out of the window, they could see the lights of towns and tried to guess where they were. James had looked at a map earlier and roughly plotted their course. They should pass near Messina, Fort Victoria, Salisbury, Fort Jameson, Mbeya, Dodoma and Arusha before beginning their final approach into Nairobi. However, most of the time, it looked as if there was little or no major habitation, as there were very few lights visible, just miles and miles of blackness.

The stopover in Nairobi was relatively short, and as it was just past midnight, local time, there was little going on and not much open. From Nairobi to London was the major leg of the journey, with another nine and a half hours to go. It seemed that the crew was intent on getting people to sleep if they could, as they turned the lights down and the temperature up to get everyone drowsy. Before he fell asleep, James took an occasional glance out of the window, but there was even less in the way of lights than they had seen from Johannesburg to Nairobi.

Katrina poked James in the ribs and told him to wake up as the crew were beginning to serve breakfast. It was still dark out, and James thought that they must be over the Mediterranean or north-central Italy. Certainly, on their side of the plane, there were no lights on the ground visible, but perhaps on the other side of the plane, they could see more. Breakfast done, the crew handed out landing cards to everyone without a British Passport; those with British passports did not need one. Dawn had now broken, and the sun was up, lighting the clouds below.

Unfortunately, it was still cloudy as they made their approach into Heathrow Airport, and James was unable to point out to Katrina the sights of London. That was a shame because the approach path took them right over the west end of London and all the places that James was familiar with from his days at college. At Heathrow, it was misty and cool, but not really raining, just enough moisture to condense on the cold outer shell of the plane and mist up the windows. They taxied up to a gate and waited, for what seemed an eternity, for the rest of the passengers to disembark.

They made their way through immigration and customs without any problems and threaded their way through the exit maze to the arrivals hall. James looked around and saw his father and brother waving to him. He pointed them out to Katrina and steered his way over to them.
"Welcome, welcome," said Mr Martin. "Did you have a good flight?"
"Fine, thanks," replied James. "Dad, Will, this is Katrina."
"Pleased to meet you," said Mr Martin, holding out his hand.
Katrina took the proffered hand but then pulled him closer and kissed him on the cheek.
"*Aangename kennis*," she said, forgetting herself completely for a minute.
"I assume that was polite?" James's father asked him.
"Oh yes, very!" he replied, laughing.
Will did not have the inhibitions of his father and gave Katrina a hug and a kiss.
"Your mother decided that she would not come with us, so that there would be more room for your luggage," reported James's father.
"The truth is she didn't want to get up so early," whispered Will to his brother. "We had to be up at five thirty to get here in time."

20

They made their way to the car park and set off for the short ride to Cores End. After the tunnel under the runway, they joined the M4 and went west to the Slough west exit, where they left the motorway and then wended their way past the Weston Wagon Wheel factory, through Taplow, past the Canadian Red Cross Hospital and Cliveden, then on through Hedsor before descending into Cores End.

"Welcome to our humble abode," said James's father. "I hope you will like it here."

"I am sure I will," replied Katrina. "It's all so green and organised."

"Probably very different to Zambia?" asked Will.

"Oh yes," she agreed. "Very different."

"Well, anyway, come on in and meet James's mother," suggested Mr Martin.

While Mr Martin ushered Katrina into the house, Will helped James with the luggage.

"You're a jammy bastard, you know," commented Will. "How in the world did you get such a knockout to go for you?"

"I'm just such a marvellous chap," suggested James.

"Huh," was Will's comment. "There must be a real dearth of good-looking blokes out there if someone like you can land someone like that. Maybe I should go out there, or are all the good-looking girls taken?"

"Well, one of them at least," commented James.

"How much stuff did you bring?" asked Will. "These bags must weigh four to five stone each!"

"Well, by the time we go home, we will have been away a month," said James. "And mine is the small suitcase, the bigger ones are Katrina's."

"When Alex said she was exotic, I thought she was just exaggerating or the photographs just made her look great," commented Will. "But she really is, almost makes Bridget look plain."

"Wait, wait a minute, who's Bridget?" asked James.

"You'll meet here this weekend," said Will. "She's this girl I work with."

"Shouldn't you be at work now?"

"I took the rest of the week off to squire you around," said Will. "Thought it was the least I could do for my new sister-in-law."

"So, what do you actually do?" asked James.

21

"Well, you know I started to work for ICI, now they have me supervising a paint line."

"Isn't that a bit of a switch from Civil Engineering?" James asked.

"I suppose so," agreed Will. "But I built the line and now I'm running it!"

"And what does Bridget do?" asked James.

"She's a chemist, checks up on what I do," Will explained.

"I'll bet she does," commented James. "In more ways than one!"

When James and his brother went into the house with the luggage, the air had a definite frosty feel about it. James looked at Katrina, his father and mother and concluded that someone had said something. Will, coming in with bags, was less sensitive to the atmosphere and merely asked Katrina if he could take the bags directly to the room that she and James would be using. James's father told him that it would be the one above the front hallway. Katrina followed Will up the stairs, and James decided to leave things for the moment and also went. He would try and find out from Katrina what was said and then decide what to do about it, if anything.

When Will had left, Katrina turned to James, and there was no need to try and get her to talk; she came right out with it.

"You know, James, your mother can be a *regtig ou feeks*!"

"Why, what the hell happened?" he asked.

"She only said that she supposed I was acceptable, even if I wasn't English or obviously not completely white!"

"I'll go down and sort it out," said James.

"No, man, she's not worth it. I thought it was only the *Boerekies* that were *verkrampte*, but apparently, there are people in this land of freedom and enlightenment that are worse."

"Are you sure? Do you want us to leave and go and stay in a hotel somewhere?"

"No, man, it's fine. The silly old *teef* can have her prejudices; it's her loss."

"What did my dad say?" asked James.

"He just looked helpless," commented Katrina.

22

"Typical," James remarked. "That's about all he can do when she goes off. You know, she'll probably ask you if you know how to eat with a knife and fork."

"No man, really?" she asked.

"Well, we're going to spend most of our time here out, and we'll take a trip to see my grandmother, so the two weeks should go fast enough," concluded James. "Look, I told them that we were going to clean up and take a nap before doing anything, so there is nothing on till lunchtime, so we might as well try and get some rest and catch up on the sleep we lost last night."

Lunch was actually fairly civilised. James thought that perhaps, for once, his father had actually stood up to his mother and told her to behave. James handed over the presents that he had brought and was gratified that they all appeared to be well received and appreciated. After lunch, James suggested that his brother might like to take them on a general tour of the area so that Katrina could see where he was brought up and what the place looked like. The tour turned out to be fairly extensive and covered ground as far as Henley, Windsor, Beaconsfield and High Wycombe. They saw the grammar school that the brothers had attended and the high school that their sister had gone to. Will took them into a pub before returning home and bought them a beer each. Katrina was a little unsure about this warm beer stuff and told Will that she preferred the Zambia Breweries Lion to Wethered's.

Will also introduced them to the new currency. While James had been away from England, the change had been made from pounds, shillings and pence to pounds and new pence. So instead of 12 pennies to the shilling and 20 shillings to the pound, there were now 100 new pence to the pound. James quickly discovered that that had been shortened to simply "p", so now something cost 50p instead of 10 shillings. Decimalisation had finally made it to the UK! However, there was no move to switch to metric measures, so miles, pounds and gallons were still in use, unlike Zambia, where officially it was all metric. However, even in Zambia, they still used an odd mixture of miles and kilometres, feet and metres and pounds and kilograms.

After dinner that night, they planned out the two weeks ahead. Alex was going to join them over the weekend, and the next week was to be filled with trips to London, Stonehenge and a river excursion. When James looked at the calendar, he realised that they would really only have the next week for visits and sightseeing as they were due to fly home the Tuesday after next. On that realisation, James's mother then started to complain that their time was really short and that it would not give her time to get to know Katrina. James was sure that she would next start to compare amounts of time spent in South Africa and England, but was spared that discussion.

The next two days were filled with short trips to places not too far afield. Friday night, Alex came down from London for the weekend, and Bridget also joined them. That put Mrs Martin into a bother because she waffled and wavered about reorganising everything and having James move in with Will so that she could put Bridget in with Katrina and Alex. Fortunately, Alex took her aside in the kitchen and told her a few home truths and then all was sweetness and light, and logic prevailed. James stayed with his wife, Alex had her own room, and Bridget was put in with Will.

Later that evening, James's father took them all out for dinner at the Compleat Angler in Marlow. James remarked in an aside to Will that the old man was pushing the boat out a little. He was familiar with the hotel as he had passed it many times on his way to the boathouse used by his grammar school. It had a wonderful location on the River Thames, just upstream of Marlow Lock. Mr Martin waxed eloquent to Katrina and Bridget about the history of the hotel, or pub as it had been, and the celebrities that had stayed there, including J. M. Barrie and Edgar Wallace.

Katrina was intrigued by the river and the system of weirs and locks that made it navigable. She could not help but compare it to the Kafue or the Lunsemfwa, where there were the ever-present obstacles of rapids, hippo and crocodiles.
"Yes, my dear," agreed Mr Martin. "I am sure those rivers are very nice, but this is the River."

24

"Shades of *Wind in the Willows*," whispered Alex to James.

"Does it ever freeze?" Katrina asked.

"Sometimes," he answered. "In fact, when the children were small, I remember taking them for a walk along the towpath between Bourne End and Marlow, and it was frozen just about all the way across."

"That must have been only cold," commented Katrina.

"*Baie koud*," James said.

"What was that, dear?" asked his mother. "You should speak English here; we can't all understand whatever it is you were saying."

"He only said that it was very cold, Mrs Martin," explained Katrina.

"What language do your parents speak?" asked Bridget.

"It depends," replied Katrina. "Some things are better said in Afrikaans and some in English, so whichever language says it best is the one they use."

"Isn't that awfully confusing?" asked Mrs Martin.

"Only for people like me," commented James. "It takes a little getting used to, but I can manage now."

"It's possible that I may have to learn some Afrikaans soon," remarked Bridget.

"Oh, why?" asked James.

"I may be moving to the explosives division of ICI sometime. Perhaps even to one of the African overseas subsidiaries," she elaborated.

"What, when?" asked Will.

"Oh, I'm not sure, they only approached me today," she said. "I'm not sure exactly what they have in mind or where."

"But," spluttered Will. "What will I do if you move?"

"We need to discuss that later, don't you think?" she said.

"Does this mean that you are going to move away as well?" asked Mrs Martin.

"Who knows?" replied Will.

"Don't worry, dear," said Mr Martin. "There will still be Alex close by."

"Not if I can help it," muttered Alex into James's ear.

"What was that, dear?" she was asked by her mother. "You shouldn't mutter, dear, speak clearly, enunciate properly."

"I was telling James to move his big feet," lied Alex.

"Don't annoy your sister, James," was the response.

"So, Bridget, when do you think you will know something?" Katrina asked.

"Next month, I believe. As I understand it, it's between me and this bloke from Newcastle," she replied.

"Well, good luck to you," said James. "Here's to Bridget, may she succeed in all her endeavours!"

"If you do go to Jo'burg," said Katrina. "I have some family there and some of my school friends live there now, so maybe I could introduce you to them?"

"That would be great," Bridget said. "It would really help to know there is someone there other than the Company."

"Well, there could be me," volunteered Will.

"That would be perfect," said Bridget. "Let's keep fingers and toes crossed and see what comes!"

"Do you think they'll get married if she goes?" Katrina asked James later.

"Probably," he replied. "Brit companies tend to be a little on the conservative side and would probably frown on just shacking up in Jo'burg."

"Do you think they would try and find him a job as well?" she asked.

"I don't know," admitted James. "I don't know that much about ICI and how they operate, so really can't say."

"Well, I hope she gets it and they go," said Katrina. "So James, what's the plan for us tomorrow?"

"Alex is driving you and me and Will, and Bridget to see my grandmother," he replied.

"What's she like?" she asked.

"You'll see tomorrow," he said. "You'll like her. She's not at all like my dad. She's much more forceful and much more fun!"

James's grandmother lived in Bidford on Avon, a small town south of Birmingham. The drive was mostly across country as there was no direct route from Cores End. They skirted Oxford and then headed towards Chipping Norton. Will kept up a running commentary on the scenery and places they passed through, and then started to ask Alex about her love life.

"Alex," he started. "Is there someone in your life right now that we should know about?"

"Why?" she replied.

"Oh, just curious to see if there was anyone to sweep you off your feet and take you away from your legal dealings."

"Well, if you must know, I am seeing Vincenzo."

"Wait a minute, I've not heard of this one before, who's he?" Will asked.

"Oh, a solicitor I know in London. He comes from Italy; you know, tall, dark and handsome!"

"Has he lived here long?" asked Bridget.

"About two years, he works for one of the law firms in London, and his family are in banking in Florence," explained Alex.

"So, wedding bells in the offing?" asked Will.

"We'll see," was the only answer he could get, and then she changed the subject and asked Katrina about the handbag they had brought her.

As they were headed through the last stretch of the road to Bidford, Katrina commented that, for the UK, it was an unusually straight road. James then explained that the current road was built on an old Roman road, Ryknild Street. Katrina added that she thought it was different to a typical English road that seemed to her to be all twists and turns, so unlike most of the southern African roads that went straight except when negotiating major hills and valleys. They reached Bidford, crossed the narrow bridge over the Avon and made their way to James's grandmother's house. She was waiting for them all, and as with grandmothers everywhere, wanted to know everything and to feed them.

"Lovely to meet you, Katrina," she said. "How do you like England? Are you all hungry?"

"Well, it's different," started Katrina, then she paused, not quite knowing how to proceed.

"Let me guess?" suggested Mrs Martin. "The weather is awful, it's cold and damp, there are too many people, and everything feels shut in! Would that be a good description?"

"Oh, no, I couldn't say that," Katrina protested.

"Yes, you can, dear. You can be honest with me. I know what it must be like coming to a new place that is so different, and let me guess, Elizabeth is being difficult."

"Well, you know Mum," added Will. "She could piss off a priest!"

"William!" interjected Alex, trying hard to appear scandalised, while suppressing her giggles.

"Well, he's right, dear," agreed Mrs Martin. "So, Katrina, what do you really think?"

"I'm enjoying all the new things, sights and places to go, but I won't be sorry to leave and go home!" she replied.

"I didn't think so. Now, Bridget, what's your news?"

"I may get a spot in Jo'burg."

"How wonderful, and will you take Will with you?"

"You know, I might just at that. I've wondered and wondered, but seeing James and Katrina together, I think it's time we did something."

"Really, will you marry me?" asked Will.

"Yes. It's just a pity that you didn't do something earlier so that James and Katrina could have come to the wedding!"

"Don't blame me," Will said. "I've been wanting to ask you for a while, but I've always been afraid you'd say no."

"And, Alex, what about you?" Mrs Martin persisted, completing the interrogation.

"I'm seeing Vincenzo Bernini, a solicitor in London."

"Italian is he, are the Italians all that we are led to believe in bed?"

"Gran!" Alex spluttered.

"Well, it's a consideration. Looking at these brothers of yours and their smug faces, I'd say they are doing pretty well for themselves. Come into the kitchen, you can tell me without the long-eared donkeys listening," she commanded. With that, Mrs Martin took Alex by the hand and, beckoning Katrina and Bridget to follow, dragged her off into the kitchen.

"Well, James, do you think Gran has anything strong in the dresser?" asked Will.

"Take a look, and if there is, I'll join you in a toast to your upcoming nuptials."

On the drive home, James and Will both wanted to hear about the kitchen conversation, but got nothing from any of the girls. All they got was a comment from Alex that she was taking Italian lessons. James was sure that later, when they were on their own, Katrina would recount the conversation. He was right. In the privacy of their room, Katrina gave him a complete blow-by-blow account. She giggled at some of the things that James's grandmother had said and the questions she asked, but she also said it was fun and they had had very frank discussions about their various menfolk. They learnt a lot about James's grandmother that even Alex had not known, and Katrina told James that Bridget's comment was that she must a been a real raver in her young days. Katrina's final comment was, "Did you know that your *ouma* said that she had once done it on a motorcycle? She said it had a sidecar so wouldn't fall over and that your granddad had the hardest time staying balanced!"

James's parents had been stunned by the announcement that Will and Bridget made when they returned on Saturday, and Bridget had left Will to answer all his mother's questions while she telephoned her own parents. On Monday, Will went back to work with Bridget and James, and Katrina went to London with Alex for a couple of days. On the train from Bourne End to Paddington, Alex told them what she had planned: a visit to the Tower, the Natural History Museum and the Victoria and Albert Museum, because Katrina had specifically asked to see those places. In London, they stopped first at Alex's flat to drop their bags, then took the Tube from Kensington High Street to Notting Hill Gate, then to Bank and Monument and then to Tower Hill. "Why didn't we just take the Circle line all the way to Tower Hill?" James asked Alex.

"Because I thought it would be interesting for Katrina to see another line, so decided on the Central line," she replied.

"Do you use the Underground much?" Katrina asked.

"Every day to go to work and then around London for various things," Alex replied.

"You don't have a car?"

"No, there's really no point, and where would I park it?"

"Will we meet Vincenzo?" asked James.

"Yes, for dinner tonight. He's cooking, so we'll meet at his flat later," promised Alex.

Katrina was amazed by the Tower of London. She could not get over the Yeomen Warders, known to most as the beefeaters, the ravens and the general antiquity of the place. To her, the Crown Jewels were interesting but not as interesting as the walls, the towers and the general fortifications. It had been many, many years since either James or Alex had been to the Tower, so having a visitor was a plus, because they were now forced to go. Lunch in one of the cafeterias near the Tower was a disappointment, and Katrina found the waitresses surly and rude. So much for encouraging visitors.

Dinner, in contrast, was wonderful. Vincenzo was a great host and made them really welcome. His flat was only a couple of streets from Alex's, so James asked her in an aside if she had thought about moving in with him. She told him that they were working up to that, and to watch this space! Vincenzo had prepared *Crostini con funghi* (mushroom croutons) as appetisers, then served *Corniglio con patate al rosemarino* (rabbit with rosemary potatoes). Alex asked him where he had found the rabbits, and he told her that he had found a butcher off Knightsbridge who seemed to specialise in game meats in addition to the regular fare.

Katrina asked Vincenzo where his family was from, and he told them that they came from Tuscany. Their house was in the hills and had olives, almonds, grapes and some citrus trees. He invited them to go any time they wished and then told them that he and Alex were planning a trip there at Christmas time. Alex confirmed that, and Vincenzo said it would be an excellent opportunity to meet his family. His father, as the head of a banking company in Florence, was aware of his social position and was anxious to see who this English girl was that Vincenzo was dating and whether or not it would lead to anything more permanent. To James, it all sounded very romantic, and he told Alex that he hoped she would have a good time there.

Alex's flat was not quite as elegant as Vincenzo's, but certainly serviceable. She did have a spare room, which meant that no one would be sleeping on settees! The following morning, Alex went back to work after giving James a key to the flat and directions to get to the museums. James thought that a little superfluous as he had lived in that part of London for three years whilst at University. He could quite easily find his way around. Katrina enjoyed the walks through Kensington Gardens to get to Exhibition Road and then spent the next two days "doing" museums. Thursday, they did the City and finally got to see the "Chambers" where Alex plied her trade, just behind St. Paul's Cathedral.

Over a drink on Thursday evening, Vincenzo asked Katrina about Zambia and South Africa. Katrina then related the difference between their last day out in Calitzdorp and their days in London. She told of driving off the road until it was no longer possible to take the car, then seeing antelope and other animals. Then she told of her experiences in London with its millions of people, all of whom seemed intent on getting in her way. For her, the country was small, there were seemingly countless numbers of people, and the weather was nowhere near as pleasant as the Zambian winter. Vincenzo also asked her if she had eaten rabbit before. Katrina then gave them a litany of all the game meats she had eaten, from scrub hare to hippo. She warned them off waterbuck as they had a strong taste, but heartily recommended eland and buffalo.

Back in Cores End, two other excursions had been planned, one to Stonehenge, a must-see on Katrina's list and a trip on the river, something that Mr Martin thought she should experience. Stonehenge was dramatic and eerie, particularly because it was lightly raining and the mist seemed to hang around the place. The river trip was short, Cookham to Marlow. The locks on the river closed down for the winter in mid to late September, so through traffic was difficult. Again, the weather was not cooperative, but Katrina did enjoy her ride. The conversation centred on the impending visit of Bridget's parents to meet the Martins. Bridget had not joined them on the boat ride; she was going to arrive the next day with her parents, who were driving from Evesham.

"I've never met Bridget's parents," lamented Will. "They'll be here soon. What do I do?"

"Don't worry, Will," James reassured him. "I'm sure everything will be fine."

"Yes, but!"

"Hey, no buts, okay," James instructed him. "If they really don't like you, you can always leave the country!"

"Sure, like you did, smart move," commented Will.

"William, James, Mr and Mrs Mortimer are here; come on down and meet them!" commanded Mrs Martin.

"Okay, here we go," said Will.

"Mum, Dad, this is Will," introduced Bridget.

"Pleased to meet you both," said Will.

"So, you're the young man who's going to take our Bridget off to the wilds of Africa," commented Mr Mortimer. "Only joking. I know she's the one pushing for this, and please call me Henry."

"Thank you, Sir," replied Will.

"And, I'm Elizabeth," offered Mrs Mortimer. "Please call me Elizabeth, or Mum if you prefer. Now, Elizabeth and Bridget, we'll let these men gossip while we go and start planning a wedding! You come too, Katrina, you've been through this more recently than Elizabeth or I, so can help a lot!"

"Bridget tells us that you are a boat builder," commented Mr Martin.

"Yes, I build mainly small wooden craft, up to thirty feet. Mostly yachts, but sometimes rowing boats and canoes, and I've done a racing shell once, an eight."

"Do you have a large shop?" James asked.

"Large enough, we employ about thirty people. We have access to the Avon and the main road, so transporting boats in and out is not too much trouble," elaborated Henry.

All in all, everyone seemed to get on well. Mrs Martin had decided that being a boat builder was not in the league of being a mere tradesman, so elevated the Mortimers in her social rankings. The Mortimers were intrigued by Katrina and plied her with countless questions about South Africa and Johannesburg. Obviously, if their daughter was going to get the job there, they were concerned for her well-being and wanted as much information as they could get. Katrina repeated her offer of an introduction to some of her extended family who lived in Johannesburg and promised to stay in touch with Bridget and Will. When everyone had gone, Mrs Martin announced that she was satisfied with the proceedings and that she really liked the Mortimers and had promised to visit them and look at Elizabeth Mortimer's paintings.

"Is there anything we should buy before we go home, *Suikerbossie?*" James asked Katrina the next day.
"I don't think so, except that we should get something for Attie for looking after the house and something for Gibson," she replied.
"Well, we have all day, let's see what we can find."
"Where shall we go?" Katrina asked.
"I'll borrow my mom's car and we'll go to Maidenhead. If we find nothing there, we can always try somewhere else," James replied.
"Should we get something for your mom and dad?" Katrina continued.
"Do you think we should?" he asked.
"Yes, something for putting us up for the past two weeks," she replied.
"Even though my mom's been a real bitch towards you?"
"Well, I've decided that she can't help it. She just has these deep-down prejudices that she can't get past. Don't you feel sorry for her?" she asked.
"Not particularly, but if it's okay with you, I'll live with it," was James's final word on the subject.

Tuesday morning, they were up early and, after breakfast, started to pack. James wondered why they were packing so early, as the plane did not leave until seven forty-five that night, so they had plenty of time. His mother hovered around giving suggestions and advice until James asked her if she could make some lunch for them all. They were joined for lunch by the rest of the family, including Bridget and Vincenzo. That set Mrs Martin into a panic once again, because she had not met Vincenzo before. She was unsure about him because to her, he was as dark as Katrina and so very 'foreign'. She started to imagine all kinds of scenarios where Alex would marry this Italian and then go off to live in Italy. Then she got onto the subject of grandchildren.

"Will I hear the patter of tiny feet any time soon?" she asked Katrina.

"I doubt it," she replied. "I don't particularly want any children."

"Well, what about you, William? Have you and Bridget talked about any family?" Mrs Martin asked.

"Don't look at us," he replied. "We haven't got married yet, and if we do go to Jo'burg, I don't see any children for a while. You'd better ask Alex if there could be any *bambinos* in the offing."

"It's *i bambini,* not *bambinos,*" corrected Alex. "And don't you think you ought to let us at least get to the stage of thinking about marriage before you lumber us with children?"

"I'll be sixty before I see any grandchildren," wailed Mrs Martin. "How can you all do this to me?"

"Now now, dear," interposed her husband. "We can't let our wishes run the lives of our children."

"But I want a grandchild!" she said. "One of you better do something before I die!"

"You're being dramatic, dear. I think that's enough," commanded Mr Martin. "We will hear no more about it. If and when it happens, we will be very pleased. But until then, it is not our concern!"

Mid-afternoon, they all went to the airport to put James and Katrina onto flight BA43, London to Lusaka with a stop in Entebbe. James joked to Katrina that it was only to make sure that they actually left and went back to Zambia. There was a surprise waiting for them at the airport. It seemed that Vincenzo had done some work for a couple of BOAC bigwigs, and they had moved James and Katrina from economy class to first class. That was really something! James and Katrina could not thank Vincenzo enough, but he shrugged it off. As far as he was concerned, this is what families and friends did for one another.

At last, they were leaving. Goodbyes were said, and there were even hugs from James's parents. The goodbyes were tearful, but there were promises made all around for visits. In fact, James's father commented that if Will and Bridget did go to Johannesburg, then they could kill two birds with one stone and visit both South Africa and Zambia. Well, time would tell.

The flight back was very comfortable. The plane was a Vickers VC-10, so nowhere near as large as the jumbo that they had flown on from Johannesburg to London. However, being moved to first class really helped. The seating arrangement in first class was only two on each side of the aisle, and they had their own steward. The service was good, but not quite up to the Johannesburg run. Perhaps the South African market was different enough to warrant the extra effort, or perhaps the jumbo was just a much newer plane and had better galley equipment, plus more staff. James was glad that they had decided on the Tuesday flight; the Friday flight would have also stopped in Khartoum, which would just make the journey a little longer and would have put them into Lusaka just after noon, after which they still had to get to Ndola. The Tuesday flight got them into Lusaka early enough to get to Ndola before noon.

We have this problem

"So, how was the trip?" asked Attie.

"Long," replied Katrina. "But James's family were not as bad as I thought they could have been."

"Yes, my mother only insulted Katrina half a dozen times; it could have been more," added James.

"*Yerra* man, that is only *mubi*, what was her problem?" asked Attie.

"I think she really believes that I should have married some English girl and not a Boer *meisie*," commented James.

"What about the rest?" asked Attie.

"Well, his *ouma* was only nice," hedged Katrina.

"And the others?" persisted Attie.

"You met Alex, so you know she is nice, James's brother seemed distracted until he proposed to his girlfriend Bridget, and his dad was just there," elaborated Katrina.

"I think my brother's problem was that he was desperately afraid of losing Bridget," commented James.

"I don't think your mom liked me too much," said Katrina.

"Or Bridget, Will's girlfriend," added James. "Particularly when she told us that she might go to Jo'burg, in which case Will would go with her."

"Drama, man," said Attie.

"Oh yes, to add fuel to it all, Alex told her that her current beau is an Italian!" added Katrina.

"I think that went over like a lead balloon," commented James. "I am only beginning to appreciate just how *verkrampte* she really is."

"Can we go home now?" asked Katrina.

"You have all your *katundu*?" asked Attie.

"*Ja, tina kona zonke*," she replied.

"Okay then, *kom ons ry*," suggested Attie.

He led them out to the car park and helped them load their luggage into the Land Rover.

"So, what's new?" asked James.

"Not much," said Attie. "You know life just goes on."

"Any problems while we were away?" asked Katrina.

"No man, nothing, it was really quiet," commented Attie. "When do you have to start back to work?"

"I go in on Monday," replied James. "I am supposed to be taking over a section in the fold area, which will be more interesting than just a regular section."

"I think they want me to go back on Monday as well," added Katrina. "But I think they're also wondering just what to do with me."

"Did you hear about the *ouk* from the mine that was killed by the hippo?" asked Attie.

"No, where?" asked James.

"I think he was up around Kasaba Bay," replied Attie.

"Do you know who it was?" asked Katrina.

"No, I only know that he got bitten and didn't survive, tipped out of his boat, I think," elaborated Attie.

It was good to be home, hot as it was. James had almost forgotten just how hot and humid October could be. Attie dropped them off, picked up his own stuff and went back to his flat. After he left, both James and Katrina changed into lighter clothes and then started to address the issue of unpacking. Attie had stocked the fridge, so there was beer and chilled water readily available to keep them cool while they worked. The unpacking only lasted so long, then their attention wandered, and the bed called. Making love in the middle of the day was hot and sticky, but satisfied their need for one another.

The next morning, Gibson returned. He was there at six-thirty, a little early for James and Katrina, who, having no need to go to work, were not even up and about. Katrina presented him with the gifts they had brought for him from England, a pocket knife and a transistor radio. Gibson was delighted with both. Katrina then spent the next hour with him, going through their travels and experiences. He wanted to know about James's folks, and Katrina was very honest with him; after all, he had known her for a long time and could probably tell when something was amiss.

The next mission was to do some shopping for food and other essentials. Attie had replaced most of what he had used, but his idea of what constituted a suitably stocked pantry and Katrina's differed. They also collected all their mail from the Post Office and took it home to pay bills and sort out things in general.

Saturday, they decided a break was in order and went out to the boat club. It was hot and humid, and Katrina fancied a swim to cool off. Once at the club, they spent a fair amount of time catching up with people they knew and reliving their trip. James was sure that he told his story of the trip at least fifty times, but Katrina told him that he exaggerated and that it was only twenty times.

Monday morning, bright and early, James reported in at the mine office expecting to meet James Ross, the Underground Manager. However, he was told to report to George McIntosh, the Manager Mining. As James had not been back long enough to even report to work, let alone make a mess of anything, this must be something different. He drove to the main offices and introduced himself to the receptionist. He was directed to the appropriate place and knocked on the door.

"Come in," he heard McIntosh say. "Ah, Martin, come in and sit down, coffee, tea?"

"Coffee, thank you," replied James.

"I think you know Colin Winter?" asked McIntosh, getting the coffee. "The others you may not know. Let's see, Duncan Brown, our chief exploration wizard, Tony Williams from the planning department and Henry Wayne from the concentrator."

"I'm sure you're wondering what this is all about?" commented Colin Winter.

"A little," admitted James. "Obviously not the section I was scheduled to be going to today."

"No, we've changed things a little, perhaps. We have this problem," said Winter. "We have been working on starting up a small mine near Mkushi, and the chap we had running things, Jim Brown, managed to get himself killed by a hippo last week."

"Yes, I heard about that," said James. "But, I didn't know who it was."

"Well, we now have a need for someone to take over right away and get the place started up," commented McIntosh. "We're prepared to give you the chance to run it if you want to."

"I'm sure that you'll have a thousand questions," commented Duncan Brown. "So, let me give you the bare bones of the project."

"Before we do that, do you have the latest ore reserve figures and maps, Duncan?" asked McIntosh.

"Right here," he replied. He then got up and spread some maps and charts out on the table.

"Okay," said Brown. "The site is near Mkushi, just off the Great North Road, not too far from Kapiri and on the same road that leads to the Italian operation at Munshimwemba. We've made a deal with the Eyeties about the mining rights on this side of the river, and we're going to re-open the Mtuga property that was mined underground in the twenties."

"We're thinking of an open pit," interrupted Winter. "It would only be a small operation with front-end loaders and trucks and a small concentrator."

"Right," added Brown. "We have much of the plant already on order and on the water, some houses built, and other work going on, and we're waiting for the mining equipment to be shipped."

"Normally, we'd have an Assistant Underground Manager run something like this," said McIntosh. "But, this is small enough that we're prepared to give you the chance to show us what you can do."

"Why don't you gather up your wife, take a trip down there today, if you can, and let us know by Wednesday if you want to do this?" suggested Winter. "We really do need to get on with things, and if you don't want to do it, we need to find someone else pretty damn quick."

They went through more details of the project for the next two hours, then McIntosh suggested that James call his wife and find out if she could take the rest of the day and the next two days off to take a trip to the mine site. Katrina quickly checked with her employers, and they were happy to agree, probably thinking, as she later commented, that more transportation of equipment to the mine site would be needed at some time, and they would probably bid on the job. In fact, they had already moved quite a lot of construction materials and some heavy equipment to the site. James was loaded up with drawings and maps and given directions as to where to actually find the site, a little unnecessary, as Katrina knew where it was. Brown and Wayne would also be going to the site and were to leave immediately after the meeting.

When James arrived home, Katrina was already there and had had Gibson put together some lunch and other food to take on the trip. She was eager to learn what this venture was all about, so over lunch, he explained as much as he knew. Gibson hovered around listening to the conversation, trying to understand what it might mean for him as well as for them.

They told Gibson that they would be back on Wednesday night and left for Kapiri. On the drive down, Katrina asked all the obvious questions, such as where would they live, were there already people there, where would they shop, *et cetera*. James told her as much as he knew and speculated on the rest. He was excited about the opportunity but also a little nervous about taking on such a responsibility.

Kapiri came soon enough, and they turned off onto the Great North Road. About fifteen miles up the Great North Road, they turned onto the road towards the Mkushi district and the Mita Hills dam on the Lunsemfwa River. Another twelve miles down that road and well into the Mkushi district, they came to the sign for the Mtuga property. They followed that track a short distance until they came to a village and a construction site. It seemed that they were expected because almost immediately they were met by none other than Hippo, one of James's acquaintances from his first days on the mine. Hippo took them to the temporary office, where they found Duncan Brown and Henry Wayne. They were already in a meeting with John Watson, a contractor from Kitwe that James and Katrina knew. It was his equipment that Katrina's company had moved to the site. John was relating progress to date on bush clearing for the mine site and pre-stripping that he was doing to remove all the top soils and soft overburden.

After the meeting, John suggested that he take Katrina on a quick tour of the site and the housing while James went with Duncan and Henry for a more thorough review of the situation. There was actually quite a lot to see. There was the skeletal structure of a complex to hold the crusher, ball mills and related equipment and a bank of flotation cells. Henry told James that the actual crusher and mills were on the water and were expected in Beira within the month. Transportation and installation would take another three to six months after the boat docked.

The next group of buildings would one day be workshops for the mining equipment. Duncan told James that Tony Williams's department had done a study that compared contracting the work to running the operation themselves, and the returns came out best when the mine ran the operation. A fleet of equipment had been decided upon and ordered with shipment dates from Peoria, Illinois, in early December.

The mine site itself was clear of bush and already had a shape as John's company had stripped off most of the softer soils. Duncan had a plan of what the open pit would be like, and from that, they worked out how far back to strip each level. James asked where the dumps were going to be and was shown a cleared area with haul roads leading to piles of dirt. His next questions were mainly about water, electricity, telephone, spare parts and people. Henry told him that the water would come from the Lunsemfwa River and that a pipeline was already laid. Electricity might be a problem because the Italians were already on the single line that served the area, and another demand on the system could cause outages. Because of that, they had provided the operation with some generators, enough to run the mill and the houses, in case of need. As far as people, he was going to have to work out his needs and a plan for how to recruit and house them.

Meanwhile, Katrina had taken the tour with John and had seen the housing and the general layout of the area. She was excited about the prospect of a move there and asked John if his company would be doing all the work. John told her that he had bid on the work but that the

41

company had decided to buy the machines and do the work themselves. All he had was a contract to do the preliminary bush clearing and pre-stripping. He would continue with the pit as long as they paid him, or until the new equipment arrived and was running.

The tours over for now, James and the others joined Katrina and John at the largest building in the nearby village for dinner. They were joined by several others who were also working on the project, including Hippo and John McFarlane, the concentrator section boss who had been assigned to the project. James vaguely remembered McFarlane from university. McFarlane had been two years behind him in the mineral technology class. Apparently, he had come to Zambia in late 1971. James wondered why he had not seen much of him around town and learnt that he had been used for various special projects that kept him out of Kitwe, something that his wife was not overly keen about. However, now that he was assigned to the Mtuga project, he and his wife were spending much more time together as she was also there on the site.

Over dinner with the rest of the construction project team, they talked about the progress to date and the challenges yet to come. The area of greatest concern was the delivery of equipment, whether it was for crushing and grinding or mining. With the expected arrival of the mill machinery into Beira in the middle of November, they had to plan for its transport to the mine site. Once the project team found out who Katrina was, she was peppered with questions about transport equipment, rates, rail versus road and whatever else they could think of that related to moving things.

After dinner, they had all been invited to John McFarlane's house, so, hoping that his wife could stand visitors, most of them descended upon the McFarlanes. John introduced his wife, Kirsty, and offered drinks. Katrina sat and talked to Kirsty for a while and was told a tale of woe. John had been away so much that she had barely left the house for almost a year, so knew almost no one and had been nowhere. She was thrilled to meet Katrina and, at last, have someone else to talk to. The

McFarlanes both came from Inverness and, at times, Katrina found it hard to follow what they were saying.

Not wanting to intrude too long on the McFarlanes, James and Katrina excused themselves and asked where they would be staying. Duncan Brown told them that they had been assigned the house that Jim Brown had been using. It had been cleaned out since his death, and his widow had not been back. The house was equipped with the bare essentials in furniture, and there was also a complete set of new bedding that had been delivered earlier. James helped Katrina make up the bed and then suggested a bath. However, Katrina first said that they needed to find a way to secure some of the extra blankets over the windows. Whoever had cleaned the house had really cleaned it and taken out all the window coverings, if in fact there ever were any.

A little later, when they were in the bath together, James posed the question that was on both their minds.
"So, what do you think?" he asked Katrina. "Shall we take the job?"
"It's your decision, but why not, it looks like it could be fun!"
"I think so. I'll talk to Duncan in the morning and tell him that we'll stay."
"What about the house in Kitwe and Gibson?" she asked.
"I expect that if we move here, we'll have to give up the Kitwe house, and then we'll have to work out what to do for Gibson," James continued.
"I'll talk to some of the others in the morning about what they do and where the boys live," Katrina promised. "Then I'll find out when they want us to move and arrange something with my company."
"What about you?" James asked. "Won't you miss the job?"
"No, it's been different since we sold the business. Working for someone else, even in the same business, is very different to running your own business. I'll be happy for a change."
"Are you sure?"
"Sure sure, *moenie worry nie!*"

In the morning, there was a knock at the door, and Kirsty was there to offer them breakfast. James and John left very soon after breakfast and went to find Duncan Brown and Henry Wayne. James gave Duncan the news that he wanted the job and asked about moving. Duncan told him that the sooner the better, but suggested that before he came, he take a quick tour of the other open-pit mines on the Copperbelt. He would arrange things so that James and two of the shift bosses could visit the other operations and perhaps learn a thing or two.

James spent the morning looking over the whole site, then went with Hippo for a tour of the existing mining operation. They met up with John Watson and talked about the bush clearing and pre-stripping. John had brought down some dozers and scrapers for the job. A couple of his dozers were busy clearing and pushing the bush and trees into piles away from the projected pit perimeter. Another was being used as a push tractor to more quickly load the scrapers. They had built some temporary haul roads to the dump sites, and John was trying to find some stone or gravel he could top them off with before the rains. The lateritic soils became slick when wet, so work often ceased in the rains, sometimes for quite a while. Topping the roads off with a layer of rock helped a lot. James asked him if he had asked the Italians if they had any crusher waste they could let him have. John thought that was worth a try and took off to their mine site.

After a quick break for some lunch, James asked Duncan Brown if he had had any contact with the Italians across the river. As the geology of the sites had to be very similar, James was anxious to see what the Munshimwemba pit looked like and how much blasting they had to do. A visit was quickly arranged, and they went across the river to the other mine. Quite obviously, they were going to need a fair amount of drilling and blasting. The Munshimwemba pit was rocky. Apart from the thin layer of soil at the very surface, it was hard rock all the way down. Theirs was definitely a drill, blast and load operation. James was intrigued by their equipment. They had Russian Belaz trucks and a few Terex R-45 trucks. They also had some Caterpillar front-end loaders and a couple of antiquated Bucyrus-Erie 88-B diesel shovels acquired from the Nkandabwe mine. The Italians were very hospitable and offered them a couple of bottles of wine, apparently from the vineyards and winery of the same family that was involved with the mine.

Back at the Mtuga site, James asked what drilling equipment had been ordered. Duncan looked embarrassed and then commented that the mine captain that Williams had had work up the equipment list had patterned things after the Rokana Mindola pit and had blithely assumed that they would be able to use scrapers to a greater depth and had left the drilling equipment to be purchased "as and when needed". Now that he had seen the Italian operation, with all its goolies and other problems, he realised that they had better do something about drilling and blasting immediately. James asked about the fleet that had been ordered and was gratified to hear that it was mostly trucks and front-end loaders. The scraping portion of the operation was already being done by John Watson, so no scrapers would be required. James added drilling equipment to the list of things to do that he was developing. He thought that he could probably get away with small mobile rigs drilling holes of only 4-1/2 inches in diameter for a while, if he could find enough crews and rigs. Larger machines would be needed later, but would cost much more and take longer to deliver.

That evening, he traded stories with Katrina, who had been more successful. There were no facilities for house servants with the mine houses, but there was an African village close by, with quite nice housing. Kirsty had found it when she was looking for a house servant and had been directed to it by one of the equipment operators. Katrina had found the village headman, and it transpired that she knew him, so had struck a deal for suitable accommodation for Gibson. It was not far from the mine, but far enough that a bicycle would be an asset. That was easy to obtain; one of the Chinese bikes that were now available in Kitwe would be perfect. James related his experiences and bemoaned the imperfections of the planning department, but suggested that the Italians might be worth cultivating.

At home in Kitwe on Wednesday afternoon, Katrina sat down with Gibson and explained that they were moving to Mkushi and would he like to come. There was no question in Gibson's mind. It was his job, his duty and his desire to come; he had seen Missy Katrina grow up and was not going to shirk his duty now. Katrina went through the housing situation with him and explained what they could do. He was happy with that and just wanted help in moving himself and his family to the new village. Katrina promised transport and then set the move date for that Saturday.

"What's Kirsty like?" James asked Katrina later.
"She's nice, if a little difficult to understand at times."
"Do you think she's happy here?" he continued.
"Now, yes," Katrina confirmed. "For a while there, with John gone so much, it was touch and go, but apparently things are better now and life is rosy in the McFarlane household."
"John told me that it had become difficult and that he had asked for a more permanent assignment several times, but nothing came up until this project," commented James.
"Well, I hope she finds something to do there, or she could go off the rails fast, like some of the other wifies," Katrina added.
"What about you?" asked James. "Will you be happy there?"
"Man, it will only be fun!" she replied. "I can try my hand at gardening, explore the country a little and who knows what else."
"What about a little fun now?" asked James.
"What did you have in mind?" asked Katrina in turn. "As if I didn't know!"

The following morning, James went to the main office to report to George McIntosh that he had accepted the job. McIntosh saw him briefly, then handed him off to Colin Winter, who went through more of the details and had him sign appointment papers, including new dumps regulations that had come into force after the Aberfan coal tip disaster in 1966. Winter then took James over to the Geology Department. Duncan Brown was already there with Hippo and Abel Mwewa, another one of James's old associates. Whereas James and Hippo had some theoretical knowledge of open-pit mining, it was going to be an adjustment for Abel. Duncan then suggested that they all go in his Land Rover on their first visit.

They drove out past the western outskirts of Kitwe, past the Rokana Mindola shaft to the Mindola open pit. A tour had been arranged, and they got an explanation of the mining method and the equipment choices. The ore body was quite different to the Mtuga prospect. At Mindola, it was stratigraphic and dipping, very well defined and overlain by a marker layer of argillite. In contrast, the Mtuga deposit was more of a collection of lenses that they would have to chase. The pit planning was, therefore, going to be more complicated. James could see why their own planners had not really thought about drilling and blasting. The Mindola pit was still using scrapers a fair way down, and they had some small mobile drills working on patterns ahead of the electric shovels. There were some larger drills planned that were due to arrive sometime in the future from Hausherr, a German company.

The Mindola shift boss answered all their questions, including details of load factors, powder factors, tyre wear, production rates and the start-up issues they had faced. One of the items that James had thought of, but had not yet formulated his own plans for, was training equipment operators. Most of the Mindola operators had not even known how to drive cars or lorries when they were recruited. So, that had been one of the early tasks of the mine, to teach everyone to drive! A local driving school had won the contract, and the town had become used to seeing their lorries around the town filled with operators in blue overalls with the red hard hats of trainees. James got the name of the school and wondered if they would operate away from Kitwe. Perhaps he also needed to check to see if there was a driving school in Kabwe, which was just a little closer than Kitwe.

The Mindola operation was almost all Caterpillar equipment, scrapers, dozers, front-end loaders, graders and some rubber-tyred dozers. They had two electric shovels from P&H, apparently made in Japan by Kobe Steel. Electric shovels were out of the question for Mtuga, one because production rates probably would not warrant the expense and two because their electrical supply probably would not stand the load. James liked the service bays and the workshops. He then looked over the tank farm for the fuel and oils. He needed to work out a deal with one of the oil companies for the delivery of diesel and lubricating oils to his own operation.

They then toured the dumps and were introduced to the niceties of dump construction and drainage, and the problems of squatter townships moving in close to the foot of the dump. The view from the top of the dump was intriguing. They could see a good part of Kitwe in the distance and in other directions a seemingly never-ending expanse of bush.

At home, James again compared notes with Katrina about their days, and Katrina told him that she had made arrangements with her company to resign immediately. Her company had generously offered to move them to Mkushi and also to move Gibson and his family. The trucks would be there on Saturday morning. They did ask Katrina to use her best offices, when appropriate, to try and get them the transportation business to move the machinery from either Beira or the railhead. James told her what he had seen and then told her that they were going to the Chambishi open pit the next day.

The Chambishi pit had more in common with the projected Mtuga pit. The ore body was significantly folded, which complicated the mine layout. It was easy to see the different strata in the pit walls; in fact, it made for dramatic photography. The equipment roster included Euclid trucks and electric shovels from Ruston Bucyrus. James took particular notice of their drilling and blasting methods, from hole sizes used to explosives and firing patterns.

They then went on to the Nchanga open-pit complex. Nchanga was in a different league. James had been there before to their overlook, but now was able to take a guided tour of the whole operation. Everything was larger than the previous two operations they had looked at. The electric shovels were larger; the trucks were of a hundred-ton capacity and were diesel-electric drive. The drills were much larger with hole sizes of up to twelve inches. There were also several smaller pits in the complex, the River Lode, Upper, Chingola, Mimbula and Fitula pits. All of these probably had more in common with Mtuga than the main Nchanga pit.

Lastly, there was a bucket wheel excavator system to strip soft overburden from the top of the pit. James was interested, but it had no application at Mtuga. He asked Duncan what other open pits there were in Zambia. Duncan went through a list of a few small operations, including the Bwana Mkubwa mine near Ndola, the Kalengwa mine, some 250 miles west of the Copperbelt, the proposed re-start of the Kansanshi mine near Solwezi as an open pit and the Maamba Collieries mine, down near the shores of Lake Kariba. This last was interesting because it had the only large walking dragline in Zambia, a Bucyrus-Erie 1260-W; as with the bucket wheel excavator, it was an intellectually interesting subject but of no application to Mtuga.

At home, James discovered that Katrina had most of their stuff packed and ready to be moved to Mkushi. All that she had left out were essentials for the night and clothes for the morning. Her old company had said that they would have a crew there by seven to begin loading. As Katrina knew nearly all the drivers and loaders, she had no doubt that they would be there at seven, perhaps even a few minutes early at the gate. They decided on dinner out and, in the way of a remembrance, drove to Luanshya and ate at the Blue Room. It was a restaurant they had been to when they had first started dating. On their way home, they stopped, as before, to look at the stars and watch the electrical storm that had blown up. There was an impressive amount of lightning and associated thunder, but no rain!

What's in the project budget?

Monday morning early, James called a meeting of the project team, in part to meet all of them, particularly those he had only seen in passing the week before and in part to get a better sense of where they were with the project. Hippo and Abel had the easiest job, for the moment, they were just observing the pre-stripping and checking on the construction of the dumps and the haul roads. James soon gave them new tasks to work out how many operators they would actually need and put a plan together for recruiting and housing. Next was John McFarlane; John was busy working with the construction contractor, ensuring that the mill and concentrator went up as planned. It looked as if he had things well under control. Then James went through with the contractor the plan for all the buildings, including the mill, equipment workshops, service bays and the tank farm. Finally, he went through the maintenance and repair items with Angus McBride, the engineer. Why was it, he wondered, that the Scots seemed to turn up in large numbers anywhere there was machinery to be built or repaired? As he went through things with Angus, they discovered that hand tools for mechanics had been overlooked, so needed to be ordered. Angus was also concerned about how he was going to divide his effort between keeping the mill and mining equipment running. James promised that they would return to that subject soon enough.

After the meeting, James pored over the documents he had been given and the files that Jim Brown had kept. He found the project file and started to go through it carefully. He asked John McFarlane to join him and then started to go through each area of the project. There was the obvious capital portion with all the major machinery and equipment, and a construction amount. Then they started to look for all the other items that would be necessary. The recruiting and training costs, the initial supplies that would be necessary before they actually produced any concentrate. It got to be almost a joke, with James asking "What's in the project budget?" and John either finding some amount or commenting "nothing!" At the end of the morning, James had a shopping list of issues to be discussed with the office in Kitwe and began to wonder if he had done the right thing in taking on this job.

He took a break for lunch and drove to the shore of the Mita Hills dam, where he sat, ate and listed in priority all the things that needed doing. The item that he put at the top of his list was some help in the area of accounting. He felt that he really needed someone on-site to keep track of expenditures. Sending data to Kitwe, then waiting for some office type to call up with silly questions, did not seem very productive. It would be better to generate the reports himself, together with the explanations and action plans, do something, then ask for forgiveness instead of permission.

Feeling a little more confident about things, James went back to the office and his paperwork. In some ways, the biggest change from his previous jobs was going to be paperwork instead of direct supervision of people. This job, clearly, was going to be more office-bound than the job he had expected to return to. Perhaps that was the price for advancement. He resolved to do whatever he could to not get trapped in the office, but to ensure that he spent a reasonable amount of time in the mine, the mill and the workshops. At the office, he arrived in time to take a phone call from Winter in Kitwe. James went through his activities for the morning, then started in on the litany of issues that he had uncovered. Winter told him to be in Kitwe on Friday, and they would go through everything with Tony Williams, his planning staff, the divisional engineer, Duncan Brown and Henry Wayne. He also promised to get some help in the accounting arena and hoped to have that name by Friday.

"How was your day?" Katrina asked when James returned home.
"Okay, I suppose, you can't believe what a *regtig gemors* it all is!"
"Why, what's wrong?" she asked.
"Oh, I'm not really sure whether the planners just didn't do a good job or if Jim Brown didn't catch things," James explained.
"Well, I heard a little about that," she commented. "Apparently, Brown was chasing one of the farmers' daughters from near here. They tell me she's not much to look at but has got a body that you wouldn't believe!"

"How do you pick up this stuff?" James asked.

"Gibson told me some, and then Kirsty and then some of the other people on the mine. It seems it was not exactly a big secret, especially when he would bring her here when his wife was shopping in Broken Hill," she elaborated.

"I know someone else who has a body that you wouldn't believe," commented James.

"Oh, who?" Katrina demanded.

"Come with me and I'll show you."

"What now?"

"Yes, now now!"

"But, Gibson's getting dinner ready!" she protested. "And I invited John and Kirsty and Angus and Morag."

"Okay, I'll show you later, that is if you're still interested?"

"Maybe, we'll see!" was her final comment.

"Who's Morag?"

"The wife of Angus, your engineer."

"Oh, how did you meet her?"

"I was having coffee with Kirsty, and she stopped by, so I invited her and her husband to dinner. Is that alright?"

"That's fine. It'll give us a chance to get to know them a little better," James thought.

After dinner and after the guests had gone and Gibson had gone for the night, Katrina asked James, "So, where is this person that you were going to show me?"

"Come with me," he replied. He led her into the bedroom and undressed her, and stood her in front of the full-length mirror. "There she is!" he announced.

"I don't think so," she disagreed. "Look, my boobs are small and I've got the legs of a weightlifter."

"I don't think so," James said, coming around behind her and running his hands over her breasts. "They feel fine to me, and your legs are fine, just what I need after a hard day at the office."

"I think you're having a hard day now, I can feel you! Get those clothes off and let's put it to good use!"

52

"Where do you think Morag is from?" James asked Katrina later.

"She told me that they're both from Glasgow," she replied. "If it's possible, I find them even more hard to understand sometimes than John and Kirsty."

"Yes, I was sure that when she said *braw* money that you'd be completely at sea!" he laughed.

"Yes, does that mean what I think, that it's good?" she asked.

"Yes, he probably gets paid fairly well, and then he's getting paid for the overtime he's putting in here, which must all mount up," confirmed James.

On Thursday night, James asked if Katrina wanted to go with him to Kitwe. She said that she would love to go and asked if Kirsty and Morag could go with them. James was happy to comply, but asked that they be ready to go at six in the morning. They were ready and at the door before six, and Gibson had come in early to provide coffee. Morag had been in the country less than three months. Angus had been recruited to work at the Mtuga property, so they had essentially gone straight there. She was looking forward to a day out in the big city. She had a shopping list a mile long, and James wondered if there would be room in the Land Rover on the way home for them and all her purchases. He drove to the mine office, then suggested that Katrina check at about three in the afternoon to see if he was still in one piece and able to go home.

James checked in and was told that the meeting had been set for ten; meanwhile, Winter wanted to see him. Colin Winter, it transpired, had been concerned about odd reports he had received back from the project and knew that all was not well. He wanted a complete evaluation of the problems and omissions and was a little surprised at what had been missed and what the extra cost would be. At ten, they met with Tony Williams, Duncan Brown, Henry Wayne and George Armstrong, the divisional engineer. James went through his findings and then watched Williams squirm a little as Winter asked question after question. Williams finally brought in the mine captain, who had done most of the work. Harry Lloyd was now in the hot seat, and it was fairly apparent that he lacked the knowledge and enthusiasm for the

53

work. Lloyd was thanked for his efforts and dispatched back to the planning department to work on ore reserve numbers for the underground mine.

Winter suggested a break for lunch and said that they would reconvene at one thirty. He then asked James if he had any plans for lunch, and if not, would he join him at the Edinburgh hotel. As Katrina and her ladies were off, who knew where, James was happy to accept. Winter then revealed a little of what had been going on. As with many large companies, it was politics. The planning department did not want the project; they had their own pet project that they would rather see the money spent on. So, they had put one of their least competent people on it. Williams reported directly to McIntosh, so it was difficult to pressure him into doing things. The best thing they could do was succeed and confound the critics. James asked about accounting help and was told that he would be joining them for lunch.

At the Edinburgh, they were shown to a table where there was already a man seated. He rose to greet them, and Winter introduced James to John Wells. John was from the head office in London and had asked for some field experience. Well, he was going to get it! Winter told James that he had pulled a fast one on the planners and had got head office interested enough to want to put one of their own people on the project, so had used the request of John as a convenient solution. John had flown in earlier in the week and had been getting familiar with the project. He had found holes and flaws in the financial analysis, which, fortunately for James, matched what he had found. Winter then gave them their marching orders; succeed!! James asked a couple of more housekeeping-related questions. Was John married? Did he have a car? Where would he live? The answers to which were, no, yes, the company would provide, and there was a spare house at Mtuga that he would be assigned to. James suggested that, if it was convenient, John follow them back to the mine that evening.

When they reconvened, the tone of the meeting was a little different. When it became known that John Wells had a pipeline back to London, Williams could not be more accommodating and concerned. James then asked for some help in the personnel area. Winter told him that help was on its way and Jerry Mwanza would be joining their team before the next weekend. James also promised to come to Kitwe once a fortnight to report, unless there was something out of the ordinary that required attention. Meanwhile, there was plenty to do!

Katrina was there at three, and James and John were ready to go. James suggested that Katrina drive back, and he would follow with John. On the way back, he tried to find out a little about his new financial help cum spy. He started with the basics. "Where are you from, John?"

"I'm from Norfolk," John started. "I went to Cambridge and joined the company about two years ago."

"What's your degree?" James asked.

"PPE, philosophy, politics and economics," John provided. "Then I did a stint in the financial analysis section of the head office in London, but it struck me that we were making decisions about people and places we knew nothing about, even where they were! What about you?"

"I was raised in the Thames Valley, went to Imperial, to RSM actually, and got a degree in mining engineering and have been here since."

"Is it really as dangerous as people say? John asked.

"No, there are risks, of course, but if you're smart, you can mitigate the risks and run a fairly safe operation. There is always the risk that someone will do something stupid, so you really are dependent on people," James elaborated. "What's your next move after this?"

"I imagine that they will put me in charge of the finances of one of the mining groups somewhere," thought John. "We'll see how well this goes. If we mess this up, things could be sticky!"

"So, you took a risk coming here?" suggested James.

"Yes, I suppose so, but, if you are half as good as Winter says, there's not much risk!" said John.

When they arrived at the mine site, they got John settled in his house, Morag and her packages unloaded, and Kirsty delivered to her house. Once at home, James asked about Katrina's day. She was not exactly a big shopping fan, so had dropped Morag and Kirsty for a while and then had got back together with them for lunch. She was curious about John Wells. "Who's the *ouk* you rode back with?" she asked.

"Either our saviour or our condemnation," commented James. "He's from head office in London and is here to help with the finances."

"Morag and Kirsty thought he was rather dishy, in a bookish academic sort of way," she commented. "Is he married?"

"Apparently not," James replied. "I don't want him distracted for a while, so tell all the matchmakers to lay low for a while!"

Saturday, James introduced John to the rest of the team and then let him do his own interviews to get himself up to date. John Watson came into the office and invited everyone to a *braai* that he was going to hold that evening. John told them that he had also invited some of the local farmers and the Italians from across the river. He was going to set something up at the temporary camp that he had built for his people while they worked on the Mtuga contract.

The *braai* was a great success. It was likely to be the last one for a while, with assured weather. The rains were sure to break soon, and then it would be more difficult to plan outdoor events. Everyone went, which was gratifying to James, as he wondered how things would go. Katrina made contact with one of the farmers for milk, butter and eggs and John Wells was invited fishing by another farmer. Hippo and Abel talked to James a little about John. They wanted to know how much to tell him. James told them to tell him everything; it was their best chance of pulling off a coup and confounding the nay-sayers. John McFarlane and Angus entertained almost everyone with their discussion about football and the pros and cons of Celtic versus Rangers. They were both invited by Hippo to go to a Mufulira Wanderers game at some time.

The farmers told them a little about the various ANC and ZIPRA camps that were in the area. The ANC, the African National Congress, from South Africa, was training people for their struggle against the apartheid regime in Pretoria. ZIPRA, the Zimbabwe People's Revolutionary Army, the military wing of ZAPU, the Zimbabwe Africa People's Union, was also training people for their struggle against the Smith regime in Rhodesia. The farmers commented that, for the most part, they were left alone by the ANC and ZIPRA people, but occasionally odd things happened. All the farmers wanted to do was raise their maize and tobacco and get it to market.

There had been problems in Lusaka with ZAPU and ZANU, the Zimbabwe African National Union; they had both sufficiently annoyed President Kaunda in 1971 that he actually evicted a number of them from Zambia. He was tired of the factional fighting between them; after all, they were supposed to be fighting the minority regime in Salisbury, not each other. One of the major differences between ZAPU and ZANU was that ZAPU and ZIPRA were essentially supported, trained and armed by the Russians, whereas ZANU and ZANLA, the Zimbabwe African National Liberation Army, were supported, trained and armed by the Chinese. This meant a difference in their approach to the conflict, the former more direct and the latter more subtle.

For almost the whole of the next week, James spent his time working on plans for the mine and resolving issues that came up with the construction. The foundations for all the major pieces of mill machinery were in place, and the roof was now on the main building. On his visit to the Mkushi Copper Mines operation, James had seen something that alarmed him a little. There, the prevailing wind blew all the dust from the crushing operations into the equipment workshops. He wondered how they managed to keep anything running well when a repair was just as likely to cause problems as solve them. He checked their own layout with John McFarlane and the others and learnt that, more by good luck than judgement or planning, their layout would not have the same problems. The prevailing wind tended to blow dust away from the workshops. He had also been fascinated with the Russian equipment that Mkushi had; the Belaz trucks and the dozer, the crane and the Gaz, jeep-like, vehicle. It all looked rather like something out of the fifties. The Italians told him that they also ran like something out of the fifties, with the exception of the primary crusher that just kept running no matter what they put in it.

John Wells was turning out to be a marvel. He knew that he did not know a lot about the business, which in some ways was good, because he would ask the most basic questions. The project team was sometimes at a loss as to how to answer, because they had not thought of the issues in that way. He caused them to go back to basics and really think about some of their assumptions. In less than a week, they now had a project timeline and spending plan and could begin to follow their progress. John McFarlane was now starting to worry about the chemicals he would need for the flotation cells, the balls for the mill and spare mantels for the crusher. They also needed somewhere to store all those things and the spare parts for the mining equipment when it arrived.

John's other big worry was the number of people he thought it would take to run the mill. His first estimate was four hundred, split among the various departments of the concentrator. He had people for the crushers, the mills, the flotation cells, the thickeners and the filters. Plus, he wanted to add a number of maintenance people to the number that he and Angus had already presented. At first, James was horrified at the size of this army, but then he thought of it in terms of three shifts with coverage over the weekends, and he realised that it was probably realistic. They also needed to establish how much support they would get from Kitwe in terms of purchasing and other administrative functions. John also reminded James that he was not Superman and that there needed to be supervisors for three shifts, so at least two more.

By the weekend, James was ready for a break, and Katrina suggested that they take off after lunch on Saturday and drive to the Wonder Gorge. She thought that they might take sleeping bags and either sleep in the back of the Land Rover or on the ground, if they found a suitable spot. James toyed briefly with the idea of inviting others, but decided against it. This was the time he needed for himself to be on his own with Katrina. They left the site at about one and drove across the river and past the Munshimwemba property. When they came to a major crossroads, they turned right and headed south. Katrina told him that the crossroads was known by the unlikely name of Piccadilly Circus, just a little different to the Circus that James knew of in London! The next landmark was Old Mkushi; James presumed that at some time in the past, the local administrative centre had been moved from there to the current site at Mkushi, on the Great North Road. Actually, the road they wanted turned off just a little distance short of Old Mkushi and went west; they then took other turns and finally a less graded dirt road that eventually led to the confluence of the Lunsemfwa and Mkushi Rivers.

The view was spectacular! A thousand-foot-deep valley with dense bush-covered slopes cut into the rocks. "What do you think, shall we stay here the night?" James asked Katrina.
"Man, it's only beautiful," she replied. "*Ja*, I think it would be a good place except for all the people."
"I noticed that," commented James. "Where are they from?"
"*Ja*, probably from Broken Hill and Lusaka," thought Katrina. "It's not too far from Broken Hill; they're also *maningi ouks* that come from Broken Hill to the bottom end of the Mita Hills dam every weekend to fish."
"Did you notice that turn-off back there that looked like it went down to the Mkushi River?" James asked.
"Do you think the river is fordable?" Katrina wondered.
"Only one way to find out," suggested James. "Do you see any people over on the south side of the Mkushi River?"
"No, *kom ons ry*," she said.

James went back a little way up the track and turned off onto the road that went down the hill to the river. The road twisted and turned as they lost altitude until they reached the riverbank. James got out and waded across to check the water depth and the going underfoot. It looked as if they would have no problem with the water depth, but the going was tricky, and he decided that it would be better to winch themselves over. He then looked around for something to anchor his cable to with little success. He noticed an older man watching him, so waved and greeted him.
"*Madala, kanjani?*"
"*Mushle Bwana, ini wena funa?*"
"*Mina funa buya lapa side, ma lo magwakwa ena mubi,*" commented James, lamenting the condition of the road through the ford.
"*Ena kona munya lapa side,*" said the man, pointing to another less obvious crossing. "*Mina azi lo ena mushle!*" he confirmed.

59

"*Sure?*" queried James, anxious that the going would be better at the other ford.

"*Sure, sure, buya na mina, tina azi buka na lo,*" suggested the man.

James went with him, and they looked at the other ford. It was not as obvious as the main ford, but, perhaps because it had been less used, it was in much better condition with a smooth sandy bottom and only small rocks, unlike the main ford, which was littered with large rocks.

"*Ena mushle,*" James agreed, then asked the man where he lived. "*Upi ena kona la kaia ka wena?*"

"*Lo ena lapa side,*" the man indicated, pointing up the slope they were about to go up. "*Lo ena kachana,*" he added, indicating that it was far.

"*Wena funa buya na tina?*" asked James, wondering if the man would like a ride up the hill at least.

"*Sure, Bwana, mina azi diniwilli stelek,*" replied the man, accepting the ride and explaining that he was very tired.

"*Ini lo gamu ka wena?*" James asked, wanting to at least be able to address him by name.

"*Silent, futi lo gamu ka lo Bwana?*" he was asked.

"James, *okay, tina azi hamba,*" he replied and suggested that they go.

Back at the Land Rover, he explained to Katrina that there was a better ford a little further upstream and that they were going to give the kind gentleman who had shown him the ford a ride up the hill. On the way up the hill, Katrina asked Silent what he did and, in turn, explained where they now lived and worked. Silent told them that he had worked at Kabwe in the lead and zinc mine until his health deteriorated and then had retired. He now lived with his sons and daughters, and grandchildren. He liked to grow things and was proud of his garden. Silent told them that many years earlier, the area had been well populated with rhino, and it was generally rhino tracks that people used to get around and that now formed the basis of the roads they used. Unfortunately, over the years, the population had been reduced to almost nothing, and the rhino had moved away to safer pastures. When they reached the top, they understood why Silent had been glad of the ride. It was quite a climb up, and James had had to use the low range of his gearbox all the way, using only first and second gears. At the top, they came to a small village, where they dropped off Silent, and they drove on to the edge of the canyon.

From this side of the Mkushi River, the view was a little different, but just as spectacular. They could make out the people on the other ridge, but otherwise, there was no one else around. James wondered how hot it would be at the bottom of the gorge or in the Luano valley below the gorge. Apart from the Lunsemfwa River, there were also the Mulungushi then the Lukusashi Rivers before the now swollen Lunsemfwa joined the Luangwa. All that water in deep valleys typically meant hot and humid conditions, and it was October, the hottest month of the year, so the valley must be pretty stifling.

It felt like rain, and the electrical storms had been as impressive as ever, but thus far, no rain. Perhaps the rains would break the following week. That thought set him to thinking about the construction site and the preparations for rain, including a sump in the pit with a suitable pump. He made a mental note to talk to John Walker about it on Monday morning. He did recall seeing drainage channels around the pit leading off into the bush. He trusted that the water would, in fact, flow away from the pit and not towards it!

Katrina broke in on his reverie and suggested that they think about dinner. James agreed and cleared a circle of ground and then built a fireplace out of stones. He gathered brush from the trees and bushes in the area and lit a fire, and attended to cooking dinner. After dinner, he put up a screen around their campsite and cleared an area for their sleeping bags. Not that they would need much in the way of coverings. It was still fairly warm, even though the sun had gone down. He thought about the possibility of rain and decided that it would be fine that night, so did not bother with anything above their heads. There was almost no moon at all, so the stars appeared brilliantly. As they lay back on the ground sheet and looked up, James tried to identify the constellations that they could see. He picked out Corvus and the Southern Cross, then started to guess the rest. Katrina helped him a little, and together they identified Virgo, Leo, the Hydra and perhaps Crater. Of the many others they could see, James thought that he would

61

need a star map or some other guide. Without the light from cities, it looked as though there were many millions more stars, even more than they had been able to see from Kitwe.

"What do you think of the job so far?" Katrina asked James as they lay star-gazing.

"Well, I had some serious misgivings for a while, especially after I heard about the politics. But, now I think we can make it, if everything arrives on time and we don't lose too much time in the rains," he replied.

"Is there anything I can do to help?" she asked.

"Not yet," he thought. "But, when stuff starts arriving in Beira, you can probably help a lot with advice on how to ship it to the mine."

"Well, if you use the railway as far as Kapiri, it's fairly easy to get it from there to here," she thought.

"I just hope the railway crossing at Vic Falls across the bridge stays open," commented James. "Without that, we'd have to use roads from inside Rhodesia somewhere, maybe even come across the Chirundu bridge."

"Well, enough of trains and things," remarked Katrina. "Why is it that I'm having to make the first moves tonight? Are you sick or something?"

"Come here and find out," he invited.

In the morning, they were awakened by the birds and by the sound of thunder in the distance. It seemed to James that the thunder was getting nearer and the sky was certainly clouding up. As they had a ford to cross before going home, he thought it was probably a good time to start and get across the Mkushi River before it rained. Katrina looked around, smelt the air and agreed.

"I can smell the rain," she commented. "We'd better go now now before it comes and the river comes up!"

"You're right," agreed James. "Let's get the *katundu* in the car and get going."

Katrina was right; they were across the river and about halfway up the slope to the road when it started to rain. First, there were just a few really large drops that made the windscreen messy. Not enough to clean it off, but just enough to smear the dust into mud and make it difficult to see. James pushed the Land Rover hard to get to the top before it really came down, and the track became difficult. They made it with about ten minutes to spare. Soon it was really coming down, and the windscreen wipers had a hard time keeping up with the amount of rain.

For the rest of the drive home, they slid and skidded a lot as the rain had turned the road into mud. Typically, the first rains showed where the problems were with the roads and such drains as there were. In another week or two, there would be deep patches of mud in those spots where the soils were poor, and driving would be an adventure again. As they turned into the mine site, James saw John Watson's crew chief, Jackson, scurrying around the perimeter looking at drainage. He found one spot that was directing the water the wrong way and got a Caterpillar D-9 tractor to redirect the water into the bush. James stopped and talked to him briefly, and was assured that they had a sump ready and a pump. When any appreciable amount of water had collected, Jackson said that he would go down and start the pump. James asked where the riser line would empty out and was directed to a drainage channel cut deep into the bush. It looked as if that would be fine.

They got into their house without getting too wet and decided to leave everything in the Land Rover until later. James and Katrina were changing when they were disturbed by a knock at the door. James went to see who it was and found John McFarlane and Angus on his doorstep.

"Come in," he invited. "Is everything alright?"

"Fine, we won't come in, we're all wet. We saw you drive in and thought we should give you a status report before you got involved in anything," replied John.

"Yes, we have a few problems," added Angus. "The levels around the workshops are not what they should be, and we need to dig a ditch across the front to stop the water going in."

"Okay, I'll get Jackson to send a grader over; that should do the job. Anything else?" James asked.

"Yes, we have the same problem with the mill building," replied John. "Can we save you the trouble of coming out and just talk to Jackson ourselves?" asked Angus.

"Of course," replied James. "Just tell him what you need done and keep a record of it so that we can talk to the building contractor tomorrow."

"We thought you'd say that," commented Angus. "We're going to get John Wells to come with us and see what we need."

"Good, it'll help us if he tracks everything that needs doing, then we can deal with the contractor with numbers," added James. "Anything else you need?"

"No, I think that's all," replied John. "We'll be off and let you know tonight how things are."

"Thanks," said James. "I'll see you later."

"It sounds as if they're pretty good," commented Katrina when they had gone.

"Yes, maybe things will turn out fine after all, if they don't get transferred away," agreed James.

The storm lasted about two hours, then the rain stopped and the sun shone again. James retrieved their belongings and then made some tea. He was checking over some drawings when John and Angus returned. They pointed out to him on the plans where the water had been flowing and where the low spots were. All in all, it was not too bad; it could have been much worse. It was apparent that around the houses that they were going to have to do something about the roads because they had turned to mud almost immediately. If James did not want all the wives complaining about mud in their houses, he would have to come up with something, and quickly. He wondered how the African village had fared and was reassured by Angus, who had been talking to Jackson, that the African village had been intelligently sited on a slight knoll, so that the water naturally drained away from it all the way around.

Monday morning it rained again, enough to halt all work in the pit and on the construction. James used the time to go through the work plans and schedules for the next few weeks and to meet with the contractor about the grading of the site and the assurance that they had been given that all water would flow away from the buildings. The contractor was embarrassed and promised to make good the work they had had to have done, and threw in a few extras to balance the books. It turned out that most of the day they spent testing the roads for safe driving, only to be forced back inside by more rain. That night it rained hard, James and Katrina lay in bed listening to the noise as it beat down onto the corrugated iron roof of the house. James thought that that was a sound he would carry with him the rest of his days.

Tuesday morning brought sunshine and bad news. Their road had been washed out by the rain, and there was now a nice deep gully where before there had been a small stream and bridge. James drove out to have a look and stood on the edge with John Watson, Hippo, Abel, Jackson and Angus.

"We need a new bridge," John commented. "God only knows where we'll get one fast enough to allow us to bring equipment in this week."

"How wide is the gully?" asked James.

"I'd guess just over twenty feet," suggested John. "Why, do you have an idea?"

"Let's try this, call up Zambia Railways and see if we can beg, borrow or steal, or perhaps even buy, a couple of flat railway wagons and use them to bridge the gap," suggested James.

"Are they long enough?" asked Angus.

"I would guess about thirty feet, and if they can take a D-9, they can certainly take our regular traffic. If we put them side by side, we can bring over even the widest loads," elaborated James.

"We could always just fill it in with a load of rock," suggested Abel.

"No," disagreed John. "Then we'd have a dam and the water would go somewhere else. We need to let it go away. But, we could use some rock as rip rap to be sure that the bridge abutments don't erode anymore."

"Okay then, I'll get onto Zambia Railways about some flat wagons. Meanwhile, John, can you get some rock and protect the banks a bit here? Also, you might grade off the top of the bank on both sides so that we can drop in the wagons when we get them," detailed James.

"Is there another way across the stream?" asked Angus.

"Sure, we can run a D-9 over a little upstream, but we couldn't use the crossing as a ford for much traffic; we'd spend all our time pulling things out of the dambo," explained John.

James called Zambia Railways and was passed from person to person until he finally reached a Mr Mwewa. As they were talking, something rang a bell in the back of James's mind about Mr Mwewa.

"Mr Mwewa, were you in Kitwe in 1969?" he asked.

"Yes, I was there with Mr Turnbull, why do you ask?" was the reply.

"Do you remember me? I was the one taking pictures of trains that were in the station."

"Ah, yes, the spy, I do remember, you are still here then?" Mr Mwewa said with a laugh.

"Yes, and with a problem that perhaps you can help me solve," commented James. He went on to describe their problem and his proposed solution. Mr Mwewa was hesitant because railway wagons were hard to come by, and to lose two would be awkward. However, he checked his records, books and notes and came up with two that they could have. They were in Kabwe, and if James could meet him there the next day, he would 'loan' them to him. Now all James had to do was get across the stream, drive to Kabwe and arrange for a couple of low loaders to move the wagons. He was already formulating a plan in his mind of how to place the wagons without a crane, and then realised that he needed some way to get the wagons onto the low loaders in the first place.

James went home quickly and asked Katrina if she could come into the office for a minute and call her friends in Kitwe and get two low loaders for the next day, to collect the wagons and deliver them to the mine site. Although the notice was short, Katrina was able to arrange things, and they would all meet in Kabwe on the morrow at ten in the morning.

The next day, they were towed across the stream by John using one of his D-9s, a little overkill, but that way the dozer was on the right side of the stream to prepare the top of the bank. When they arrived in Kabwe, Mr Mwewa was ready, and the good news was that he had a crane. He had brought out a railway crane that they had in the workshops, and it was a simple matter to lift the wagons off their bogies and onto the low loaders. James took the opportunity to talk to Mr Mwewa about the loads that they anticipated would be coming from Beira in the next months, and they arranged to meet to discuss unloading at Kapiri Mposhi.

Placing the wagons at the bridge site was actually fairly straightforward. James had asked Abel to find them two tall trees that needed to come down as part of the bush clearing, and they used those as shear legs to pull the wagons across the stream using dozers on each side for lifting and placement control. It only took a couple of hours, and they were back in business with a nice bridge. They tested it by running the D-9 back across the stream, and everything was fine. John and Hippo had brought in rock and protected the bridge abutments, so, for now at least, the crisis was over.

The next crisis occurred quickly enough. The following day at about noon, they lost power. James checked with the Italians, and they had also lost power. It seemed that someone had skidded off the road in the mud and had knocked over a power pole. The wires had crossed and knocked out the whole line. Angus had their generators up and running quickly, then started to decide what loads to put onto them. The offices and houses he connected quickly, and then provided some power for the contractor working on the buildings. James checked again with the Italians, and they had done essentially the same thing. They had a Caterpillar package for the concentrator and the mill, and a Russian system for the houses. Apparently, that was quite a system, and generally, things evolved into a small party when they started it. James got onto the electricity supply company and added his pleas for a quick response to put the line back up. He got a promise of a crew the next day, but they had to find a new pole and get that to the accident site. They also had to dig out the old pole and place the new one. James offered help with digging, but was informed that they were 'quite capable' of fixing their own problems.

It was actually Sunday morning before power was restored. The broken pole had not been the only issue. Some of the wires had been damaged and needed replacing, so the whole job had taken longer than anyone had anticipated. James was happy to hear that all was well and set some meetings for Monday morning to check on what had gone well and not so well in the past week. He doubted that these were the last crises they would see and wanted to see what they might do better in the future. He had called Kitwe on Thursday afternoon and moved their scheduled fortnightly review back a week. Apparently, something the people in Kitwe were about to do anyway for some reason.

Sunday, Katrina made lunch as Gibson was off for the day, and after lunch, they sat on the *stoep* watching the rain. It came off the roof in sheets and was forming quite a nice channel in front of the house.

"Are you sorry we came?" James asked Katrina.

"No, it's been fun," she replied. "It's never boring, there's always something going on."

"I like the rain, don't you?" he asked.

"*Ja*, this time of the year it's only *lekker*," she agreed. "By the time we get to April, though, I'm ready for a break."

"Do you remember when we went out past Kamfinsa and it rained on us?" he asked.

"*Ja*, but I think there're too many people around here to do that again," she laughed.

"We could always go inside?" he invited.

"Man, you're only a randy old goat, will you always be like this?" she asked.

"Only with you," he promised.

"*Ag* man, so you say. What did you have in mind?" she asked.

"Well, I could help you out of those wet clothes and then. . ." he started.

"What wet clothes?" she interrupted.

"These," he said, grabbing her and pulling her into the stream of water coming off the roof.

"Look, man, we're all wet now," she said, spluttering and laughing.

"I know, let me get you inside and out of those wet clothes," he offered again.

"Okay, but you're going to have to work extra hard now to pay for your sins!" she threatened. James found that her idea of working hard was not particularly arduous. He helped her out of her wet things and dried her off, then she pushed him down onto the bed and then straddled him. She moved up his body, offering herself to him, and his tongue quickly found her. She moved in time with his attentions and came with a shudder, after which she moved down and lowered herself onto his penis. This time, she took longer to come, and James was hard-pressed to contain himself. He failed and had to finish her with his hands.

"I love you," he whispered in her ear, now that she lay sprawled over him.

"I know," she said. "How long before we can do that again?"

"Maybe ten, fifteen minutes, maybe half an hour," he said.

"Good, because I want to try something different," she promised.

What that might have been, James did not find out that day, because they were disturbed by a persistent knocking at their front door. James got up and dressed himself, and went to see what could be so important on a Sunday afternoon. At the door was a man from the Kapiri Mposhi post office with a telegram. He had actually ridden his bicycle in the rain and mud to deliver it. James thanked him and offered him hot tea or coffee, but he declined, saying that he was expected at the African village and would be taken care of there.

"Who's it from?" Katrina asked.

"Will," replied James. "Let's see what it says; Married Saturday stop Bridget got job stop Arrive Cape Town Nov 29 stop Need be Jo'burg Dec 8 stop Advise route stop Will."

"We should get them to stop and visit with my folks," she suggested.

"Great idea, I'll call in a telegram tomorrow and suggest that, anything else?" he asked.

"No, the route you took would be fine," she thought. "Why don't you suggest they meet my folks in George on December 1st, and then my dad can help them from there?"

"Okay, I'll also send a telegram to your dad asking him to meet them at, where, I need a landmark in George?" he asked.

"What about the Slave Tree on York Street?" she suggested.

"Good idea, I'll let them both know," he agreed.

"Now, how about some afternoon tea?" she suggested. "I'll make it and bring it to you on the *stoep*."

They had visitors soon afterwards, all enquiring about their telegram and was it good news or bad. Katrina ended up serving tea to about fifteen people in the end, and by then, the whole community knew of their news.

During the next week, James had meetings with John Watson, the building contractor and his own staff. They received news on Wednesday that the boat with the mill machinery had docked in Beira and then started the process of tracking its progress. Fortunately, it had all been purchased as CIF Mkushi, or carriage, insurance and freight paid to Mkushi, so the job of actually organising transport did not fall on their shoulders. By the time James and John Wells were ready to go to Kitwe for their delayed fortnightly review, they were able to confirm that all the equipment was on the rail and somewhere between Beira and Bulawayo.

Katrina, Morag and Kirsty all wanted a trip to Kitwe, so tagged along on the ride north. James and John got Katrina to drop them at the mine office and then found their meeting. This time it was not only Winter, Brown, Williams and Wayne, but also McIntosh and another man whom John Wells knew, but James did not. He was introduced as Colin Beauchamp, and he was from the London office. Apparently, he was a financial type and had been concerned by the extra appropriations that James had asked for and had come to hear the story for himself. That explained the quick agreement to delay the review for a week, as Beauchamp had been expected.

James went through everything, and then Beauchamp did the unthinkable; he looked to John Wells for confirmation or denial. James was surprised that he would do that, at least overtly; usually that kind of confirmation was sought privately. That had to be his way of sending a message of dissatisfaction to the mine management. Fortunately for Winter and James, John confirmed all that James had said, then went on to praise the team for what they had done in the past two weeks, including replacing the bridge to the mine. With the stroke of a pen, Beauchamp then approved the extra expenditures and asked James if he thought they would have any more surprises. Unable to give an answer beyond the fact that all the known problems had been addressed, James hesitated to speculate on what might happen next.

On Saturday, James suggested a day trip out on Sunday to the Kundalila Falls. He asked his team if any of them would care to join him. Hippo and Abel said that they were going off somewhere to watch a football game. John McFarlane told him that he was going fishing with Kirsty and one of the farmers, but Angus and Morag and John Wells said that they would love to go. They left just after eight on Sunday morning and drove up the Great North Road, the 150 miles to the turnoff, arriving at the falls just in time for lunch. Katrina gave the guided tour while James set things out for lunch. The others were amazed by the view from the top of the Muchinga escarpment and took rolls of pictures. None of them felt like climbing down to the bottom of the falls, which was a shame because from the bottom, the view of the 270-foot falls was spectacular. Fortunately, the weather favoured them, and it did not rain until they were well on their way home. The last ten miles were entertaining as the Land Rover slid around on the slick and muddy road, and once or twice, Katrina was sure that they would end up going backwards.

ZIPRA

For the better part of the next week, things proceed apace. Despite rain, construction of the building went ahead, and they even managed to get some work done in the open pit. As they stripped away the top and sub-soils and got more into digging rock, the going actually became easier. They received daily bulletins as to the whereabouts of their mill equipment, and James met with Mr Mwewa to organise the use of a siding at Kapiri Mposhi to unload the wagons. They had a day or two of anxiety because the train was held up at the border at Victoria Falls. James could never determine if the hold-up was with the Rhodesians or with the Zambian customs people. Eventually, whatever the problem was, they had a resolution, and the wagons were allowed to proceed. He and Katrina met with the contractor to go over transportation from Kapiri Mposhi to the mine site, and they also met with the local police inspector because some of the loads would be large and might require an escort.

Jerry Mwanza, Hippo and Abel brought in a few driving schools for interviews and selected one that they would use to teach their operators how to drive. They also met with a housing contractor and set about building the needed accommodations for the operators. They got more definitive numbers from John McFarlane and Angus as to the number of mill operators and mechanics, electricians, etc., that would also need to be housed. They would end up with quite a sizeable village. Fortunately, they had a house design already, and there was precious little in the way of planning permissions to get. Their greatest challenge was laying water and sewer pipes and stringing electricity lines. They had to keep the electrical service to each house to a minimum because the supply was not that reliable or robust, and too much load could cause failures. Not that the houses would be anywhere near the load of the primary crusher, but it did all add up. Water and sewage treatment was something neither Hippo nor Abel knew much about, but John McFarlane stepped in to help with the contractor.

John Wells was kept busy with keeping track of all that was going on, from daily earth movement logs of John Watson's people to cubic metres of concrete poured, steel erected, and roofing put on. He seemed to James to be a little distracted one day, and James asked him what the problem was. John thought for a while, then obviously decided to take the plunge.

"Well, I'm not too sure how to put this," he started. "But I'm not a monk and I wouldn't mind meeting someone a little fairer than you once in a while."

"Ah, female company," James commented. "Maybe it's been my fault. I told the ladies no matchmaking for a while, because I wanted to keep you trapped and focused."

"Thanks a lot," commented John. "What can one do around here anyway?"

"Well, there are several of the farmers who have daughters," offered James. "If you like, we can arrange for you to meet some of them."

"Setting me up on blind dates," John cringed. "I'm not sure I really like the sound of that."

"I'll ask Katrina who there is and if they're attached or not," promised James.

"I heard that Jim Brown found himself someone," commented John. "Who was that?"

"One of the farm girls," replied James. "It depends whether you're looking for a quick roll in the hay or something a little more serious."

"I've thought about that," said John. "If she would shag Brown, knowing that he was married, who else is she shagging. I don't think I would want to be part of that."

"Okay, I'll ask and let you know," James promised again. "Not to be too indelicate, are we talking white or black?"

"I'd not thought of that," replied John. "I feel like I'm turning you into some kind of procurer of services, so sorry, but I don't think I'm quite ready for one of the black girls. It would be too much like a colonial convenience arrangement."

Later that day, James put the problem to Katrina. "I thought you told us no matchmaking?" she remarked.

"I know, but he must be feeling a little lonely; he even told me he wasn't a monk," he replied.

"Poor *ouk*, he must be only frustrated by now," thought Katrina, then she started to giggle, then to laugh.

"What's so funny?" James asked.

"I can just see you and John fencing around the topic. I would've loved to have been a fly on the wall!" she replied.

"Just as well you weren't," he commented. "I'd have been really embarrassed."

"Are you frustrated and in need of companionship?" she asked teasing.

"That's one of those questions that if you answer yes or no, there're problems," he replied.

"Why?" she asked.

"Well, if I say yes, you'll tell me that we make love almost every day and isn't that enough, and if I say no, then you'll tell me that we obviously are making love too often, so I'm damned if I do and damned if I don't," he replied.

"You could always just say that you love me and always want to be with me," she suggested.

"I do love you," he replied. "It's difficult for me to imagine life without you now. You make my days come alive, you make me laugh, you continue to surprise me, and I think I love you more now than I did when we first started to go out!"

"We were interrupted the other day," she said. "Come here and let me show you what I have been thinking of!"

For the next couple of days, James walked around with an inane grin on his face. He felt a little sorry for John. He had Katrina and was really enjoying life with her. John had no one yet, so must be getting lonely and frustrated. Katrina arranged a party over the weekend and invited most of the singles in the area to attend. After that, it was John's problem. She would provide the venue and the possibility to meet; if nothing came of it, there was not much she could do. James wondered if his next challenge would be to be a father confessor to someone. He thought sometimes that he had been educated in the wrong things. All his dealings with his biggest problems, people, could not be solved by equations and formulae.

Monday morning, early, James received a telephone call from Mr Mwewa to tell him that their mill machinery had arrived in Kapiri Mposhi. James detailed John McFarlane to go with the contractor and keep an eye on things. They had arranged for a crane to be at the siding and for another to be at the mine site to start placing pieces of machinery as they arrived. James looked through the process flow chart to re-acquaint himself with all the steps, then went into the bays and imagined where everything would be going. He was certain that they would find something that they had forgotten in the way of a conveyor or feeder, but small items were available from the Copperbelt, so there should not be much in the way of delay.

He was going through the list of railway wagons and loads when John Wells came in.

"So, John, *howzit?*" he asked.

"Fine, thank you," John replied. "Do you have anything for me?"

"Yes, you can have all this stuff," James indicated, pointing to the pile on the corner of his desk. "How was the party on Saturday?"

"Ah, yes, I thought you'd ask," replied John, smiling. "Actually, I have a date tomorrow night with Elena."

"Who's Elena?" queried James.

"She's one of the daughters of Mr Petalas," John replied.

"Okay, this is obviously going to be twenty questions; who's Mr Petalas?" James continued.

"Oh, he's a farmer. Grows maize and some tobacco, I believe. Has four daughters, which I'm sure his wife would like to marry off, and lives not far from Piccadilly Circus," elaborated John.

"And is Elena, oldest, youngest, middle?" James continued with his probing.

"Number two in the line-up," replied John. "The oldest is spoken for, but Elena is, for the moment, free as a bird."

"So, date tomorrow night?" confirmed James. "Remember to be in by eleven," he continued, laughing.

"Don't laugh!" said John. "I have to have her home by eleven or Papa will come looking for me."

"So, where will you go on this date?" asked James, intrigued.

"She suggested the farmers' club, so I imagine things will be fairly well chaperoned and reported on to the community by Wednesday," bemoaned John.

"Ah, well, the joys of a small community," James sympathised.

Jerry and Hippo were his next visitors. James had wondered what Hippo's marital status was. He learnt that Hippo was not yet married, but that he had a prospective wife in Kabwe and was working on getting the *lobola* together that he would have to pay as the bride price. Hippo and Abel currently shared one of the houses in the village, but James suggested to Jerry Mwanza that Hippo take one of the empty houses to be ready for his new wife. While they were on the subject of houses, James went through with Jerry reports on progress for the new village they were putting up for the mine and mill operators, then asked if they had enough housing in the village currently used by the management and supervision. Jerry thought they would need another ten houses there, so James told him to add it to the current construction contract and build ten more of the type that Hippo and Abel were currently sharing.

James then asked Hippo to get some crushed rock organised to repair the road. With the heavy loads that they were going to bring in, they were bound to damage the road. He suggested that Hippo patrol the road twice a day and arrange to have any damage repaired quickly. They had a small lorry that they could use for transporting the crushed stone, and they had a small labour gang that was for general purposes. This would be a perfect task for them to work on until everything was delivered.

The following afternoon, James was watching his people unload the main components of the primary crusher when he found Gibson at his side, obviously anxious to talk to him.

"*Ini lo indaba* Gibson?" he asked.

"*Lo indaba ena na lo Madam,*" Gibson replied.

"*Ka ini, lo Madam ena mushle?*" he asked, now concerned.

"*Wena azi lo Madam yena hambili lapa* Mkushi?" Gibson continued.

"*Sure, yena hambili na* Mrs McFarlane and Mrs McBride," agreed James.

"*Skati yena buya lapa mugodi fanika yena azi bambili na lo ZIPRA,*" explained Gibson. That set James thinking. Katrina and the other ladies had had some kind of run-in with a ZIPRA group.

"*Yena mushle manje?*" he asked, now really concerned.

"*Sure, sure Bwana, zonke ena mushle, ena kona lo madala, yena kulumini na lo ZIPRA,*" explained Gibson. James wondered who the person was who had intervened in the situation, and was relieved to hear that all was now well

"*Upi ena kona lo Madam?*" asked James.

"*Yena azi buya manje manje so,*" said Gibson. James thought that if they were going to arrive soon, he should go home to meet them and get the story from them. He told John McFarlane and Angus McBride that something had gone on, and it would be a good idea to meet their spouses when they returned.

"Gibson, *buya na mina, tina azi hamba lapa kaia,*" he said. He and Gibson then drove back to the village and the house to wait for Katrina and the others. It was about half an hour before they arrived. Katrina got out of the Land Rover and ran up to James and hugged him. Kirsty and Morag went off with their respective spouses, and James took Katrina in to get the story.

"Are you alright?" he asked.

"No, man, I'm fine, I could use a drink, but yes, I'm fine," she replied.

James got her a rum and Coke and then sat next to her to hear what had happened. Gibson hovered in the doorway, also anxious to know what had happened.

"Well, you know we went to the Mkushi *Boma?*" she started.

"Yes, I think it was to sort something out with Morag's identity card," said James.

"Well, all that went well then when we were driving back almost to Piccadilly Circus, there were all these people in the road in uniform with guns; men and women, most of them women," she continued. "I think the men were Zambian Army based on their uniforms, but the women, I think, were all ZIPRA. They blocked the road, and we had to stop."

"What did they want?" he asked.

"Some character who identified herself as Comrade Freedom shoved a gun in the window and said that we were interfering with a ZIPRA exercise and were under arrest," she said.

"I thought that they left us alone?" James said.

"Apparently not," she replied. "Anyway, we had to get out of the Land Rover with our hands over our heads, and then they started haranguing us about being agents for the racist regime in Salisbury."

"But, anyone who knows us knows that all we want to do is run this mine," complained James.

"I know that, you know that, but apparently Comrade Freedom didn't know or believe that," she said bitterly. "Stupid bitch!"

"But, how did you get away?" James asked after a moment's thought.

"You remember the *madala* that we gave a lift up the hill by the Mkushi River?" she asked.

"Yes," James recalled.

"Well, he's no more a retired miner than I am. He came by in a Zambian army Land Rover and proceeded to yell at the Zambian Army guys for ten minutes," she said. "I think he must be an instructor or some senior officer because all of them jumped to attention when he yelled."

"What did he say?" asked James.

"I don't know, he lost me after the first minute, but he was very nice to us. He calmed Morag and Kirsty down and apologised for the incident and guaranteed that it would never happen again. I think he was embarrassed by Comrade Freedom," she replied. "But how did you know something had happened?"

"Gibson told me that you were in trouble," he replied. "So I thought I should come home and see that you were alright."

"Thank you, Gibson," Katrina said to him.

"*Aziko indaba Madam, wena kona mushle manje?*" he asked.

"*Mina shala mushle manje, kanjani wena inzwili na lo?*" she said that she was fine now and asked how he had heard about the problem.

"*Mina azi ena kona lo indaba, mina aikôna azi fanika,*" he replied. So, he knew but had no idea really how. James thought it was another example of how news seemed to travel very quickly and without apparent means. He had long given up trying to explain it; it just was.

For the next couple of days, Katrina was unwilling to go far from the mine site. She believed what Silent had said, but wondered what would happen if he were not around. James, however, was busy and spent a lot of time with his people as the major pieces of machinery were brought in and placed. There were just over forty loads that were eventually delivered, including the primary, secondary and tertiary crushers, the ball mills, the flotation cells and all the various clarifiers, thickeners, conveyors, feeders and hydrocyclones needed for the process. John McFarlane was going to be busy with the contractors for a while installing all that equipment and connecting up electrical supplies, water supplies and instrument lines. Hippo repaired the road a dozen times in four different places; at least now they knew where the problem areas were.

On Thursday, James took some time to drive to the Mkushi *Boma* and sat down with the district officer. He went through the problem that Katrina and the others had had with the ZIPRA people while driving home and told of their saviour. He told the district officer that he wanted to express his gratitude to that man, whom he only knew as Silent, and asked what could be done to avoid such incidents in the future. The district officer was sympathetic, but he was reliant upon the Zambian army and their relationship with the ZIPRA hierarchy. He promised to talk to the local commander and see if they could not better monitor the comings and goings of the ZIPRA people so that their paths would not cross. James told him where they were with the project and roughly who would be travelling where and when.

As he was leaving, he saw Silent, who came over and talked to him. James learnt that he was actually Colonel Mulanga in the Zambian army, and he knew who all the people on the mine were and was kept abreast of the comings and goings. The colonel then told James that he had instructed the ZIPRA people to do their training closer to their own camp and east of Old Mkushi. That way, there was no possibility of meeting them on the road to the Mkushi *Boma* or to the farmers' club. He asked if James could pass on the message to the Italians that if they had any reason to go east of Old Mkushi, they would first contact the district officer, and he would make sure the message was passed on to the appropriate people. James thanked him again and told him where they were with the project. Colonel Mulanga knew about the contact with Mr Mwewa and had had one of his people checking on the loads as they were delivered.

The next day, James and John made their fortnightly pilgrimage to Kitwe. This time, the ladies elected not to go but stayed at home getting their hair done by one of the ladies from the Italian operation. James was never sure who discovered that one of the Italian village residents was a hair stylist, but they had all gone trooping over the river for a morning out. In Kitwe, they reviewed progress and then related the various incidents that had occurred in the past two weeks. James was a little annoyed because it seemed that the geologists had been given word of the ZIPRA movements but had neglected to pass on the information. Winter took James and John to lunch at the boat club, probably to see if there was anything else he needed to know. James gave him a few more details, but essentially, they had already gone through a complete briefing, so there was little else to add. Winter congratulated them on their progress and was delighted with the solution to the bridge problem. He even suggested that the mine in Kitwe give two flat wagons to Zambia Railways in exchange for the two that James had been given by Mr Mwewa. That James approved of wholeheartedly, as it assured his good relations with the Railways people.

On the way back to the mine, John asked James if things were always this exciting. James commented that as a lowly section boss or shift boss working underground, he rarely saw the light of day, except on Saturday afternoons and Sundays. He also did not have to deal with half the issues they were now concerned with. Certainly, there was no active ZIPRA presence in Kitwe, and because the mine was well established, all the ancillary services were already in place, such as housing, mine club, hospital, stores and all the infrastructure needed for a large operation. They had none of those and had to either build for themselves or make do somehow. James then asked John about his date with Elena.

"Well, to be honest," began John. "I'd rather been expecting someone who was just a pretty face, but she's an expert on horticulture and has been helping her dad with crop yields. I now know more about maize and its variants than I'll probably ever need to know!"
"How did she become an expert?" James asked him.
"She read horticulture at university and then did a one-year master's program in Brazil, so she speaks Portuguese as well as Maizese," he replied.
"Does she speak Greek as well?" James asked.
"Yes, rather makes me look like a duffer, only speaking English and a little grammar school French!" John lamented.
"You have to be careful with these colonial women, John," James cautioned. "You never know what they can turn their hand to!"

When they got back to the mine, Katrina was waiting with a telegram. It was from her father to confirm that Will and Bridget had made it as far as George, and they would be spending a couple of days in Calitzdorp before going on to Johannesburg. James thought that if Bridget really wanted to learn a few words of Afrikaans before starting work in her new job that she could not be in a better place.

December 4th did not seem as if it were a day of any particular significance until James received a call from the Italians to join them in a Santa Barbara day party. He had not known, until then, that Santa Barbara was the patron saint of miners. Well, a party seemed like a really good idea. He asked who he could bring with him, and the invitation was extended to anyone who wanted to go. He did get the impression, though, that what they meant was any one of the European staff. He then debated about how to put this to his team.

He sat down with Hippo and asked what plans Hippo had for the evening. As it happened, James was saved by football. Hippo was coming to see him anyway about getting off a little early so that he, Jerry, Abel, John McFarlane and Angus could all go to Kabwe for a football match. James breathed a sigh of relief and agreed, but did offer the alternative of the Santa Barbara party. It was clear that Hippo then also struggled with how to respond, and James helped him out by suggesting that perhaps he and Abel might not feel as welcome as the others in the staff. Hippo agreed and said that he was sure that James would understand. They then had a short philosophical discussion about how long they thought it would be before all the barriers were truly down. Hippo thought it would be the next generation. Already, it was the junior school children who were having parties with children of all races. As they grew up, unless they were otherwise indoctrinated, those attitudes would stay, and they would continue to mix without conscious thought. Hippo said that he and his contemporaries struggled with mixing probably as much as James. Some of the problem was a holdover from Colonial days; some were just a lack of common interests.

In the end, it was James and Katrina, Kirsty, Morag and John Wells who went to the party. The Italians certainly knew how to have a good time. As he enjoyed the *festa*, James wondered how it would be if Alex did marry Vincenzo. He wondered if they would have such parties and whether they would stay in England or move to Italy. In his heart, he rather hoped that they would move to Italy. He had never been there and, having met a few Italians, now thought that he would rather like to visit and see how they lived in their home environment.

The following day, James received word from the Caterpillar dealer that their equipment had left Peoria and was on its way to the East Coast of the US. They gave him a vessel name and a sailing date from Baltimore. The scheduled arrival in Beira was January 11th. The next bulletin he would likely get was the arrival in Beira and then the transport to Zambia. Now it was more urgent that they look to operators and training. Hippo and Abel had been quietly selecting potential operators from among the many that applied. They had been running tests of reflexes, aptitude, eyesight and, because of an incident at one of the Copperbelt mines, a hearing test. These tests had weeded out the numbers fairly drastically, but they were confident that they would find enough. The driving lessons had begun, and the driving school had turned up with two International Harvester trucks to take out trainees. Apparently, this was all very reminiscent of the Rokana operation, the main difference being that the Mtuga trainees were unlikely to be driving around any towns, whereas the Rokana trainees probably terrified the residents of Kitwe on a regular basis.

John McFarlane was happy with the progress on the crushing and grinding machinery installation. He and Angus were busy with maintenance schedules for the various mills and were trying to sort out just what spare parts they had and what they were likely to need. With everything going so well, James began to feel a little as if he were intruding at times.

He decided that, as things were reasonably well in hand that he would learn to operate the earth-moving equipment that they would be receiving shortly. He talked to John Watson and was set up with Jackson, his crew chief, who was to be the instructor. They started with a scraper, and James learnt how to basically drive it and how to operate the various levers that controlled how the bowl was filled and emptied. He was a little confused at first because Jackson would say 'diesel too much' and James would back off on the throttle, only to discover that what Jackson meant was 'put your foot down hard'. After the scraper, they moved to a dozer, which looked simple until James tried to push soil down a slope and finished up with a roller coaster. It took a lot more expertise than he had imagined to cut just enough off to maintain a nice working area and do useful work, but also not enough to bog the dozer down completely.

His efforts on the motor grader were entertaining. There were so many possible ways in which the grader could be adjusted that James wondered how on earth the operators managed to achieve what they did. He began to have a fair degree of respect for the equipment operators and a much greater appreciation for the difficulties they were to face in the months to come. The only items that he could not try out were a front-end loader and a truck. John Watson told him that the truck was simple enough, but that it might be worth learning how to run a front-end loader at some time.

"Your shipment left Baltimore yesterday, the 12th," the Caterpillar rep told James. "I gave you the vessel name before, but if anything changes, I'll let you know."

"Do you have a trainer that can be assigned to us for a while?" James asked.

"Yes, that was part of the purchase agreement," the Caterpillar rep replied. "He'll be there about a week after the equipment arrives."

"What about spares?" asked James.

"I've been through the lists with Angus," was the reply. "There should be a fair number of crates of parts with the machinery shipment."

"Is there anything else we need to think about?" James continued.

"Well, we have this oil analysis program that you might want to consider," was the suggestion. "It allows you to detect bearing failure and other issues early by sorting out metals in the oils."

"That sounds like a good idea. Would you talk to Angus about that?" James requested.

"Sure, will we see you in Lusaka in the near future?" he was asked.

"Perhaps, I'll see what the schedule looks like," promised James. "Well, stay in touch, and if there are any issues, please let me know."

"Sure thing," the rep promised, then signed off with "Have a good Christmas!" James thought that the rep must be spending a lot of time with Americans, as he was picking up odd Americanisms.

James received another call, this one from South Africa. It was Will calling to tell him that he and Bridget were in Johannesburg and were in a house in one of the suburbs. Bridget had started work, and Will had been given a job in the paint division. Will related a little of their experiences in Calitzdorp and their drive north to Johannesburg. Will cut the call short as it was at the expense of the company, and although they were happy for him to make the call, they had set limits. Will was well within the limits.

At home that day, James told Katrina his news that Will and Bridget were in Johannesburg and well and that his equipment was on the water and should be all at the mine in about a month. She, in turn, had news of her own.

"You know that little operation that's near Mkushi River that digs up clays?" she asked.

"Not really," James replied. "What about it?"

"Well, they're looking for someone to sell their clays, sands and other minerals," she elaborated. "I see the *ouk* tomorrow and find out what it's all about."

"What do you think it will mean?" James asked.

"I don't know yet," she replied. "I'll find out tomorrow."

"How did you hear about the job?" he asked.

"Kathy, who delivers the milk, told me and arranged for me to meet," she replied. "She told me that they dig the stuff up near the Mkushi River and sell it to all kinds of people."

"You know, you just reminded me," thought James. "We were supposed to be getting a geologist to help us. I wonder what's happened?"

"They probably think you don't need one yet," commented Katrina. "You see, you'll get one just now."

"Actually, we could probably use one now now," remarked James. "I don't think just now is going to be soon enough!"

On Thursday, when James was putting together his papers for the routine fortnightly meeting the next day, John Wells came in and asked if it was all right for Elena to ride with them to Kitwe. Apparently, she wanted to do some Christmas shopping and thought that Kitwe might have more choices than Kabwe. James thought that that would be fine and wondered who else might be going. Katrina was going, he knew, but he needed to check on Kirsty and Morag.

James checked with Katrina in the evening, and she did indeed want to get to Kitwe. She also had news of her interview with the Mkushi River clay people. She had met with a Stewart Forbes, who had put together the operation and was paying royalties to the farmers on whose properties the clay deposits were found. Forbes had offered her the job of representative, which she had accepted.

"How do you get paid?" James asked.

"It's all commission," she replied. "I get so much a kilo for each of the minerals that I sell, plus travel expenses."

"I suppose this will mean some travel?" he asked.

"*Ja*, he told me that the paint and tyre factories are in Kitwe. The china place is in Lusaka, and the glassworks is close by in Kapiri," she explained.

"Well, have fun and drive carefully. Do you think you'll ever be gone overnight?" he asked.

"It's possible," she thought. "In Kitwe, I can always stay with the Watsons, and I'm sure that there are people in Lusaka that I know."

On Friday, they did indeed have a full house. James and John, together with Katrina in the front seat of the Land Rover and Kirsty, Morag and Elena in the back seat. On the way north, Elena gave them only the basics, where she was born, raised and schooled and where she went to university. She told them a little of her aspirations but made no real comment about John or any previous relationships. James was certain that as soon as he and John were out of the way then the conversation would change and more details would either be forthcoming or would be extracted.

The progress review was fairly straightforward. The installation of the equipment for the process plant was going well and on schedule. They had, in fact, gained a few extra days, partly because they had been able to get deliveries from Kapiri Mposhi very quickly and partly because John and Angus, working with the contractor, had come up with clever solutions to allow them to work even when it was raining. James reminded the panel that he needed two more supervisors for the concentrator. When they went to a three-shift operation, he could not survive with only John McFarlane. After about an hour, Colin Winter called for a break and suggested to Duncan Brown that it might be a good time to introduce them all to his new geologist. Duncan disappeared for a few minutes, then came back in and very dramatically made the introduction.

"This is Rita," he started. "Rita Ryan, geologist extraordinaire, late of Trinity College, Dublin and your expert on all things geophysical, geochemical and probably metallurgical, with apologies, of course, to Gilbert and Sullivan."

"Please come in," invited Colin. "Welcome to our cabal. That is James Martin, the project leader, and John Wells, the fount of all things financial, also of the project. You'll be spending most of your time with them. As to the rest of us, this is Henry Wayne from the concentrator, Tony Williams of planning, George Armstrong, our divisional engineer, and of course, you know Duncan and myself."

'When did you arrive?" asked James.

"I flew in yesterday," she replied.

"All set for the great challenge then?" asked Henry. "How do you think you'll manage in the bush with no shops or beauty parlours?"

"I'll be fine, I think," she replied. "I did some of my master's work in the Olduvai."

"Oh, you're a palaeontologist then, not an exploration geologist?" asked Tony Williams.

"She's very well qualified," intervened Duncan. "I have worked with her before, before she did her master's, and that was all economic geology!"

"We were thinking that Rita could ride back with you this afternoon," Colin suggested to James.

"Oh, fine," James said. "How much stuff do you have?" he asked Rita.

"Not too much," she replied. "Only three suitcases and a rucksack."

"Well, that'll be fine," commented James. "I'll put them on the roof and cover them with a tarpaulin."

"I hope Elena and the others didn't buy too much," muttered John in an aside to James.

"I presume you have a place for Rita to live?" asked Duncan.

"We'll manage," said James at the same time, privately wondering who he was going to lean on to take Rita in for a couple of weeks before the other houses were ready.

"Rita, is there anything that you really need to do before we go to the mine?" James asked after they left the meeting.

"Not really, but I wouldn't mind the chance to change into something less formal for the drive," she replied. "I'll just use the loo and be back in ten minutes. Those are my bags; I don't need anything else out of them, so if you need to load them, you can."

"I wonder how long we'll have to wait for the others?" commented John.

"I suppose it all depends on how well the shopping went," suggested James. "How much do you bet that Rita's back before they arrive?"
"Even money, I think," John laughed. "No, I should have put some money on it, here they come now!"

The drive south was almost a repeat of the drive north, except now there was a new subject for interrogation. James never ceased to be amazed at the questions the women asked and seemed to get answered. Introductions had been made all around, and Katrina had looked at James with raised eyebrows in query when he commented that he was going to have to find somewhere for her to live for a couple of weeks. Morag saved the day. She reminded them all that Angus was due to be gone for the next week at a maintenance and service class, so she would be glad of the company.

Rita did ask one question of them, "Is that idiot Henry Wayne always so condescending?"
"Oh, yes, the bush, shops and beauty parlour question," commented James. "I suppose he can't help it. He's a product of his generation and upbringing."
"Some of these men forget where they would be if we were not there to bail them out!" added Katrina. "Let me tell you, Rita, before I knew James, he had some of those silly notions!"
That got them all talking, and James and John were showered with abuse, fortunately good-natured abuse for the next few miles. John then added fuel to the fire by commenting that if they felt strongly for the cause of women's liberation, he had no objection to their removing their bras and burning them.

Christmas

"Have you thought about what you might like for Christmas?" Katrina asked James.

"Not really," he replied. "I can't think of anything that I really want."

"But there must be something?" she persisted. "Something that you wouldn't normally buy for yourself."

"No, not really," he said. "I have everything that I need."

"I'm not talking about what you need," she persisted. "I'm talking about what you might want!"

"Okay then, what do you want for Christmas?" James asked in retaliation.

"A new camera," Katrina suggested. "I would really like to take some pictures of this place, and I don't have a camera."

"I'll see if Father Christmas has you on his list," James promised. Actually, he was quite relieved because he had taken a guess on what she might like based on conversations with Kirsty and Morag and had picked up a camera the last time he was in Kitwe. Now all he had to do was think of something for himself that he could suggest to Katrina.

"Why is it that you are always so hard to buy for?" she asked.

"I don't know," he admitted. "Perhaps because my needs are simple and there really isn't anything that I have to have."

"Yes, but what about something frivolous, just for the hell of it?" she asked again.

"I don't know; I'll think about it," he promised.

"You're a *groot kak*," she commented. "Why must you be difficult?"

"I'm not being difficult, *Suikerbossie*," James protested. "I just can't think of things like that quickly."

"Well, you'd better tell me soon, or you'll get what you get, you've got less than a week!" was her final shot.

"How is the new job?" James asked Katrina, changing the subject

"I'm still learning," she said. "I'm still trying to find out what the different minerals are."

"I thought it was just clay?" he asked.

"Yes, but clay that you'd take to the china factory," she elaborated. "They also have some sand that goes to the glass factory near Kapiri and some other stuff that goes to the paint factory and the tyre factory."

"Maybe you should talk to Rita?" suggested James. "I'm sure she could help you with the different minerals."

"I did," Katrina said. "She was actually really helpful."

"Do you think there's any reason why you would go down to Old Mkushi or thereabouts?" he asked.

"What, and run in with those ZIPRA characters again?" she asked in turn. "No, man, I don't think so. I can't see any reason to go near there, unless I take the wrong turning at Piccadilly Circus!"

"Okay then; when's your first trip?" he continued.

"After the New Year, I have an appointment in Kitwe on January 3rd," she replied. "Now you need to get going or you'll be late for your meeting!"

The big news at James's morning meeting was that their new mine Land Rovers were to be delivered that morning. They had had them painted brilliant yellow, borrowing the idea from Mindola, and had fitted radios. The radio base station was also due to be delivered that day, and then they would see what the range was and if there were any blind spots around the pit. At least now, James no longer had to use his own vehicle for travelling back and forth to Kitwe and for running around in the bush on the pit perimeter. The next big topic of discussion was call signs; who would be what, a number, a name or the vehicle number? James asked John Watson what the other mines used, and the answer was the classic 'it depends'! In the end, they decided to stick with names. There were not that many of them, and there seemed to be no point in using numbers that reflected the hierarchy; that seemed a little pretentious to James. The use of vehicle number supposed that a particular vehicle would always be used by the same person; something that James doubted would always be true.

At about ten in the morning, a procession of brand-new Land Rovers pulled into the site. There was a station wagon that James would use to cart visitors around, mainly, and the balance was open back, long wheelbase types. James and the rest of the staff looked them over, and there were obvious differences between his Land Rover. Whereas his was a Series IIA, these were now Series III. The most obvious difference outside was the use of a plastic grill to protect the radiator. "Pretty useless for grilling in the bush" was the only comment he heard about that. Inside the cab, the instruments had been moved behind the steering wheel, whereas before they were low down and in the centre of the dashboard. Also, the whole dashboard was now some form of plastic foam-padded material. 'Well, there goes the bottle opener!' was the comment he heard on that change. On the older models, the metallic curl of material under the dashboard shelf served as a handy bottle opener anywhere along its length. The one less obvious difference that the Land Rover dealer pointed out was the all-synchromesh gearbox that replaced the old box that had crash gears on first and second.

James then assigned the vehicles to each of his staff, and they had two left as spares. Apparently, when they had been ordered, several months earlier, Jim Brown had been thinking of a larger staff than James now had, or thought necessary. Angus had already set up a maintenance routine for all of them and had asked them, please, to try and stick to it. That way, the vehicles would actually last longer.

After lunch and after the Land Rover people had all left, James and John Wells had a series of meetings with tyre people. They knew very well that tyre wear and tear would be an expensive item. What they were looking for was the best deal they could get, including, if possible, someone on site regularly, if not permanently, to keep an eye on the tyres and advise if their mining methods were accelerating tyre wear. Finally, they struck a deal with one of the suppliers with a promise of a man to be there one day a week to check and replace tyres when necessary. They already had compressors on site and had an inflation cage arriving shortly. So, by the time that the equipment actually arrived, they would be ready.

That evening, James and Katrina invited Morag and Rita to dinner. Or rather, Katrina worked out something with Gibson, who cooked for them. Rita told them a little of her career up to date and had been surprised when the mine had offered her the post of production geologist. James suspected that it had only been possible because there was no underground operation at Mtuga, so the traditional prohibition against women working in the mine did not really apply. Rita came from a small town near Nenagh in Ireland that actually had a lead and zinc mine. She had been down that mine a few times and had been into other operations in France, Germany and England, but had not been down any of the Zambian mines.

Katrina asked Morag and Rita if they had any plans for Christmas. As neither of them did, Katrina invited them to join her and James for the day. For Morag and Rita, it would be a different Christmas, being in the middle of summer instead of the dead of winter. From Katrina's point of view, she had never known anything different, and the notion of a 'White Christmas' was something that existed only in songs, films and Christmas cards. Morag told them that she had heard from Angus and that he would be back in time for Christmas. The course he had been taking had been going well and would, in fact, finish early, so he would be home a little sooner than originally planned.

At about two, the following afternoon, a convoy of cars came into the construction site. James was surprised to see Tony Williams, Henry Wayne, George Armstrong and Duncan Brown all get out of the cars together with about six others that he did not know. Tony Williams came over to where James was waiting and opened the conversation on an odd note.

"Ah, Martin," he started. "We've brought some of the planning department and a couple of real shift bosses and mine captains from underground to see what kind of mess they are going to have to clear up!"

"Why would there be anything to clear up?" James asked.

"Because I know that you and your collection of neophytes are going to make a real dog's breakfast of this project and we are going to be called upon to fix things!"

"The project is on schedule," commented James, not knowing whether to be amused or seriously irritated. "Unless there are serious unknowns that no one told us of, I don't foresee any issues!"

"Don't go accusing me of leaving anything out!" shouted Williams. "I'll have you know that I've always been against this colossal waste of money, and if I had my way, we would cut our losses and stop now!"

"I see," said James. "If there's nothing else, perhaps you and your team would like to leave?"

"Don't go telling me when I can leave or stay, and don't go looking for your saviour to protect you!" Williams continued.

"Tony, don't get apoplexy now," cautioned George Armstrong. "Why don't you come along now and let's go back home?"

"Oh, I suppose you are in support of this mess now as well?" accused Williams.

"Hey, Tony, knock it off!" interrupted Duncan Brown. "You're just making yourself look like an idiot in front of these people."

"Don't call me an idiot!" shouted Williams.

"George, we'd better get him out of here before he says something he'll really regret," commented Duncan.

"You haven't heard the last of this," Williams threatened as the others manoeuvred him into the car. "I'll do my best to shut this place down and stop the waste of money!"

As they drove off, James heard one of the mine captains comment, "That's what comes of drinking at lunchtime!"

"He's nuts," was the comment that James heard most from the others after the entourage had pulled out and left. He was left wondering just what project Williams had favoured, had been shelved to permit the expenditure on the open pit. John Wells was actually able to answer that question. He later told the team that Williams had been working on a sub-vertical shaft that went from the 3500 level of the main mine to a new 5200 level, making it a fairly deep mine for copper in that it reached down to 5,200 feet. Apparently, according to John, the problem was that the ore reserves at those depths fell largely into the category of possible. There was a little in the proven category and even less in the probable, but to move any quantity of reserves from possible into the other two categories would require either a substantial increase in the market price of copper or a substantial reduction in extraction costs, neither of which scenarios looked likely in the near future. Simple economics would not justify the expense of sinking the new shaft when there were returns to be had from much closer to the surface at the Mtuga project.

James wondered if he should include the visit in his weekly report to Winter, but decided to leave things well alone. He was sure that Winter would hear from someone, and he could make his own mind up about the significance of Williams's threats and rants. He did say a silent prayer that there were no hidden issues that might surface and create difficulties.

At noon on Saturday, James called a halt to everything and had a short meeting before the Christmas break. There was so much to do that they were going to start back to work on December 27th, but until then, peace and quiet would reign. Most of the contractor employees left immediately to go back to Kitwe or other Copperbelt towns for the holiday, and soon the only people left were the mine employees who lived in the two villages.

At home, Katrina was in a deep conference with Gibson. As far as James could tell, they were going over meals and plans for Christmas. Katrina was trying to get Gibson to agree to take the time off, and Gibson was arguing that he needed to be there to make sure that they and their guests were properly cared for. In the end, a compromise was reached and Gibson agreed to come in early on Christmas day but promised to go home to his family by noon.

"So, *Suikerbossie, alles is reg?*" James asked.
"*Ja, alles is reg,*" Katrina replied. "How about you? Will you finally take some time off?"
"For the next couple of days, I'm all yours," he promised grandly.
"You're all mine already," was her comment. "What I want to know is, will I have your undivided attention, or will you be worrying about that open pit of yours?"
"Promise, no pits, no crushers, no trainees, nothing," he committed.
"So, if it doesn't rain tomorrow, let's go fishing," she suggested.
"Okay, where and how?" James asked.

"John Watson lent us his boat," Katrina elaborated. "It's on a trailer in their camp, and we could tow it to the ramp on the dam and spend the day."

"What about this afternoon?" he asked.

"Well, if it rains, we'll stay in and find something to do," she promised.

"What do you mean, if it rains?" he asked. "Look at it; it's going to pour down any minute!"

"Gibson," she called. "*Mushle wena hamba lapa kaia manje manje, lo com com yena buya. Tina azi buka wena kusasa.*"

"Okay, madam," Gibson replied. "*Mina azi buya kusasa. Upi skati wena azi hamba lapa lo dam?*"

"*Kabanga* nine," Katrina thought. She had told Gibson to go home as it was about to rain, and then she had told him that they were going to leave at about nine in the morning to go fishing.

After Gibson had gone, it did rain, hard enough to reduce visibility such that it was not possible to see the next house. James took a quick look outside and assured himself that the water off the roof was running away well. Then Katrina took his arm and suggested a bath before dinner. Now he knew why she had dispatched Gibson off to his own home early. They were not to be disturbed. Katrina had filled a bath and had some wine poured, she had also put on some music, not that they could hear it too well because of the noise of the rain on the corrugated iron roof. In the bathroom, she undressed quickly, climbed into the bath, then waited for James to do the same. Once in the bath, things got a little out of hand, and water went splashing everywhere.

"We need to get a larger bath," suggested James, laughing.

"*Ja,* that would be good," agreed Katrina. "But, if it is too large, you'll be too far away."

"Too far away for what?" he asked.

"If you don't know now, you never will," she commented.

"Why is it that we always sit at the same ends?" he asked.

"What, do you mean, why do I always sit where the taps are?" she asked.

"Yes, is it like one of those hand-holding things, it only works comfortably one way and if you change it feels wrong," he elaborated.

95

"Why don't we try?" she suggested. James ducked down as Katrina climbed over him and sat down at the other end.

"No, it's not right," she agreed. "We seem to be most comfortable the other way around. Let's change back." As she stood up to climb back over James, he stopped her in her tracks and buried his face between her legs. "That's not fair," she commented. "I can't reach you from up here."

"Well, just relax," he commented, taking a short break from his ministrations.

Later, after they had mopped up the floor and dressed, Katrina poured them some more wine, which they actually drank, unlike the first lot that had ended up in the bath. The rain had stopped, and they took chairs and sat out on the *stoep* listening to the night noises.

"What do you think all your people would say if I told them what a randy old goat you really are?" Katrina asked James.

"I think most would be jealous or not believe you," he replied.

"I wonder what goes on in some of the other houses?" she pondered.

"Probably very much the same as in our house," he suggested.

"You're probably right," she agreed. "Who's that coming our way?"

"Looks like Rita to me," James replied, and then he got up to greet their visitor.

"*Howzit,* Rita."

"Good evening, James, Katrina, I hope you don't mind me dropping in like this," said Rita.

"No, not at all, can we get you a glass of wine or a beer?" asked Katrina.

"Thanks, Katrina, that would be wonderful, a beer, please."

"I'll get it for you, have a seat," James offered. He then went in and got Rita a beer and another chair for himself. He wondered if this were purely a social visit or if there was something that Rita wanted to discuss. Rita solved his question for him.

"I've been looking at the drill logs," she started. "There is an area with much higher iron than copper."

"Would that be by the old iron mine that is close to the dam?" James asked.

"I don't know anything about an old iron mine, but yes, it's close to the dam, that way," she indicated, pointing.

"Is there enough to make it worthwhile to dig up?" James asked.

"I'm not sure yet," she said. "I've looked over the copper values and we're alright there, so maybe this could be a bonus."

"But, I don't know of any iron or steel operations in Zambia," offered Katrina. "The only ones I know of are in Rhodesia or South Africa."

"That's true," agreed Rita. "Maybe it's too small to warrant anything, but it seems a shame to waste it."

"Why don't we ask Duncan when we're next in Kitwe?" suggested James. "They may have already noticed the iron and done studies on feasibility."

"Possibly," agreed Rita. "But I think that Williams and his group would have just buried the data and ignored any opportunity."

"What else might we find?" asked Katrina.

"Well, I was talking to the geologist over the river at the Italian place, and they have found quite a few emeralds," Rita commented.

"I'm not a jewellery fan, but I wouldn't mind a nice emerald from here if you find one," said Katrina.

"We'll keep a lookout," promised James.

"Another beer, Rita?" offered Katrina.

"Thanks, that would be great," she replied.

"I know you've only been here a week," commented James. "But, what do you think?"

"It's fun and I expect that as you actually start mining, it'll get more interesting," Rita explained. "What about you?"

"It's more of a challenge than I thought," admitted James. "And there are days when I wonder if I didn't bite off more than I could chew."

"That's not what I hear from the others," Rita commented. "They all seem to think that things are going well."

"Will you stay for dinner?" offered Katrina.

"Are you sure?" Rita asked.

"Of course," Katrina assured her. "James is running the *braai* tonight, so unless it rains again, we won't have to do anything except sit and be waited on!"

Later, after Rita had gone, Katrina commented to James that it must be difficult for a single girl on a small mine like theirs to find anyone to go out with. Having just been through the same issue with John Wells,

James agreed but was not sure what, if anything, he could or should do. He suggested that they leave things for the moment and perhaps Katrina could get to know Rita a little better and find out where the wind blew in her case.

As planned, Katrina and James spent Christmas Eve on the Mita Hills dam fishing. At first, James was not sure that they would ever get things underway, as it was raining lightly when they collected the boat and the boat ramp was, to say the least, a little muddy. However, James managed to get the boat launched and his Land Rover parked well out of the way. Once out onto the lake, they were caught in another rain shower and were drenched. James suggested that they head back in, but Katrina insisted that the sun would shine soon, and then they would dry out. Meanwhile, James sat and shivered as he fished. It was obviously not his day as he caught nothing while Katrina caught seven good-sized fish, and a fish eagle swooped past him twice to snatch a fish out of the water. Katrina was right about the sun; it did shine, and they were able to dry out just in time for the next rain shower. This one was heavier than the first, and this time, Katrina was the one who suggested that they head back in.

Getting the boat out was quite a challenge as the boat ramp was now very wet, and any traffic on it quickly turned it to mud. James took the precaution of attaching his winch cable to a good-sized tree, which, as it turned out, was a good idea, as the Land Rover lost traction on all wheels trying to pull the boat out of the steep ramp. There were also a couple of dambos they had to cross before reaching the road home, and the rain had turned them very sticky, so going was difficult. James did not want to have to get help from either his own people if he bogged down, or from the Italians; it would be something hard to live down. With care and caution, they made it back to the mine and more firm going.

Christmas Eve night, everyone was invited to the Italian village to watch a film. They brought films in every week or so from Lusaka. The screen was interesting. The Italians hung a bed sheet up by using beer bottles along the top of a dividing wall. The resulting picture was pretty good unless there was too much wind, and then the screen became rippled and the action sometimes looked a little peculiar. The film was good except everyone was a little lost until they worked out that they had been watching reel four instead of reel two. However, it did not spoil the evening, and things finished up with Christmas carols, both in English and Italian. Fortunately, there was not far to drive home as none of the Mtuga contingent were in much of a state to drive far. Only one driver left the road, and he was quickly pushed back onto the graded surface with no damage or injury.

Christmas morning came, and James and Katrina both regretted the night before. Too much wine had been consumed, and now they were paying the penalty. After a very light breakfast, consisting mostly of coffee, they swapped presents. Katrina was delighted with her new camera, and for James, she had got a new shortwave radio. While Katrina busied herself in the kitchen with Gibson, James fiddled with the dials on his radio and found all manner of odd stations. He had been a fan of LM Radio for a while and generally preferred their music selection to Zambia Radio. However, it had changed during the year, and James had learnt that after the takeover of the radio station by the South African Broadcasting Corporation, content and format had changed, not for the better in his opinion. So he was looking for another station to listen to.

Their guests arrived earlier than they had hoped, a little before noon and were actually pretty chipper. Angus was in heaven, he not only had Morag in the house he also had Rita. James hoped that nothing would develop to upset the balance of things in that household. Katrina and Gibson had prepared a late lunch, which was for the newcomers to Zambia a most un-Christmas-like lunch. No turkey, no Christmas pudding, just light fare with an abundance of salads and cold meats. Not that there was not plenty to eat, it was just different food and probably better suited to the hot weather than the heavier British and Irish style of fare. Katrina's only concession to tradition was mince pies and sherry, which she served late in the afternoon as the sun was setting.

Border closure

Boxing Day, a traditional British holiday, had been adopted by the Zambians as one of their holidays. For the Mtuga project team, it was time to catch up before returning to the construction challenge. For James and Katrina, it was a quiet day, only made exciting when Katrina saw a black mamba outside the kitchen. She told Gibson to stay inside and then watched until she saw it slither off into the bush. Gibson had wanted to take a more typical Zambian approach to the snake and kill it, but Katrina was not convinced that he could have killed it quickly enough to not put himself in danger.

Construction started up again on Wednesday morning with a flurry of activity. James took the time to get an exact count on just about everything because he had a scheduled review meeting in Kitwe on the Friday of that week. Katrina was going with him because they had an invitation to a New Year's Eve party. James talked to John Wells and asked him if he had anything planned for the New Year. If not, then he, and Elena if he wished, would be welcome to join him and Katrina at the party to which they were invited. John checked with Elena, and after clearing up where she would be staying, said that they would be delighted to go with the Martins. Katrina had arranged with John Watson for them all to stay at his farm outside Kitwe. They had been able to assure Elena's father that she would have her own room; however, James reasoned that even though the room was available, whether she chose to use it was up to her and John.

On Friday at their review meeting, Colin Winter opened the proceedings with a request from Tony Williams for the reason for his visit to the project just before Christmas. He prefaced his request with the comment that the convoy had been seen by George McIntosh, who had been curious as to the purpose of the outing. Williams hedged with his explanation and looked to the others for help. Henry Wayne came to his rescue and said that they had been to the project to check on the process flow for the concentrator. Winter suggested that in the future, they check with him before invading the project with so many people.

After that, the review was fairly perfunctory with few questions. James was now convinced that they had made an enemy of Williams and probably Wayne as well.

On Saturday, James and Katrina took John and Elena to the boat club for the day. It was clear that John and Elena had hit it off. Katrina remarked to James when they were alone for a few minutes that she could see there being an empty room that night. The only question James had was, whose room, John's or Elena's? Katrina gave the matter some thought and announced to James later that John's room would be empty as Elena would make the first move and invite him to join her. She was proven correct, and for the next three nights, John and Elena went off to bed early.

Back in Mtuga on Tuesday, James returned to work, and Katrina started to collect her samples to take with her the next day for her appointments in Kitwe. It seemed a shame to James that she had come all the way back to Mtuga, only to return to Kitwe so soon, but that was the way she had planned it and wanted it, so he left it alone. At his office, James went through progress with his people and then, after the rest of them had left, asked John about his weekend.
"John," he started. "You remind me of a bloke I used to work with in Kitwe, Bill; he used to come to work looking as shagged out as you do."
"Ah, well," John began. "It was quite a weekend."
"So, would it be impertinent to ask where things may go with Elena?" James asked.
"Who knows," John continued. "We'll have to see. Certainly, I think it could go further, but you never know."
"Just don't get too distracted!" James cautioned.
"No, I don't think that will be a problem," John promised. "I think we'll only be able to get together on weekends."

Katrina returned on Friday with exciting news. She had sold quite a lot of mica to the tyre factory, other minerals to the paint factory and some sand to one of the water treatment companies. She had also set up some appointments with the glass and china factories in Kapiri Mposhi and Lusaka, respectively. She regaled James with tales of her trips to the different factories and the tours she had been able to take to see how they used the products she was selling. She had really enjoyed herself. James also had some news. The boat with all its earthmoving equipment aboard was off Durban and headed north towards Beira.

The following Tuesday, James was out on the construction project when John Wells came looking for him. Apparently, there was an urgent telephone call for him from Kitwe. James hurried back to the office and picked up the telephone. It was Colin Winter with some startling news. The Rhodesians had closed the border, and the Zambians had retaliated by also closing the border. What that meant for James was not immediately clear, but Winter told him to drive to Kitwe immediately for consultations and to bring John Wells and Katrina. James went home and told Katrina that the border had been closed and that there could be problems. He told her that he had been summoned to a meeting in Kitwe and that she had been invited to attend, he guessed to talk about transportation alternatives.

Later that day in Kitwe, they held a council of war and reviewed the latest information. Apparently, the Rhodesians were making some noises about backpedalling a little, but the Zambians were adamant that the border would remain closed. The company representative in Lusaka had talked to the various ministries and had no good news. In the meeting, Williams was delighted.

"Now, you'll have to cancel this project," he crowed.

"Not necessarily," commented James.

"What do you mean?" demanded Williams. "The borders are closed, you can't get your equipment from Beira, so you're up the creek without a paddle, as they say! And, why is she here?" he continued, pointing at Katrina.

"Mrs Martin has a little more experience with transportation than the rest of us," replied Colin Winter. "It might be useful to hear what she has to say. James, please."

"We've been going over things," said James. "Katrina, why don't you give us the transportation options?"

"Well, your boat is between Durban and Beira," she started. "Obviously, we can't have it go back to Lobito and use the Benguela Railway."

"Of course not, that's about the most idiotic thing I've ever heard," interrupted Williams.

"True, but we have three other options," continued Katrina. "We could continue to Beira or divert the boat to Nacala or Dar es Salaam."

"Then what?" asked Williams.

"Well, from Beira or Nacala we rail everything to Salima in Malawi and then road everything from there, or from Dar we convince the Chinese to help us by railing everything to Makambako, then we road everything from there," she elaborated.

"Why do you think the Chinks would help us?" Williams asked.

"Mainly because it embarrasses the Rhodesians, the South Africans and the Brits," commented Duncan Brown.

"Have you worked out how to actually do this?" Colin Winter asked Katrina.

"I have a basic plan that we worked out on the way up here," she replied. "I need to go over the routes more carefully and decide which is the best option."

"Fine, you do that," Winter suggested. "Meanwhile, I'll get the office in Lusaka to contact the Chinese, Tanzanians, Portuguese and the Malawians and see what we can work out."

"What about the route through Malawi?" Henry Wayne asked, a little behind everyone else

"It's possible," commented Katrina. "But, I need to look at the condition of the different railways and then the roads, including bridges, which will probably be the main problem."

"Okay, James, you, Katrina and John go over the routes and get me your recommendation by tomorrow afternoon. I'll tell the Cat people that we may have to divert the boat north to stop at either Nacala or Dar, depending on your recommendation, and I'll call London with the good news," decided Winter. "The rest of you, nothing changes in the schedule or the support I'm looking for from you!"

For the better part of the next morning, James, Katrina and John camped out at the boat club and studied maps and transport logs that Katrina had borrowed from her old company.

"As I see it," she concluded that afternoon. "It's about 1,065 kilometres from Salima to Mtuga, the hills we'll have to go up and down mean a total climb of about 4,100 metres and a fall of about 3,500 metres, where we'll have to worry about braking, and we have the Luangwa bridge to deal with."

"What about from Dar?" James asked.

"About the same from Makambako, if we can get the Chinese to cooperate," she replied. "It would be about 1,100 kilometres from Makambako to Mtuga, we would gain about 4,000 metres, lose about 4,500 metres, and I don't remember any particular bridges that would be a concern."

"Which do you think would be the better way?" James asked her.

"I'm not sure," she started. "Each way has its problems. From Beira to Salima is probably the best rail route, from Nacala the railway link to Malawi and Salima is iffy, and Dar is congested, and the Great North Road is pretty beaten up."

"What else?" John asked.

"Well, from Salima we have to worry about the Luangwa bridge," she continued. "It's a suspension bridge, and I'm not sure it'll take the load except one truck at a time."

"Could we knock down the banks of the river and ford it?" James asked.

"No, I think the banks are too steep, we may have to do that on some of the smaller crossings anyway, but the Luangwa is a big river!" she thought.

"But, what about roading the equipment?" James asked. "There aren't that many low loaders around."

"You only use low loaders for the tractors, the slow front-end loaders and the graders," she explained. "The trucks you drive."

"I'll have to check with Jerry, Hippo and Abel to see that we have enough drivers," thought James.

"So, what do you think?" James asked Katrina.

"Either way has its problems," she reiterated. "But, I've driven the Salima route a couple of times and have better knowledge of that road.

I also think that with the border closure, everyone will try to divert to Dar, so I think we should stay with Beira."

"We'll have to get someone in the Lusaka office to clear up the contract details with the Cat dealership; they'll probably declare *force majeure* because of the political situation," added John. "As I remember, the purchase from Cat itself was CIF Beira, so there won't be problems there. Local delivery charges were to be in Kwacha and payable to the local dealer."

"Are we stepping on their toes?" James wondered, "By moving too fast."

"I talked to the dealer in Lusaka yesterday," said John. "Basically, if we can come up with a viable plan, they said they'd be happy to go along with us, because they didn't have an immediate solution."

"Alright, what else do we need?" asked James.

"Well, we'll need fuel bowsers, Zambia Police escorts, buses for transporting the drivers to Malawi and some agreement from the Malawians to let the drivers in, probably without passports," commented Katrina. "I doubt whether any of the drivers you will get have such an item as a passport. We'll also need a crane to put the pans on the trucks at Salima."

"How much fuel will we need?" asked John.

"We should take about 20,000 litres with us; those trucks of yours could use a fair amount on the trip," Katrina replied.

"What about the spare parts, dozer blades and all that sort of stuff?" James asked.

"It goes in the back of the trucks," said Katrina. "Oh, and one more thing, we'll need to work out how to feed all our drivers and take some tents or something for overnight stays."

"Anything else, *Suikerbossie*?" James asked.

"We'll need a truck with a welding set, just in case," she added.

"A welding set, what for?" James asked.

"Oh, you know, bridge railings, other things, you never know," she elaborated.

"Who are you married to, James?" asked John. "Mata Hari or some other secret agent."

"I'm beginning to wonder," James commented. "But, then again, I told you before, John, you have to watch these colonial women, you never know what they can do!"

105

"*Voetsak* James," was Katrina's comment to that witticism.

"I have all the details here," said John. "Why don't I put it all together?"

At four, the council of war reconvened, and James laid out the options. He made the recommendation that they have the boat dock at Beira and transport the equipment by rail as far as Salima. He then went through the balance of the items that they would have to take care of to collect the equipment. Colin Winter told them that the Portuguese and Malawian embassies had committed to help in every way possible. Henry Wayne interrupted the proceedings with an important question.

"I thought the Luangwa bridge had fallen down?" he asked.

"It did," replied Katrina. "In 1968, the bridge collapsed, but it was replaced by a new bridge, I think by Cleveland Bridge."

"So, is it open and usable?" Henry pressed.

"Yes," replied Katrina. "There have been problems with the construction, but it is open and usable."

"What kind of problems?" asked Henry.

"Oh, some of the bolts have been failing, and that may limit the weight it can carry in time," Katrina elaborated. "But, if we take the vehicles over one at a time and limit the speed so as not to build up a vibration load, we'll be fine."

"Fine, what else do we need?" asked Colin Winter. James then laid out a brief list of what they would need that they did not have at the mine site. He looked for commitment to getting various items. George Armstrong promised to get them four diesel bowsers, a lorry with a welding set and a bus, to be delivered to the Mtuga site before Wednesday, January 24th, in time to drive to Salima.

Katrina estimated that the boat would be off Beira by January 12th, and then there was at least a week to ten days to unload and entrain for Salima. Colin Winter said that he would talk to the Caterpillar dealer and that they would work out things with CFM, Caminhos de Ferro Moçambique, to get a train organised. James wanted to be at the railhead to meet the train and have time to assemble the trucks before leaving for Zambia. There were a myriad of small details to be worked out, and Winter suggested that they adjourn the meeting and let the project team get back to the mine site and sort everything out.

Once back at Mtuga, James pulled his team together and issued marching orders. John McFarlane was to focus on the construction of the concentrator; the balance of his team, with the exception of John Wells, whom he placed in charge in his own absence, were co-opted to be part of the transportation team. Hippo was assigned the task of meeting with the Zambia Police and arranging an escort vehicle and team. Abel was instructed to produce one dozer operator to load the tractors onto the low loaders and twenty-eight truck operators, twenty-four for the trucks and four spare. It was quite a challenge for Abel, but he did have some help in that the Copperbelt mines were coming to their aid and had offered a similar truck for training for the next couple of weeks. Angus was told off to collect grease guns, the right kinds of oils, some spare tyres and a lorry with a compressor fitted. Jerry Mwanza was asked to put together a menu and supplies to feed the transport drivers, both for the outbound journey and the return. James told him not to forget the Zambia Police escort, who would most likely also need feeding and watering and probably a similar Malawian squad. James asked Katrina to take a couple of weeks off from her selling job and plan the route in detail, including overnight stops, with places to park the fleet off the road.

Katrina arranged with her old company, the Caterpillar dealer and a couple of the mines for eighteen low loaders to be ready to go on Wednesday, 24th. They would use five for track-type tractors, five for front-end loaders, two for rubber-tyred tractors, one for the crane, three for graders and two spare for parts or other items. The Caterpillar dealer was also going to provide a team, consisting of driver instructors, mechanics and electricians. When James added up the whole contingent, he told Jerry he had better cater for sixty-four people plus the Zambia Police escorts, probably another four or six. Altogether, he counted up twenty-nine vehicles going to bring back the equipment, counting on the fact that twenty-four pieces of equipment were going to be driven back under their own power; that made a total of fifty-three vehicles on the return journey, quite a convoy! He was certain that they would find out that they had forgotten something, but they had become used to improvising, so he was sure that if anything did crop up, they would find a way to cope.

Confirmation was received that the vessel was scheduled into Beira on January 12th and a berth had been reserved. The Portuguese were cooperating and had rearranged the berths so that they could avoid demurrage charges and get the vessel in and unloaded quickly. The usual fortnightly review in Kitwe was cancelled, but they did receive a visit from Colin Winter. He came on the Friday to look over progress with the concentrator and to see how plans were coming for the transportation of the mining equipment. He seemed in no hurry to return to Kitwe, and James asked him if he would like to stay at the site for the night and return the next day. Apparently, that had been his plan, so James set him up in their guest house and invited him to a *braai* with his project team.

Later that night, when they were sheltering from the rain and hoping that the steaks had been cooked enough before the rains came, James asked Winter how things were going.

"If you can pull off this transportation and keep to the schedule, I would say very well," he replied. "I think you have done a really first-class job here."

"Thanks," said James. "But, the credit really goes to all of them," he continued, pointing to his various team members.

"Perhaps, but it's leadership that counts," Winter commented. "But, before you start feeling too good about yourself, you have to remember you're 'B' stream!"

"I'm sorry, 'B' stream, what do you mean?" James asked.

"Well, you have a mining degree, work out here in the mine and will progress up the normal chain of command if you stay here," started Winter. "But, the ones that really succeed are those that go to Cambridge, read history, or art or PP&E like your man Wells, and then go to the head office. Those are the 'A' stream types in this company. Look at me, I'm 'B' stream, I'm older by far than Beauchamp, but have to answer to him!"

"So, you're saying there's no real future here?" James asked.

"No, there's always a future and a good one at that, but you'll land up answering to your man Wells before you know it!" Winter explained.

"I suppose that's always a possibility," said James. "But, at the moment, I just want to get through the next month."

"What else do you need to get done in the immediate future?" Winter asked.

"I need some drilling equipment," James thought.

"I'll get the people from Holman, Atlas Copco, Ingersol Rand and Gardner Denver to call in next week, and you can discuss with them what you need," Winter promised. "As you said before, you can probably start out with small mobile units, but you are going to need something larger!"

"I need to construct a magazine too," added James. "So, I'd better check the regulations for magazine siting and construction. Then I need to arrange for some explosives to be delivered and also get a powder truck for hauling it into the pit."

"Let me know if you need any help in Kitwe to get any of that done," offered Winter. "Now perhaps we should join the rest of your party, or they'll think we're plotting something."

The following week was busy! Hippo and Abel worked diligently to have the operators ready in time for the expedition to Malawi. James met with the different suppliers of drilling equipment and found out that there were enough demonstration units in the country that he could get almost immediate delivery. John McFarlane and his contractors made significant progress on the concentrator, and Jerry went shopping for food and other commodities for the trip.

On Friday, the 12th, James received word that the boat had docked in Beira and unloading had commenced. The CFM representative reported that the equipment was being loaded onto the flat railway wagons, but that the train was unlikely to arrive at Salima before Saturday, the 27th. It was a question of getting enough flat cars moved around the system to accommodate the load. Later that day, a bus and four diesel bowsers were delivered to the mine site, and the bowsers were actually full of diesel, a minor miracle of organisation. The bus had been borrowed from the local bus company and still carried the signs of CARS, Central African Roadcars, a holdover from Federation days. James presumed that the bus would make it all the way to Malawi, but in case it did not, he made sure that Angus put enough towing cables, shackles and other useful things into the pile of miscellaneous items they were taking with them.

The normal fortnightly review was moved up to Tuesday and was held at Mtuga. The five managers all travelled down together and were there relatively early. Because the review was being held at the mine site, James took the opportunity to have each of his team give an update as to where things stood. With the exception of John Wells and, to James somewhat surprisingly, Hippo, all of them were nervous and were concerned that they did not make a hash of things. As far as James could tell from the meeting and from the questions, none of them had anything to be nervous about. After the meeting, they all took a tour of the construction site and were able to see for themselves that things were as presented. James now thought that he understood why Winter had been down some days earlier. If he had not been satisfied, the review would have been in Kitwe with no plant tour.

Hippo had arranged with the driving licence examiners to be at the mine to issue driving licences to all the operators. This was useful because it also gave them a document with a photograph in it to present to the Malawian immigration people, apart from the list that they had put together. Hippo was living up to James's opinion of him, that of Mr Fixit.

Wednesday morning, early, a convoy set out from the mine to rendezvous with some of the low loaders at Kapiri Mposhi. There, they also picked up the Zambia Police escort, two Land Rovers in the charge of an inspector, Mr Phiri, two sergeants and two constables. For much of the drive to Lusaka, Mr Phiri rode with them and had all kinds of questions about the mine, the people on the mine and this particular project. He had been detailed by headquarters in Lusaka to escort this convoy to the border and there await its return. Now he understood why there was an escort; the thought of twenty-four of the mining

110

trucks careering down the road without supervision was not something he relished. At Lusaka, their escort guided them through the town and took them to the rendezvous with the Caterpillar dealer's team, led by Phil Eastman. From Lusaka, the extended convoy headed out on the Great East Road towards Chipata, Fort Jameson, for old timers. Katrina had proposed that they stop at the Luangwa and camp overnight. It would give them a chance to check the brakes on the low loaders after the long descent into the Luangwa Valley.

Just before the Luangwa bridge, Katrina indicated a turn off to the north, which they followed until it too came to the river. Here, at least, was space enough for all the vehicles to turn around and park, without obstructing the road. Now Jerry's organisational abilities were revealed. Apparently, he had met with Hippo and Abel and had found cooks among the ranks of the operators. He had also set others on the tasks of laying out the camp and the tents, setting up tables, portable showers and digging toilets, all of which were done with much gossip and laughter. James was amazed to see that within two hours of stopping, they were eating dinner under cover with the promise of hot showers and beds to sleep on. The Zambia Police contingent joined them for dinner, and James learnt that Mr Phiri had grown up in Chipata and had moved up the ranks until he was put in charge of an area of Zambia about the size of a reasonable county in England. He ran this whole area with sergeants and constables scattered among the small communities.

The following day, it seemed like a long drag back up out of the Luangwa valley to Chipata. They had been held up for a short while at the bridge by the Zambia police and army checkpoint, but Inspector Phiri had quickly sorted that out. The road went up and down across water courses that fed into the Luangwa, and there seemed to be an endless number of culverts and small bridges. Just past Kacholola, the road surface got poor. It was essentially a gravel road with occasional bits of tar. With the rain that was falling, Katrina warned that this could be sticky on the way back. She also told James that they were paralleling the Moçambique border and because of FRELIMO activity, they might expect to see more Zambian army people checking on travellers. James had been surprised to learn the night before how close they were to the

Moçambique border. From the Luangwa bridge, it was a relatively short distance downriver.

The convoy eventually passed through Chipata, and Katrina called a halt. Mr Phiri had suggested a good site for their camp just past the town and before they reached the border. After setting up the camp, the police all disappeared into town, to visit relatives, friends or just a bar. James had made it clear to his team that there were to be no town or bar visits; he wanted an alert, sober crew for the whole trip.

The drive to the Malawi border was very short, and they were there by seven the following morning. There was a line of buses, cars and lorries, and at the rate they were proceeding, James could envisage spending a day just waiting. However, he had not counted on their police escort. Incensed at having made such good time to the border, only to have his charges sit, Mr Phiri took his police Land Rover and drove up the line to the post. James and Katrina watched him go into the building and wondered how long it would be before he emerged. It was about thirty minutes, but when he did come out, it was to go to the Malawian border post, not back to the convoy. That took another thirty minutes, but this time he came back with a Malawian police inspector and two others. He waved his own people forward and obviously issued instructions. A sergeant came back and told the convoy to cross the border and wait. He also instructed Phil Eastman, James and Katrina to take all the passports, driving licences and lists of people and vehicles, first to the Zambian station, then to the Malawian station. That all took another two hours as each side wanted to record everything, in long hand, even though they were given typed-up lists of people and vehicles.

By ten, they said farewell to their Zambian escort and, in the company of their Malawian escort, moved off again. They arrived in Lilongwe just after noon. Perhaps not the best time to be going through a major town, but the escort helped, and before long, they were headed downhill again, this time to the shores of Lake Malawi and the railhead at Salima. At the station, they were told that the train was expected in late the next day, so they had the best part of a day to kill. The

Malawian police escort suggested that they drive to the lake shore and set up camp on Senga Bay. That sounded to everyone like a great idea, and by five in the afternoon, they had a campsite set up. Before releasing everyone to their own devices, James insisted that each low loader was checked out thoroughly, and all the support vehicles also got a going over.

"Well, James, we're here," announced Katrina. "Now what?"
"We wait," he replied. "The train should be here tomorrow, I gather that it has a priority on the route."
"I wonder what that'll cost," she pondered.
"I'm sure somewhere, someone will receive their appropriate recognition," he laughed.
"Oh, is that the word for it?" she asked.
"What about the road conditions?" he asked, changing the subject as some of their people came around for instructions.
"It doesn't look too bad," she thought. "I would arrange the convoy to send all the regular vehicles first and have the mining trucks follow with our rear escorts trailing them. That way, if there is too much road damage, we won't hang up a low loader."
"Okay, you're the boss," James agreed. "Jerry, did we bring any beer?"
"No," said Jerry, who had come in with the rest of the team. "I thought it best not to have any with us, one because I don't fancy anyone drunk driving one of those big trucks and two because I didn't want problems at the border."
"Hippo, do you think you could find us a beer each? And I do mean only one each," James asked.
"Sure," Hippo said, "I'll be back soon."
"Is it always so hot here?" James asked Katrina after Hippo and Jerry had gone.
"Always!" she confirmed. "And, wait until the sun goes down and the mosquitoes come out, then you'll find out why we brought nets!"

Saturday afternoon, James, Katrina and Phil went to the station and were in time to see the train arrive. James had learnt his lesson in Zambia and, even though the locomotive was an interesting steam engine, took no photographs. He would have liked to because it was of

113

a type not found in Zambia and was likely to be replaced with diesel traction shortly, as the Malawians were dependent on coal from Wankie, which lay in Rhodesia. The station master joined them and discussed the unloading process with James and Phil. They agreed to have low loaders at the station the next morning at six, even though it was Sunday. They also set up a base yard in which they could do the assembly of the trucks.

Getting everyone up in time to be at the station at six in the morning was a challenge, but they made it, just! As each piece of equipment was unloaded, it was fuelled and either driven to the base yard or, in the case of the track-type tractors, loaded directly onto a low loader. Once at the base yard, Angus and the Caterpillar dealer people went about placing the pans onto the trucks, fitting the outer rear wheels and the cabs to make driving easier. James had also decided to equip one rubber-tyred dozer with a blade and one front-end loader with a bucket in case they had road building to do on the way. The balance of blades and buckets was loaded into the backs of the trucks. As each truck was readied, Katrina hovered around keeping a record of what was loaded into it so that when they got to the border, she could tell the customs people what was what. The whole process took three days, so that by Wednesday, January 31st, they were ready to leave.

With the Malawi Police escort leading, the convoy climbed up the long slope towards Lilongwe. The climb took a little over three hours, and then they were able to relax a little during the gentler up-and-down journey to the border, with the last climb up into the Mchinji Hills.

At the border, the Malawian escort said goodbye, and the customs and immigration people waved them through. On the Zambian side, things went well until one of the customs people suddenly stopped reading the manifests and jumped up.
"You must come with me," he announced, pointing to Phil and James. Once inside the office, he showed the manifest to his supervisor and then asked his question. "Why are you smuggling guns into Zambia?"
"We have no guns," protested Phil.

"You tell lies," accused the customs officer. "Your own documents betray you!"

"But, I'm telling you we have no guns!" Phil protested again.

"It says, quite clearly on your documents that you have guns," repeated the officer.

"This doesn't make sense," James said. "May I see the manifest?"

"There, there, you see?" the officer said, pointing to the line item that said "Guns, grease, twenty."

"Oh, I see," admitted James. "May I ask one of my people to bring one of these guns in for you to see?"

"So, you admit to having guns," the officer crowed. "We'll send you to Lake Benguela for a long time!"

"May I get one for you to see?" James repeated.

"No, I will have one of the people you have get one!" retorted the officer. He disappeared then reappeared with Hippo. "These people say that you have no guns in your equipment, but this paper says you do!" he said accusingly. "They say you must get one to show me!"

"Sure," agreed Hippo. "Do we know which box they are in?"

"This paper says, truck number five," the officer announced. "I will come with you and see if that is true!" On that note, he went out with Hippo, leaving James and Phil under the watchful gaze of his superior and three other officers who had come to see the action.

Hippo came back in about twenty minutes with the customs officer and Mr Phiri, their escort. He had in his hands a box and a grease cartridge. In front of the assembled crowd, Hippo removed the grease gun from the box and held it out for all to see.

"What is this?" asked the customs chief.

"This is a grease gun," began Hippo. "It is loaded with this cartridge like this and used to lubricate the equipment and also your cars."

"How?" asked the chief. "Come with me to my car and show me."

Leaving James and Phil with an unwilling subordinate, everyone else left and went with Hippo to grease the car. When they returned, it was clear some kind of deal had been made, because James and Phil were told they were free to go with their convoy. Hippo later told them it had cost them six grease guns.

The border proceedings had taken about four hours, so it was late when they finally all got through into Zambia. Mr Phiri had anticipated the problem when he saw the convoy arrive and encounter problems. He had picked out a site for the night and had posted his second Land Rover there with his own officers. Although it was almost five by the time they were at the campsite, records were broken for setting up the camp and organising a meal. By six-thirty, they were eating! James told the whole crew that they would not start so early in the morning and that there would first be a check of all the low loaders and trucks before they started upon the long downhill journey to the Luangwa crossing.

Things went well the next day until they hit a soft spot in the road between Petauke and Nyimba. The road had broken up because of the heavy traffic, and heavy rain had worsened the situation. The fourth low loader bogged down, and the whole convoy came to a halt. James walked down the line of vehicles to take a look, and what he saw was not encouraging. After a brief conversation with Phil and Hippo, James had the finished rubber-tyred tractor unloaded, and they towed the low loader free of the trouble spot. Then they unloaded the finished front-end loader and went back up the road to a spot that James had noticed earlier. Using the front-end loader, they took gravel to the soft spot and spread it around. The rubber-tyred dozer was used to compact the gravel into the road and smooth it out. After two hours work, James judged the road good enough to continue. They loaded the equipment back onto the low loaders and started off again. They had now been on the road for eight hours, and James thought it was time to call a halt. Kacholola seemed like a good place to stop, and James consulted Mr Phiri, who agreed and went ahead to find a location.

That evening, after dinner, James sat down with Mr Phiri, Katrina, Phil, Angus and Hippo and discussed the road ahead. Katrina told them that the surface from Kacholola to Lusaka had always been better than to Chipata, so they should expect better going from thenceforth. James just wished it would stop raining. It was hard to see sometimes in the rain, and there was the ever-present risk of a washout in the road. Mr Phiri assured them that the road would be fine and he was trying to work out whether it would be better to go straight through Lusaka or take some side roads around to the east and the north. Abel then entered the conversation and asked if it would be possible to go home on the other road that went north, just east of Rufunsa and came out by Piccadilly Circus. Katrina knew of the road, but she pointed out a few problems with the route. First, the road surface was dirt, varying from gravel to laterite and probably plain mud. Second, they would have to cross the Lunsemfwa, and finally, the climb up from the Lukasashi Valley to Fiwila would be quite a challenge. Her comment on the suggestion was that it was a great idea to avoid Lusaka, but the crossing of the Lunsemfwa was just not feasible.

The next morning, they made the trip down to the Luangwa bridge in short time, then took each low loader and truck across one by one, then began the long climb up towards Lusaka. Things went well until they were partway up the long haul towards Rufunsa. James happened to look back and see one of his trucks belching clouds of black smoke. They found a convenient place to pull over, and he went back down the convoy to see what the problem was. One of the operators was most distressed. He told James that his truck had just lost power. The Caterpillar crew arrived, and the operator repeated his story.

"Just shit," said Phil. "The turbocharger's gone!"

"What does that mean?" James asked.

"It means this truck has low power and will probably not make it without help!" he explained.

"Shit, what can we do?" asked James.

"Why don't you just tow it?" suggested Katrina.

"What do you mean tow it?" James asked.

"Hitch it to one of the other trucks and tow it," she repeated.

"Can we do that?" James asked Phil.

"Well, theoretically yes," he replied. "But, do we have anything to tow it with?"

"Of course," replied Katrina. "Angus has all sorts of gear in one of the trucks."

"Why did the turbocharger go?" James asked.

"The oil feed," Phil said. "Unfortunately, there is a weakness in the design and the oil feed to the turbocharger has been known to fail. No oil, so there goes your turbocharger!"

"Okay, I'll get Angus, and we'll get this truck hitched to the one in front. What else?" James decided.

"We'll disconnect the drive train but run the engine to provide steering and brakes, we'll blank off the oil feed to the turbocharger so we don't lose all the oil. Who's the best operator you have?" Phil asked.

"Chazeema," James said without hesitation.

"Okay, he's the one we want driving this thing, and the next best needs to be driving the one towing it!" Phil elaborated.

"Fine, I'll fix that," James agreed. "Let me know when you are ready to go again."

At the pace they were going, it looked as if a stop in Lusaka would be necessary. Mr Phiri thought it best that they stop east of Lusaka and then go through the city early in the morning. He asked James and Katrina if he could go with them, and they would ride ahead and make the necessary arrangements. They found a suitable location and Mr Phiri made sure that the local police squads knew that he was there in charge of things, so that they would not be bothered. They then sat back to wait. Eventually, the convoy arrived with no additional breakdowns, and they set up camp.

Fortunately, the Great East Road and the Great North Road meet on the northern side of Lusaka. So the following morning, they missed the real centre of the city, but even so, Mr Phiri had organised some extra police officers to man the intersections and particularly the roundabout where the two main roads met. They closed the roundabout to all other traffic and let the convoy through on the wrong side of the road, ensuring that nothing would either collide with the centre of the roundabout or get hung up on the island. Then it was all speed to Kabwe, or at least as fast as was sensible. James recounted to Katrina his impressions of driving that same road a little over three years earlier, when he had first arrived in Zambia. It seemed the same to him in some respects, but the novelty and strangeness had gone, and it now was the norm rather than something out of the ordinary.

After they passed through Kabwe, everyone began to get more excited. There was only Kapiri Mposhi left; then they would turn off onto the

Great North Road, and fairly quickly after that, the dirt road to the mine. James just hoped that the mine road was in reasonable condition and that the low loaders would not bog down on the last stage of the journey. John Watson had anticipated things and had patrolled the road a few times and made repairs where necessary. He met them at the road end and assured James that all would be well for the last few kilometres.

At the mine site, everyone turned out as a welcoming committee as the trucks pulled in. James was pleased to note that construction of the concentrator had obviously proceeded apace while they were gone, and progress was apparent. John Wells had laid on a *braai,* and James decided to leave unloading everything until Monday. Most of the operators were anxious to get home after their trip and left as soon as James told them that there would be no further work that evening. He invited Phil and his crew to stay and join them, and then looked around for the drivers of the low loaders. Katrina told him that they had already gone and were headed for the local African village. She hoped that they would all be sober enough on Monday morning to drive and help unload.

"So, *Suikerbossie,* how was the trip?" James asked Katrina later.
"I'm glad to be home," she replied. "But, it was fun, wasn't it?"
"I'm not sure that it was all fun," he commented. "For a while there, I was a little concerned about being shipped off to be detained at President's pleasure at Lake Benguela."
"I suspect they weren't as ignorant as you might think," she explained. "I think they just wanted some form of gift, bribe, facilitating payment, call it what you will."
"In that case, we were lucky to get away with only half a dozen grease guns," James commented. "What do you fancy doing tomorrow?"
"Nothing!" was Katrina's announcement. "I've been in your company now for eleven days, and there hasn't been any opportunity to get friendly! So, Mister Martin, be prepared!"

Unloading and final assembly of the mining fleet began in earnest on Monday morning, and James took the opportunity to meet with John Wells and John McFarlane to get up to date with events at the mine.

119

The Johns agreed that it had been marvellously uneventful. John McFarlane did have one piece of news. Their tank farm was ready, and if there was any diesel left over from the trip, it would be wise to discharge it into the tanks. Later that morning, James said goodbye to the low loader drivers, the diesel bowser crew and the bus driver. Their CARS bus had made it to Malawi and back with barely a hiccup. It looked as if they would be able to start mining with their own machinery by midweek. Although they were still in the overburden removal stage, it would not be long before they started to extract copper ore, and James was anxious that the concentrator be ready. He also needed some drilling equipment on site immediately, so set about organising that and the crews to run the drills and the explosives he would need.

There was one other item that needed attention before production in the mill started. They needed at least a holding pond for the effluent from the flotation cells and would need a real slimes dam at some point. James asked Rita and John McFarlane to a meeting and told them that he wanted to know where would be the best site to locate a holding pond and a slimes dam. They looked over topographic maps and geologic maps and settled on a small valley that lay to the south. It was not too far to pump the slimes, and there was no water course in it to complicate matters. James suggested that they go and take a look before settling on the location, and was gratified that it fit the bill. He asked John if he felt comfortable designing the dam and the spillways. John was honest enough to admit that civil engineering was not his strong point, so James sat down with him and they sketched up a design. Before they proceeded with construction, James wanted to check with the engineers in Kitwe and also get some liner to put in the bottom of the ponds they would create to stop migration of the chemicals into the lake. They decided to use waste rock from the mine as their main building material, so would need a fair amount of it crushed into smaller sizes to form a water-tight barrier.

Favoured son

As James and John Wells drove north on Friday morning early they were confident that they would get a good reception in Kitwe. The concentrator was coming along nicely. The mining fleet was all assembled and operating. They had started actual mining and had even found some ore that was worth mining, and had stockpiled it until such time as the concentrator was operational. There were a few things that James wanted to go over with the management team in Kitwe. He needed some supervisors for the concentrator. When the plant was fully operational, it would be around the clock, and John McFarlane could hardly be expected to be there at all times. James also felt that he needed another two shift bosses for the mine, so that he could have two on each of two shifts. Angus needed more mechanics, and although these had been promised, they had not yet been assigned to the mine. He also wanted some better lights to enable them to operate at night more efficiently.

At the offices in Kitwe, they found the meeting room and had a few minutes to wait before the management arrived. A secretary poked her head around the door and seemed surprised to see them there already. She vanished quickly, and a few minutes later, the managers came into the room. Apart from the regulars, there was a newcomer, George Bullock. James knew George, having stayed in his house for a while, and the Bullocks were away on a long leave. George McIntosh introduced him to John Wells but said nothing more at that time. James went through progress to date and gave them all the news. George Armstrong thanked them for the return of the diesel bowsers and the bus and asked if there was any diesel left over from the trip. James danced around the question and said that yes, there was a little, and he had transferred it to the tanks at the mine. He then made his request for the extra supervision, and Winter assured him that people would be assigned the following week. As for lights, Armstrong told them that they had lights on order and that they would be delivered within the month.

John Wells went through the accounting and finance issues and showed that, even though they had had to innovate and adapt because of the border closure, they had stayed within budget. All around the room, congratulations were murmured, then George McIntosh called for attention.

"I'm pleased to be able to introduce to you the new Open Pit Manager for Mtuga, George," he started. "George is currently an Assistant Underground Manager and is slated for an Underground Manager slot, and it is felt that he would benefit from a spell at Mtuga to broaden his experience."

"What will be my role?" asked James.

"Ah, yes, Martin," continued McIntosh. "You will take over the mine, and George Walker will take over the concentrator. Walker will be assisted by McFarlane and two others we're sending you, Mike Smith and Ken Brown."

"I'm sure we can rely on you to fully support George in his new role?" asked McIntosh.

"Of course," lied James. "I'll do whatever I can."

"By the look of it, just keep on doing whatever it is you have been doing," laughed George.

"What about housing and all that sort of stuff?" asked John Wells.

"Ah, well, because Martin, you are in the manager's house, you will need to move to one of the others and allow George to move in shortly," ordered McIntosh. "Also, give him the Land Rover you have been using and take one of the others for yourself."

"Will Walker require transport?" John continued.

"No, give him and the others houses, but no vehicles, the concentrator people don't need to be running around the mine," replied McIntosh.

"When will you be joining us?" James asked George.

"I'll be there with my wife on Monday, so if you can be moved by Sunday night, I would be happy," he replied.

"Fine, I'll do that," agreed James.

"Well, that's that," announced McIntosh. "George, please join me for lunch, and we'll go over the details of your assignment."

After they had left, James and John sat for a while looking at each other. Duncan Brown, Henry Wayne and Tony Williams had quickly left after

McIntosh, as though they were embarrassed by the proceedings. Colin Winter stayed with them but for a while said nothing.

"Will you two join me for lunch?" Winter finally asked them. "I may be able to tell you what is going on."

"Thanks," agreed James, although he was clearly agitated and annoyed.

"It's okay, you can actually say it to me," said Winter.

"Alright, what the fuck was that all about?" asked James angrily.

"I'm sorry to have to tell you," began Winter. "But, Bullock is earmarked for great things, and the General Manager has instructed us to give him a spell at the open pit to broaden his experience."

"If he's so wonderful, why don't they send him to some other mine then?" asked James.

"Unfortunately, we no longer have that option," explained Winter. "He works for the Zambian company, as do you, and the other countries where the parent has operations won't take people from here."

"How long will he be at Mtuga?" asked John.

"Probably a year," replied Winter.

"Then what, do we get another favoured son?" John asked.

"Careful, lad," warned Winter. "I understand your frustration, but if you let the others hear you say that, you might be back in London sooner than you think."

"A word to the wise, Mr Winter," commented John. "I do not need their approval, and they would be well advised to remember who will be doing what one or two years from now."

"I'm sorry, I don't follow you," said Winter, a little nettled by Wells's attitude.

"My father is a major shareholder, so I know what it is to be a favoured son," stated John. "I did this assignment mainly to get some experience that I thought would be useful when I take over managing his portfolio."

"Ah, I see," said Winter, a little set aback. "I trust that we have lived up to your expectations?"

"Indeed," agreed John. "One of the main things I have learnt is that it is hard to find good operating people and if you do, don't lose them through stupidity!"

"Can we go to lunch?" asked James, interrupting this exchange. "I need to get back to Mtuga and move!"

"There is one more thing before you go," interrupted Winter. "We have a nurse for you for the clinic."

"Great," commented James. "Is she married? What's her name?"

"Florence Hill and she's single, one of the sunshine girls," Winter said. "She'll move down next week, and you'll also get a visit once a week from one of the doctors from our hospital here."

"Fine," said James. "We've enough people now that we could use some help. We'll take care of the housing for Florence and see that she gets settled in. Does she speak Bemba?"

"I doubt it," thought Winter. "You'd better plan on getting yourselves a Zambian nurse as well to translate for you. I'll leave that up to you and Jerry."

The ride back to Mtuga was quiet. James was seething and was also very disappointed. He felt that he had done a good job, but that seemed not to account for anything. He thought he had been promised the job himself, but it seemed that whatever promises had been made did not count.

"What the fuck am I going to tell everyone at the mine?" James asked.

"Just tell them the bare facts, James," suggested John. "It won't serve you to say anything else."

"What do I tell Katrina?" James continued.

"Tell her everything we know," advised John. "She deserves to know what we do."

"You're probably right," agreed James. "What a bunch of bastards!"

"Bullock is one of the select few who have already been identified as high-potential candidates," commented John.

"How do you know?" asked James.

"I've seen the lists," John said. "They are typically updated every year and include all the assistant managers who are thought to be candidates for promotion."

"Who puts them on that list?" asked James.

"Those annual reviews that you are supposed to have been going to," stated John. "The results of those go to London, and high potentials are selected."

"Well, why doesn't he go and be high potential elsewhere?" complained James.

"Unfortunately, this part of the operation only has one open pit and no one else wants Bullock," commented John.

"How the hell do you know that?" asked James.

"Winter said as much, in a very roundabout way," explained John. "Just because London identifies him as high potential, doesn't mean that the local people all agree."

"Really, I can't have been listening," thought James.

"No, you had enough on your mind," agreed John.

"That's *kak* man," commented Katrina later when James broke the news to her. "What a bunch of bastards!"

"You're telling me!" agreed James.

"What are you going to do?" she asked.

"I'm on a contract," he replied. "If I break the contract, I stand to lose quite a bit."

"Man, what a *doës* McIntosh must be," she remarked. "What about Bullock?"

"Do you remember the *doës* whose house I stayed in that didn't want me to have overnight guests, before we were married?" he asked. "That's who he is. Who knows what he's like to work for? I never really had much to do with him when I worked underground; he was at a different shaft."

"Shame, and just when you thought everything was going well!" she said.

"Well, tomorrow we'd better organise our move to the spare house and get out of here," he added.

"I'll get Gibson and some of the others to organise it," she promised. "Don't worry about it, what about Mrs Bullock?"

"Oh, that'll be a riot here with John chasing Elena and Rita and Florence being single," he replied. "I'm sure she'll have something to say about that."

"Maybe we should leave a mamba or two in the house?" she suggested.

"I like the thought, but probably not," James commented. "If he died of shock, who knows what kind of idiot they would saddle us with next!"

At the meeting, he called the next morning, the news was greeted with shock, disbelief and protest. James had had to take John McFarlane

125

aside before the meeting and break the news to him directly, and let him know that he now had a new boss, George Walker and two new cohorts. James went through with them all the facts that he was moving house that day and that he was taking a spare open-bed Land Rover and ceding the station wagon to George Bullock. He also made the usual speeches about supporting the new manager, however hypocritical he felt about it himself, and told them that he would be concentrating on the mining. It looked as if Angus was the only one who had dodged a new manager, but who knew what the powers that be might do next.

By the time James went home, Katrina had moved house, and they were now ensconced in a new home. Gibson had made sure that the old house had been cleaned. He was having no one criticise himself or the madam for anything relating to the house. The new house was on the opposite side of the village and had no greenery yet or any other plantings. They were now back to square one with window coverings and the other small amenities that made living comfortable.

Monday morning, James had his usual staff meeting, and then everyone went about their business but did not go far, all waiting for Bullock to arrive. At about ten, a car and a lorry laden with stuff pulled into the site. James met with George and assigned Abel to show the lorry driver where we needed to go to deliver the household stuff. George introduced his wife, Mary, and she then went off in the car to the house to supervise unloading. George then called a staff meeting and was introduced to everyone. He informed them that George Walker and the others would be arriving after noon and asked if there would be houses ready for them. Hippo confirmed that there was and asked if there was a Mrs Walker. Apparently, there was, Susan by name.

Bullock then wanted to tour the construction site and check over the concentrator, the workshops and all the other buildings that were underway. He said that he was going to leave actual mining operations until the afternoon. James listened as John McFarlane went through the process and each item of machinery used, and when it would be operational. Although he, James, had had to swat up on his knowledge of comminution, he was streets ahead of Bullock, who seemed to have no clue. In the workshops, Angus kept up a patter in the broadest of Scots, and James wondered if Bullock actually got more than about ten per cent of it. He did understand one thing, and that was if they wanted the fleet to run efficiently, the maintenance schedule needed to be adhered to and respected.

After lunch, James and Rita met with Bullock, and they took a drive around the pit perimeter. Rita explained the orebody type and pointed out various lenses and outcrops that they had already started to mine and stockpile. John Watson still had people there pre-stripping, and he came over to introduce himself.

"How long are you people going to be here?" opened Bullock.

"Probably another three weeks or so," John estimated. "It depends on the rain. Too much rain and we cannot work."

"Why not, are your operators afraid to get wet?" Bullock asked.

"No, but I don't want to lose any of them or any equipment in a smash, which is what we could have with slippery roads," John replied.

"Well, how much time have you already lost?" Bullock continued.

"About eighteen work days this rainy season," thought John. "You have the detailed breakdown of hours worked and time lost."

"Why haven't you paved everything to make it safe?" Bullock asked.

"We have covered the major haul roads with crushed rock, and they are pretty much all weather, but the working areas and the dumps we cannot pave because we are digging them up or building them as we go!" John supplied.

"Martin, do you have a working plan for this pit?" Bullock asked.

"Yes, you can see here; this is the perimeter, these are the benches we have excavated, and this is the area we are working on now," James offered.

"I can't make head or tail of this," Bullock complained. "I need to see separate drawings of each level to see where we are!"

"Okay, we'll get that for you," said Rita, looking at James and raising her eyebrows in a 'What the hell kind of idiot is this that can't read a cutting plan', look.

"Walker should be here by now," Bullock thought. "We'll go back to the office and see him."

"I met George when I first arrived in Zambia," commented James. "But I've no idea what he has been doing."

"He did some time in the smelter, then in the concentrator," Bullock replied. "He's just got back from a long leave with his new wife."

"Well, if this is her first experience of Zambia, it should be interesting for her," thought James.

"When we get back to the office, perhaps you could get us some coffee?" Bullock said to Rita. She looked at him a little archly and told him politely that she had a meeting with two Government geologists and was needed elsewhere immediately. As James had never heard of any Government geologists, he rather thought that this was a polite way of telling him to piss off and get his own bloody coffee. This was obviously going to be an adjustment for everyone.

At the office, they found George with his wife, Susan, together with Mike Smith, Ken Brown and their spouses, Violet and Rose and Florence Hill. James made arrangements for the spouses and Florence to be shown where they would be living. Susan had already complained about the fact that the nearest reasonably sized shops were in Kabwe, some 124 kilometres away. James then rubbed a little salt in her wounds by pointing out that power failures were not uncommon and that sometimes the road became almost impassable. That only seemed to heighten her sense of isolation, and James almost felt sorry for George and a little guilty about his treatment of Susan. When John McFarlane arrived, he went through everything again with the Georges, then took George Walker and his two new cohorts off on a tour of the facility. Bullock next asked to see John Wells and wanted to see the numbers. He had several complaints about items having been omitted from the original plan, and finally, John had to point out to him that it had been the planning department in Kitwe that had been guilty of the omissions, not the current staff.

"I see we have radios in the Land Rovers," commented Bullock. "What is the system for identification?"

"We have just used names up to now," replied James.

"We'll change that," stated Bullock. "I'll be one, you're two, George Walker will be three and I'll decide on the rest later."

James thought that was a little pretentious. One did not really need to be told every day who was the boss and what the hierarchy was. James wondered what else Bullock would change. Things were not off to a great start, and he began to wonder if he should ask for a transfer elsewhere. He discussed that idea with Katrina later, who suggested that he wait a while and see what transpired.

For the next couple of weeks, James and George Bullock went through their transition. James had to work hard not to appear too impatient with the questions and ideas that George had. It surprised him a little that George actually knew so little about surface mining issues. Also, perhaps because the mine was small, remote and new, there was little in the way of infrastructure, clearly something George had been used to and seemed to be a little lost without. For someone who had been identified as a high flyer, he seemed to be singularly lacking in leadership qualities. Perhaps, James thought one day, they were all being rather hypocritical, as all those on the mine site had learnt by experience and sometimes by trial and error, whereas George was having a crash course.

John McFarlane was having an easier time with George Walker. At least he understood the theory and practice of comminution and concentration very well and was able to actually contribute ideas and guidance very quickly. John found that he was actually learning a lot and enjoying the experience. Having Mike and Ken to help him also made the job considerably easier. James had been happy to dump onto George the slimes dam project, promising the equipment for earth removal and the transport of waste rock to the site to build the dam. George quickly got in touch with the engineers in Kitwe, and they were happy with the basic design that James had sketched up, only making a few suggestions for anchoring at the base of the dam and the wings where it blended into the hillside. However, they also directed that James should construct the dam, so he got it back again!

James dumped the issue of a Zambian nurse into Bullock's lap, and he promptly turned around and dumped it onto Jerry Mwanza. It turned out that the solution was quite easy. Hippo's wife-to-be was a nurse and was happy to move from Kabwe to Mtuga and join the mine payroll.

The wives were a different issue. Mary had illusions of grandeur and wanted to lord it over the balance of the spouses in the village. Her idea of socialising was afternoon teas held on her *stoep*, to which she invited select groups at different times. After her first experience, Katrina found reasons to be absent when the tea parties were planned. Mary and George had been in Zambia for eight years, so had arrived just after independence, and Mary considered herself an expert on all things Zambian. Katrina reported to James that Mary was a racist worse than almost any South Africans that she knew, and treated her house servants like dirt. No wonder, Katrina commented to James one day, Mary was unable to keep a house servant for more than a few months. They all quit as soon as they could, and she was then back searching for new help. Susan, however, was completely new to the country, and after she had got over the shock of the isolation of the mine and the road conditions to Kabwe, she found that she actually was starting to enjoy the experience. She made friends quickly with Katrina, Kirsty, Morag and Rita and found reasons and excuses to go on expeditions with them as often as she could. Katrina, or rather Gibson, helped her find a house servant, an older man who clearly had been a house servant before and was now looking for something closer to his village.

James found that George Walker had changed over the past three or so years. Whereas when he had first met him, James had thought George to be something of a know-it-all, George now admitted to much that he did not know. He also had softened his attitude towards the Africans and others who were there. Afrikaners were no longer "as thick as two short planks, ugly with unpronounceable names". James rather suspected, as he had learnt underground, that George had actually learnt a lot from different people in the concentrator and the smelter and had come to appreciate others.

The next fortnightly review was not held in Kitwe but at the mine site. McIntosh, Winter, Armstrong, Wayne and Brown all made the trek to the mine and announced that they would stay the night and suggested a *braai* be held on Friday night with the local management and their spouses. George Bullock talked it over with James, and they decided that the prospects for fine weather were good, but, in case of rain, they made a plan to gather in the workshop if necessary. The next problem was where to house so many visitors. In the end, they just allocated one to each of five houses, so James got Winter, George Bullock took McIntosh, George Walker took Wayne, Angus McBride took Armstrong and John Wells was lumbered with Brown. Bullock decided that billeting Brown with Rita just would not look right. The whole escapade rather cramped the style of John Wells, who had been planning a romantic weekend with Elena. Perhaps, James suggested to him, that would still be possible if they could get the *bwanas* out of there before lunch on Saturday.

George Bullock and John Wells presented the review, and apparently, all must have gone well because the balance of the management was invited to lunch with the senior staff. James wondered where the lunch had come from, as he had heard nothing about preparations beforehand. McIntosh enlightened them all to the fact that he and his party had brought lunch with them and the crew to prepare and serve it. That accounted for the extra vehicles that James had seen arrive just before lunch.

The afternoon was taken up with tours of the concentrator, workshops and the mine. Bullock took the lead and pointed out everything that "he had done", much to the amusement of the rest, until they realised that he was taking credit for much that he had not done. Things were actually well on schedule, even ahead in most areas. The main crusher was running, and the balance of the crushing and grinding circuit behind it was undergoing tests and trials, and the flotation cells were ready to receive their first material. By the first or second week of March, they would be in business in terms of concentrating ore, and the pressure was now shifting to the mining section to find and win ore. They had been lucky and been able to find some lenses very quickly and get those extracted and stockpiled, but to hear it from Bullock, one would imagine that he had personally gone into the mine and pointed out where to dig. Rita was clearly less than impressed and decided to let him hang himself with predictions of what they would mine next.

The *braai* was a little more relaxed. It was held in the middle of the management village, and all residents were invited. George and James were both relieved to see that their weather prognostications had been correct and there was no rain. Mary Bullock tried to be the grand dame, but the senior managers present stole the limelight and attention was focused away from her. The same crew that had arrived to handle the lunch was on duty for the *braai*. It was not quite the amateur affair that the mine staff had staged for themselves in the past. But with a catering staff, it meant that the mine project team did not have to cook.

"So, how are you now?" Colin Winter asked James.
"Fine, thanks," he replied. "I'm busy enough with the mining, and I've spent a fair amount of time with George bringing him up to date."
"Thank you for that," commented Winter. "I would say from today's briefing that things are still going better than expected."
"Mrs Martin, I understand you're in the industrial minerals business?" Duncan Brown asked.
"True," she agreed. "I've had a few lessons from Rita on the basics and can now identify micas, feldspars and china clays."
"What's it like living out here in the wilderness?" Duncan asked.
"Fine," she replied. "I think some of the others feel a little isolated at times, but I'm enjoying it."
"Any more issues with the ZIPRA folks?" Winter asked.
"No, since the one time, we haven't seen them much, except in the company of the Zambian Army," Katrina replied.
"I think our contact with the colonel really helped," added James. "But I think there could still be issues with some of the farmers, because I think the ZIPRA chaps see them as spies for the Rhodesians."
"Just watch yourselves," reminded Duncan. "We don't want any incidents!"
"Have you seen anything of the Chinese?" Winter asked.
"Yes," James replied. "We often see convoys of their green lorries going back and forth on the Great North Road."

"Well, they're certainly coming on with the railway," Duncan commented. "It won't be too long, and they'll be connecting with the Zambia system at Kapiri."

George and Mary Bullock joined their little group, and the conversation shifted to how Mary was adapting to the small settlement and the lack of amenities.

"I don't know how people were able to cope in the twenties and thirties," she started. "Imagine having almost no shops, bad roads and no electricity?"

"I suppose, like all people, they managed," suggested Duncan. "After all, if you don't know what you don't have, you don't miss it."

"What about you, Katrina?" she asked. "What was it like when you grew up here?"

"As Duncan said, I didn't know anything different, so for me it was normal," Katrina replied. "I remember getting electricity, crossing the Kafue on the Ndola road by pontoon and seeing lots of game on the road."

"Most of that's gone now," commented Winter. "Population pressure has driven it all away."

"Yes, but what did you do about culture?" Mary persisted. "It seems to me that it must have been a pretty culturally barren place."

"Not when I was younger," Katrina replied. "We had the Little Theatre in Kitwe and the bioscope, Rhodwins on the Mufulira road and other things."

"Yes, but what about the symphony and opera?" Mary insisted.

"Let's face it, Mary, we just couldn't afford it, could we?" Katrina asked.

"I suppose not," she conceded. "I just love going to all the concerts I can when we take our long leaves to London. It just heals my soul!"

"Perhaps you'll excuse us?" James interrupted. "I need to ask George Armstrong a couple of things."

"What things?" Katrina asked him after they left the group and were headed towards Armstrong.

"Nothing in particular," admitted James. "I couldn't stand the pretence any longer, after all, in her book I'm probably a cultural Philistine and you're probably just a *Boer meisie* that is getting used to wearing shoes."

"So, James, how is the new boss?" Armstrong asked.

"Fine," commented James.

"He always struck me as a bit of a wanker," Armstrong added. "I could never really get on with him."

"Well, as I'm stuck here, I'll have to try," James thought.

"Rather you than me, chum," laughed Armstrong. "Just make sure he doesn't piss off Angus too much. He's too good to lose!"

"What's your next move?" James asked.

"Consulting engineer in the Johannesburg office, probably two to three years from now," Armstrong thought. "That is, of course, if you chaps don't make a mess of this or the world economy goes haywire."

"What do you mean?" asked Katrina.

"Well, if the price of copper drops twenty-five per cent, then we have an economic problem at most of the mines, this one first," he explained. "I'm sure your man John Wells has models that look at copper price and mining costs to see where the break-even point is."

"Yes, we do," acknowledged James. "It would be better if we could get some computer time to run the models."

"That's hard to come by," Armstrong agreed. "The accountants spend all their time worshipping at the fount of all knowledge and poring over the reams of paper that the computers spit out. We never get a look in!"

McIntosh came over and joined them as he made his rounds of the staff. James was a little surprised that he had staged this *braai*, as usually McIntosh was never seen by mere mortals. Still, it probably helped to boost morale, and it did not hurt to introduce the others, like Hippo and Abel, to the likes of McIntosh and Winter. James found, and he was sure that it was even more the case for the shift bosses, that the open pit business was very different to the underground side of the operations. Underground one was invisible, with only occasional visits from the hierarchy. In the open pit, everything was visible, and it was far too easy for senior officials to drive to the pit edge, look over and then start asking questions. The pressures on the lower supervisory staff were different and, in some cases, too much. James had heard of shift bosses on some of the other mines requesting transfers back underground, where they could at least be in charge of their own world. James thanked the stars that their pit was at least a good drive away from Kitwe. He pitied those who worked on the Copperbelt itself, where access was almost immediate.

Saturday morning, only George Bullock was required for the meetings, and they finished by eleven. No one was sad to see the *Bwanas* go. They did rather throw a blanket of apprehension over everything. John Wells was particularly happy to see George and Mary Bullock also leave, headed to Lusaka for the balance of the weekend. Now he had a little more leeway in entertaining Elena. James had told him of the experience he had had staying in the Bullock house while they were away, and John was a little surprised at the moralistic attitude that they had shown.

James and Katrina invited John and Elena to go fishing with them, with the idea that they would camp overnight. Katrina had begged the use of John Watson's boat, and they had a couple of tents in case it rained. Elena thought the idea was marvellous and soon after the Bullocks had gone, James met with his shift bosses and, deciding that all was well in hand, felt that it was safe to leave for the lake. The boat ramp was muddy but not rutted enough that it made launching the boat too difficult. Elena asked to drive, and she proved to be expert. She explained that during her stay in Brazil, she had piloted many boats on the rivers there. That left James, Katrina and John plenty of time to fish. John had done a little fishing before, but he explained that it had been mainly fly fishing on exclusive rivers in Scotland. Trolling with spinners was a new experience for him. He kept the rest in gales of laughter as he described the typical British river where coarse fishing was common. He described the hunched-over figures wrapped up against the seemingly ever-present rain, watching floats on lines cast into muddy waters, with an occasional burst of activity when something happened and the float bobbed. It seemed that fishing below the outfalls of power stations was good and much sought after, because the warmer water influenced the size of the fish.

Katrina told Elena where to head for the campsite, and they made their way down the lake. When they reached the site, they were disappointed to see several people already there. James recognised Colonel Mulanga, whom they had met previously. He thought it would be impolite to merely turn about and head off to another part of the lake, so they pulled into the bank and greeted the others.

"Colonel, how are you today?" James asked.

"Fine, thank you and you?" he replied.

"I think I can speak for us all and say that we are well," James committed.

"I'm sorry; did you expect to camp here?" The colonel asked.

"Don't worry, there are plenty of other places on the lake," James reassured him.

"I'm also sorry that we must ask you to stay at the north end of the lake and on the west side," the colonel continued. "We have some training exercises at the moment, and we would not wish you to become involved."

"Thanks," said James. "We'll be on our way."

"I understand you have a new manager at the mine," Colonel Mulanga commented. "I hope he will be as easy to work with as you have been."

"I'm sure he will," thought James. "I'll let him know you are in the area."

"Thank you, *hamba gahle*," admonished the colonel.

"*Shala mushle*," responded James.

Katrina told Elena to turn the boat around, and they headed back up the lake.

"What did he say at the end there?" asked John.

"He told us to go well, and I told him to stay good or well," James replied.

"Who were those people?" John asked.

"Well, the colonel I talked to is with the Zambian Army, and I presume that most of the others are ZIPRA," James thought.

"Not ANC?" John asked, looking for clarification.

"No, they wear different uniforms," explained James. "And the ANC camp is not as close as the ZIPRA camp."

"Well, where shall we camp for the night?" Elena asked, anxious to steer the boat in the right direction.

"It'll have to be somewhere towards the top end of the lake," thought James. "There are a number of inlets that we could try."

Katrina directed them towards a long inlet on the western side, which she told them was fed by a good-sized stream and which was probably navigable up to five miles from the lake. She thought it would be a likely spot as it was well away from the southern end and was large enough to have other features. Katrina was right about the inlet; it went quite a way from the main lake and had smaller bays scattered along its banks. She suggested to Elena to just pick one of the bays and try it. The first bay that Elena tried was not too successful. It rather reminded James of the scene from the *African Queen*, where Allnut was dragging the boat through the reeds. They backed out of there fast and tried the next bay. That was much better, and they were able to edge up into the bay a little before tying up to a large tree on the bank.

Later that night, after dinner, John started asking Elena and Katrina about the night noises and the stars. He had not been out at night before in Zambia and was intrigued by all the different sounds. Between them, the girls pointed out owls, hippo, leopard, jackals, hyæna and bats. John was a little concerned when he heard about the leopard and the hyæna, but was reassured that it was highly unlikely that they would be bothered in any way. James did hear him move his sleeping mat closer to Elena's, if that were possible! Things took a turn for the worse when it started to rain, but James and John got shelters strung quickly between two large trees, and they moved into dryer quarters. It was a very pleasant interlude away from the favoured son and his autocratic approach to things.

Assessment panel

In the office on Monday morning, Bullock passed on a piece of information that he had learned on Saturday morning. James was to report to the office in Kitwe on Thursday morning for an assessment panel. Apparently, there was a management panel meeting late in the week, and they wanted to see all the mine captains. The panel was to consist of managers from each of the mines in the group and the personnel manager from the office in Lusaka. However, before James went to the interview, there were forms to be completed. Bullock told James to be back at lunchtime, and they would go over the forms and the assessment that he, Bullock, was giving. That just filled James with delight. Here was someone who had just taken over the job he had been doing and was now going to pass judgment and have that judgment reviewed and commented on by other managers in the group.

James left the office and drove out to the pit rim to check on progress. They had taken delivery of several small mobile drill rigs, and he wanted to lay out a drill and blast pattern with Abel. Rita joined him on the pit rim, and they drove down together to meet with Abel. To some extent, the drill pattern was going to be a matter of trial and error as they learned what worked. It was all driven by the bucket size of the loaders they had. The Caterpillar 988 loader had a nominal 6 cu yd bucket, so there was an optimum size of broken rock for easy loading. James decided, for now, to try a three-by-three-metre pattern and see if this gave good results. He had noted at the Mindola pit that they were using a four-by-four pattern, but the Mtuga pit was different, much more rocky and fractured. They would see after the first blast or two if they needed to enlarge the hole spacing or bring them in a little. Too much breakage was a waste of explosive, and too little meant the inevitable 'goolies' and the necessity of secondary blasting with its attendant waste of time. He also surmised that when they got larger drilling equipment and could increase the hole size, then the spacing could also increase. For now, they only had machines capable of drilling 4 ½" diameter holes, so would make do.

Abel gave his instructions to the drill crews and then came and sat with James while they worked out the explosive load for each hole and the detonation sequence. Unfortunately, they were not permitted to use electrical blasting because of the fear of lightning strikes and premature detonation, so would use safety fuse plus Cordtex with in-line delays. They would also try and use ANFO wherever possible to reduce costs. They had two types of delays for the blasting circuit: 15 milliseconds and 20 milliseconds. The trick was to time the blast right to get the best effect. Rita was interested, which is why she had tagged along and asked questions that related to the fracturing of the rock that was already there and how that affected the blast. James was concerned about that but had no real way of gauging the effect until they had had a trial or two.

They set the blast for three the following afternoon, by which time they would have enough holes drilled for a reasonable amount of material. James told Abel to let him know when they would be starting to load the holes, and he would come down and check on the blast conditions. Then he went back to the office for his meeting with George Bullock.

It seemed that George Walker was also on the docket for a panel because he was leaving Bullock's office as James arrived.
"Hey, James," George began. "You have to see Mister high and mighty as well, do you?"
"Yes, how was it?"
"Not too bad, he really doesn't know me, and he knows even less about the concentrator, so he's in the dark," concluded George. "Watch out for the snide little digs, though. When does your panel meet?"
"Thursday, and yours?" asked James.
"Wednesday, in Broken Hill of all places," George complained. "Susan was looking forward to a day out in a little larger town, still, I suppose Broken Hill's better than Kapiri!"
"You're right about that. Why Broken Hill?" James asked.
"I don't really know, unless they've arranged a visit to the lead and zinc processing plant," George replied, then continued. "Why don't you come and see me in the concentrator after your meeting and tell me how it went?"

"I'll do that," thought James. "I'll also give you some idea of what we'll be digging up and sending you in the next few days."

"Great, see you soon!"

James knocked on the door to Bullock's office and was told to enter. Bullock was obviously finishing a telephone conversation with someone, and the topic was concentrate deliveries to the smelter. He was asking about road transport because he and James had been told that it would be provided, but apparently, now they were going to have to do it themselves, judging from the questions and answers that James could hear.

"Can you imagine that?" Bullock asked. "They tell us all along not to worry about shipping the concentrates, now they change the rules and tell us that we have to ship and include the freight in our costs!"

"I suppose there was no adjustment to the credit we receive for the concentrates?" James asked.

"Not on your life!" protested Bullock. "The bloody smelter manager is just trying to wangle lower costs so that he comes out looking better!"

"When do we have to make our first delivery?" James asked.

"In about a month," was the reply. "I suppose we can get some kind of transport by then, do you know what the Eyeties use?"

"Well, I've seen a Kenworth tractor with a trailer and a Peterbilt; I'm sure they would tell us what their experience has been delivering to Rokana," thought James.

"When we're done here, why don't you pass this good news on to Walker and let him work it out?" instructed Bullock. "Now let's get back to the business at hand. You have this panel on Thursday, and I'm supposed to send in all this paperwork ahead of time. The annoying thing about it is that I really know nothing about what you've done except the job here, which is quite remarkable by the way. What do you think?"

"I think we've done fairly well so far," started James.

"I would agree with that, I've put all my comments on this form, have you any comments?" Bullock asked, passing over the forms.

James went through the pages and had to admit that George Bullock had been fair. He had only one question. "What do they mean by does he dress well?"

"I've no idea," George admitted. "It was always a mystery to me."

"Would it be inappropriate to ask you to make a change there?" James asked.

"What do you want to say?"

"What about, he dresses in accordance with the requirements of the job," suggested James.

"That sounds reasonable," George agreed.

"What do they normally ask at these panels?" James asked.

"It depends who's on them. Sometimes it seems pretty stupid, other times they actually ask intelligent questions. They'll probably want to ask about your aspirations and career thoughts," opined George. "What do you think of Walker?" he continued, changing the subject completely.

"George, well, he's alright," countered James.

"Look, I know most people think I'm unapproachable and a bit autocratic, but you can actually talk to me," George Bullock continued.

"Well, I've not really seen much of George since we first started with the mine, but when we first started, he seemed to think he knew a lot," James offered.

"Well, I think he still thinks he knows a lot. I'm a little disappointed in his attitude; he seems to think he is the fount of all knowledge when it comes to the concentrator. How much do you know?" George asked.

"I'm a little rusty, but I can manage," James replied.

"Brush up a little, I want some second opinions in the staff meetings I plan to start next Monday," ordered George. "Oh, and by the way, although you've been told to report at nine on Thursday, you'd better go the night before, get to the office at eight and be prepared to wait all day before they get to you!"

"Thanks, shall I give the news to George about the transport changes?" asked James.

"Fine, would you also ask John Wells to step in for a minute? I've some items I need to go over." Bullock requested.

James passed on the word to John Wells and then went off looking for George Walker. He found him on the concentrator floor, discussing something with John McFarlane. James waited until they finished and then dropped the transportation bombshell on them.

"Hey George, I'm supposed to pass on a message, you'll have to organise transport to get the concentrates to the smelter," he said.

"What?" George asked.

"Apparently, the smelter people have fixed things so that the cost of transportation is to our account, so you'll need trucks or something," James explained.

"Well, that's just ducky," George commented, then did the obvious thing. "John, you'll need to organise transport to the smelter in time for the first delivery."

"Thanks a lot, George," John complained. "James, do you think Katrina could introduce me to some people who could help?"

"Of course, stop at the house later and tell her what you need. I'm sure she'll find a way to help you."

"So, James, how did the session go with our lord and master?" George asked.

"Not so bad," James replied. "He was probably distracted by the transport issue."

"You said something about ore and values?" George commented.

"Yes, you should be getting about 10,000 tonnes with an average grade of about 2%," James committed.

"What about grade variation?"

"The best we can determine is that the range is between 1.5% and 2.2%, so not too great a range, certainly no really low-grade stuff, and nothing really rich," James explained.

"Did you get that, John?" George asked.

"Yes, I'll tune the cells when it starts to come in."

"Well, I need to go and check on our blast for tomorrow," said James. "I'll see you chaps."

James went back to the open pit and found Rita watching the drilling and occasionally grabbing samples of the cuttings that were coming out of the holes.

"Anything interesting?" James asked.

142

"I was wondering if we could relate penetration rate to hardness and give you something like an algorithm to calculate explosive load," she replied.

"What are we drilling into now?" James asked.

"It's pretty mixed," she started. "Over here it's mainly gneisses, whereas over there, there are some quartzites, and over there it's a mix of granites and gneisses."

"This is a weird orebody, isn't it?" James asked.

"It is indeed, it's a whole series of intrusions into the country rock, we could probably get half a dozen PhDs written on this deposit and the irumide belt in general," Rita thought.

"Is there a way to relate the air volume coming out of the hole to the fracturing that's already there?" James asked.

"Maybe, but I'm not sure how we'd actually do that," Rita admitted. "You'll just have to try and see how things go."

Abel and Hippo came over to join them. It was shift change time, and they were doing their handover. James went through with both of them the blast they were setting up, and Hippo committed to have all the drilling done that night so that they could load the holes in the morning and set off the blast at shift change the next day. Shift change was a good time for the blast, as all the equipment would be out of the pit.

At home, James broke the news to Katrina.

"*Suikerbossie*, I have to be in Kitwe on Thursday for an assessment panel. Do you want to come with me?" James asked.

"What's that?" she asked.

"Essentially, an interview with different managers from the group to see if I'm still sane and what I think my prospects might be. Do you want to come?"

"Oh, sorry, yes, I'd love to come. I can visit with the tyre and paint people while you're busy. Do you know how long you'll be?"

"No, Bullock told me to be there at eight and be prepared to wait all day," James replied.

"Where will we stay Wednesday night?" she asked.

"I've no idea, what do you think?"

"I'll call John Watson, it'll be better than the Nkana Hotel or even the Edinburgh," she thought.

"Will you let Gibson know that we'll be gone Thursday?" James asked.

"*Ja*, it'll be *lekker man* to just get away for the day with you, I've not seen much of you lately," she complained.

"I'm sorry, we've been pretty busy lately. I think things should settle down now," he promised.

"Well, let me just tell Gibson he can take off now and we'll see how sorry you really are," she said.

"You're really grubby from that mine of yours," she commented when she returned. "I think a shower is in order!"

"Whatever you say," he agreed.

They had installed a shower outside, screened from all sides but open to the sky. Their intention had been to provide for cleaning off when working in the yard or, as was the case now, coming back from the mine covered in dust and dirt. Unfortunately, there was only cold water, but with air temperatures as hot as they were, cold showers were not always unwelcome. Katrina turned on the shower, then tapped her foot impatiently as James undressed and got under the shower with a gasp as the cold water hit him. Then she stripped off and came in with him.

"There's plenty of room in here, isn't there?" James commented.

"More than enough! Give me the soap, man, and I'll clean you off!"

"Where's the shampoo?" he asked. "I can do your hair for you."

"Here," she replied, handing him the bottle. "Now turn around so that I can do your back."

"Stop wriggling," James complained after he turned back around to face her. "How can I wash your hair if you're always moving around?"

"Because, if I stay still, you'll get ideas."

"What ideas?"

"If you don't know, I'm not going to tell you!" she laughed. Then she turned her back to him and pressed herself up against him. He could feel her buttocks up against him and, cold shower or not, his erection was almost immediate. James gave up on the hair washing and put his hands on her hips and whispered in her ear. "Move your legs apart and lean forward." Katrina did that, then reached down between her legs

144

and found him and guided him into her. They tried that for a while, then she pulled off him and turned around to face him.

"If we're going to do that again, we should put something closer for me to hold on to or lean against," she said.

"I'll see what I can do," he laughed.

"Can you lift me up?" she asked.

"I'll try," he groaned, but only in jest. He picked her up, and she wrapped her legs around him and her arms around his neck. She kissed him deeply as he thrust himself back into her, and they stayed locked in their embrace until they both came.

"That's hard work," James commented.

"Yes, but worth it?" she asked.

"Every time," he laughed.

"Maybe we shouldn't make so much noise," Katrina suggested. "Who knows what the neighbours will think?"

"Do you care?" James asked.

"Not really, it's none of their business," she commented, dismissing public opinion with a wave of her hand.

Gibson had left some dinner cooking in the oven, which they enjoyed; then Katrina wanted to know more about the assessment panel and what it entailed. James went through the discussions he had had with Bullock and speculated on what they might ask him. Then he asked Katrina if she would like to see their first blast that they were going to set off the next day. She thought that might be interesting, rather like driving out of Kitwe on the Ndola road to watch the Rokana people pour slag onto the dump. At night, it was spectacular to see the molten material cascading down the dump face in rivers. The main road had been moved a couple of times because, over time, the slag dump encroached upon the road and it was no longer safe. James asked her to be at the mine office at two, and she could drive out with him to the viewing point.

The next morning, James and Abel checked on the work Hippo had finished overnight, and all the holes were completed. Now came the charging. First, they took a Pentolite booster and poked a hole in it through which they ran the Cordtex. The booster they lowered into the hole, and then poured in ANFO until it was a few feet short of the top. There was always debate about whether to fill the last couple of feet of the holes with dust and dirt, so James told Abel to fill one half of the blast and leave the other and see if there was any noticeable difference. With all the holes filled, they started to connect up the Cordtex into the lines that would control the blast pattern and sequence. After lunch, James went back and watched Abel connect the fuses that they would use to actually fire the shot. They agreed on the time of the blast, and James went back out of the pit to make sure everyone was clear. On the pit rim, they erected barriers so that no one would drive down the ramps. He went to the office and found Katrina, plus about eight others who wanted to witness the first blast. James found hard hats for them all, even though he knew that any reasonably sized rock would make short work of the hard hat and the head in it. Still, it would protect against small fragments and satisfy the regulations.

At the viewpoint they had prepared, James and his entourage joined George Bullock, George Walker and Rita. All of whom had come to watch the excitement. He was sure that the novelty would wear off pretty quickly, and soon it would be very much a matter of routine. James contacted Abel on his radio and told him when to light the fuses. Then he started the siren they had installed to provide a warning to anyone passing by that a blast was to occur. They all watched as Abel got out of his Land Rover, lit the fuses, watched for a few seconds to see that they were burning properly, then headed for the ramp. James had had Hippo also go down, so that if one Land Rover broke down for some reason, they always had the other. The two shift bosses arrived at the viewpoint and joined the rest.

"How long do we have to wait?" asked Bullock.

"Well, we used nominally six-minute fuses," explained James. "And, four minutes have gone, so anywhere from 120 to 150 seconds from now."

"That much variation?" Bullock asked.

"We tried some experiments the other day," James explained. "And we discovered that the twelve-foot fuses were going off anywhere between six minutes and six and a half minutes. We tried forty fuses and got quite a scatter."

"Okay, any time now," Abel promised and was rewarded with an impressive bang and cloud of smoke. The smoke and debris blew away from the viewpoint, and the small particle debris that was put up by the blast landed mostly in a zone of about fifty metres from the blast site. As far as they could see, all the holes had gone, and the rock pile looked nicely fragmented. James shut off the siren and then, after a few minutes, they made their way down to the blast site for the post-mortem.

Hole spacing needed to be closed up a little, and a few more delays would have been helpful. But all in all, for a first shot, it was not too bad, only a few 'goolies' to be broken with secondary blasts. Hippo got a bulldozer and pushed them off to one side to be dealt with when they did their next blast. Then followed the clean-up of the ramps and area around the blast and the detailed analysis of what they had achieved. James and Rita checked over the rock pile and showed Hippo where the ore lens occurred and what to separate in terms of waste and ore. The waste would go to the dump, and the ore to the crusher. James was a little surprised by the mineralisation. He had expected to see more oxides, as close to the surface as they were, but it was nearly all sulphides and therefore suitable for their flotation process.

Wednesday afternoon, Katrina loaded bags of samples into the back of their Land Rover, and they drove north to Kitwe. They were between Ndola and Kitwe when they were waved down by a policeman. He came up to them and asked if they had a jack. It seemed that the police Land Rover that was by the side of the road had a flat tyre, and they were trying to change it, but their jack did not have enough travel. James went and had a look and quickly concluded that his jack would not help. The police driver had pulled off the road and parked over the ditch so that any jack would need support underneath before it would have any effect. James noticed a number of men lounging in the back of the Land Rover, all dressed in an off-white kind of uniform. He asked the policeman who they were and was told that they were prisoners. James looked at the Land Rover, the ditch and the men and then asked the policeman if the prisoners could not be prevailed upon to just lift the one corner of the Land Rover enough to get the wheel off. This really appealed to the policeman, and he detailed off his charges.

When James had loosened the wheel nuts and announced that he was ready, the policeman issued an order, and the Land Rover magically rose up. They held it up long enough for James to pull off one wheel and replace it with the spare, and then, and only then, were they permitted to lower it. James tightened up the wheel nuts and checked the tyre pressure. It needed some air, so he got his foot pump out of his own vehicle and proceeded to start to pump the tyre up. The policeman stopped him and detailed one of the prisoners to do this work. With all back in order, James was thanked, and they proceeded on their way.

A little further down the road, they came across a police roadblock. They set these at times to check for safety issues, registration, and sometimes even wanted to see if the speedometer worked. As James pulled up the police he had helped pulled up behind, and there ensued a conversation in Bemba, which he did not understand, but the upshot of which was that they were waved through with a snappy salute. Katrina told James a tale about someone she knew who had taken their windscreen wipers off, only to have the police ask for them to be demonstrated. Thinking quickly, her friend had told the officers that the windscreen wipers only worked when there was rain and as the police had no water handy to test that claim, he was waved through with a lot of head shaking and wondering about the marvels of modern technology.

John Watson was waiting for them in Kitwe and offered to take them to dinner. He wanted to try a new restaurant in Chingola. It turned out to be not quite what he expected and was passable at best. Still, it did mean an excursion out, which was always a pleasant adventure. He was interested to learn about the panel that James was summoned to and also the appointments that Katrina had set up with the tyre and paint factories.

The next day, James reported to the office at eight and was told to wait with the others. There were ten of them altogether, three of whom

James knew, the rest came from other mines in the group, and he had not met them before. The first victim was only in front of the panel for ten minutes before he reappeared with a long face and announced that he had been told to get some more experience before his next review. James was reminded of Hornblower stories about examinations for lieutenants and the situations that the boards asked the candidates to imagine, then shot them down for almost whatever answer they gave.

The next in lasted a little longer, fifteen minutes and came out looking puzzled. He announced that things had either gone very well or very badly and cautioned the rest that the panel was really interested in how each one being reviewed would handle misfires on a large scale. James suspected that no one else would get asked anything about misfires; it was just one of the many issues that they faced day to day.

More reviews were held until a break was called for lunch, and the rest of the interviewees were asked to come back at one-thirty for their turns. James asked the others what they fancied for lunch, and the consensus was the Edinburgh. At one-fifteen, they were back waiting to be called, which was just as well because the panel started early at one-twenty. James was the second person in the hot seat after lunch and entered the room with some trepidation. All the others had reported being roughly treated.

"Ah, Martin, come in and take a seat," one of the panel members invited. "Let me introduce you to everyone. On my left, Colin Winter, whom you already know, George Hall, on my right, Moses Mwewa, Andrew McKenzie, Phillip Becket, and I'm Henry Moore, no relation to the sculptor, I'm chairing this panel."
"Tell us about this start-up you were involved in?" invited George Hall. "We've heard good things. Is it all true?"
"I don't know what you've heard," started James. "But, we've managed to bring the Mtuga project in on time and to budget, thanks mainly to the team I had."
"You don't have to be that modest," admonished Henry Moore.
"What's next for you?" asked Andrew McKenzie. "Where do you see yourself in the long run?"

"That's difficult to say," temporised James.

"You realise that you've rather cast your lot, don't you?" interrupted Phillip Becket.

"I'm sorry, I don't know what you mean," replied James.

"Well, the open pit is a little out of the mainstream underground operations, and we don't really look to get you back there," explained Becket.

"But, I was only doing what was asked of me," James commented.

"That's as maybe," Beckett continued. "Perhaps your local managers should have better explained that you were stepping out of the regular promotional route."

"We were unaware that such a position would be taken," commented Winter. "I think we need to discuss this further after Martin has left!"

"What is there to discuss?" Moore added. "Martin's done a good job, but he's now got less underground experience than mine captains his junior and we need underground managers, not open pit pansies."

"I beg your pardon?" said James, getting a little nettled. "What was that comment?"

"Well, we all know that you open-pit types like to swan around in your Land Rovers and won't work if it's raining," accused Becket.

"Hey, you two, have a heart," interrupted McKenzie. "The poor bastard pulled us out of the fire, and now we're saying piss on you! What kind of wankers does that make us?"

"Thank you, Martin, you may be excused," said Moore.

James left, and even as he was closing the door, he could hear the row that started. Winter was decrying the behaviour of Becket and Moore and McKenzie, Mwewa and Hall were joining in. No doubt a referee would be needed before that quietened down. The next person on the panel looked at James in alarm and asked what he had done. James told him that he might expect to wait for a while and then not to expect a benign group when he did get invited in. On that note, he left and went off to find Katrina. She had borrowed John Watson's Land Rover for her sales calls and said that she would be at the boat club when she was finished.

Katrina was sitting outside under a *chitenge* when James arrived. She looked up from her paperwork and immediately knew that all was not well with the world.

"What happened?" she asked.

"That bunch of bastards," he began. "They just told me that I had done a good job, but that that would be the end of it because I had taken myself out of the underground mainstream."

"What does that mean?" she asked, puzzled.

"It means that as far as they're concerned, they'll promote some other chap over my head because he comes from the underground side and not the open pit," he explained.

"What a bunch of bastards," she agreed.

"I wonder if the same kind of crap goes on with the NCCM people and the Nchanga management, where the open pit essentially is the mine?" he pondered.

"But didn't you just do what they wanted?" she asked him.

"True, but that's in this division, not the group and the rest could care less," he thought.

"What are you going to do?" she asked.

"Nothing, yet," he replied. "We'll wait and see for a few months. We might as well enjoy our swanning around while we can."

"Our what?" she asked.

"Oh, one of the idiots said that all the open-pit people do is swan around in their Land Rovers and hide from the rain, not like the real men who work underground," he explained.

"Did he actually say that?" she asked, appalled.

"Not in so many words, but fuck them all, maybe I'll get John Wells to fuck them all up at the London office," he fantasised. "But, for now, a beer would do fine."

"John, two Castles please?" Katrina asked a waiter who had been hovering just out of earshot.

"What about your day?" James asked.

"Much better than yours," she said. "I sold tons of mica to the tyre factory and tons of feldspars to the paint factory. I just need to work out now how I'm going to get it dug up and delivered by next Friday."

"Not this week, surely?" James asked.

"No, next Friday, so I have just over a week," she commented. "*Alles sal reg kom.*"

At four, James suggested to Katrina that they should probably be going if they were to get back to the mine at a reasonable hour. She agreed and went to find John Watson, who was in the bar, to return his car keys and thank him for the hospitality and use of his vehicle. She returned with John, the waiter who had their bags and announced that she was ready to go.

The following morning, James checked in with George Bullock and gave him a summary of the panel review. Bullock had heard from Winter the previous afternoon, so had heard all the gory details of the argument that followed James's panel. He had also come to the realisation that he was affected and that he was now lumped in with James as one who had left the mainstream. Needless to say, he was not thrilled. It also rather conflicted with the notion that he was one of the high-potential managers. He asked what James thought.

"Well, I was thinking last night that if they told us that we would put ourselves in a dead end by coming here, then no one who was really any good would come, and they would have only the lesser lights," offered James.

"You're right, it would be another special rejects," commented Bullock, referring to the special projects office by its other, less polite, name.

"Well, the cat's rather out of the bag now, isn't it?" James asked.

"You're right again," Bullock agreed. "What a bunch of bastards!"

"So, we're probably stuck here for a while, so why don't we make the best of it?" suggested James.

"I was rather thinking of something a little more direct," commented Bullock. "Do you think we can get the production economics to the point that it really embarrasses them?"

"Without high grading?" James asked.

"I don't have a crystal ball to know when we might leave or the mine might get closed, so we'd better not screw ourselves, so no, no high grading for a while at least," Bullock thought. "Why don't you work with Ryan and Walker and get a plan together, one that we won't share with the pricks in Kitwe?"

Full production

The first day of the new regime was hardly auspicious; it rained all day, and production was next to nothing. Fortunately, there was some ore in the stockpile so that the concentrator was able to keep operating. James met with Rita and George and passed on his news and the directive that Bullock had given him. They all speculated on what Bullock was actually doing and reached the conclusion that he was starting to look elsewhere. He had only about a year to go before his current contract expired. Given that conclusion, James was surprised that he had not told them to begin high-grading the pit. Perhaps that would come in the coming months. George suggested that it would come when Bullock could see his way clear to having a string of months with ever-increasing production and improving performance. That would look good on any curriculum vitae.

James and Rita met with Hippo and Abel, and they reviewed the cutting plan and the pockets of ore that they would expose. Hippo commented that they had had to slow down the trucks in the last few days because the ramps were becoming rough. James left the office for a few minutes and came back with George Walker. He then asked George if their crushers had the capacity to take some waste rock for a while to make road materials. George looked at the production schedules and thought about the quantities that they were currently processing, and then asked them how much they would need. James did some quick calculations and asked if they could get five thousand tonnes of crushed rock quickly, crushed to about fifteen centimetres. That would give them enough fines to form a nice roadbed on the main haul ramps, better in fact than the road from Kapiri Mposhi. George did his own calculations and suggested that they start delivering waste rock in the morning, and by Monday, they would have enough to build all the roads they wanted. He asked that the waste rock not contain really large boulders, as that would slow up the process.

Hippo and Abel promised delivery of good materials and then asked how they would get the crushed rock back down into the pit. George told them that he could discharge from the primary crusher into a pile outside the building, accessible to a front-end loader. They worked out the details of where and how, then assigned a front-end loader, two trucks, a wheel tractor and a grader to the work. Hippo and Abel laughed at now being in the road-building business but agreed that it would speed up the trucks and lessen tyre wear, so all in all was not a bad idea.

Rita asked James and George if either one of them had a good statistician in their ranks. Neither of them did, but James remembered something Angus McBride had said once and suggested that they talk to Angus about whatever Rita had in mind. Rita told them that she was trying to build some models of the ore body from the old diamond drilling logs and from the assays of the chips that they got from the blast holes. Unfortunately, the diamond drill exploration holes were too widely spaced to give anything other than a general view of the ore body and the values; what they needed was more local information, down to the ten metre or better grid range. There was some ancient history from old reports and an electrical survey done in 1925 and 1926 by A. B. Broughton-Edge, but that focused on the area now being mined by the Italians and to the east and as such was not that helpful.

Angus had indeed some expertise in statistics and was intrigued by the idea of using the drill cuttings data to interpolate between holes and get a better view of the ore pockets they were after. Rita worked out with Hippo and Abel a program for getting grab samples of the cuttings and thought about what kind of information she could get from quick assays to give to Angus. Angus, for his part, bemoaned the fact that the company computers were in Kitwe and that access was limited to the finance people. He felt that this was a problem that would fit well with the concepts and capabilities of computers. For his own interests, he actually got more from Caterpillar through their scheduled oil sampling program than from the company's computing staff.

When George started to deliver crushed rock, James gave Hippo and Abel some hints on how to crown the haul ramp and make sure that rainwater would run off to the drains. He also got into super-elevation on curves so that the trucks would not have to slow down too much as they entered corners. James had worked on a motorway site before going to university and had noted some of the construction techniques. He told his shift bosses that he would test their roads by driving around the corners with his hands off the steering wheel of his Land Rover. He said that he would be happy if he could do this at forty miles per hour on the flat and not run off the road. He then went on to caution Abel and Hippo not to try this method of test until and unless they were confident that the road was built appropriately. The last thing he wanted was one of them sailing off into the pit from a road test. They both laughed and assured him that they were not about to try any hands-off stuff; they both really liked the idea of both hands firmly on the steering wheel.

Road building went well, causing only minor inconveniences with production of ore and waste until Thursday. Then, it rained. It really rained! It came down hard enough that they could see drops of water bouncing six inches up off the concrete pathways and aprons. For several hours, everyone from the mine stood under the overhang on the office buildings and watched the rain come down and wondered what it was doing to the new roads they had just built. When the storm finally abated, the rain gauge showed 75mm of rain, and James estimated that most of that had come in the space of the first hour. George Walker came over from the concentrator and complained bitterly about roof leaks, even into the office he had had constructed on a mezzanine floor above the flotation cells.

That evening, when Gibson had gone for the night, James asked Katrina about her day and if it had been as soggy as theirs.
"No man, but it only rained," she started, using the peculiar habit South Africans had of beginning a positive reply with a negative. "When I was at the Mkushi River diggings, I thought I was going to get bogged down for sure until they pulled me out with the front-end loader."
"What about the road between here and Piccadilly Circus?" he asked.
"It was bad in places," she commented. "But, there's something else."
"What?" he asked.

"I got the feeling that there were people off the road watching," she replied. "I don't know if it was those ZIPRA people again or someone else."

"Did you see anyone?" he asked.

"No, I just had this feeling that the road was being watched," she said.

"You think watched in general or specific?" he pressed.

"I think watched in general," she thought. "Someone wants to know who and what goes along that road."

"Do you think the Rhodesians are checking out the ZIPRA camp?" he asked.

"Maybe," she thought. "But I didn't think they were operating outside Rhodesia. I know they have been having problems lately with terrs coming in from Moçambique, but we're a little far from that border."

"Maybe I should see if I can find Colonel Mulanga and see if there's anything we should know," thought James. "Meanwhile, maybe you should go to Mkushi River the other way."

"*Ja*, but it's much further that way, I'd have to go almost back to Kapiri, then take the Great North Road up to Mkushi Boma, then to the River," she complained.

"Better safe than sorry," James commented.

"You're right. Man, I hate this, it's such a bloody nuisance," bemoaned Katrina.

"You're beginning to sound just like a *Rooinek*," kidded James. "Such a bloody nuisance!"

"*Ou pas niefie jy soek my?*" was her reply to that, asking James if he was looking for trouble.

The following day, George Bullock called from Kitwe, where he was attending the regular fortnightly review and told James that the engineers in Kitwe had approved his preliminary design for the slimes dam and had provided detailed drawings. There were a few differences, but nothing of great note, and they had given their approval to start with the preliminary drawings. James wondered if the changes had been made to justify the time spent reviewing his drawings and if they had actually been reviewed at all. He was a little concerned that they had merely made a few cosmetic changes, but had not really looked at the engineering of the dam. He would hate to build the thing and then have it fail in years to come and dump all the slimes into the Mita Hills dam. Still, he had to assume that the Kitwe office was responsible. Now he could set about constructing the dam. He had already looked at the waste coming from the pit and calculated how much they would need to build the dam wall. The membrane material that would form the water barrier had already been delivered, so the next task was to clear and grade the dam site and the retention pond site.

He arranged to meet Hippo and Rita at the location of the future dam wall and laid out where the wall would be and indicated to Hippo the extent of the projected pond that would form behind it. That area all needed clearing of trees, a windfall for the local charcoal producers who would now have a ready supply of felled lumber for a while. They would have to chop it up into suitable lengths and sizes, because Hippo would merely have the trees knocked down and pushed into piles. Rita wanted to have some pits dug so that she could see how far down they would have to clear before coming to rock good enough for the foundations of the wall. A better way would have been to drill a number of exploratory holes and look at the cores recovered. However, they did not have ready access to a diamond drill, so over-engineering was probably a good alternative. Hippo looked at the area to be bush-cleared and said that he did not have enough spare capacity with his dozers to do the work in a short time. He asked if it would be possible to get John Watson to do the work for them.

James called back to Kitwe and found George still there. He checked with him about retaining John Watson and received the all-clear. In fact, he was told to 'just build the bloody thing'. Bullock admitted that they had the budget for the construction, and he did not care whether they spent it outside the company. It almost seemed as if Bullock's mind was elsewhere. James reasoned that it probably was, focused on his own career and where it would take him next. James arranged to meet with John the following morning, and because it would be Saturday, John suggested a boat trip afterwards on the Mita Hills dam, that is, if it was not raining. That sounded a lot like bribery and corruption to Katrina when James told her later what the plan was for the day.

John was at the mine bright and early, or by eight anyway, which meant that he had had to leave at six in the morning. He arrived with his wife, Carol, whom he dropped off with Katrina before coming on to meet with James and with Attie, who had come along to actually supervise the work. Together, James, Hippo, Rita, Attie and John looked over the dam site and the preliminary drawings that James had put together. Rita asked about pits to check soil conditions, and John suggested that, rather than have crews dig by hand that he just bulldoze out some trenches that she could then examine. It would be quicker that way and also give her the opportunity to walk the site, as it were, and see what conditions were. He told Rita to point out to Attie where she would like the trenches to be dozed out, and he would ensure that it would be done on Monday. James and John then left Attie and Rita to the job of laying out the new dam and went to make use of the existing Mita Hills Dam.

On the water, Carol asked Katrina if they had noticed any shortages in the shops in Kabwe. As Katrina had not been shopping in a while, she had to admit she had not. But that raised the obvious question: what shortages had Carol noticed? Carol ran down a list of items that seemed to be in short supply in Kitwe, most of which were basic commodities, such as rice, flour and cooking oil, plus a few luxury items like wine. John added that they were also having problems getting the right kinds of lubricants for their machines and asked James how much he had in stock of various types. James admitted total ignorance and said that he had better check with Angus. John told them that the problem seemed to be congestion in Dar es Salaam, which was holding up shipments to Zambia. That meant that any shipment that did arrive quickly disappeared unless you knew just when it would arrive. Obviously, the border closure was having some effect on the Zambians as well as the Rhodesians.

After the boat trip, James arranged a *braai* and invited the Watsons, Attie, Rita and whoever else wanted to come. Hippo, Angus and John McFarlane had already left for a football match in Kabwe, but Morag and Kirsty both decided that any event was better than football widowhood. Abel would have liked to have also gone to the football match, but he had the afternoon shift that week and so was occupied. John Wells had gone off for an assignation with Elena, which left only the Georges. The Bullocks declined, saying that they had planned an evening in, but the Walkers also accepted, happy for any event that broke up the week.

James rather thought that the Bullocks had decided that they really did not want to mix with the riff-raff, particularly local yokels. On the other hand, Susan Walker was delighted to meet someone new and seemed eager to learn more about the history of the country and what the circumstances were that had everyone being in Zambia. She learned that the Watsons had, in fact, both been born in what was then Northern Rhodesia and never seen a reason to leave, for to them it really was home, which also explained why they had both become Zambian citizens after independence. Attie was the son of South Africans who had migrated north in the early 40s looking for a better opportunity. He saw himself as one day leaving and heading south towards George, a town that he liked, but he had no immediate plans.

Katrina had invited John and Carol to stay the night, but they now also needed a place for Attie. Rita surprised everyone by saying that Attie could use her spare room. That set all the tongues wagging, and speculation was rife about what that might mean. Did it mean that Rita and Attie had something going or was she just being hospitable? Heaven only knew what the Bullocks would make of that. When James had been single, he had stayed in their house while they were on leave, and they had issued a no overnight guests prohibition. But, as this was Rita's house, it would be pushing the limits of mine management to start dictating whom she might entertain. When everyone else had gone, Katrina and Carol both commented on Rita's invitation and asked their respective spouses if they thought it meant anything. Neither James nor John would commit, both only saying that time would tell.

Monday morning, James told Abel what the plan was for the dam and that he would let him know when to start directing the waste rock from their dumps to the dam site. He then went out to the site and met with

Attie. Although it was still early, there were already great swaths cut through the bush as Attie and his crew cleared the trees and bushes from the retention pond boundary. Rita had staked out where she wanted trenches dug, and there was a dozer busily digging slots across the line of the dam wall.

"So, Attie?" James asked. "What's the story?"

"What story?" he parried.

"The story with Rita, *ou maat*?" James pressed.

"No man, I could only go for her," Attie admitted. "Do you think she'd be interested in me?"

"Why don't you ask her?" suggested James. "She's not attached that I know of, and you're not such a *losgat*."

"*Voetsak* James," was the reply. "*Ja*, maybe I should ask her out, she was nice the other night, let me use her spare room, but I'm telling you, James, I didn't know whether to push it any further or not."

"Maybe because you didn't, she thinks you're a nice bloke," James suggested.

"James, don't ever let anyone know that you called me a nice bloke," Attie said, horrified. "First, I'm not sure I know what a bloke really is and second, whatever happened to *potent ou*?"

"Well, are you going to ask her out or not?"

"*Ja ja*, I'll do it later today when she comes to check on her trenches," Attie promised. "Man, you should see the way she walks, even in boots. She has this sway to her that is only *lekker* man. I wonder what she looks like in shorts?" he added dreamily.

"Just focus on building my dam for me, Attie," James commented. "Time enough for your love life when I can spare you or Rita!"

James related his conversation to Katrina later, and she thought that they would make a good match. Attie might not have a university education, but he was smart, had a good job with John, owned his own business on the side and a house and had all the prospects that fathers usually look for in prospective sons-in-law. She then told James that Gibson had told her that in the local African store, they were out of bread flour and cooking oil, and he had asked her to check in Kabwe if she was going soon and to get some for him. The African store did have rice, *mealie* meal and *kapenta*, which would provide for most families.

160

James had also talked to George Bullock and Angus, and they had checked on shipments of parts and lubricants and discovered that it was all on back order. So, who knew when any of the orders would actually arrive?

Katrina mentioned to James that there were some Somali traders who stopped by the Italian operation about once a month. They drove from Dar es Salaam in a dilapidated old blue lorry but seemed to be able to get anything. She suggested that the next time they were in the area that they give them an order and try them out. James agreed and wondered what fell off the back of which lorry to make it into the manifest of the Somalis, but he admitted that perhaps he was being grossly unjust. They were probably just good itinerant traders who had discovered a niche and were fulfilling a need to everyone's advantage.

Now that the production levels were increasing, James felt that it was time to take a closer look at their blasting practices. He had started things out on a 3m x 3m hole pattern and had made a few minor adjustments based on the first few blasts. Now they had enough experience to change the pattern a little more. He planned to try opening up the spacing between holes in rows parallel to the open face, so a 3m x 3.5m pattern. He was also going to try some different delay patterns using more in-line delays than they had used in the past.

Unfortunately, Rita had not made enough progress with her analysis and modelling to give them any better picture of what the rock looked like below the surface, so it was still trial and error. James had also spent some time across the river at the Italian operation. They had some larger self-propelled drills from Gardner Denver and Ingersoll Rand that he wanted to check out. If they worked well, he felt that they would be a suitable size to specify for acquisition. Although the hole sizes drilled did not seem that much larger, 6" versus 4-1/2", the actual difference in hole volume was quite substantial, over seventy per cent larger in fact.

The Italians were most helpful and gave James chapter and verse on the two drill rigs, both performance and maintenance. James then contacted the local dealers and talked to them about price and delivery.

He then wrote up a specification and asked for quotes from the two dealers to include delivery time and method. Obviously, with the border to Rhodesia closed, the machines would have to come in another way. It was back to the problem he had had earlier in the year, of Beira and Salima, Nacala and Salima, or Dar es Salaam. He decided to leave it to the distributors but added a penalty for late delivery. Not that penalties really helped when he was faced with drilling deadlines, but perhaps they would be motivated to find ways to get the machines on site. He was looking for two machines plus spares, so the order, while not large by Nchanga scales, was still reasonable.

Thursday, Katrina left for Lusaka. She had a visit planned to a pottery there and was hoping to sell some china clay, which was, after all, the main product of the Mkushi River Clays. She was in a hurry to go and decided not to stop and have James take the spare wheel off the bonnet of their Land Rover, where it usually sat, and put it in the back. She had discovered before that the wheel was just too heavy for her to lift off the bonnet, so normally had James put it in the back for her, from where she could manhandle it into place. As it transpired, her decision was not a good thing. On her return the next day, just east of the Kapiri Mposhi turn-off, she got a puncture. Swearing, she pulled over to the side of the road and waited. Surely someone would pass and offer assistance. That day of all days, traffic was light; the only vehicles on the road seemed to be the Chinese trucks from the railway construction. They looked at her but drove on by.

Finally, a *madala* on a bicycle happened by and asked if she needed help. While Katrina jacked up the Land Rover, the *madala* lifted the spare wheel off the bonnet and rolled it around to the back. When the wheel had been changed, he offered to put the wheel with its flat tyre back on the bonnet, but she demurred, pointing out that back at the mine they would want to take it off to repair it anyway. He would accept nothing for his help and left on his bicycle, wishing her a good day.

Back at the mine, Katrina related this story to James and others who had come to see her, each with their expectations of what she had managed to get in Lusaka. Angus offered to get the tyre fixed and took it off with him, then Katrina sat down to the task of sorting out all the shopping lists she had been given and what she had actually been able to find. Lusaka was a little better stocked than Kapiri or Kabwe, but still, flour and cooking oil were in short supply, and even rice was hard to find. She had seen some ridiculous advertisements in the Lusaka paper for commodities, even an offer of champagne for potatoes.

There were obviously shortages everywhere, and people were offering bizarre exchanges. However, Katrina had managed to find most of what was on her lists, with the help of the pottery manager, who had taken her to a couple of traders that were well stocked. The prices were a little above the norm, but not outrageously so, which would probably come if the shortages continued.

Monday, March 19th, brought a letter from Will and Bridget. They were doing well in Johannesburg. They had decided to live in Bedfordview. It was about halfway between Modderfontein, where Bridget worked and Alberton, where Will now worked. He had managed a transfer to the Dulux facility there, so was still in paint. From Bedfordview to each of their places of work meant a commute, but it was not far. It also meant two cars, but apparently, that was not a problem. Bridget was finding things very different and sometimes a little difficult. Women in the explosives business were rare enough, and one in a chemical engineering role of telling others how to better run the process was unheard of. Still, apparently, she had already proven her worth, and the managers of the different lines were now actually asking for her help and no longer muttering when she was assigned to them. For Will, it was much simpler. He came from a paint background and knew enough about the products and processes that he was accepted immediately. Katrina asked James if he was going to reply and when! James danced around the subject a little and then promised that he would put pen to paper within the week.

The next project that James decided that he had better tackle was a new magazine. They had a small temporary magazine set away from the village and the mine, but it was hardly the place to store any quantity of explosives. He talked to George Bullock, who asked why they really needed a new magazine, and only agreed when he realised that he would be the guilty party if the mines inspectorate decided to look at their current facilities and find them inadequate. While he was with Bullock, James also asked about the survey help they had been promised. Bullock waved that off with the comment that, as James could already use a theodolite and a level, then they could get by and save the money.

The existing magazine was some way to the south of the operation, and James saw no reason to move it far. The orebody did not extend much in that direction, and there were no villages or farms. They had already cleared a fire break around the old building, but that would need extending a little to accommodate a larger facility and more explosives. James started his project by laying out the foundations for the building, then staked out the revetment that he would surround the new magazine with. The revetment would be simple enough, essentially dirt and rocks piled up and then planted with grass to form a barrier so that any untoward explosion would go up and not out. There had been some impressive, explosive incidents in the past. Katrina had told him of one in Kitwe in August of 1950, where a train and an explosives truck had collided on a level crossing on the line to the Mindola shaft. That had created an impressive bang and lots of debris from the destroyed steam locomotive and the explosives truck. There was also an explosion at the Kafironda factory in December of 1971 when a shunting accident set off explosives in railway wagons, killing many people. There was a folklore tale about an accident that the Italians had had involving the transportation of explosives in one of their Belaz trucks. It was alleged that the heated bed of the truck and the poor road conditions led to an explosion. James had been unable to confirm or deny this rumour.

What he did learn out of all this was that the greatest risk seemed to be the transportation of the explosives, rather than the storage. Therefore, he took a second look at their explosives truck, as they would have to collect explosives from Kafironda and transport it the 230 kilometres to the mine. Their truck did not look too bad. The only additions he resolved to make were new signs and new anti-static chains.

With work on the new magazine now progressing, James went back to the pit to check on their next blast. They were now down to the 40m bench and were chasing an ore lens down to the 48m bench. He checked with Abel, and they went through the blast sequence and arranged the delays in the firing lines appropriately. With some minor alterations in the hole spacing, they were now getting good fragmentation, and loading was going well. Rita kept herself busy staking out areas of ore and directing traffic. Normally, they would have had a sampler to do this, but Bullock was holding onto the purse strings pretty tightly and would not countenance extra people, no matter how little he had to pay for them. In his mind, better to have an expatriate, for whom he was already paying a lot, do the work than a local employee who might cost less but who would be an extra head.

The following week brought a crisis. Their water line from the river obviously had broken somewhere, because water stopped flowing to the mill and the houses. James and George Walker drove down the rough track that paralleled the line until they found the break. They did not so much find the break as drive right into the puddle created by the break. James stopped quickly enough to be able to reverse out before they became mired down. Then he got on the radio and told Angus where the break was and waited for him to arrive with the lorry that had the welding gear on board, plus pieces of pipe and other equipment. Satisfied that the problem was in good hands, James drove back to the mine, but something nagged at him.

"Why do you think the pipe broke, George?" he asked.

"Beats me, probably just shitty thin-walled pipe," was the reply.

"I don't think so," James countered. "The walls looked thick enough, but did you notice the marks around the pipe and the tracks in the bush outside of that big pond the leak created?"

"No, are you saying someone cut the pipe?"

"It's a possibility, but who? Who would want to either take the water or disrupt the mine?" James asked.

"We'd better ask around," thought George. "I'll see if I can find out anything."

The pipe took about eight hours to repair, and the housewives were bemoaning the lack of water for toilets, cooking, etc. James had organised for the water cart, normally used for dust suppression in the mine, to load up with water directly from the river and deliver it to the two villages. He also issued a warning that the water was not filtered or clean and should be boiled vigorously before use. The last thing he wanted was half the workforce off with some waterborne disease or parasite.

The next thing to fail was the power supply. This was much simpler to understand; a car had skidded off the road and taken down a power pole where the line crossed the road. It was still quite a feat to get the car that far off the road with enough speed to knock the pole down, but it had been managed. James wondered how long the power would be out this time and immediately contacted George Walker and Angus to be sure that their generators were up and running.

"Shouldn't old Bullock be doing all this?" Katrina asked him.

"Probably, but he seems a little distracted, and I can't get him to focus on anything," James complained.

"Probably that nurse he's seeing in Broken Hill," she commented.

"What nurse?" was the obvious question.

"Oh, I saw him I Broken Hill a little while ago, hanging onto a nurse," she elaborated.

"But, weren't they both in Broken Hill this last weekend?" he asked.

"*Ja*, who knows what these *bwanas* get up to?" she laughed.

It was two days before the main power was restored, and that came as a relief because one of the generators had started to give some trouble. James had been pressuring Bullock to make up his mind about switching off the village and leaving only the plant running. Bullock was wavering about what to do and was relieved when he no longer had to make any decision.

James went home in disgust and there found the Somali traders with their dilapidated blue lorry. Katrina was going through a shopping list with them, and there were a few others lined up to also hand over their orders. The traders would take no money until the goods were delivered, but did agree on prices as they took the orders. So they must have had enough margin in their prices to cover whatever variations in their costs would be in the next month. They told the assembled group that they would also be bringing back a variety of things not on the list, and those would be at market prices at the time. Well, if one really needed something, then cost was secondary; it would quickly sort out the need to have from the want or nice-to-have items. The Somalis promised to be back in a month and left in a cloud of dust and exhaust fumes.

Was it ZIPRA?

"Do you know what day it is today?" James asked Katrina.

"Wednesday!"

"True, but what's the date?"

"April 4th, what's special about that?" she began, then remembered. "It's our wedding anniversary!"

"Three years already, *ou frou*," he commented. "How many more do you think?"

"How long will you live?" she asked. "Probably not too long if you keep up the *ou frou* comments!"

"What kind of day do you think we'll have?" he asked.

"Looking outside, I'd say the last remnants of the rains and the usual routine," she thought.

"What would you like to do tonight?" he asked.

"I'll cook up something special," she promised. "Then we'll see if the past three years or so have improved you or not!"

"I'll see you later then," James promised. He drove to the pit viewpoint to get a sense of where they were before going to the office, and Katrina was right; there was just a brief shower before the sun came out and banished what was left of the clouds and dried up the ground very quickly.

When James arrived home in the late afternoon, Gibson had already left, and there was a table set for dinner. However, Katrina told him that there was no rush for dinner as it would keep. She suggested that he take a shower and then join her on the *stoep* for a beer. Much refreshed and cleaner, James sat down next to Katrina and accepted the proffered beer.

"Happy anniversary!" Katrina toasted.

"Happy anniversary," echoed James. "Here's to many more!"

"Where do you think we'll be next year?" she asked.

"I don't really know," he replied. "Probably still here."

"I like it here," she announced. "It's peaceful, except for the ZIPRA *ouks*."

"You don't miss the big city?" he asked.

"What Kitwe?" she asked. "Kitwe is a small town, and I like it because I grew up there. But as for being a big city, it's not Jo'burg or London, and I'm not sure that I would really like to live in a big city."

"No, I can understand that," agreed James. "There's a peace about the bush, even with wild animals, that's hard to beat."

"What's your favourite position?" she asked, changing the subject completely.

"What do you mean?" he asked.

"What's your favourite position? Do you like to be on top, do you like me to be on top, do you prefer to be behind, what?" she pressed.

"Oh, I see," he said, the penny finally dropping. "I think you on top, kneeling astride me."

"Fine, that's how we'll start," she announced. "And then we'll see if there is something else that might be fun! It's our anniversary, we need to celebrate."

"But, what about dinner?" he asked.

"Do you want me or dinner?" she asked, brushing up against him.

"The dinner can wait!"

The next day, the rains were officially declared over when the meteorological office announced on the radio that "there will be no more weather until October". Because the days were now going to be essentially the same with no rain, there seemed little point in making a daily broadcast. From then, April 5th until October, the overnight temperatures would drop, sometimes to almost freezing, but by ten in the morning the skies would be clear blue with no clouds to be seen and the temperature would climb to between 75°F and 80°F. When October came, the humidity levels would rise and the days would then be hot and sweltering, giving rise to the soubriquet for October as "suicide month".

James put away his rain gear and planned his next excavations in the pit to drop the sump to an appropriate level for the next rainy season. The sump level was determined by the ore volume they wanted to extract for the period from November until April of the following year, such that the ongoing operation would not flood. Deepening the sump during the rains was a messy operation and could lead to real problems. He got required production rates from Bullock and then went through the extraction plan with Rita. She pointed out where the ore could come from, and James then worked out how much overburden he would have to move to expose the ore. This gave him his cutting plan, which he could then translate into monthly and weekly work schedules. With the sump currently at the 56m level, he calculated that he needed only to drop it to the 64m level, but the pit would grow in length and breadth, so that the capacity of the sump and the pumps needed to be increased. Some iteration was required as the orebody was not uniform, and the concentrator ran best with fairly steady feed rates.

It was as well that he had done this work because the regularly scheduled fortnightly review was moved to the mine site, and all the *Bwanas* showed up at ten on the Friday morning ready to hear about the plans for the year. It took them a little while to fully understand that, unlike the underground operations, where the weather conditions on the surface had little impact, in the surface mine, the weather greatly influenced the production schedule. After an hour of presentations and discussion, they all wanted the tour and were driven out to the viewpoint where James explained the bench system, the ramps and the current and future sump locations. He also pointed out on the surface where the new pit perimeter would extend over the next year. After a brief discussion about blasting and powder factors, or explosives used per tonne of rock blasted, it was the turn of George Walker, and he had the pleasure of their company for the balance of the visit. The report from Bullock later was that all had gone well and that he had been complimented on his management of the operation.

Shortages of flour, cooking oil and potatoes continued, but Katrina and Gibson, between them, had managed to work out which stores had which commodities, and they combined shopping lists. The next issue that arose was with the fuel and oil supply. The diesel fuel came from the refinery in Ndola, which was fed by a pipeline from Dar es Salaam. For the most part, the fuel was acceptable, but their local Mobil representative stopped by the mine to warn them that they might see higher-than-normal sulphur levels in the fuel for the next few weeks. Apparently, a batch of fuel oil had been received at Ndola that was not the best. The refinery was trying to make the most out of it, but there were limits. Angus decided to increase the frequency of his oil sampling program for the mine equipment to more quickly detect any problems caused by the extra sulphur. It seemed as if it were one problem after another. They all wondered if things would ever settle down to a routine with no or few issues to address.

On Saturday morning, just after the staff meeting, John Wells informed the assembled group that he would be away for the weekend in Lusaka. James caught up with him as they left the meeting and asked the obvious question.

"Are you going alone or will you have company?"

"Ah, yes, Elena is coming with me. I'm leaving now to collect her, and we'll drive straight to Lusaka," John explained.

"Where are you staying?"

"The Ridgeway."

"First class," commented James. "So, is this getting serious?"

"I think so," John admitted. "It's going well, and I'm working up the courage to pop the question."

"Well, good luck and have fun!"

"Oh, we will!" John promised.

After work, James relayed his news to Katrina, who already knew about the trip. She had learned of it from Gibson, who knew the house servants at the Petalas farm.

"Do you think they'll get married?" James asked her.

"*Ja*, she told me the other day that she's just waiting for John to ask!"

"Well, he's plucking up the courage to do just that!" James commented.

"Perhaps this trip to Lusaka will do the trick," she thought.

"What do her folks think about her probably going to England?" he asked.

"Apparently, they think it's great," she replied. "The farm can't support four daughters and their families, so they're anxious for all of the girls to find husbands outside the farming business."

"Well, John won't want for money," he commented. "So, she'll be well provided for. I wonder what his family will think?"

"It depends, whether they are as *verkrampte* as your mother?" she wondered.

"You're right, to my mother being Greek is probably almost as bad as being Afrikaans or African!" he agreed.

Sunday morning, James and Katrina were disturbed by someone knocking at the door. It was Gibson.

"*Inindaba wena aikôna sebenzili lo ki kawena?*" asked Katrina, wondering why Gibson had not used his key.

"*Indaba madam ena kona lo mkulu ndaba,*" Gibson replied, telling them of a big problem.

"*Ka ini?*" she asked.

"*Lo farm ka lo madam Elena, zonke ena bulayili,*" he announced, clearly very agitated, having to announce the deaths of everyone at the farm.

"*Ubani ena bulayili yena?*" she asked, wanting to know who had done the killing.

"*Mina aikôna azi,*" he admitted to ignorance of the perpetrator. "*Kabanga lo skelms, kabanga lo muzungu or kabanga lo ZIPRA, mina aikôna azi.*"

"Oh shit, James," she said. "Who the hell would want to kill the Petalas family? *Gibson, ubani ena kona lapa farm?*"

"*Ena kona four madam, lo donna Elena yena hambili lapa Lusaka, futi lo donna Alexis yena hambili lapa Ndola,*" he enumerated, accounting for all the family.

"I wonder if we should try and reach the Ridgeway?" she asked James.

"Probably should," he agreed. "Let's go into the office and see if we can find them."

"Okay, Gibson, *tina azi kuluma na lo donna, futi tina azi buka wena kusasa,*" she concluded.

It had always struck James as odd that there were really no words in ChiKabanga for thank you and please, but then it was a command language, and there was probably little demand for those expressions. Gibson went back home and would be back on Monday, and James and Katrina drove into the office. They speculated as to who may have done this and how. They called the Ridgeway, but Elena and John had already left and were on a tour of Lusaka before heading home.

"What do we do now?" Katrina asked. "It seems a little cold to just let her drive into the farm and discover the police there. I wonder who found them?"

"I've wondered that," James agreed. "It's Sunday, so I don't suppose it was the house servants, unless they have the poor chaps come in every day."

"Call Kathy and see if she knows anything," Katrina suggested.

"Who's she?" he asked.

"You know, the lady we get milk, eggs and butter from," she explained.

"Do you know her number?" he asked.

"Yes, hang on a minute," she said. "I have it here in my bag. Here you are."

When the phone was answered, Katrina asked for Kathy and learned from her that a passing neighbour had become suspicious of the incessant barking of some of the dogs and had gone to investigate. He had discovered a couple of dead dogs and then had looked in the windows and seen the family shot to death. Kathy said that the neighbour had surmised that the guns had been poked through the windows that were open, only protected by burglar bars, and had shot the sleeping family. Kathy also said that the police were there in force, all two of them, but that an inspector from Kabwe was on his way.

As Katrina finished her conversation, George Bullock came into the office. He had just heard of the tragedy and wanted to see if anyone knew any of the details. Katrina told him what she knew. He wanted an answer to the obvious question: who had done it? Was it a burglary gone bad, Rhodesian security forces operating within Zambia or even ZIPRA? Katrina told him that the police were on the scene with a senior officer on his way from Kabwe to investigate. The problem was that each scenario seemed as improbable as the next. With everyone dead, it would have been no problem for burglars to break down doors and gain entry, but there was no evidence of damage to any of the doors. Why would the Rhodesian security forces attract attention to themselves by murdering a local farmer and his family? And why would ZIPRA antagonise everyone by killing off a local maize farmer, unless they were certain that he was a spy for the Rhodesians and actually passing information to them, in which case, why not let Colonel Mulanga take care of things with a deportation notice? Perhaps it was none of the above and was instead a disgruntled employee or ex-employee. The problem with that was, as far as anyone knew, relations between the family and all their farm workers were good, and no one had been discharged in the past three years. The final alternative, presented by George, was perhaps that one of the workers had made a play for one of the daughters, had been rebuffed and had sought revenge for his slight. Whatever the reason, it remained a mystery for now as there was no obvious evidence to support any of the scenarios.

George asked James if they had been able to get hold of John and Elena, and then suggested that it might be better to meet them on the road before they got to the farm. That meant that someone was going to have to stand guard for the better part of the afternoon at the mine site road end, but it would work, particularly if they switched duties every hour or so. James agreed, and they contacted others and set up a roster. George took the first hour, probably because there was little chance that John and Elena would be back so soon. It was about four in the afternoon when they were finally spotted and flagged down by Rita and Attie. She relayed the news to them and gave them the option of stopping at the mine instead of going back to the farm. Elena said that she wanted to go but that she would probably be back later, not seeing herself staying at the scene overnight.

John and Elena were back a little after eight. They had given statements to the police but had learned little of value beyond that which Rita had already conveyed. The police had the house cordoned off and sealed up as a crime scene and were expecting detectives on the morrow to look for fingerprints, cartridge cases, footprints and all the other possible clues that might be found. Soon after their return, the mine village was also visited by the police inspector. It was Mr Phiri whom they had dealt with before when they moved the mine equipment from Malawi into Zambia. Mr Phiri met first with George Bullock and then asked generally for any help that anyone could give him. James asked him if he had talked to Colonel Mulanga and learned that they had been in close contact and that the colonel was investigating any ZIPRA involvement. Katrina debated about relating her feeling that the road from the Mkushi Boma was being watched, but decided that the colonel would probably know if that was ZIPRA people or the Rhodesians.

Katrina asked Elena if she had been able to contact her sister and relay the news to her. Elena told them that the police had been very helpful and had tracked down Alexis in Ndola and that she was staying there rather than returning to the farm. Elena said that she would stay with John until they decided what to do. The police investigation was likely to continue for a while, but she was not holding out much hope that they would actually come to some resolution. If it turned out to be ZIPRA, it would be quietly swept under the rug and lost in the intrigue of politics. If it were the Rhodesians, it would be easy to blame some nameless operatives and just wash their hands of the affair. If it were actually just local criminals, they would probably deflect blame onto ZIPRA or the Rhodesians, so the Zambia Police were faced with a difficult situation. Privately, James thought that inside a week they would probably know who had actually done it, but proving it and or having the political will to do something about it was another matter.

The following morning, James heard twenty different theories as to the circumstances behind the shootings; however, the one common thread was that ZIPRA had been involved. Whether for political reasons or for personal revenge was a matter for hot debate. About half of his operators were in the camp of the political assassination group, and the other half thought it was linked to more personal motives. Within those two major groups were sub-groups that tended to differ only in the details. Apparently, Mr Petalas had had words with the ZIPRA cadres earlier and had warned them off his farm and its environs. He apparently also had ties to tobacco farmers in Rhodesia, and there was speculation that he was passing information to them and thence to the Rhodesian security forces. James tried to convince himself that this was all total speculation because the shootings had only occurred two days earlier, and the matter was still being investigated. But, he also had to admit that the bush telegraph was uncannily accurate most of the time. Needless to say, the other farmers were nervous and were looking to the

Zambian Government for assurances. Elena had told John that she was convinced that the killings had been personal because one of the senior ZIPRA cadres had been offended by her father and had lost face with his people. She was also absolutely convinced that nothing of consequence would be done, and the matter would be left to quietly fade away.

Katrina told James that she thought that part of the problem was that nearly all the farmers had a "cheeky *kaffirs*" attitude. By that, she meant that they tended to look upon the black Zambians as hired hands that they could abuse verbally and physically sometimes and that any response by the farm hands put them in the category of "cheeky *kaffirs*". Obviously, as James knew from experience, such attitudes could bring physical harm or death in the mines where it was all too easy to sneak up behind someone and deal a heavy blow. So, in recent years at least, it was less prevalent in the mines than on the farms. Katrina's opinion was that the attitude was also more prevalent among the newer British settlers, those who had come out to Africa post World War II. In her view, some of the problems that the farmers had they brought upon themselves. She doubted whether that was the case with Mr Petalas, but would not rule it out. She also would never suggest it to Elena, who was convinced that their farm was the model of co-operation and understanding.

What would happen to the farm now that only the two daughters were left was a matter of great debate. Although Elena had the knowledge to run the farm, it was assumed by most that she would not actually do so, preferring to marry John and leave the country and go to England. Alexis had absolutely no interest in the farm. She was happy with her boyfriend and his trading business. So the conventional wisdom was that the two girls would wind up the operation, terminate the lease on the property and sell off the stock and the equipment. Already, there were rumours of the other farmers lining up to take a look at the tractors and other machinery items that were on the farm.

The funerals for the Petalas family were held, and most of the farmers in the area attended. James saw Colonel Mulanga in the back of the crowd and made a point of saying hello after the rites. He had hoped to learn something about the killings but came away disappointed. The colonel was not giving anything away. However, James did learn from the colonel's driver that several of the cadres from the camp had been moved to a camp in Tanzania; whether that was mere coincidence or as a result of the shootings, he was left to speculate.

Saturday brought a letter from Alex. She and Vincenzo were getting married. Unfortunately, James and Katrina would be unable to attend as the wedding was planned for early June, and they had no leave due. Alex also announced that after the wedding that they would be moving to Italy and living in Florence. Apparently, Vincenzo had a position to go to with a well-known international firm that had interests in Italy and the United Kingdom. Alex was also hoping to work, but first, she had to improve her Italian, so was enrolled in a language school. She bemoaned the fact that her wedding was being organised by her mother to an extent that made it almost intolerable, but took solace in the knowledge that she would be leaving England and the interference in June. She complained that since Will and Bridget had left, she had received frequent visits in London and was tired of the heavy hints about grandchildren.

"What do we get them for a wedding present?" Katrina asked James.
"I've no idea," he admitted. "Maybe send them a nice copper bowl or something?"
"That might work," she agreed. "Next time we go to Kitwe, I'll talk to some friends and see what we can come up with."
"You know we never sent anything to Will and Bridget," he commented. "Maybe we should get two copper bowls and send one to them as well?"
"What's this?" she asked. "You're actually coming up with ideas today!"
"I'm in a creative mood," he replied. "I'm on a roll, so what else do we need?"
"We could get some copper items for ourselves as well," she thought. "We really don't have anything, and I can see us leaving at some point and not having anything from here!"

"Who do we know in Kitwe that makes or can get us something nice?" he asked.

"I know a couple of coppersmiths," Katrina said. "So, it won't be just the ashtrays that come from the smelter. We can get beaten copper bowls or plain bowls that are nicely formed."

"You're nicely formed, you know," James told her, running his hands over her body.

"Don't change the subject," she warned. "We can get to your wandering hand troubles later. First, we need to reply to Alex and wish them well and apologise for not being there!"

James duly wrote his letter of apology and sent it off to Alex, then he turned over the task of securing and sending wedding presents to Katrina. He also sat down and tried to compose a telegram to send to be read out at the reception that would pass whatever there was in the way of censorship in the Zambian and British post offices. He had plenty of time for that, but it was going to be a challenge.

The following Wednesday, George Bullock again left for Kabwe, citing some mysterious meeting with the local government officials.

"It's his floozie he's going to see," remarked Katrina. "There's no meeting, except for two hot, sweaty bodies."

"I wonder if his wife knows or suspects?" James asked.

"Probably, if he keeps this up for much longer, he'll run out of excuses to go," Katrina thought.

"You said before that it's a nurse he's going to see?" James asked, seeking confirmation.

"*Ja*, a tall blonde with boobs," she confirmed.

"Perhaps, they're just friends?" he suggested.

"Friends! I don't think so," she announced. "Friends don't do what they were doing!"

"But how did you get to see?" he asked.

"I was looking for a tree to park under and found them instead," she explained.

"Did he see you?" he asked.

"No, she looked at me briefly as I drove by, but where his face was between her boobs, there was no looking up!"

"So, how do you know it was him?" he pressed.

"He used the mine Land Rover, which is a little hard to hide, as it's bright, bright yellow with bloody great numbers on the side!" she elaborated. "Then I saw them later walking into a shop, both looking a little ruffled."

While they were without their illustrious leader, James and George Walker had a minor crisis to resolve. One of the equipment operators managed to run his truck into another, and one of the mill operators overcharged the ball mills and caused spills all over the place. Both it seemed upon investigation were intoxicated. James had begged a few breathalysers from the Zambia Railways people, as they were among the few people in the country who used them. They got good positive results from the tests and were ready to dismiss the employees on the spot, but the rules said that Bullock had to approve the action. That meant a wait until Bullock decided to reappear from his tryst in Kabwe. For the interim, they parked the miscreants in the change house and told them to wait, even if it took until late in the evening. Fortunately, there were plenty of witnesses to the events and the subsequent testing, so the paperwork was complete, and Jerry Mwanza had signed off on the judgment and the proposed actions. All it needed was the final signature from Bullock, which was quickly given when he arrived back from Kabwe.

The other mission for Bullock was to approve the completion of the magazine. The building had been constructed with lights, ventilation, blow-out panels and locked doors, and the revetment had been built up around it. There were already some weeds and small bushes growing on the soil they had covered the rocks with, so James guessed that by the next rainy season, it would be well covered and the slopes stabilised.

On Sunday, the Somalis and their dilapidated blue truck arrived. They were back as promised, almost to the day. They had obtained all the items that were ordered and were quickly besieged by all those who had requested things. They charged exactly what they had quoted when they took the orders. Then they unveiled the other items they had brought with them. They had everything from kitchen knives and scales to olive

179

oil and red wine. Katrina bought the kitchen scales. She told James later that she was tired of just guessing weights. She also bought some red wine and wondered how they had managed to bring all this stuff through the Tanzanian and Zambian customs posts. James was convinced that they either bribed the border guards or used a side road that crossed the border well away from the manned posts. Either way, they were very enterprising and were happy to take orders for the next month.

Emeralds

The May Day holiday was celebrated, which rather broke up the week as it fell on a Tuesday. James was happy to have the day off, particularly as he had spent the last few days on a drive to clear up the haul roads of their collection of BFRs. One of the issues he had noted was the increase in the number of large rocks present on the roads, which led to tyre damage, so he had instructed all and sundry to clean up the roads and, if they saw a big rock on the road, to get it moved. It seemed that this was one of those items where periodic reminders were necessary. He himself had stopped numerous times and shoved large rocks to the side of the road, sometimes even requiring the use of a grader as the rocks were too large to be manhandled. Such rocks were known in the business generally as BFRs, and on some of the mines, failure to remove such could lead even high officials into deep and hot water.

James had thought of taking a day out on the lake, but Katrina was a little leery after the farm shootings and suggested instead that they take a trip more to the west. She had always wanted to see the Lukanga swamp area, so they set off early and drove into Kabwe, then west through farmlands to the swamp area. It was a peculiar area with streams draining in from the north and east and eventually draining out to the west to the Kafue River. Some of the local folklore had it as a meteor strike area, but that theory was open to much discussion. When they arrived, the first thing that struck them was how flat the general area was. It was no wonder that water collected and seasonally flooded a large plain; it was a large, oversized dambo. There were birds in abundance and, unfortunately, some flies and mosquitoes. Still, it was worth the drive and was peaceful enough. No ZIPRA and no traffic. Indeed, their approach to the swamp area had been via marginal tracks with a good deal of sliding around, even with the Land Rover in low range and four-wheel drive.

"What do we have for lunch?" James asked Katrina.
"What did you make?" she replied.

"I thought you were making lunch!"

"Well, you know what happened to the man who thought, don't you?"

"I'm sorry I didn't make anything," James admitted.

"Just as well I did," she commented. "Why do I always have to be the one to remember to do these things?"

"I did remember to bring something to drink," he offered. "I've got beer, wine or can make tea, if you'd rather?"

"Lion or Castle?"

"Either or a Simba!"

"Where did you get the Simba?" Katrina asked.

"Some of the operators had been to Lubumbashi for some nefarious purpose and brought a few cases back; they thought I might like some."

"I'll try a Simba, *monsieur* James, *s'il vous plaît?*"

"For *mademoiselle*," he said, handing over a beer.

"What are you trying to do, *Monsieur*, seduce me?" she asked.

"But of course, *cherie*, what do you think?" James replied in his best Maurice Chevalier voice. "I remember once that you asked me, *Voulez vous coucher avec moi?*" he reminded her.

"Well, the Maurice Chevalier bit needs improvement, but other than that, you won't have to try very hard, and I wasn't thinking of actually sleeping; there are no beds around, so the groundsheet will have to do!"

"Do you think there is anyone around?" he asked.

"Judging by the birds, I don't think so," she thought. "Unless they've been here for a while, lurking quietly in the bushes."

They finally had lunch about an hour later and had just started to eat when three middle-aged Zambian ladies walked past with hoes over their shoulders. They all looked over at James and Katrina, smiled broadly and obviously made comments, in ChiBemba and English, about the activities that had just ended. Katrina understood just enough of the ChiBemba to blush beet red. The ladies left laughing and in deep and rapid conversation with each other.

"How long have they been around?" James asked.

"Long enough, judging by their comments," Katrina confirmed. "They think you're quite the man and were wondering if I would lend you to them for a day. They wanted to casserole you!"

"They wanted to what?" he asked.

"It's a joke," she said. "There's a Rhodesian *ouk*, Wrex Tarr, who tells ChiLapalapa stories, and one of them is about an *mfazi* called Suzie who fancies an RAR sergeant major and wants to casserole him. Her friend, Violet, keeps trying to correct her English until she defines casserole as 'do slowly for two hours'. So that's what the *mfazis* have in mind!"

"Do we need to leave?" he asked.

"No, they were happy for the show and now their husbands had better look out!"

"Are there any other people lurking around?" he asked.

"I don't think so," she thought. "I should have guessed that someone was coming when the birds started up about fifteen minutes ago, but I was otherwise occupied!"

"I wonder what they think of *muzungus* who engage in *lo jig a jig* out in the middle of nowhere in the middle of the day?" he wondered.

"Probably think it's quite natural," she thought. "Although they might be inclined to be a little more discreet!"

"Well, *ou frou*, should we be starting back?"

"I suppose so, but less of the *ou frou* bit, I thought I was *mademoiselle?*" Katrina complained.

"Ah, well, that was before, this is now, the deed is done, I've had my way with you!" he said, after which he had to duck as Katrina threw empty food containers at him. Fortunately, she was laughing hard enough to spoil her aim, and she missed.

As they drove into Kabwe, it was apparent that something was amiss. There was a line of cars backed up from the railway crossing. James talked to the driver in front of him and learned that the train had derailed near the crossing, and it was likely to be some time before they could clear things up.

"How well do you know Broken Hill?" he asked Katrina. "We need to find another crossing."

"We have a choice of north or south," she replied. "Let's try to the north. Turn around and go back to the hospital, just after it turn right and head towards the Bwacha township, there's a crossing there that should bring us back to the main road, eventually."

"If it's a long train and that crossing is also blocked?" he asked.

"I think it's the other way around," she commented. "Look, the engine is just north of the crossing, so the train extends to the south, which means that the mine crossing is probably also blocked."

James followed Katrina's instructions and crossed the line near the Bwacha township. Then they had a quick right and left turn before joining the main road again on its way out of Kabwe.

The rest of the drive home was uneventful until they turned onto the dirt road that led to the mine. Not far down that they came upon a bus stopped in the road. James pulled up behind it and got out to see what the trouble was. Then he saw all the people on the bus waving at him and pointing towards the road in front of the bus. He saw what the problem was. A lion was lying in the road watching the bus and now him. However, it did not seem overly concerned with him or the bus. James slipped up behind the bus and then worked his way down the side until he could climb on. The driver told him that they had been there for about thirty minutes, and he did not want to aggravate the lion because there was no door on the bus and no one wanted an extra passenger. They had tried hooting at it, but it just lay there and looked at them and occasionally yawned and showed off lots of teeth. There was no way they could drive around the lion because the bush on either side of the road was too thick for the bus to drive through.

James worked his way back to his Land Rover, very carefully, trying to keep the bus between him and the lion and yet keep an eye on what it was doing.

"So, *ini lo ndaba*?" Katrina asked.

"A bloody lion lying in front of the bus," James replied. "What do you think, should we try running at it and see if we can scare it away?"

"It's a pity the bus is right in the middle of the road," Katrina thought. "It means we'll have to run on the side where it's softer; we don't want to bog down."

"Perish the thought," James commented. "The last thing I want to do is bog down while our friend is there. Which side looks better to you, *Suikerbossie*?"

"Reverse a little and let's look at each side and see if one is better than the other," she suggested.

After a minute or two of reversing and advancing, they both agreed that the left-hand side of the bus would be better. So with the Land Rover in four-wheel drive, headlights on and horn blaring, they raced past the bus and appeared in front of the lion. This affront was just too much for him, and he jumped up and ran off into the bush. The people on the bus clapped, and then the driver made haste to go as fast as he could away from that spot. James stayed in front of the bus, not wanting to be caught in the dust cloud that followed every vehicle on the dirt roads. Finally, he lost the bus as it started to stop to let people off to go to their own villages. Some of them would stay with friends and only go back up the road when they had news of the lion and where he had wandered off to.

On the way home, Katrina told James a story about a lion in the Luangwa Valley. Some years earlier, in the late 1950s and early 1960s, one of the game wardens, Norman Carr, had adopted two lion cubs. He had taken these cubs to the Luangwa Valley to try and teach them to survive on their own with the aim of returning them to the wild. He would transport them in and on his Land Rover, and they became quite used to riding around on the roof. One day, a visitor had been driving in the valley, and a lion had jumped onto the roof of his Land Rover. Unfortunately, it was a canvas-topped version, and the lion came through the roof. The driver got quite a start and punched the lion on the nose. The poor lion was quite unused to this kind of treatment and left. The visitor later related this story to others and was dismayed when he learned that he had not been so brave after all, but had seen off a lion that had been habituated to people and Land Rovers. To James, it was still a brave act. The lion may have really taken offence and turned on the visitor, making short work of him.

Thursday of that week, James was inspecting the dumps when he saw a strange Land Rover near the foot of their largest dump. He worked his way down to it and discovered that it was Colonel Mulanga. Apparently, the colonel was taking a break from the rigours of training.

James went through the usual polite talk, then broached the subject that still troubled him.

"Can you tell me, Colonel, who was responsible for the Petalas family deaths?" he asked.

"Ah, well, that is a good question, my friend," began the colonel. "I am a little confused about this. The Zambia Police have given no opinion and have no suspects, but the people all know who did it!"

"Do the people know or do they assume?" James asked.

"Ah, that is the question!" the colonel continued. "Perhaps this is one of those matters better left alone!"

"I hear that some cadres from the camp have moved to Tanzania," commented James.

"For more training, you understand," explained the colonel.

"Have you seen any Rhodesians in this area?" James asked.

"Not yet, my friend," the colonel began; then continued, "But, I think they will come one day. They will break all the international laws and attack us, even though the camp is a refugee camp for people displaced by the illegal regime."

"If it is a refugee camp, why did the people that my wife met on the road have guns?" James asked.

"A few must have the proper arms and training to keep order in the camps," explained the colonel.

"I see," said James, not seeing at all but realising that this conversation would go around in circles with no real answers. "Well, Colonel, I wish you a good day and a good life, stay well!"

"*Hamba gahle,* my friend," wished the colonel, then he drove off in the direction of Old Mkushi and the ZIPRA camp.

James recounted his conversation with Colonel Mulanga to Katrina that evening, and she thought that what it really meant was that they had done the deed and been quietly moved out of the country to avoid any complications. James was inclined to agree with her, but wondered if the colonel had not been in the job too long and was just naturally cagey.

Rita announced later that week that she was going to host a deputation from the Government Geological Survey Department. There were some seventeen geologists who were making a trip to the Mkushi mine and to their mine. They were coming because the geology of the area was of great interest to them and was quite unlike that of the Copperbelt. Rita asked if each household in the village could take one or two of them overnight, and she also checked with Bullock about feeding them lunches and dinners. He told her that he did not care what they did. He would be in Kitwe for the day for the fortnightly review and would be back late. When they arrived, it was in five Land Rovers, all from the Geological Survey department. They had already been hosted by the Italians, and two of them were most excited because they had found emeralds in the Munshimwemba mine. Rita was sure that they would be anxious to see if the same conditions existed in the Mtuga property and if more emeralds might be forthcoming.

Rounding up geologists was a challenge. They had a habit of wandering off and chipping off chunks of rock in the strangest of places. Ensuring that they had on safety boots and hard hats was a never-ending task. Perhaps it was the nature of the beast and their very personalities that led them to be a little 'scatterbrained' in James's book. When they broke for lunch, one of them set a rock on the table, and for the next hour, opinions were shared as to what it really was and how it explained the deposit that was being mined. James was intrigued by the number of differing opinions and the vigour with which each theory was attacked and defended. It made for very entertaining watching.

James had to chase the geologists out of the pit in the afternoon so that they could do their normal blasting. After the blast, they all went back down again to look at the broken rock and see what had been exposed. It was only after dinner, when the party had moved to James's and Katrina's house and nearly all of the camp residents had gone home, that Rita broke her big news. James thought afterwards that she had kept it to herself because the crowd was too large and there would be too many expectations. There were only he, Katrina, John Wells and Elena, Rita and the visiting geologists. Rita's big news was that she had found a small cache of emeralds. She gave one to Elena, one to Katrina, kept one for herself and gave one to the leader of the government party. That ensured smooth passage of the paperwork needed to possess uncut emeralds. Katrina and Elena were delighted, and both began to discuss where they might get them cut and set. Elena wanted hers as a ring, but Katrina wanted hers cut and set as a pendant, believing that she would actually wear it more that way.

The geologists expounded at length as to why there were emeralds in the area and then went on to discuss other precious and non-precious stones that they had seen and dealt with. There was a fairly high traffic in malachite, some of which actually came from across the border from the Congo. There was quite a lot of amethyst near Lake Kariba, and there was talk of a commercial venture to exploit the finds. The only diamonds any of them had come across, they believed, actually came from the Congo or from the Williamson mine in Tanzania. The Congo diamonds tended to be more along the lines of industrial stones, whereas some of the Williamson stones were very nice.

When the geologists left in the morning to drive back to Lusaka, James tallied up the damage and realised that he would have to get some more beer in the house. The party the night before had completely depleted his stock, and there was now nothing in the house, no beer, no spirits and no wine. It was just as well that these visits were infrequent!

On Monday morning, Katrina left for Kitwe to make some sales calls on the paint and tyre factories. She had already received orders from them and was wondering how the material had performed and if they wanted more. She also had some bags of other material that came from a different streambed. This material was more of a yellow clay and had more sand in it. She wondered if there might not be a use as a drilling mud or a water filter media. At any rate, she was going to make a few calls in Kitwe to see if there was any interest. She told James that she would be staying in Kitwe for the night and returning the next day. James was not thrilled that she would be gone overnight, but would rather she stayed in Kitwe than drive back in the dark. One never knew what might be on the road, particularly trucks that had broken down and just left with a few broken branches in the road as a warning. That worked in the daylight but at night it was of no use.

After Katrina had gone, Gibson brought more coffee, and James planned his day. He knew that Abel and Hippo had things well under control in the pit, so he decided to spend some time with Angus and the arcane world of equipment maintenance and repair. They tracked equipment availability, but he had no real knowledge of what actually failed on different machines and whether there was any pattern, driven either by the environment, the operators or the method of use. When James left for work, he reminded Gibson that Katrina would not be back that night and that it would only be him for dinner. Gibson was most concerned by the fact that he, James, might be late for work because he was leaving later than normal. Gibson wanted to know at what time James normally started and why he was later that day. James would learn later on that the issue was that the other house servants had made remarks about him being late to work, and Gibson was not about to let that happen again. He came in earlier after that and made sure that James was up and breakfasted before six-thirty.

Angus was a mine of information. The equipment used in the mine went for regular servicing every shift and got a wash down, then a fuel and grease session, then a tyre check. At set intervals, each machine was pulled aside for a longer series of checks and filter replacements. If the oil sampling data that came back from Caterpillar indicated a potential problem, they then sent the machine to the main workshop and actually pulled that part of it to bits to have a look. Breakdowns were handled as they arose, and the challenge was to fit everything into a schedule that made some sense.

"So, Angus, are there any patterns to the breakdowns that we get?" James asked.

"It's hard to say, I've got a lot of data but not much information," was the answer. "I need to really get some programmer's time in Kitwe and see if we can get some sort of routines to look at the data."

"Is there any way to do that on the kitchen table without submitting everything to the computer department?" James asked.

"I've tried that," Angus commented. "But, I think I need a little help."

"Do we need to make a trip to Kitwe and see if we can get the computer *ouks* to do something for us?" James asked.

"I'd like to," Angus agreed. "But, I think old Bullock would baulk at the cost, because you know they won't do anything without a cost centre to charge it to!"

"Maybe we can try bribery and corruption?" suggested James.

"How?" Angus asked.

"Well, I've got a couple of cases of wine from the Italians. Let's see if we can't appeal to some baser sense," James elaborated.

"Great idea! I know a couple of the programmers," offered Angus. "Let me find out who's the most vulnerable and would do the work on the sly for a small consideration. We should try a bottle or two first, there's no point in letting on that you have cases of wine to trade, not yet anyway!"

Katrina came back from Kitwe with orders for sand, clay and more. She also brought some copper bowls for approval that they would send as wedding presents, timely and belated, to Alex and Vincenzo and Will and Bridget. The task of packing and mailing, she turned over to James and then went on to talk about her trip.

"I went into Lentin's jewellers in Kitwe and talked to Gerry Lentin about my emerald," she commented.

"Did he have any suggestions?"

"No, man, he was really helpful. He gave me the name of someone who could cut it, and then he suggested a mount for it that would look good in a pendant."

"What sort of mounting?" James asked.

"Really simple, something that doesn't detract from the stone and hide it in too much gold and filigree stuff."

"How much?"

"Not too much, I'll pay for it out of my mineral sales!" she promised.

"It's funny," commented James. "I never really thought about Zambia as being a place where you could find emeralds. I've always equated emeralds with Colombia."

"*Ja*, but they also have them in Rhodesia, and they found them here back in the late twenties near the Kafubu stream," Katrina explained.

"Where's that?"

"It's west of Ndola and southwest of Kitwe, you go out to Kalulushi and then south. It used to be Miku Enterprises, but I think it's all run by Mindeco these days."

"With the government involved through Mindeco, that ought to be a roaring success," James thought. "How is it that you know so much about Zambian emeralds? Wait a minute, didn't your dad take his money out of the country in durable goods? Would the durable goods have been emeralds?"

"James, that's illegal! How could you imagine such a thing?"

"Oh, so that's how he did it. *Slim kêrel!*"

On Wednesday, Bullock made his pilgrimage to Kabwe. It was becoming noticed now, and speculation was rife in the village as to what he was really doing in Kabwe and if his wife knew. James and Katrina had not passed on what Katrina had seen, and, as yet, no one else had been witness to anything. Bullock was also becoming more detached from his job, almost as if he had already moved on to another opportunity. It seemed unlikely that he had already found another job, but anything was possible. James did wonder who Bullock would take with him when he left, his wife or the lover in Kabwe. Katrina told him that it would obviously be the wife, unless of course she found out and decided to take action. But who knew, perhaps this was a pattern for them and passed as a normal situation.

On Saturday, Elena finally moved in with John Wells. She and her sister had set things in motion to dispose of the assets of the farm and were giving up the lease. Neither of them had the desire to continue trying to run the operation, particularly with ZIPRA operatives still active in the area. Mrs Bullock did arch her eyebrows in disapproval, but was ignored by all. John was delighted and told James that he was helping Elena get over the shock of the killings, but that intimate relations were slow to come back to their previous level. By that, James interpreted John as saying that he was on short rations for a while until Elena had gone through her mourning period. John also told James that a wedding was planned for July 15th, to be held in Lusaka at the cathedral. Invitations would be forthcoming, and John wondered if James would step in as best man if his brother from England could not be there. James was happy to oblige and inquired after the brother. Apparently, he was with

191

a law firm in the City and was well known for acquisition and divestiture transactions. It seemed that he was actually quite wealthy, but that his time was in great demand and he sometimes had trouble sorting out work and family obligations.

Another week of May evaporated away, leaving James and Katrina wondering where the time went. Their lives were by no means humdrum, as there was always some new challenge to face. The next challenge came late Saturday night. At a little after eleven, James heard a Land Rover come into the village either in a tearing hurry or with some serious mechanical problems. He went out to investigate and met Angus and Morag, both as white as sheets and visibly shaken.

"What's up, Angus?" James asked.

"There's been another shooting," Angus gasped out. "We were coming out of the farmers' club and people started shooting at us."

"Was anyone killed?" James pressed.

"At least two," Angus thought. "They got the drivers of the first two cars, then it became pandemonium."

"Come in and let's get you something to drink," James ordered. "Are you both okay?"

"We're fine," Morag said as she got out of the Land Rover and was ushered into the house by Katrina.

"Was it the ZIPRA *ouks* again?" James asked.

"If you ask me, yes," Angus said bitterly.

"How did you get away?" James asked, now curious.

"We basically just *bundu* bashed. I drove off the road and through all the small brush and a couple of mealie fields. I've no idea if I buggered up the front end of the Land Rover, but quite frankly, I didn't give a fuck, I just wanted to get us out of there!"

"Was anyone else from here at the club?" James wondered.

"No, it was just us. What I want to know is why. Why did they ambush the club and start shooting guys?"

"I don't think we'll ever get a good answer to that," commented James. "But come on in and let me get you something."

"Thanks, James, I don't think we'll be going to the farmers' club for a while!"

"I'll see if I can find Colonel Mulanga and see if I can't get some answers," promised James. "Meanwhile, you and Morag get over and see Florence. I need to know that you're both okay!"

At their Monday morning meeting, Bullock told the staff what he knew, which was precious little. Two farmers had been shot in an ambush outside the farmers' club, and suspicion again pointed to ZIPRA, but no one would actually own up and confirm that. He strongly suggested that the mine staff stay well clear of the farmers' club for a while and not use the roads to the east that led to Piccadilly Circus. All their supplies came in from the west, and there was just no necessity to put themselves at risk. He also suggested that anyone with business in Mkushi go in convoy with at least one other vehicle and carry a gun of some sort. That alarmed Angus and John McFarlane, neither of whom had ever handled a gun and certainly did not own one. As far as James could see, it was just a sensible precaution, but he was also concerned about Katrina's trips to Mkushi River to visit the clay diggings.

Next, they turned back to the more pressing business of production. Bullock told them that he had received word from Kitwe that they were to increase production rates. James went through the cutting plan and concluded that they were well-positioned except for drilling and blasting. They really needed the new drills. John Wells chimed in that he had word from the dealer that the drills would be delivered on May 30th, which was only just a little over a week away. They would need a couple of days after that to train the operators, and it should be possible to put them into service at once. They had enough drill bits and explosives for a month at least. They would have to run the units for a while to see what bit wear was actually like, but it made sense to get some additional bits on order right away in case their predictions were wrong.

After the meeting, James sat down with Angus and went through equipment availabilities. Whereas the trucks were performing well, the front-end loaders had problems. They were lucky to get 75% availability out of them, which calculated out to being about one loader short.

Angus was trying hard to discover why they were having so many problems, but commented that Rokana reported that their availability on their five units was hovering around 70%, with slightly lower numbers in the rainy months. In fact, their only good month had been June of 1972, when they reported 90%. Some of the problem was tyre wear, but there were also a host of other minor issues, generally around the hydraulic systems and bucket wear. James suggested that they get a spare bucket from somewhere and prepare it for service so that they could quickly change out the bucket and not park a machine just for bucket maintenance. Angus thought they could get a bucket from one of the other mines that had just crashed a machine. He promised to contact one of his friends and work out a deal.

That evening, James told Katrina what Bullock had said about driving to Mkushi in convoy and asked her what she thought about driving to Mkushi River. Katrina replied that she had noticed an increase in Chinese truck traffic and that the smart thing to do would be to attach herself to one of their convoys. They never travelled except in groups of at least three to four trucks, so it would be safer. It might mean waiting at the road end for a while, but she knew some of the people at the glassworks in Kapiri and thought that she could get notice of their passage and time her journey to meet them. James thought that sounded great except for the obvious question: how would she get back? Ah, that was the problem. He asked her what she thought about approaching Elena and asking her if she fancied riding along with Katrina. One of them could drive, and the other could carry a gun. Katrina liked that idea and promised to talk to Elena in the morning. There was always the slight chance that Elena might go off the rails and start shooting at ZIPRA folks, just because they were ZIPRA and in her mind responsible for her parents' deaths. So, perhaps the smart thing to do was to have her drive and have Katrina ride shotgun.

Monday morning, Attie asked the Georges to go with him to inspect the new slimes dam. It had finally been completed and was now ready for use. He had even installed a small catchment downstream of the normal outflow to catch any sediment before it went into the Mita Hills Dam. George Bullock came back from the site and asked James and

Rita to go and inspect the work and then to sign off on acceptance. Rita commented that Bullock did not want to have his name on anything that could come back and haunt him. As Rita had been close to the construction all along, she was satisfied with the job and felt that Attie and his crew had done well. Now all that remained was for George Walker to organise the movement of the slimes from the temporary holding ponds that they had been using into the permanent tailings dam. That was a question of pipes and pumps, and both Rita and James were happy to leave it to him.

On May 30th, two low-loaders pulled into the mine at about ten in the morning with the new drills. James, Hippo, Abel and Angus crowded around to check out their new machines. The drills were self-propelled, diesel-powered, with hydraulic jacks for levelling. Unlike their smaller drills, which were percussive, these were rotary drills so were equipped with a rotary drive motor that travelled up and down a mast. The operator had a cab from which he could drive the machine when tramming and also operate it when drilling. The cab was offset to one side so that the operator could also see the hole being drilled and the pile of cuttings that were being ejected. Unfortunately, the engines were not Caterpillar, like the rest of their fleet, but Detroit Diesel, but at least they were of a model common enough in Zambia. James turned Hippo and Abel loose and told them to get the selected operators the required training. The distributor had provided an application engineer for that purpose, and he would be with them for the next week. James told Hippo to arrange with Jerry Mwanza where to accommodate the engineer.

No sooner had they unloaded the new drills when the Somali traders arrived. James was sure that their truck was worse each time he saw it, but it made a run from Kapiri Mposhi to Dar es Salaam every month without fail. He had no idea what other business they did along the way, but was sure that they did a roaring trade, this month quite literally, as the silencer on the truck had been damaged and it was quite noisy. Angus offered to help them get it repaired and told them to come to the workshops after they had been to the villages and completed their transactions. Bullock griped about this a little, but everyone else pointed out that the traders could get almost anything they wanted, and it paid to keep good relations with them. They also had all the news from the Great North Road and knew what was going on in Zambia and Tanzania.

Another chance!

The first Wednesday of June, Katrina and Elena went to Kabwe to get supplies and came back with an interesting tale. They had seen George Bullock in town at about ten and then again at one. The second time, he looked as if he had had an encounter with someone other than his lady friend. According to Elena, it was the husband who had discovered the two in *flagrante delicto* at their house and had taken action. Now she and Katrina were speculating as to how Bullock would explain his black eyes and bruises to his wife. James commented that instead of making movies like Peyton Place about society in America, it would be better to make movies about African colonial and expatriate goings on. Kenya had had quite a reputation for a while, and Zambia now had its share of misdeeds and liaisons.

"So do you think Bullock will go back to Kabwe next week?" James asked Katrina later that evening.
"I doubt it," she thought. "It would be a bit risky. Don't you think?"
"Maybe they'll rent a room in Kapiri," suggested James.
"That would be entertaining," she thought. "But I don't think so. I think he'll look for another floozie now."
"Do you think the *ouks* in Kitwe will hear of it?" he asked.
"Maybe, it depends on who the husband is. The real question is, if they do hear about it, what will they do, if anything?" she replied.
"To their chosen son, probably nothing except to tell him to keep his pants on for a while," commented James. "I'm afraid I don't have a lot of faith in our high and mighty *bwanas*."

Alex married Vincenzo at the Hedsor church, which surprised James a little, one because Alex was not known to frequent churches and two because it was Church of England and not Catholic. He had wondered if Vincenzo was a practising Catholic or not, and whether the choice of church would be left to Alex. He had duly sent his telegram of congratulations, worded such that it would pass the censors of both the Zambian and British post offices, but also with enough double entendres to create a laugh when read aloud. He was sure that Will had sent a similar telegram from South Africa, so they were both represented at the wedding, in spirit if not in person.

The verdict on George Bullock came soon enough. He did not make his weekly pilgrimage to Kabwe on the following Wednesday but did go to Kitwe on the Friday for his fortnightly review. At about ten that morning, James was called to the office for a telephone call. It was Colin Winter calling.

"James, I want you to take over running the mine for a while," he started. "George Bullock will not be returning."

"I see," said James. "Will this be a temporary thing?"

"As far as Bullock is concerned, no, don't expect him back. As far as you're concerned, we need to see. I'll let you know," Winter promised.

"Have you been in touch with Mary Bullock?" James asked.

"Yes, we've given her the lie of the land, and she wants to move away from there. We've promised a moving truck will be there tomorrow," Winter explained.

"Is there anything else I need to know?" James asked.

"Not for now. I'll send someone down with the appointment papers for you to sign, and we'll get you acting pay as from today," Winter promised. "Well, I need to take care of some things here. Keep up the good work!"

James hung up the phone and then went off to see first John Wells and Jerry Mwanza, then George Walker and John McFarlane and finally Angus, whom he found with Hippo and Abel. He needed only to track down Rita and let her know the news, then the whole staff would know. The only person who was not delighted with the news was George. Perhaps he felt that, as he had started with the company at the same time as James and held the same pay grade that he should have been considered. However, that was not the decision made, so, for now at least, he had to live with it. There was, of course, much speculation as to whether this would be a short-acting role for James, who would then be replaced with another substantive assistant underground manager, as before, or whether he would be placed in the role permanently. Privately, James rather suspected that the former was more likely to happen. There were just too many assistant underground managers, all looking for the next step up in the promotional ladder.

Later that day, James related his news to Katrina. He then had to repeat it to Rita, who came in from a day in the bush looking at rocky outcrops for signs of mineralisation. Neither was surprised; in fact, Katrina already knew. She had heard from Gibson that a *mkulu skopu*, or big boss, in Kabwe had been offended by the behaviour of his wife and George Bullock. He had registered a complaint with his company, and the word had gone up and then back down to the Kitwe management of their own company. They had done the intelligent thing and removed Bullock, lest there were repercussions.

The next morning, a lorry arrived to take away the Bullock's household possessions, and a driver came with papers for James to sign. For the moment, James decided to leave the house vacated by the Bullocks as a guest house and instructed Jerry Mwanza to organise furniture, cookware and such so that it would be usable in the near future. He also had a long meeting with George Walker and reviewed the status of the processing plant. George was doing a good job, and the recovery results were better than James had hoped. He made a point of telling George that he had no intention of interfering and trusted him to run the facility to his best ability. George then indulged in a little speculation as to what might happen in the future.

"You know, James," he started. "I think those bastards will send us another wanker, so that he can chalk up his open-pit experience."

"Possibly, I really don't know what to expect any more," agreed James.

"It could even be a *churra*," teased George.

"What do you mean, who?" James asked.

"Well, there's that chap, Patel, in the planning department who is an assistant underground manager, except no one wants him underground," George explained.

"I've met him; he's pretty smart," James protested.

"Yes, but totally lacking in management capability," George added.

"Really?" James asked.

"Sure; I've heard that he's been threatened by several people. They all want his opinion when they're in trouble, but no one wants to deal with him otherwise," George said.

"Yes, but why here?" James asked.

199

"How much damage can he do? There's only a few of us, and all the supervisors are pretty bright, so could probably identify with him a little better," George said.

"Well, I suppose we'll find out in the next week or so," commented James. "I need to go and see Rita about which lenses we need to mine next to keep feeding all this machinery of yours, George. Now that the Bullocks are gone, why don't you organise a village *braai* to celebrate?"

"Okay, that's a great idea. See you, James," George said.

"So, *bwana mkubwa,* what do you want to do today?" Katrina asked James on Sunday morning.

"I'm not such a *bwana mkubwa,*" commented James.

"Well, you are for a while, no matter what the *ouks* in Kitwe decide to do," she insisted. "So, again, what do you want to do?"

"You told me once about a couple of sunken lakes," he suggested.

"*Ja,* there's one up by Ndola and the other is near St. Anthony's Mission, just a little past Mpongwe," she replied.

"That sounds like a plan, let's try the one near Mpongwe, *kom ons ry,*" he said.

They were there by eleven, and apart from birds, the lake was deserted. James was intrigued by the place. The lake was generally circular in form and had steep rock sides, giving it the appearance of having sunk. Katrina told him that there were many local legends associated with the lake and that it was very deep. As far as she knew, no one had yet established just how deep, but certainly deeper than most scuba divers had been. The water was very dark. It looked almost black in certain lights. James wondered if there were fish in the lake, and Katrina told him that there were, but that the local legend was that if one caught a fish from the lake, it would never cook. If James had had any plans with Katrina, other than just a day out with lunch, they were quickly dashed as several other cars arrived. Judging by the licence plates, they were all from Ndola or Luanshya, and neither he nor Katrina knew any of the people.

"No casserole today, *Suikerbossie,*" James kidded Katrina.

"Well, at least not here," she agreed. "Perhaps we should make our way home. At least there we can shut the world out!"

"True, but don't you agree there's something romantic about making love in the open air?" he asked.

"*Ag man*, you are only right. We should put up a tall fence around part of the yard so that I can sunbathe *au naturel*," she suggested.

"I can probably arrange that," James agreed. "It'll help you with that slight tide line you have around your hips and boobs."

"Just leave my boobs out of this! Are we going home now or do I have to wait hours to see if you are ready and available?"

"For you, I'm always available," he promised.

The week under his management started well enough for James. He had a quick staff meeting and then set about going through the files that Bullock had kept. As it transpired, much of what he needed to know was readily available from John Wells or Jerry Mwanza, and it was only on the technical aspects of running the mine and the mill did he need to concentrate. James ruefully commented to John that each step up took him further away from the operations. However, he was determined not to be desk-bound and turned as much of the administration as he could to John and Jerry.

By lunch time, he was free enough to take a tour. He decided to start at the end of their process and work backwards. So, he arranged to meet George and Mike Smith at the dock they had set up for loading concentrates. It was fairly crude because they had no storage bin that would discharge into a truck, so they essentially kept the concentrate in a large pile, under a roof, until they were ready to load it into trucks. Then they would call up Hippo or Abel and borrow a front-end loader for a short time and load the trucks. George explained that at the current production rate, they were loading three trucks a day with concentrate to go to Kitwe. They would need to increase the rate to five per day fairly shortly, so would need another two trucks and trailers. He also said that they really needed their own front-end loader as they could not keep borrowing from the pit. James was a little concerned about damage to the road, particularly as the Kapiri to Ndola and Kitwe road was breaking up already. They might have to go with lighter loads and more frequent journeys to minimise damage.

From the concentrate stockpile, they then moved slowly back upstream, past filters, thickeners, flotation cells, hydrocyclones, mills and crushers to the coarse ore storage. George kept up a continuous patter about recovery, liberation and re-circulating loads. James remembered enough of his mineral technology classes to get the gist of the conversation, but the finer points of the balance of the system he decided to leave to George and Mike. Throughout the process, there were samples taken and adjustments made on the basis of test results. George and Mike both commented that it would be better if their analyses were more real-time to remove the delay from sample time to reaction time. But that degree of automation costs quite a lot, and the company had been unwilling to go that far. Both were also convinced that they could demonstrate economic payback with increased automation. James promised to see what he could do and asked them to be ready with project proposals. He was also concerned that the shortages that had occurred with household products, lubricants and other items had also affected the availability of such things as balls, reagents and spare parts. George detailed those areas where they had been having supply problems, but said they had managed to work around most things, even trading items with some of the other mines. For the moment, at least, there were no constraints to production.

At the primary crusher, they watched a truck from the pit discharge a load of ore. Just after the primary crusher, there was a large stockpile. Whereas the mill ran around the clock, the mine only worked two shifts, and the deliveries of ore were intermittent. They needed the stockpile to smooth out the lumpy deliveries into a process stream. For a few days in the rains, they had drawn down this stockpile to almost exhaustion and had come close to shutting down the mill. George did not like to do this as restarting everything took care and attention, and close monitoring of the electricity demand. Running at steady state was one thing; start-up loads were a different matter.

From the primary crusher, James drove off into familiar territory. At least the mine he understood well. He drove down to the loading faces where the front-end loaders were busy loading blasted rock into the trucks, then back up onto the benches to look over the drilling and blasting. Abel joined him, and they went through the projected blast for the day and the plans for mining the next three ore lenses. James also wanted to know how the new Gardner Denver drills were performing. Abel was delighted with them and was getting good results with not as much bit wear as they had anticipated. They were still experimenting with blasting patterns and planned to open up the hole spacing a little as they were getting over fragmentation. That meant it was easy to load but was costly in explosives.

Rita was hovering and came over quickly enough to point out the extent of the ore lenses and give an opinion on which to mine next. At least now she did not have to go through the cutting plans level by level and day by day. That was something George Bullock could never get the hang of, but which James found quite simple to follow. To him, it was just a simple exercise in three-dimensional geometry, and he could never understand the difficulties that Bullock had. His last visit was to the outlying area of the open pit and the dumps. The dumps regulations required that they be properly constructed, and James was checking to see if they had any slippage on the outer slopes. Although they had a good plan for dumping waste material in appropriate lifts that ought to be stable, he still wanted a visual check to reassure himself.

In Wednesday's mail was a letter from James's parents. They announced that they were going to visit Africa! Their plan was to first visit Will and Bridget in South Africa, then come north to Zambia before returning to England. All this was scheduled for July. They planned to arrive in Johannesburg on July 11th and Lusaka on July 21st, with their final departure on July 28th, so all in all, not a very long visit to either location. Just enough time to say hello, take a quick look around and then leave again. James needed to check with the Kitwe office to see if he could take that week off, or else Katrina would be saddled with his parents. He was certain that neither Will nor Bridget would get time off; they had not been in their jobs long enough. The best they would probably be able to do was a long weekend. Still, they could always arrange a trip to somewhere like the Kruger Park and have a guide take them.

James spent the next couple of days trapped in the office. He was working on the plans that he had to present to the head office in Kitwe for the next year. It was a little early for annual plans, but the copper marketing people wanted some visibility of potential production levels. Although James had done the mining plan before, he had never done the milling and concentration plan. He called George in a few times to go through milling rates and recovery rates based on different run-of-mine grades of ore. Fortunately, there was not much variation from the numbers that Jim Brown had worked out as an initial project plan. All that had changed were expense levels. Shortages had driven costs up almost across the board, and John Wells was forecasting that world copper prices would really drop in 1975. So, they ran a few exercises with varying copper sell prices to get a sense of the break-even point of the mine. If they could improve the copper recovery of the system by only one or two percentage points, it made a real difference to the break-even point. John Wells ran some sensitivity analyses, varying tyre, fuel, explosive, reagent and ball costs. These he plotted out on a series of graphs, and both James and George commented that they would lay money on the fact that no one in the Kitwe office would have the faintest idea what the graphs portrayed.

James commented to Katrina later that his new job was nearly all paperwork. He tried to make a point of driving through the pit every day and walking through the concentrator, but there were days when those visits were short. It was different. In his first three years in Zambia, he had spent most of his time with drillers, lashers, section bosses and timber crews. He knew them all personally and could describe their capabilities and failings. Now, he was lucky to know twenty of the drivers who were running equipment in the pit and even fewer operators in the concentrator. Putting names to faces was a challenge, with only the really outstanding, good and bad coming to his attention.

The next Thursday, James and Katrina left for Kitwe, James for his meeting on Friday and Katrina to make some sales calls at the tyre and toothpaste factories. They had arranged to stay with John and Carol Watson and arrived in time for dinner. John was interested to learn what they thought of the current Watergate scandal in the United States and also whether they thought anything would come of the discussions between the Briton, Denis Greenhill, the Rhodesian government and Bishop Abel Muzorewa. Of the Watergate scandal, neither James nor Katrina knew very much. Of the discussions in Rhodesia, neither James nor Katrina thought that anything would come of them. The Smith regime was not yet ready to talk and was still confident that it could defeat the terrorists' threats militarily. They told John and Carol what they knew of the purported ZIPRA involvement in the killings locally, and John commented that it was because if they crossed the Zambezi, they were in an immediate firefight with the Rhodesians, whereas the local farmers had little in the way of defences. He had told his people working in the area to stay well west of Piccadilly Circus and not to use back roads to get to the Mkushi Boma or Mkushi River.

At seven thirty on Friday morning, Katrina dropped James outside the main mine offices. She left to visit her customers, and James went to his meeting. He had to wait a while until the regular attendees arrived. When all were present, he quickly went through the report for the past two weeks and then asked for two more trucks to transport the concentrate. Before anyone would commit to additional trucks, there were some questions about production levels. They wanted to know what the anticipated levels would be compared to the current level and for how long that might last. As with everything, the answer to that was, 'it depends'. It depended mainly on the sell price of copper and what the mine costs were. He went through the analyses that had been run on the mine and the sensitivity curves. The only thing he could not really predict was the future market price of copper. Obviously, this was something they had all been discussing as well, because Tony Williams from the planning department had reams of charts with numbers for the underground mines. But he, like James, had no answer to the question of future copper prices. As far as buying two more trucks, the direction was given to subcontract some of the transport and get a local haulier to do the work. It was also suggested that he rent a small front-end loader for the time being. It seemed that they were looking to hold to a minimum additional capital expenses.

After the regular meeting ended and Williams, Brown and Armstrong had left, McIntosh and Winter asked James to stay a little longer. James assumed that they wanted to discuss whether or not he would stay in place as the manager or be replaced. They did not keep him in suspense too long.

"James," began McIntosh. "We want you to know that we really appreciate all you've been doing at Mtuga. We also want you to know that the decision on who runs the mine is a difficult one.

"I understand that," agreed James.

"We're about to promote Jim Ross to an underground manager slot, and he asked for open-pit experience," McIntosh explained.

"But, there are also other considerations," added Winter.

"Quite," agreed McIntosh. "We don't want to keep churning people through there and disrupting the organisation."

"I can see that," agreed James.

"We've also had a request from Tom Slater to take the slot," added McIntosh.

"I don't think he likes me very much," commented James.

"You're right about that," said Winter. "In fact, he intimated that if he got the job, you would be moving on!"

"We don't want those kinds of disruptions," McIntosh announced. "So, we want you to stay in the role you are now."

"Does that mean I'm the new assistant?" James asked.

"Not exactly," McIntosh replied. "We are having a difficult time with the corporate office. You're just too young and haven't been either in the job long enough or with the company long enough to be made substantive assistant underground manager. We'll have to keep you acting for a while."

"I see," James said, not seeing at all.

"Look, James," Winter tried to explain. "The corporate personnel people have charts of age and job grade, and you are disturbing the status quo!"

"So, you see, James, the best we can do is keep you acting for at least another six months, or until they have another situation that causes them to re-think their time in grade charts," explained McIntosh.

"You will, of course, continue to receive the acting pay for an assistant," promised Winter.

"Thank you," said James. "Is there anything else?"

"No, that's it for now. Thanks for understanding and keep up the good work!" was McIntosh's final word.

"We'll see you in two weeks, then, James?" asked Winter.

"Of course," James agreed. "I was wondering if I could get a week off in July, around the 23rd? My folks are coming out from the UK and I would like to show them around a little."

"Of course," agreed McIntosh. "We'll see you in two weeks then."

On that note, McIntosh and Winter left, and James was left with his thoughts for a while until a secretary informed him that they needed the room for another meeting.

James left the office and found one of the mine police. He asked if he could get a ride to the boat club. As he had been seen in close company with the Manager Mining, a *mkulu skopu*, if there ever was one, the mine police were only too happy to transport him to wherever he wanted to go. The boat club was the venue that James and Katrina had agreed upon as a place to meet. The guard at the gate leapt to attention when the mine police Land Rover pulled up, and he delivered a snappy salute. James thanked his chauffeurs and walked on into the bar. Katrina was not yet there, so he ordered a beer and a sandwich and went outside to sit. Under a *chitenge* looking out over the dam, he reflected on the morning. On the one hand, he was pleased to be given the opportunity to do the job, but on the other hand, he was annoyed that they were so bound by rules, traditions, or whatever that they could not do what he thought was the right thing.

When Katrina arrived, he gave her a quick recap of the morning. She was happy that he was staying in the same job, at least for a while, but unhappy that they had not made the promotion substantive. James explained that it was rather like a brevet commission in the army. They gave you the commission in the heat of battle, and then some bureaucrat in the rear echelons of the army took it away from you when the crisis was over.

Saturday morning, James told the rest of the staff at the mine what the decision was regarding managers and then told George that no new trucks were forthcoming and he had to contract for hauling and to rent a small front-end loader. George was not surprised and had already sounded out a couple of companies that had expressed interest in the work. It would be steady work and over good roads, for the most part, not like the 'hell run' to Dar es Salaam. And while they were speaking about hauliers, the Somali traders arrived. They had brought all the items ordered on their last visit and had a few extras that they were now trying to sell. James had discovered that Katrina liked kitchen gadgets, so if they had anything that looked remotely like something one would use in a kitchen, she wanted a look and, if possible, a demonstration. James did wonder if the Somalis took anything back with them, or whether their traffic was all one way. He doubted that they would want to carry copper wire bars, as their lorry looked barely capable of making the trip empty, let alone with tons of wire bars. Elena said that they sometimes took tobacco with them, but that was a seasonal crop, and she had no idea what they did the rest of the year.

Monday and Tuesday were government holidays, Heroes Day and Unity Day, celebrated on the first Monday and the first Tuesday of July, respectively. The mine followed the practice of the parent company and worked on the days. All it meant to them was no banking and no post. James was a little hazy on who the heroes were who had died for the freedom of Zambia, but given the colonial regime, there had to be some. Unity Day was in recognition of the formation of the OAU, the Organisation for African Unity, not that there seemed to be that much unity on the continent, even among members.

With his parents due to arrive shortly, James asked Katrina if she thought that her parents might make a trip to Johannesburg to meet them. Katrina thought that was a great idea and sent a telegram to them asking them if they could be available to go north to the Transvaal for a day or two. She also sent a telegram to Will and Bridget explaining things and asking if it would be possible for them to accommodate an extra two people. The next task was to sort out what places it would be good to show the Martins when they came. James had suggested the Livingstone memorial, but that was rather out of the way. It was close to a drive of 180 miles to get to the memorial, so a little too far for a day's outing. They could add a trip to the Luangwa National Park, but only if they were able to use the track that went down the escarpment from south of Mpika. Still, that might be an adventure in itself and give them a taste of 'Africa'. Katrina thought that that sounded like fun and suggested that they go to the memorial and then cut through the Lavushi Manda National Park to pick up the Great North Road and then take the road down to the Luangwa valley. The road, or track as it might better be described, was far enough east of the ZIPRA camps that James did not anticipate any problems, but he thought it might be wise to let Colonel Mulanga know what he was doing and when. He and Katrina had decided to finish off the trip by driving through the Luangwa National Park, joining the Great East Road and finishing up in Lusaka in time to put his parents on the plane back to London.

James took his Land Rover into work on Wednesday and asked Angus to check it out thoroughly. He did not fancy taking the track down the escarpment and having a breakdown on the way. He also asked Angus to get him a couple of new spare tyres, tubes, radiator hoses and fan belts. He decided against extra springs but did make sure that he had the high-lift jack on the Land Rover and a new rope for the winch. Angus had suggested that they take another Land Rover as well so that they had two vehicles in case something went wrong. He offered to lend them his as he did not think it appropriate that they drive around Zambia in a bright yellow Land Rover with large numbers on the side, which is what it would be with a mine Land Rover.

Things at the mine were going well. There had been no crises for a while, and production was steadily increasing. James was still concerned about the performance of the front-end loaders and their ability to keep them running. He and Angus had found a candidate in Kitwe who could be bribed with Italian wine to do some programming for them. James had dropped off all the data they had on his last trip to Kitwe, and now they were waiting for results. James had made arrangements with John Watson to rent a front-end loader for George to use when loading trucks with copper concentrate, and George had contracted with a haulier to transport the concentrate to Kitwe. That actually worked out well because now they could give their own trucks proper servicing, something that had not been easy with the delivery pressures they had been under.

Replies to telegrams arrived, and Koos and Sussana would indeed travel to Johannesburg to meet James's parents. Will and Bridget were pleased to be able to return hospitality and, yes, did have room. That settled, James now had a good two weeks before he had to worry about his parents again. They would be in the capable hands of his younger brother, and Koos and Sussana might even be persuaded to take them to Kruger.

On Friday, James went with Katrina to the Mkushi River diggings. One, to provide her with an escort and two, to visit the Mkushi Boma to see if he could meet up with Colonel Mulanga, ask what he knew about the shootings outside the farmers' club and pass on his travel plans. They stopped briefly at the Mkushi Boma on their way to Mkushi River, and James let the District Officer know that he was looking for the colonel and that they would be back at about two in the afternoon. Then, they went on to the diggings. Katrina was anxious to check on orders that she had received and when the material was to be delivered. Back at Mkushi Boma, Colonel Mulanga was there with his driver. James suggested that Katrina make small talk with the driver and find out what she could while he talked to the colonel.

"Good afternoon, Colonel," he said. "I hope I didn't pull you away from anything important?"

"No, my friend, it is fine," promised the colonel. "What can I do for you?"

"I was curious if you had any information about the shootings recently outside the farmers' club?" James asked.

"Ah, yes, the farmers' club," the colonel parried. "I wonder what the Zambia Police have to say?"

"I haven't heard," James responded. "Somehow I don't think they'll find the perpetrators."

"Perhaps you're right," sighed the colonel. "These are difficult times, and we are all dealing with difficult situations. I understand that you are back in charge of the mine. Is that permanent?"

"I don't know," James admitted. "They're telling me that I'll be acting for probably another six months, but who knows?"

"Tell me, are there others at your mine that seek recreation in Kabwe?" the colonel asked.

"Not that I know of," commented James, wondering how the conversation had been neatly turned away from the shootings to morality at the mine.

"Is there something else I can do for you?" asked the colonel.

"Yes, we are planning a trip with my parents to the Livingstone Memorial and then are going to drop down through the Munyamadzi corridor to Luangwa. From Luangwa, we're going to Lusaka to put them on the plane back to London," James explained.

"I will make sure that you are not interfered with in any way," promised the colonel. "If that is all, I regret that I must quickly leave you because I have an appointment in Lusaka with the general that I must not miss."

"Go well," said James.

"Stay well," replied the colonel. Upon which note, he signalled his driver and they left.

"Well?" queried Katrina. "Did you get anything out of him?"

"Not a word," bemoaned James. "He's a master at changing the subject."

"Well, I got from the driver that five of the male instructors at the ZIPRA camp had suddenly been transferred and that five of the cadres had been moved to Tanzania. The excuse is that the ZIPRA men are not happy that the Zambian instructors are getting on too well with the ZIPRA women!" Katrina explained.

"Do you believe that?" James asked.

"The bit about the women and the instructors, yes," she concluded. "As for the farmers' club shootings, another convenient transfer to Tanzania!"

On Saturday, James was visited by Jan van de Venter, the Lusaka representative of the local dealer that handled the Gardner Denver line. He came to see how the drills were working and also brought along a friend.

"James, good to see you again. How are the drills working out?" asked Jan.

"Fine, thanks," James conceded. "They've actually exceeded our expectations, and we're on our schedule."

"I'd like you to meet George Murphy," Jan said, introducing his visitor. "George is the area manager for James & Brown."

"Pleased to meet you," James said. "I'm afraid we don't have any of your equipment at this site, and there isn't much on the Copperbelt. It's mainly Bucyrus and P&H stuff."

"Don't I know it," George agreed. "We've been trying to break into this market, but those guys have a good position, and it's hard without a machine population on the ground."

"So, George, where are you based?" James asked.

"I work out of Jo'burg," he replied. "I'm taking a tour of the hinterlands at the moment, trying to drum up business and get some fishing in with Jannie."

"Would you like some coffee?" James asked.

"Thanks, that would be great. What about you, Jannie?" George asked.

"*Ja asseblief*," agreed Jan.

"Okay, I'll be back in a minute," promised James and he left to get some coffee organised. Back in the office, he found Jan and George studying his cutting plan, with Jan explaining what the drills were doing and where the pit was expanding.

"Say, this is a nice little operation you have here, James," George commented. "How long have you been here?"

"At this site, almost nine months and in Zambia, a little over three years."

"Any chance of a tour?" George continued.

"Of course," promised James. "Here's some coffee, let me give you a quick synopsis of the operation, then we'll take a tour."

Over coffee, James went through the basics of the operation from the mine to the concentrator, including the essential statistics of reserves, run-of-mine ore grades and production rates.

"Jan tells me that you had to bring in the equipment yourselves?" George asked.

"Only the mining machinery, the crushing and grinding equipment, was already here when we got caught in the border closure problems," explained James. "So we brought everything else in by road from Salima, except, of course, the drills from Jan that he delivered."

"Must have been quite a deal," commented George.

"Not really," James said. "We just rounded up operators, took them to Salima and drove everything back. It all made it fine except for one truck that had a blown turbocharger."

"That's what I like about the Brits," George said to Jan. "No big deal to them, just another day running the empire!"

"Where are you from?" James asked George.

"Born and raised in Denver, joined the company right out of college and worked my way into the Africa slot," George elaborated. "I like the place, could get used to the way of life. I even learned a few words of Afrikaans and Fanagalo to make life easier."

"For a Yank, he's not too bad," admitted Jan. "George at least will listen before he tells us how fucked up we really are!"

"Well, shall we take the tour?" offered James.

"Great, lead on, Macduff," George accepted.

As they toured the mine, James explained the workings, and George fired off questions. He would have liked to have seen at least drills from James & Brown, but admitted that their smallest size was a little too big for the operation. He also agreed that the shovels were just too large, except for some six-cubic-yard diesel shovels they had. He pointed out that the Italians had similar pieces of equipment made by Bucyrus-Erie. James knew that and commented that those units were obtained used from the Nkandabwe coal mine and were not in the best shape. When they worked, they were fine, but they needed a lot of care and attention. The Italians seemed to have a welding truck permanently assigned to the two shovels. They also needed service and repair in the pit, which meant that if he used similar equipment, he would have to get another service truck and probably a crane. For the moment, at least, the front-end loaders worked well enough to do the job and provide flexibility.

As the Mtuga mine was a little far from any town, it was customary to offer visitors lunch. James extended the invitation and took George and Jan home for lunch. Jan and Katrina had met before, and their conversation quickly changed into Afrikaans, which left James time to talk to George. George was happy to talk about his company and his aspirations. His job gave him the opportunity to visit mines in South Africa, Swaziland, Lesotho, South West Africa, Rhodesia, Botswana, Zambia, Zaire, Angola and Mozambique. He had to admit he was less than keen about travelling to Zaire and the Portuguese territories, but he had to maintain contact with all the mining operations. His predecessor had done little to build up the business, so he was starting a long way back from Bucyrus and Harnischfeger.

"Excuse me," interrupted Katrina, switching back to English. "I'm forgetting my manners. Can I get you something, George?"
"A beer would be great, thanks," he replied. "What were you and old Jannie talking about?"
"I was telling him about the latest shootings," she explained.
"Rather you than me," admitted George. "I'm happy to be in Jo'burg."
"Do you have a family?" Katrina asked.
"If you mean am I married? Yes. If you mean, do I have kids? No," he explained.
"Does your wife ever get to travel with you?" James asked.
"She doesn't really like anything that's less than five star," complained George. "So, Mtuga for her would be out. I guess even Lusaka would take some convincing before she came."
"Does she get lonely in Jo'burg by herself?" Katrina asked.
"I guess that sometimes she does, but she has a pretty full social life and I don't really fancy the afternoon bridge parties, so I'm happy to go walkabout occasionally."
"Do you get back to the States often?" James asked.
"The company has us back once a year for vacation and meetings, and I get to go with customers, so I guess I'm back maybe four to five times a year." George thought.
"That's a lot of travelling!" said James. "How do you stand it?"
"It's not so bad. We get to travel first, so are not back in cattle class and service is pretty good on SAA," George explained.

After their visitors had gone, Katrina asked James about the company James & Brown. James explained that it was a mining and construction machinery manufacturer from Wisconsin in the US. It was difficult to rank them against the other manufacturers because each one had a different mix of equipment. Certainly, they were a company not nearly the size of Caterpillar, but sold larger equipment and generally only competed with Caterpillar in their construction machinery business.

For the next week, James watched John Wells as the wedding neared and the realisation began to hit home to John that soon he was to actually be married. There was one surprise; John's parents were flying out from England to be at the wedding. They were due to arrive in Lusaka on the Friday before the wedding and had announced that they would be staying for a week after the wedding. James suggested that they use the guest house so that they would not be imposing on the newly married couple. John thought that was a great idea! His parents had booked a suite at the InterContinental in Lusaka and had also booked rooms for John and Elena and for James and Katrina.

The regularly scheduled fortnightly review was held in Kitwe, and James asked John to go with him. It was largely a formality as the operation was running well, they were well within budgetary norms, and production was steadily increasing. The *Bwanas* in Kitwe, ever anxious to ingratiate themselves, all took a proprietary interest in John's marriage. None of them wished to be caught napping if a major shareholder arrived at the door. There were no questions of substance at the review. Everything had been covered previously, and the Mtuga team were on schedule. James suggested that they might extend the review period to a month, but the panel in Kitwe wanted to keep the schedule as it was. It was explained to him that the only real information they got was the fortnightly reviews, and they needed to know what was going on. John suggested to James later that what they meant was that they had no network of spies in the camp. There were just too few people there, and James could easily keep track of them all, and there were no telephones, except the ones in the office, which John could monitor.

Saturday, John drove to Lusaka with Elena. James and Katrina followed later in the day. He had wanted to be sure the planned activities for the weekend were in hand before they left. He was confident by now that

215

Hippo and Abel would manage the pit activities without problem and that George could manage the concentrator without his help. James named George as the acting manager while he was gone, but there would be no additional compensation for George, as the time was too short. Once in Lusaka, they all checked in at the InterContinental, and John made contact with his parents. A dinner was arranged so that they could meet Elena and either approve or despair.

Elena was approved of. Katrina commented to James later that it was no surprise. Elena was intelligent, well-travelled and a delightful person all around. The fact that she was of Greek extraction did not bother the Wells one iota. John's father was anxious to know when John planned to return to England, as he had a future mapped out for him. John had hedged around that question and suggested at least another year, if not two. Mr Wells had accepted that, but did offer an overseas leave when John's local leave came due. Elena said that she thought that would be delightful, so it was agreed.

The cathedral was open when James and John arrived on Sunday morning. The wedding had been planned to follow the early Sunday services, so it was set to begin at nine. There were guests at the wedding, most of them farmers who had driven in from the Mkushi area. Katrina commented to James that they all had to have got up early to be there in time. After the ceremony, there was a reception at the InterContinental, which was cut short by the desire of most of the guests to be back in Mkushi before dark. In fact, the wedding party also wanted to be back, so a convoy left Lusaka just after two for the drive back. It would be a long day for everyone who had driven in that morning, but all those whom James talked to were pleased that they had made the effort. James also suspected that it had also given some of the farmers a chance to get together and work on the purchase of goods and chattels from the Petalas farm.

James offered to take John's parents back to Mtuga with them, as John and Elena had a mountain of gifts to take home, and their Land Rover was full. During the ride home, Katrina pointed out places of interest and recounted a little of the history of Zambia. Mrs Wells was a little horrified by the dirt road off the Great North Road, but Katrina assured her that there were many worse roads in Zambia, and in fact, their road was fairly well-maintained. Mrs Wells wanted to know as much about Elena as she could learn and pressed Katrina for details. Katrina told her what she knew, which was actually not very much outside the basic facts. She did relate the story of the shootings and the investigation that had followed, and the general lack of an official conclusion.

For the balance of the week, John and Elena dutifully collected his parents and took them on day trips around the area and then returned them in the evening to the guest house. James was co-opted to do a mine tour, and George did the concentrator tour. They did have visits from Kitwe by McIntosh and Winter, who came to be sure that their major shareholder had got the right impression of the place. By Friday, Katrina was beginning to fret about her visitors due to arrive shortly. She gave detailed instructions to Gibson about cleaning and supplies she wanted for their trip. James gave his instructions to Hippo and Abel and appointed George to act in his stead while he was away. Winter had brought the appointment papers with him, so all George had to do was sign, and he was in charge and responsible. That afternoon, John's parents said their goodbyes and James and Katrina drove them to Lusaka. They were meeting James's parents off the plane from Blantyre at around noon on Saturday, so they had to go to Lusaka anyway.

The visit

"How was your flight?" James asked his parents when they finally appeared from immigration.

"Fine, fine," commented his father. "It's no distance at all compared with flying from London."

"Elizabeth, how are Will and Bridget?" Katrina asked.

"Oh, they're doing just wonderfully!" she exclaimed. "You should see their house, it's so big, with a wonderful garden. Oh, and we met your parents too, Katrina, such lovely people!"

James took all this gushing to mean that she was still a little nervous about being there and was covering it with over-enthusiasm.

"Do you have all your luggage?" James asked.

"All present and accounted for, son. Where to now?" his father asked.

"We'll drive to the mine and get you settled, then we thought we'd take a trip for a few days, finishing back here in Lusaka. How does that sound?" suggested James.

"It sounds exciting," commented Elizabeth. "Will we see wild animals on this trip?"

"Of course," promised Katrina.

"Did you go anywhere other than Jo'burg?" James asked.

"Oh, yes!" Elizabeth exclaimed. "Sussana and Koos took us to the Kruger National Park. It was magnificent! Your father took roll after roll of pictures."

"Did you see much of Will and Bridget?" Katrina asked.

"Not enough, dear. They were working. But we still had a good time with them. We went to Pretoria with them last weekend!" she replied.

"Do you hear anything from Alex?" James asked.

"Oh, yes!" she replied. "She's having a lovely time, but I think she's hearing too little English. Sometimes she actually forgets herself and talks to me in Italian! Don't you think she's missing England, William?"

"I don't think so, dear," he said. "I think she's really happy there and enjoying Florence."

"Well, here's the car," indicated James. "Let's get your luggage loaded, and then we can be off."

218

"There are no motorways here in Zambia?" William asked, stating the rather obvious.

"None," agreed James. "There really isn't the traffic volume, and once we're out of Lusaka, there's even less traffic."

"How far is it to your house?" William asked.

"Well, it's about 130 miles to Kapiri and then another forty or so beyond," James explained.

"Are there any big towns on the way, James?" Elizabeth asked.

"Only Kabwe, which is hardly a big town by UK standards. It's mainly there because of the lead and zinc mine," he explained.

"I thought the mine was at Broken Hill?" William asked.

"The name of the town was changed to Kabwe," Katrina explained. "There were several towns that were renamed after independence. There was Fort Jameson, now Chipata, Fort Roseberry, now Mansa and Abercorn, now Mbala."

"How confusing!" Elizabeth thought.

"It's not bad, Mum," James commented. "Most of the towns, like Kitwe, Ndola and Lusaka, all kept their names."

"When will we get to your house?" Elizabeth asked.

"I just need to quickly stop by the Caterpillar place and pick up some parts," apologised James. "If any of us are in town, we run errands!"

"Will there be room?" William worried.

"They can go on the roof rack," James commented. "There will be a few boxes, and to answer your question, Mom, probably by six tonight."

On the drive to the mine, Katrina repeated her tour guide piece that she had delivered the week before to John's parents. Elizabeth was comparing what she had seen in Johannesburg to Lusaka and noted that it was nowhere as big a city, nor did it have the huge dumps from the gold mines that dominated parts of the Johannesburg skyline. The difference really being that Johannesburg had grown up as a mining town, whereas Lusaka had become the administrative centre of the country after the territorial capital was moved from Livingstone in 1935.

Kabwe failed to impress except that they were held up at the railway crossing, and Kapiri Mposhi was hardly identified as a major crossroads. They were only diverted off the road a couple of times. The road surface had broken up, and there were diversions into the bush to go around the damaged areas. William was curious about the deep ditches along the side of the road, but understood when Katrina explained how hard it could rain in the summer and how quickly those ditches could actually fill with water.

Not far past the turn-off from the Great North Road onto the dirt road, they came upon an ancient Land Rover. It was parked just off the centre of the road with the bonnet up. James pulled over to see who it was and if they needed help.

"Chazeema," he greeted, recognising one of his operators. "*Kanjani, ini lo ndaba?*"

"*Eh, Bwana, lo machine yena aikôna funa hamba!*" complained Chazeema.

"*Upi wena hamba manje?*" James asked.

"*Lapa kaia ka mina, lo ena duzi duzi na lo mugodi,*" he replied.

"*Mushle tina azi donsa wena,*" James offered.

"*Mushle sterek Bwana, mina shalili lapa kudala!*" Chazeema complained.

"What's the problem, James?" asked Elizabeth.

"It's one of my operators," he explained. "His Land Rover is broken down, and we're going to tow him to the mine. He says that he's been there a long time, probably no one else has come along today."

It only took a minute to attach a tow rope, and they were on their way again. While they travelled, Katrina regaled James's parents with the tale of the bus and the lion that they had encountered in May. Towing the other Land Rover slowed them a little, but they were still at the mine by six just as the sun was setting. They dropped Chazeema and his antique off at the mine where he could get further help, unloaded the spare parts and then drove on to the village.

"Is this where you live, James?" Elizabeth asked.

"Yes, not bad, is it?" he replied.

"Is this all the houses?" she persisted.

"For the managers and supervisors, yes," he explained. "We have another bigger village for the operators just over that way," he indicated.

"But, what about shops?" she wondered.

"We generally go to Broken Hill once every two weeks or so," explained Katrina. "We just plan ahead and buy in bulk. We can also get milk and eggs locally, and most of the time, some fresh vegetables."

"Well, I never," was Elizabeth's comment to that. "What do you think of that, William?"

"It looks all right to me," he commented. "I imagine it's what you get used to."

"Why don't you go inside with Katrina, and I'll bring the luggage?" James suggested.

"Gibson, *lo ena lo baba futi lo mama ka lo Bwana James*," said Katrina introducing James's parents to him. "*Mushle wena hamba na lo Bwana futi bamba lo katundu.*"

"What was that, dear?" Elizabeth asked Katrina. "That didn't sound like Afrikaans."

"Oh, I just introduced you as James's parents and asked Gibson to give James a hand with the luggage," she replied.

"Katrina, does Gibson speak English?" William asked.

"Probably a lot more than we think!" she replied. "We've put you in this room here, you'll have a nice view of the bush."

"What's that noise?" Elizabeth asked.

"Oh that, that's the mine. You can hear the trucks coming out of the mine to the dumps. It goes on until about eleven at night," explained Katrina. "Why don't you wash your hands and face and come out onto the *stoep* for a sun-downer before dinner?"

"What's a *stoep*, dear?" asked Elizabeth.

"Oh, sorry," apologised Katrina. "It's the porch in the front of the house."

"Lion, Castle or wine?" James asked when everyone arrived on the *stoep*.

"I'll have a Lion, please, James," Elizabeth ordered. "I discovered those in South Africa and quite like them."

"They may taste a little different here," warned Katrina. "Ours are made by Zambia Breweries, not South African Breweries."

"Dad?" James asked.

"I'll try one of those too."

"Katrina?"

"Castle, please, unless you have any of that Simba left?"

"I've got a couple of bottles hidden away," he admitted.

"What's a Simba, dear?" asked Elizabeth.

"Congolese beer," he explained. "I acquired a case a little while ago, but it's nearly all gone. Do you want to change?"

"No, thank you, dear, I'll stick to the Lion," she said.

Katrina noticed Gibson hovering near the doorway and got up to talk to him. They conversed for a few minutes, then she came back out onto the *stoep*.

"Gibson wanted to know if you have any washing that needs doing before we leave for our trip," she explained. "Do you need anything done?"

"We couldn't ask him to do that," Elizabeth protested.

"No, man, really, it's fine," promised Katrina. "He really wants to help, and he says that because we're going to be gone most of the week, he wants to come in tomorrow to make sure things are right."

"Well, if you're sure, dear, and it won't be too much trouble?"

"*Moenie worry nie*," Katrina emphasised. "It'll be fine, man."

"*Moenie worry nie*?" William asked.

"Oh, sorry," apologised Katrina. "It's something my dad always told me not to do: mix the two languages. *Moenie the twee languages op mix nie*!"

"Well, I'll just go and sort out the washing," announced Elizabeth. "Katrina, can you come and help me with that and talk to Gibson for me?"

"Well, James," started William. "How are you doing here?"

"Fine, Dad," he replied. "I think sometimes that the management in Kitwe makes some pretty odd decisions, but all in all it's okay."

"How much longer will you be here?" William asked.

"My contract has another two or so years to run, but it may all depend on the copper price and if this operation becomes uneconomic," James thought. "If that happens, I'm not sure what the next step is."

"Any thoughts about returning to the UK?" William asked.

"I don't know," hedged James. "It'll depend on what happens here."

Sunday morning, James took the family on a tour of the mine and the concentrator. Not much was going on in the mine, which meant that they could get out and wander around on the benches without risk or without getting in someone's way. James explained the operation and pointed out the different ore lenses that they were chasing. They had a front-end loader and a couple of trucks working on the sump so James's parents could see some of the equipment in action. For the tour of the concentrator, James had recruited George. The concentrator was working, so they were able to see the minerals sparkling in the froth on the flotation cells. George did a good job of describing the process without going into too technical an explanation.

Lunch was served at one, and Gibson informed Katrina that all the washing was done, ironed and delivered back to James's parents. They were amazed by that and could not understand how he could have done all that and prepared lunch as well. James just shrugged and said that he had long ago given up wondering how many things were done; he was just thankful that they were and wondered if they were paying Gibson enough. After lunch, James suggested a short siesta and told his parents that they had a *braai* planned for that evening and that most of the village would be attending. That raised the question of what to wear. Both James and Katrina emphasised casual, and that meant Zambian casual, no ties or suits; shorts and shirt or safari suits were actually quite formal in their way.

The first to arrive for the *braai* was Rita, accompanied by Attie, who had come down for the weekend. Shortly after them came John and Elena, and then the balance in quick succession. James was pleased to see that Hippo and Abel had also both come with their respective spouses to be. James and Katrina knew Susie, their nurse and Hippo's wife, to be, and were introduced to Mary, Abel's prospective bride. James knew that Hippo was still working to get the *lobola* together and suspected that Abel must be in the same situation. He saw them later in discussion with his father and wondered what they had found to talk about. Abel asked James later if he had heard anything more about the shootings in the area, and he related the story of his meeting with Colonel Mulanga. Abel's viewpoint was that it was ZIPRA and they were doing it because if they crossed the Zambezi into Rhodesia, they immediately were in trouble with the Rhodesian security forces, mainly because they used the same crossing points each time. Frustrated at their inability to make progress in that arena, they took it out on the local white population. Abel was also frustrated because he felt that it gave the Zambians a bad name and made the whites suspect any black face that they encountered.

People drifted off to their homes at about ten, and by eleven, everything was cleared up and Gibson had gone home.

"Your colleagues seem very nice, James," Elizabeth commented. "Do you often do this kind of thing?"

"We try and do something at least once a month," he replied. "It helps keep the team together. Plus, we usually have informal gatherings after lunch on Saturdays to review the week."

"That John Wells seems such a nice man," Elizabeth added. "His wife, where's she from?"

"Elena, she's from here, her family is of Greek extraction," explained James. "They met here and got married only a week ago."

"That's what I understood," said Elizabeth. "Is it true that her family were shot in their beds?"

"True enough," confirmed James. "We just cannot say definitely by whom."

"Is that what you and that black fellow were talking about?" she pressed.

"Yes, Abel feels that it was the local ZIPRA characters, and I think he's a little embarrassed by it all," James replied.

"Well, we need to be up early in the morning," Katrina reminded everyone. "We've a bit of a drive ahead of us."

Gibson was in early on Monday and had coffee and tea ready by six thirty. He was packing lunches when James surfaced and went out to check over his Land Rover and that of Angus. Both vehicles had full fuel tanks, and Angus had provided extra jerry cans of fuel, petrol for James's Land Rover and diesel for his own. Gibson brought out boxes with food and utensils, and James stowed them in his Land Rover. Lastly, James's father brought out suitcases, and those were also stowed.

Packing done, James went back into the house for breakfast. Katrina gave her final instructions to Gibson, then James's parents said their goodbyes.

"Which one do you want to drive, *Suikerbossie?*" James asked Katrina.

"I'll drive ours and you can drive that noisy diesel of Angus's," she said.

"Who wants to ride with whom?" James continued.

"I'll drive with you for a while," William said. "Elizabeth, will you keep Katrina company?"

"Alright, we'll switch tomorrow," she agreed. "That way we'll get a chance to talk to both of you."

"So, see you at Kundalila Falls?" suggested James.

"Fine, just don't go haring off and leave us," Katrina ordered.

Once out onto the Great North Road, they stopped for a quick conference before the one-hundred-and-fifty-mile drive to the turn-off to the falls. There was little traffic on the road except for Chinese trucks and Hell Run Fiat trucks hauling copper wire bars to Dar es Salaam, so progress was fairly rapid. They pulled off the main road at Serenje to fill up with fuel, as the stations were few and far between in that part of the country and then went on to the falls. For James and Katrina, it was the third time they had been there, but the view out over the Muchinga escarpment across the Luangwa valley was still magnificent to them.

"What's over there?" asked William, pointing out over the valley.

"Well, there's the Luangwa Valley in front of us, and if you went far enough, you'd be in Moçambique," James explained.

"What's special about the Luangwa Valley?" Elizabeth asked.

"Well, it's a major river valley; the Luangwa feeds into the Zambezi. It's also a rift valley like the Great Rift Valley system," James replied.

"It's also the site of four national parks," added Katrina. "There's North and South Luangwa, Luambe and Lukusuzi."

"Are there many people?" Elizabeth asked.

"There are no really big cities, if that's what you mean," Katrina replied.

"There's Chipata and a few small towns, but it's mainly small villages."

"Are there wild animals?" William asked.

"Lots," Katrina confirmed. "Probably the best game viewing in Zambia, maybe in central Africa, but then I'm biased!"

"So, where to now?" Elizabeth wanted to know.

"The Livingstone Memorial," James announced.

The road to the Livingstone Memorial involved a short backtrack south on the Great North Road, and then they took the road to Samfya, which would bring them close to the memorial. They were not far off the main road when they started to see antelope. There were puku by the score and some hartebeest. James had learned from some of his operators that further north on the way to Samfya, one could see vast herds of lechwe, particularly on the flats that surrounded Lake Bangwuelu. However, because their time was limited, they would not get that far on this trip.

The Livingstone Memorial was no longer an imposing edifice. It had been damaged in 1948 and still showed signs of neglect. The tree under which Livingstone's heart had been buried had long since been cut back and was no longer evident. They stayed long enough to take pictures and read the plaques, and then moved on to a campsite in the Lavushi Manda park. The campsite was not exactly how Elizabeth would have described where they stopped. Facilities in the Lavushi Manda park were non-existent, and officially camping in the park was not allowed, but James found a nice spot and they strung a line between the two Land Rovers and hung mosquito nets from it. He built a fire and laid out sleeping bags, and then started on preparations for dinner.

"Where's the campsite, James?" Elizabeth asked.

"This is it," he replied.

"But, there's no fence, no walls, no guards! Won't we get eaten by lions or something?" she worried. "In the Kruger Park, they had little villages with fences around them so that you were safe at night!"

"No, it'll be fine," he assured her. "We'll just keep the fire up to keep the hyæna away."

"But, won't there be lions and other animals?" she asked.

"Probably," Katrina confirmed. "But they're more afraid of you, so they'll leave us alone."

"What was that?" Elizabeth asked; in the distance, some hyæna had called to one another.

"It's hyæna," Katrina identified.

"But, won't they come here?" Elizabeth worried.

"No, they're a long way off," Katrina reassured her. "We'll be fine!"

James and Katrina slept well, but James was less certain about his parents. They said they had slept well, but he rather thought that the whole experience had been rather overwhelming. At least they were hungry enough to eat a good breakfast. James heated water so that they could wash and used the hot water left over to clean up the breakfast dishes. Later that morning, after they had crossed the Great North Road and were headed generally southeast, James's mother asked him what the funny-looking hills were.

"They're inselbergs," he explained. "Inselbergs are granitic intrusions that are common here."

"Will we have to sleep out in the open again tonight, James?" she asked.

"No, we're staying in the Lodge. The Luangwa parks do have more facilities, and there are government lodges and game guards," he reassured her.

"So, how long before we get there?" she asked.

"A couple of hours to the park boundary," he thought. "We have to go down the escarpment and ford a couple of streams."

"Will the road be like this all the way down?" she asked.

"I doubt it," he thought. "This is a good road, I'm sure it'll get a lot worse when we drop over the edge and start down."

"That's hardly reassuring, dear," she commented. "This hardly seems like a road to me here. I can't imagine it'll get worse."

"Don't worry," he commented. "We'll get there and it'll be a fun drive!"

About thirty miles from the main road, they stopped for a tea break and talked about the road ahead. They could see that it was starting to drop and wind its way down the escarpment. They could also see areas where the road had been washed out by the previous rains, and care would be needed to negotiate gullies. Katrina suggested that James take the lead, and she would follow. James's parents were both a little nervous about the whole enterprise and asked if many people used the road. Learning

227

that few people actually drove either up or down this track, they were alarmed and asked what would happen if something untoward did happen! Katrina assured them that everything would be fine and that one of the reasons they had come in two vehicles was to provide a safety backup. James's father then said that he wished that he'd brought a cine camera as no one he knew would ever believe what he was about to do!

The drive down was not overly difficult. There were a few washouts to negotiate, and in places the going was rough and progress was slow, but the reward was the view from the track. The track wound back and forth across the escarpment and descended through the trees at an amazing rate. In places, the growth was lush enough that it brushed along the sides of the Land Rovers, and a couple of times, James actually got out and climbed onto the roof rack of the Land Rover that Katrina was driving to see that all was still there tied down. Once or twice, William asked them to wait while he sprinted ahead and then took photographs of them as they came down the road. Once they stopped to watch a sable antelope that crossed the road and wandered off into the forest. On some of the turns, the road was steep enough that it seemed that the Land Rover would tip over forward, and James saw his mother hanging on as if for grim death.

Eventually, the track flattened out in the valley bottom, and they drove on to the Mutinondo River. This they had to cross before going any further. There were approaches already cut into the banks, and all they needed to do was assess the depth of the water and the condition of the bottom. James and Katrina both looked up and down the river for signs of crocodiles or hippo, and then James found a long pole and waded out across the river. The water depth varied a little, and he probed the bottom to check for holes and soft patches. The deepest part of the river was below waist height, and it was flowing fairly placidly, so he foresaw no particular problems.

James first took the precaution of removing the fan belts from the Land Rovers and installing the wading plugs. As his was petrol-driven, he particularly did not want water flung around the engine compartment and over the ignition system, and the wading plugs kept the clutches dry. He and Katrina had a quick discussion, and she elected to go first in Angus's diesel Land Rover. The diesel was less likely to have problems, and once across, she could help James if he got into trouble. With engine revolutions high and in low range and four-wheel drive, she waded the Land Rover into the river. It set up quite an impressive bow wave, and water came in through the door bottoms almost to the seats. Once across, she turned it around and told James to come on over. Having seen the water depth, James first wanted to ensure nothing got wet when the water came in. He moved the luggage to the roof and lifted everything else as high as he could inside the Land Rover. Once in the river, James tried to keep the same line that Katrina had followed. At least that way, he knew how deep the water would be. His mother had her feet up on the dashboard, but his were in water as it came through the bottom of the doors. His father was busy taking more photographs and was hopping around like a schoolboy.

"That was fun," he exclaimed. "Do we have more rivers to cross?"
"At least one," James promised him.
"I hope my pictures come out," he worried. "I think I got some great shots of your mother looking horrified when the water came in on the floor!"
"You're enjoying this, aren't you?" Elizabeth accused him.
"It's not what I imagined, but I wouldn't have missed it for all the tea in China," he said enthusiastically.

Safely across the river, the fan belts were reinstalled, and they drove on a few miles to a turnoff. The left-hand fork went to Nabwalya and a pontoon that crossed the Luangwa to the Luambe park, straight on went to the South Luangwa park. They took the straight-on option, and another few miles brought them to the Chifungwe Game Scout Camp. This was the boundary of the South Luangwa National Park. One of the game scouts hunted around and found a receipt book, and James paid the entry fee. Then he enquired about the water level in the Mupamadzi River.
"*Kanjani lo magwakwa lapa side?*" he asked.
"*Lo ena mushle Bwana,*" the scout confirmed.
"*Ena kona maningi manzi lapa lo Mupamadzi?*" he asked.

229

"*Ena kona,*" the scout agreed. "*Munya skati ena kona maningi, manje ena kona.*"

James took this to mean that there had been a lot of water in the river, but that the level was down. This was to be expected; they were several months into the dry season, so the water levels should be falling. They said goodbye to the game scouts and drove on to the river crossing. They also had to ford this river, so they went through the same process as before and checked the river for crocodiles and hippo before James ventured out to check the depth and bottom conditions. This river was a little deeper than the first one they crossed, so James decided to pre-install a towing bridle on his Land Rover that he hitched to the top of the bonnet. That way, if he did have problems, he would not have to fish for the bridle attachments underwater.

Katrina in the diesel went first and made it across. James noticed that she had had to go a little slower to avoid getting a bow wave that washed over the bonnet, so it was quite a bit deeper than the Mutinondo. When it was James's turn, he did well until they were about two-thirds of the way across, and then he hit a hole that he had not seen and the engine spluttered and died. Several attempts to restart the engine were fruitless, and James gave up in disgust.

"Fuck!" was his only comment.

"James!" his mother exclaimed. "Such language, this isn't the mine you know!"

"Sorry," he apologised, but only half-heartedly. "Okay, what I need you to do now is slide over here and steer when I signal. Just aim straight for the other Land Rover."

"You're leaving me here in the middle of this river?" she asked.

"I'm going to get out, bring the winch cable down from the other Land Rover and hitch this one up," he explained. James then climbed over the back seat and got out of the rear passenger side door, which was on the downstream side. He waded over to the bank, where Katrina had already paid out the winch cable. She handed him some gloves, and he pulled the cable into the river to his Land Rover. Whether he had just been cautious or prescient, having the towing bridle already in place made connecting the towing cable simple. Meanwhile, Katrina had secured her Land Rover to a couple of large trees behind it, so that it would not be dragged towards the river. It took only a matter of minutes to tow the disabled Land Rover out of the river, but almost an hour to get everything dry enough for it to fire again. While James was busy drying out all the electrics, Katrina lit a fire and prepared tea and lunch.

"Why did the Land Rover die there in the river?" William asked.

"I got a little off the line Katrina had followed and hit a hole," James confessed. "It was just a little too deep, and we were finished."

"Does the water level get higher?" William asked. He had missed the conversation earlier with the game scout because it had been in ChiKabanga.

"Oh yes," confirmed Katrina. "This would have been really difficult in the rains or in May or early June. It'll be much lower by September or October."

"Obviously, this road isn't used much," commented Elizabeth. "What would have happened if we were really stuck?"

"No, man, we were fine," Katrina assured her. "I've never had to walk home, and I don't intend to start now!"

"Well, how far is it to the Luangwa Valley?" William wanted to know.

"We're in it," Katrina announced. "Keep your eyes peeled now for game that might see."

"Where will we stay tonight?" Elizabeth wanted to know.

"We're not supposed to be roaming around in the park at night, so we need to make the Mfuwe Lodge before sunset," Katrina explained.

"How far is that?" William asked.

"I'd say about 45 miles," thought Katrina. "Perhaps four hours, if we're lucky, so we should be there by five or just before sunset."

"Why so long to only go 45 miles?" asked William.

"We don't know what we might meet on the way," Katrina explained. "We've also got river beds to cross, so sand if not water, and if we see game, I'm sure you'll want pictures."

"What will we see?" Elizabeth asked.

"I can't say for certain," admitted Katrina. "But the Luangwa is famous for elephants, puku, impala and buffalo."

"What about lions?" Elizabeth pressed.

231

"Perhaps," Katrina thought. "Keep a watch for vultures, and we may be lucky."

For James, as well as his parents, this was their first time in a Zambian national park. He had seen odd game before, but never any great concentrations. The drive took them a little east and then almost straight south, actually on the five-degree line, which was why the road was known as the '05' road. It was not long before they saw evidence of elephants, first trees that had been ripped up and then piles of dung. They came upon the elephants quite suddenly. There were probably about twenty of them, and they were suspicious of the Land Rovers and moved off quite quickly. Katrina explained in a shouted conversation between the two Land Rovers that poaching had increased and that the elephants had become leery not only of people but also of vehicles. They were crossing a dry river bed when they saw a couple of giraffe, which Katrina explained in another shouted conversation, after the giraffe had left, that they were Thornicroft's giraffe, a rare subspecies and one of the reasons the park had been created. For the rest of the drive to the all-weather road and then the Mfuwe Lodge, they saw herds of impala, groups of puku in company with troops of baboons, kudu, some zebra, a few eland and a large herd of buffalo.

Katrina had made arrangements with the Lodge for three nights, and she was looking forward to a decent wash. She was sure that the others all shared her view and would welcome the chance for a decent shower or bath. The Lodge had been built many years before, but it was still quite elegant. Situated in the park, it was ideally located to watch game moving towards the river and the water. Some animals needed to be close to water and never strayed far from the main watercourse; other species were better adapted for the dryer parts of the park and could be found quite a distance from the river.

They made it to the Lodge in plenty of time and, after a brief stop to check in, deferred the showers and baths and drove on to the Luangwa bridge for the sunset. Once on the bridge, Katrina pointed out the hippo in the river below, the crocodiles lying on the mud flats and the elephants crossing the river in tight family groups. The sun went down, almost seeming to fall into the river as it finally dropped below the horizon. William and Elizabeth were amazed at how quickly it went down. They had seen in South Africa the generally short duration of twilight, but further north in Zambia, it was even more apparent. William later commented that he took shots as fast as he could wind on his camera and could see the differences from picture to picture. James was now anxious to get back to the Lodge before dark. Fortunately, it was only a short drive and they were in plenty of time.

It was good to have the opportunity for a shower and a good clean. It amazed James how dirty one could get, even just driving along the dirt roads. He lost his apparent sun tan in about five minutes of washing and was back to a much paler hue by the time he finished. The Lodge provided a dinner which was as good as anything they had cooked the day before, and better still, there was no washing up to be done. James's parents both commented that they would sleep well. They were in a more secure, familiar environment and did not feel as exposed as they had the night before.

For the next two days, they roamed the park on game drives, and William eventually ran out of film. Katrina was called upon to identify everything which worked well with mammals, but when it came to birds, she admitted to ignorance and the bird books at the Lodge were used a lot at lunchtime and in the evenings. One of the game rangers at the Lodge told them that the time for birds was in December, when all the migratory species were there, as well as the normal residents. They saw lions when they happened upon a kill. The lions had pulled down a kudu and were making a meal of it. Hovering around the kill site were hyæna and jackals, and overhead, the vultures had gathered and were waiting. Katrina told them that by the next day, there would be very little to show of the kudu, only the stain on the ground where it had bled.

Katrina also introduced them to the great art of tracking. She admitted that she was an amateur compared to the African game guards but was able to point out various *spoor*, including lion, hyæna, hippo, leopard, zebra and buffalo. Then she got them onto the great challenge of dung reading. William, in particular, was fascinated by what the various piles of dung, or sign, told them. He shied away from sticking his fingers in but poked at things with a stick to see what he could learn. He heard one expression from Katrina that he just loved and repeated it often; to him, the word *drolletjies* or *bok drolletjies* that she used to describe the neat little pellets that impala left was just perfect. However, the stark calcium-rich white sign of the hyæna that they found looked almost out of place in the general scheme of things, where everything else was brown. With the lion sign, they tried to work out what had been eaten and agreed that, among other things, it had been porcupine, evidenced by the quills that were present. As for other signs, Elizabeth was able to quickly identify buffalo and zebra, one being obviously bovine and the other equine.

Over dinner on their last night at the Lodge, James's mother got onto the subject of children.

"When are you two going to have your family?" she asked.

"We have no plans," James replied.

"But, you must want to have children at some time," she persisted.

"Why?" he asked.

"Because it's only natural,' she commented.

"But, what if we don't want any children?" he asked.

"Everyone wants children, dear, unless, oh dear, I hope I haven't put my foot in it, you can't have children, Katrina?" she queried.

"I'm fine," Katrina assured her. "It's just that James and I have talked about it a lot, and we just don't want children."

"What do you think of that, William?" Elizabeth asked.

"If that's what they've decided, dear, then that's the way it is," he replied.

"Well, I think it's rather selfish," she remarked.

"It's not our lives, dear," William said. He wanted to get her off this subject and back to the safer territory of mammals, f-stops and focal lengths. He had been bemoaning the fact that his telephoto lens was only a 200mm lens, and what could he do with a 500mm lens? "Eat your dessert, dear and let's talk about something else!"

"Where are we going tomorrow?" she then asked.

"We'll start the drive to Lusaka," James promised. "We'll probably have to stop somewhere on the way and stay overnight."

When they left the following morning, their first call was for fuel. Katrina had made arrangements to refuel before the drive to Lusaka, and they drove out of the park to the appointed rendezvous. With tanks and spare jerry cans now full again, they had the decision of whether to drive into Chipata and then west to Lusaka via Petauke or take the less-travelled direct road to Petauke. William had not had his fill of bush roads yet and suggested the Petauke route. It would mean about 120 miles of bush roads, much further than the road down from the Great North Road, but with less of an escarpment to climb.

For about twenty-seven miles, they followed the river until the turn-off for the Nyamaluma pontoon. To their left, they had been following a line of hills down which came a few small water courses, but none of significance that would require wading across. They were all surprised at the number of elephants they encountered on the way and the odd little groups of buffalo. James had imagined that most of the animals would be inside the park. He had forgotten that they probably had home ranges that took no account of artificial boundaries drawn on a map, any more than national borders were just lines drawn by colonial powers with little regard for the local populations. From the pontoon turn-off to the Lusangazi gate was only a short drive, and the road then took a turn towards the south and followed the Lusangazi River for a while.

They now started to climb up out of the Luangwa valley, and the track was fairly indistinct and progress was slow. As they climbed up the number of elephants they saw dropped significantly, and smaller antelope were now more common. There were the solitary bushbuck near the small water courses they crossed, and a few duiker and once they saw a group of eland moving off quickly into the bush. They took a tea break, and Elizabeth commented on the change in number and types of antelope they were seeing. Katrina explained that as they moved away from the permanent water, they would see different species that had adapted to getting water from the browse they ate. William

235

then waved towards the surrounding hills and paraphrased the famous comment.

"It's really wonderful here, I'll even bet that there's gold in them thar hills!"

"There is or was," James agreed. "There was an early mine not far from here, the Sasare mine, that produced gold from about 1906 until 1942."

"Really?" Elizabeth asked. "Is it far from here?"

"I'm not exactly sure where it was," James confessed. "But I think it was in that direction, somewhere in those hills," he added, pointing to a line of hills in the middle distance.

"Maybe you should buy it and reopen it," William joked. "Then we wouldn't have to work again!"

"I don't think National and Grindleys or Barclays would ever lend me that much money," thought James. "And I'm not sure if the economics would be right now."

"Well, it's a nice thought, dear," said Elizabeth. "But don't you think we should be moving on?"

About forty miles from the Nyamaluma pontoon turn-off off they came to a road junction and the road improved significantly. They were now climbing fast, and the vegetation was changing. Instead of the large trees that were common closer to the Luangwa River, there were now innumerable smaller trees and bushes. The villages that they saw along the route were groups of round huts with thatched roofs, almost like something out of the history books. William had bemoaned the fact that he no longer had any film for his camera and had borrowed James's camera. Elizabeth, who was travelling with James that day, was just talking about the latest village they had come across being something out of King Solomon's Mines when she was rewarded by a line of ladies walking back to the village, all with items balanced on their heads. Some had bundles of firewood, others tin cans, others large cloth bundles with who knew what inside them and even one with a kettle. Utterly delighted, she kept up a monologue on the benefits of head carriage for the posture until they reached Petauke.

Petauke boasted a police station, a petrol station, a government rest house and a small motel. James and Katrina had driven past the turn-off to Petauke on their way to and from Salima earlier in the year, but had not actually been into the town. This time, they had to drive through the town and took the opportunity to fill up at the petrol station and get some beer and other supplies for the night. Between Petauke and Nyimba, they came upon the road repairs they had made on their trip to Salima. They must have done a good job because the section they had repaired was in better shape than the areas around it.

Just before Nyimba, they were stopped at a Zambian army roadblock. James told his mother not to worry and to just sit tight. The soldiers wanted to know where they were going, where they had come from and also wanted to see identity cards and passports. Fortunately, James had kept all the receipts from the Luangwa lodge and would be able to prove where they had been. His parents had their return tickets to London, so it was obvious where they would be going. One of the soldiers beckoned for James to go with him, and they went to the tent that served as the headquarters for the roadblock detail, where he was introduced to the officer in charge. The officer, a captain, asked again where they were going and where they had been, then he consulted a list he had on his desk. He suddenly shot up and saluted, and apologised for the delay and inconvenience and escorted James back to his Land Rover, apologising all the while. He ordered his troops to lift the barrier and waved them on their way with a snappy salute.

"What happened there, James?" his mother asked.
"I think that the colonel I know at home must have sent something out about us," he thought.
"Why would a British colonel have anything to do with these people?" she asked.
"I don't mean in England," James explained. "I mean, in Mkushi where we live"
"But that's not your home," she insisted. "You're British and home is in England."
"Not anymore," James told her. "Home is where Katrina and I are living."
"But, one day, you'll return to England?" she asked.
"I don't know, I doubt it," he parried.

237

"But you can't stay here," she said.

"In the long term, probably not," he agreed. "But the opportunities in England are rather limited, and I have no desire to work for the National Coal Board or any of the steel companies."

"You could always teach," she suggested.

"I don't think so," he disagreed. "I have no desire at all to teach at a grammar school, and most universities want their professors to have PhDs, and I don't really see myself taking another three years to get a doctorate."

They were stopped at another Zambian Army roadblock at the Luangwa bridge, but word must have been passed down the line because they were quickly waved through. They crossed the Luangwa and drove past the turn-off to the campsite they had used in January. James had considered camping there for the night, but, because they were so close to the Moçambique border, had dismissed the idea. When they had come in January, there had been a large convoy and a police escort. Now there were just the two Land Rovers and no police escort. He and Katrina had discussed other possible stopping sites earlier and had agreed on Rufunsa if there was not enough time to get to Lusaka before dark.

It was a long haul uphill to Rufunsa, and they were glad of a break. Petauke was small, but Rufunsa truly was a dot on the map. It had the usual police station and a petrol station, but little else. It was one of the possible ways into the International Game Park (Lower Zambezi), but not the easiest way in. From Rufunsa, there was quite a drop-off down the Zambezi escarpment to the river, and the park and guerrilla activity along the river made it an unattractive proposition for travel.

Just west of the town, the road cut through a small line of hills, and they found a suitable spot to camp for the night. James strung lines between the two Land Rovers and hung their mosquito nets. He then collected rocks and built a fireplace while William and Elizabeth collected firewood. After dinner, Elizabeth asked James about the stars. There was very little moon visible, so the stars were very evident. James pointed out the constellations that he knew, Crux, or the Southern

Cross, Corvus, Sagittarius and Aquarius, but there were a great many bright stars that he could not identify. Elizabeth wanted to know where the Plough was, and James had to explain that it was not visible from Zambia, just as the Southern Cross was not visible from England.

An early start in the morning meant that they were in Lusaka by nine. Fortunately, the Ridgeway Hotel was obliging and allowed them to check in early instead of making them wait until the afternoon. This gave them the opportunity to wash off the grime from the trip and take a break before lunch. Lunch they took on the terrace outside the main dining room. Although it was mid-winter in Zambia, the temperatures were still in the high seventies, and it was quite comfortable.

"How did you enjoy the trip?" James asked his parents.
"It was wonderful," gushed Elizabeth. "Although I did have some qualms about crossing those rivers where there were no ferries or bridges!"
"Oh, that's quite common in Zambia," Katrina reassured her. "We're used to it and have learned to deal with whatever happens, even with husbands who manage to stall in the middle of rivers!"
"I hope the pictures I took come out," William commented. "Because there should be great shots of the road down the escarpment and of the Land Rovers fording those rivers."
"Will you send us some?" James asked.
"Of course," William promised. "I tried to take a least two of each shot so that you would be able to have some. Will you give me the films from your camera as well so I can get them developed at the same time?"
"That's a good idea," Katrina thought. "Make sure that you take copies of the pictures from James's camera before you send them back to us."
"I wish we'd come for longer," said William a little wistfully. "I could have spent more time in the Luangwa Valley, and I wouldn't mind visiting other parts of Zambia."
"You need to come again," suggested Katrina. "You should see the Falls at least."
"How far is it to the Victoria Falls from here, dear?" Elizabeth asked.

"About 300 miles," she replied. "It's a good day's drive from here, or you can fly on Zambia Airways to Livingstone, or I suppose take the train."

"Did you ever take the train, Katrina?" asked William.

"Oh yes," she replied. "When I went to school, we had a special train that took us from the Copperbelt across the Vic Falls bridge and on to Bulawayo."

"That must have been really exciting," Elizabeth remarked.

"I suppose so, but it was just what we did at the time. Now, there is a girls' high school in Kitwe, so the need to go away to boarding school is no longer there," Katrina explained.

"What do we need to see in Lusaka before we leave?" William asked.

"It depends what you're interested in," Katrina commented. "Lusaka has all the embassies and there's the cathedral across the road, the InterContinental hotel and all the government buildings."

"So, not too much then?" Elizabeth asked.

"Well, it's a fairly new city by European standards," Katrina explained. "There hasn't been that much time to develop a lot of museums, art galleries and such."

"No, I suppose not," agreed William. "And we didn't come to Zambia to see buildings, but to see you and James, and as a bonus, we got the wonderful trip you took us on!"

"It might be an idea to wash and change before we go to the airport," suggested James. "We have plenty of time."

"Good idea," agreed William. "And I'm not travelling home in a tie, like I did coming out here. I felt uncomfortable."

"Well!" was all Elizabeth would say.

James and Katrina dutifully delivered his parents to the airport in time to catch their plane home. They saw them walk across the tarmac to the plane and then waited to actually see it take off.

"I want to be sure that they've actually gone," James joked. "So, what now, *Suikerbossie*?"

"I think some dinner and then bath and bed," she suggested.

"Where shall we eat, the Ridgeway or somewhere else?" he asked.

"They've got that rooftop restaurant at the InterContinental, you fancy trying that?"

"Let's stick to the Ridgeway, that way you won't have to drive anywhere," she thought.

Fire!

"Good to see you back," George told James on Monday morning. "Have a good trip?"

"Actually, yes," James admitted. "I had half expected it to be a real chore, but it turned out quite well. How were things here?"

"No problems at all," George was pleased to say. "Production is going well, we're making concentrate by the tonne and getting it shipped."

"Anything of consequence in the review last Friday?" James asked.

"No, they all came here, worse luck," George complained. "That meant the whole place was in an uproar because they wanted tours of everything."

"Anything I need to do right now?" James asked.

"There are a few things that need doing this week," George informed him. "But, nothing that can't wait until tomorrow."

"Great, let's take a tour, shall we?" suggested James.

They left the office and walked to the loading area, where their rented front-end loader was busy filling a truck with concentrate. It had struck James before that the concentrate was actually quite a nice colour, and the greenish tinge probably reflected the copper content. The trailer that it was being loaded into groaned a bit as each bucket was dumped into it. James wondered if they would ever overload a trailer. George assured him that they had done the calculations quite carefully and knew how many buckets it took to fill the trailer. The thing to keep an eye on was whether the buckets were heaped or struck, rather like a cooking recipe that called for heaped or struck tablespoonsful.

On their walk through the mill, James noticed a few places where spillage was starting to pile up and commented on it to George. He, in turn, pointed out a couple of clean-up crews that were busy shovelling and generally cleaning the place up. Apparently, what James was seeing was just the result of the weekend's work, and George pointed out that that was the reason for the large crew sizes. It seemed that no matter how well one constructed the conveyor transfers, there was always some spillage.

242

In the pit, the situation was a little different. Somehow, in the week he had been gone, they had managed to accumulate a considerable collection of goolies that now needed secondary blasting. He was at a loss to understand what had changed and went looking for Hippo and Rita to find out if the blast pattern had been changed or the rock type had changed. He found them both at one of the excavation faces where Rita was pointing out ore horizons to Hippo and his section boss.

"Hippo, Rita," he greeted them. "What's with all the goolies?" he asked, waving his hand towards the pile.

"George told us to try a wider pattern to lower the cost," admitted Hippo.

"Why would he do that?" James asked.

"You'll have to ask him," Hippo replied, passing the buck. "He didn't really give us much explanation."

"So, now what?" James asked. "How much of the next blast have you drilled?"

"Only the front line of holes," Hippo began. "We're about ready to move to the next line. Should we go back to the old spacing?"

"Absolutely," ordered James. "And you might get rid of that pile of goolies in the next day or so."

"Okay, boss," Hippo said, smiling.

"James, I think you need to talk to George," suggested Rita. "I got the impression that he was just passing on instructions that he had received from Kitwe."

James went back to the concentrator and found George.

"George, is there anything about last week that you forgot?" he asked.

"Oh yes," admitted George. "I got a phone call from Kitwe on Monday from Tony Williams with some changes. He told me that they had been going over our figures and data from the other mines and instructed us to change the blast pattern in the pit and the reagent addition rate in the cells."

"And?" James pressed.

"Well, I passed on to Hippo and Abel the blast pattern change and then took a look at the reagent change," George admitted. "He made it sound as if the instructions came from the very top," he added in self-defence.

"Well, we have a real fuck up in the pit now with goolies," James complained. "What about here in the mill?"

"I tried it for a short while," George said. "But, it just wasn't going to work, so I went back to my own numbers."

"It's a pity you didn't do that in the pit as well," commented James. "I think in the future, ignore all directives from Kitwe unless they come from Winter himself! The problem we have is that we only blast once or twice a week, and by the time we find out that something is wrong, we have a real *gemors* on our hands."

"I'm sorry, James, I was given the impression that you knew all about this and had agreed," George said, explaining himself. He had been expecting a dressing down for this incident and was relieved to be let off lightly.

"I'd better find a way to get Williams out of our hair," thought James. "You know the bastard knew I would be gone, and he probably assumed that you wouldn't have that much experience with blasting, so interfered just to be an arsehole!"

"I'm sorry, James," George said again, contritely. "I probably should just have been out when he called."

"We'll work it out, George," James promised. "This afternoon, come with me and we'll start blasting for beginners so that you don't get taken advantage of again."

James returned to his office and debated whether to call Williams and yell at him or to call Winter and complain. Neither option was very attractive. If he called Williams, it would be to yell at someone higher up in the company, and Williams would probably appeal to McIntosh by saying that he, James, had been rude and insubordinate. If he called Winter, he might be viewed by other managers as a crybaby who ran to his boss any time things went wrong. He decided, at least for the time being, to do nothing and wait until the issue was raised by Williams.

Katrina agreed with his decision and suggested that he wait until the next review in Kitwe and then quietly raise the subject with Winter. James also wanted to bring up the subject of two more shift bosses for the open pit. Hippo and Abel were covering things for the moment, but if either one of them was out or needed leave, he would be in trouble.

The Somali traders were back on Tuesday with the orders from the previous month and with some additional items for sale. They complained bitterly about the losses they had experienced at the border. Apparently, whatever route they used had actually been manned on this trip, and they had had to bribe their way through. They preferred to do this with goods and not cash, so were short a few items that they would have liked to sell. It seemed it was the Tanzanians who were being difficult. They had imposed port surcharges at Dar es Salaam and were also imposing extra duties on items crossing the border into Zambia. So much for brotherly unity. It was very much take advantage of your brother when he is down and must use your facilities. Their argument in their own defence was that the extra Zambian imports were creating congestion in the port and requiring additional manpower and equipment, all of which had to be paid for.

Katrina collected her order, then placed another order for the next month. She had absolute confidence that they would be back and with everything she wanted. She asked them about return traffic, and they told her that there was little going north that they could carry, but occasionally they had been asked to ferry a few people. That must have been an uncomfortable ride for whoever was in the back of the truck.

The next blast was significantly better than the previous two, and the fragmentation was good, without many goolies. James had begun to think that they might actually be better off decreasing the hole spacing even more, to over-fragment the rock and make loading easier. Their repair bills on the front-end loaders were mounting up, and he and Angus were becoming fast convinced that it was related to the stresses they were placing on the loaders with large rocks. Unfortunately, it was not one of those things that one could measure in a week; it would take a month or two for any changes to be obvious. Still, it was worth a try, and if the availability on their front-end loaders went up, then perhaps it was doing some good. Explosives had not gone up in price anywhere near as quickly as spare parts for the loaders, so he decided to give it a try. He met with Hippo, Abel and Rita and laid out a new drilling pattern and a new blast sequence. Now only time would tell. Their greatest challenge was going to be keeping the bureaucrats in Kitwe focused on the system cost of extraction rather than the individual cost accounts.

A week later, when James was driving to the open pit, he noticed a column of smoke coming from the general area of their magazine. Brush fires were actually quite common that time of year and, in fact, would increase in number before the rains. Some of the fires were started by lightning strikes, but these early fires were started because the Zambians used them to clear areas for crop planting. However, this particular column of smoke looked a little too close for comfort, so James went to investigate. As he neared their magazine, he could see the fire off in the middle distance. A quick check of the wind direction confirmed his worst suspicions. The fire was headed for the magazine! They had no fire engines anywhere near, so would have to improvise. He raced back to the pit and found Abel. He explained to Abel that they had a fire headed towards their explosives and that they needed to create a large fire break quickly. Abel told the operators of the rubber-tired dozers to follow him and drove out to the magazine. James rounded up the water carts that they had and followed.

Once at the magazine, they started clearing the brush away and creating an effective fire break. It needed to be wide enough that the wind would not cause the fire to jump the break and continue around the revetment. As the dozers cleared the brush, James had the water bowsers soak the area as an extra precaution. When the fire neared, they actually had the water carts run parallel to the dozers and soak down the machines and the operators. The fire was really hot, so this turned out to be a sensible precaution. When they could no longer push brush and trees away from the advancing fire, they retreated and watched. They were lucky; they had caught it in time for the fire break to be wide enough that even with the strong winds, the fire did not jump the gap and restart.

On Friday, when James was in Kitwe for the fortnightly review, he was able to report that they had stemmed that fire and another that had threatened the management housing. He told the review panel that he had instituted daily patrols looking for evidence of fires and that they had also met with the local village headmen and asked them to let them know if and where they planned to burn. At least that way, they could build fire breaks before it was a panic situation. A little later on in the meeting, Williams brought up the subject of blasting patterns.

"How is the new hole spacing working out?" he asked.

"The wider spacing gave us more goolies and therefore more secondary blasting," James reported. "So, we closed the spacing back up again."

"But I specifically ordered a change in the pattern," complained Williams.

"I realise that," James retorted. "But, it wasn't working, so we dropped the idea!"

"Why did you order this change?" Winter asked.

"Because they are spending too much on explosives," Williams explained.

"Yes, and now we're spending even more because we are doing a lot of secondary blasting and, by the way, our maintenance costs on our front-end loaders have skyrocketed!" James complained.

"Where did you get data from to be able to compute a new drilling pattern and explosive loading?" Winter asked of Williams.

"I got some information from Nchanga," he explained.

"Fine, but they use large electric shovels and one-hundred-ton trucks," James commented. "It's hardly an equivalent situation."

"I agree," commented Winter. "Please, in the future, refer any suggested changes to me for approval before dictating to the operations. You have a job in planning; please leave the operating to me!"

That was about a direct a set down as James had ever heard Winter use to anyone. It remained to be seen if Williams actually listened. But, at least now, he could legitimately call Winter to confirm any changes before he implemented them. James could not resist adding fuel to the fire and brought up the required reagent change as well, which brought Henry Wayne into the fray. Wayne was adamant that no changes were to be suggested or implemented until he and George Walker had agreed on them, and he suggested that Williams stick to planning underground mines and stay out of the concentrator business.

As the meeting adjourned, Winter asked James to stay and meet his two new shift bosses, Henry Zimba and Pete Maynard. Both had been to university in the United Kingdom, Henry at Nottingham and Pete at Newcastle. They had also both spent the past year working underground as section bosses, so this was their next step up. They were to start on Monday, so would be moving to Mtuga over the weekend. James asked if transportation of household goods had been arranged and was told that a lorry had been laid on for the morrow. He asked to use the telephone and talked to Jerry Mwanza and John Wells, and confirmed that they had two houses available. Winter left them to the administrative tasks and told James that he would see him in two weeks. James asked Henry and Pete if there were spouses and children. Henry told him that he was married and that his wife's name was Mabel and that there were no children, yet. Pete also confirmed that he was married to Katherine, and that he had two children, David, four and Margaret, three. They would be the first children that they had in the management village. In the village for the operators, there were any number of children, and Jerry had had to make arrangements with the local elementary school to take some of them, but the two arriving were too young for that to be a concern yet.

The shift bosses with spouses, children and household goods arrived on Saturday and were shown their houses. James had decided to pair Pete Maynard with Hippo and Henry Zimba with Abel. That put Pete on the day shift on Monday and meant that Henry was not on call until the afternoon. However, James suggested that they both attend his staff meeting on Monday morning so that they could get a taste of what was going on. Both Pete and Henry asked if they could be shown around on Sunday, and if possible, take their families with them. James asked Hippo to arrange that, considering it safe because they had no blasting planned for Sunday and the charged holes could easily be roped off.

Monday brought some different visitors. James was out in the mill when he got a call asking him to go back to the office. At the office was parked a green military-looking Jeep-like vehicle. In the office were four Chinese men. One of them introduced himself as the interpreter for the cadre, Mr Lao. Apparently, Mr Lao was in charge of building the

TanZam railway section from Serenje to Kapiri Mposhi, and he was looking for ballast. He had made arrangements with the Italians for some ballast, but he wanted more. James offered them tea and then called in George Walker, and they went through the request again. George asked what size they wanted, and the Chinese already had a specification sheet and some samples of desirable sizes to hand. George then asked them how much fines they could tolerate, and that took a little translation. Eventually, he took the party to the mill and showed them the output from the crushers and the size distribution that they got. The cadre and one of the others, who had to be a civil engineer, judging by his questions and reactions, understood long before the interpreter and pointed out on the graphs where they wanted the cut-off to be. George commented to James that in order to meet their desires, they would need to put in a couple of vibrating screens to take out the fines and small-sized fractions and the large-sized rocks, leaving only the stones that would make good ballast.

Satisfied that they could meet the requirements, the next discussion was cost. The cadre turned to the fourth man and let him do the negotiating. Playing tit for tat, James and George turned over their negotiating to John Wells. All that George provided to John was an estimate of the screen costs and the cost associated with running waste and not ore through the mill. They had enough raw capacity in the crushers to deliver the requirements to the Chinese, but were constrained on where it would sit until it was collected. That led to another discussion on how often the Chinese would collect the stone and how it would be loaded into their trucks. The Italians had said that they would use one of their front-end loaders to fill the trucks. George said that they would also load the trucks for the Chinese, but it would be with the smaller front-end loader they used to load the concentrate trucks. While this conversation had been proceeding, the price negotiations must have been concluded because there was a handshake, and the deal was done. The next move by the Chinese floored everyone. They produced cash in advance! They literally handed over 50,000 Kwacha in notes to John. With that, they finished their tea, said their good-byes and promised that their trucks would be there the following Monday for the first shipment.

Once they were out of the room and away from the mine, John came back into the office waving the money.

"We need to get rid of this," he commented. "We need to get it into a bank quickly before anyone finds out we've got this much cash lying around."

"I agree, John," James confirmed. "The problem we have is that we don't have any local accounts. You know that the payroll people come once a month with cash for those that want it; otherwise, everything else is handled by accounting in Kitwe."

"What do you think the people in Kitwe will say when we tell them that we've made a deal to sell rock?" George asked.

"No idea," James admitted. "I suppose at least someone will give us a difficult time about making a deal without consulting them, but if we give them the cash, they may be happier."

"They ought to be happy," John added. "After all, you're selling what to us is a waste product!"

"Don't count on logic," George kidded them. "They'll probably tell us that we're a mine and not a quarry."

"When are you going to take the money to Kitwe?" John asked.

"Actually, I think you'd better take it tomorrow, John," James thought. "Take Jerry with you and make sure it gets into the right hands. Oh, and make sure it gets applied against our expenses and not some general miscellaneous overhead account!"

When John and Jerry came back from Kitwe, they told the rest about the confusion they had created in the office. Apparently, no one knew how to handle the sale of the rock to the Chinese. Finally, John had suggested that they use the existing other income account, which had originally been created for sales of anode slimes and other transactions. They also had other news. They had been contacted by the computer programmer whom they had bribed, and he had results. He had managed to write a program that sorted out the data that they had and presented it in the form of a series of graphs. It essentially confirmed what James and Angus had begun to suspect. The front-end loaders were failing because the use that they had been put to was more severe than had been anticipated. James was convinced that changing the blasting pattern and getting a more uniform rock pile that was easier to handle would actually put less strain on the loaders and give them higher availability. Obviously, only time would tell, but for the moment, that was the plan that he would follow.

The following Monday, the first Chinese trucks arrived to collect the crushed rock. They were interesting trucks, described by Angus as similar to International Harvester trucks from the 1950s. Apparently, there had been a problem at the Italian operation. The first load of rock dumped into a truck by their front-end loader had gone right through the floor of the truck and buried the running gear. That truck had been cleared and sent back to their camp for repairs, while the rest were sent over to the Mtuga mine with instructions to load them gently and only half full. George listened to the story and decided that he had better be very careful with the trucks unless he wanted a repeat of the problem they had had at the Italian site. Each truck only received the minimum load, and even then, the springs were loaded down to the stops. The Chinese were going to have to find another way to collect their ballast. It raised the obvious question of how they had managed to get ballast for the railway they had built so far. They were unable to communicate with the drivers of the trucks well enough to get an answer to that question.

At the fortnightly review on Friday, there was a change in the members of the review group. Williams was gone, replaced by Patel. No explanation was given, only that Williams had left to pursue other interests. John told James later that that was a euphemism for being dismissed.

James was grilled about his decision to sell crushed rock without consulting Kitwe. He made the obvious comment that selling a waste product was always better than not, and the subject was quietly dropped. It was difficult to criticise success, and their production rates were up, with operational costs per ton down. Things were going well, and everyone knew it! After the meeting, Winter treated James and John Wells to lunch at the Edinburgh.

251

"I understand that you've had some programming done by the computer section," he commented.

"Who, us?" James asked innocently.

"Yes, you!" Winter laughed. "You know, you all remind me of myself when I was starting out. Do and then ask for forgiveness. Did it tell you anything?"

"If there had been anything done, we believe it would have shown us that the solution to our front-end loader problem was related to basic overloading," James explained.

"Ah, I see," Winter said. "And have you changed anything?"

"We've closed up the blasting pattern hole spacing," James explained. "It's early yet, but it looks like the system costs are actually coming down."

"What about your other request?" Winter asked.

"Which one would that be?" John asked.

"The one that relates drilling information and seismic data to the blast pattern," Winter elaborated.

"Well," James began. "We've actually not made any real progress on that front. It's not just a question of sorting data to get information. We have to construct a model that predicts what's going to happen, and so far it's eluded us."

"Well, keep trying," Winter encouraged them. "If you manage to solve that one, it'll be of great value. What is this wine like that you hand out?"

"We have a little with us if you'd like to try some?" James offered.

"Thank you," Winter accepted. "I wish you'd been here after John and Jerry dropped off all their cash last week. It created a furore all around, except with the cashier, who was happy to get the money."

"What are you doing this weekend?" James asked John when they were driving back to Mtuga.

"Elena and I are going to Ndola to see her sister. Have you anything planned?"

"I'm not sure," James admitted. "Katrina had been talking about an outing, but I don't know what she had in mind."

"Well, stay away from Piccadilly Circus," John cautioned. "I've reason to believe that the ZIPRA chaps have something on at the moment and you wouldn't want to run into them!"

"Have Elena and her sister finished with the sale of the farm?" James asked.

"Yes, that's part of the reason we're going," John explained. "They're going to divvy up the proceeds."

"Is it all in Kwacha?" James asked.

"Unfortunately, yes," John remarked. "It would have been nice to make some kind of arrangements to get money out of the country, but none of the farmers have interests enough overseas to even think of that."

"Without being impolite, are we talking a lot of Kwacha?" James wondered.

"Too many, actually," John thought. "Over time, I may try and convert some to other currencies if I can find any or to precious stones or something that we can carry out when we leave."

"You will be leaving then?"

"Yes, perhaps in a year or so, it depends when they want me back in London, or when the copper price drops enough to shut Mtuga down."

"Do you think that's likely?" James asked, a little concerned now.

"Absolutely, I've been tracking leading indicators for a while now, and I predict a fairly steep rise in the price of copper from now into 1974 and then a real drop in 1975," John elaborated.

"Then what?" James wondered.

"Oh, then the company will start examining all its contracts and cutting people as fast as they can. I feel sorry for the local Zambian workers because when it happens, they'll just get pushed out onto the dole," John explained. "Then, because it will affect all the mines and Zambia is essentially a single commodity economy, the government will be in trouble."

"What about after 1975?" James asked, curious now as to how far John was prepared to predict into the future.

"I think the drop in 1975 will be steep, and then I see a slow and steady decline for a while before the price turns around again," he predicted.

"How are you actually doing this crystal ball gazing, John?" James asked.

"Well, I have a number of economic models that I track and a set of leading indicators. So far, they've been pretty close. But, there's always the chance that things will change, say another war, a major mine disaster and closure or a coup that will upset the apple cart and change my models," he explained.

"Well, if you're right, maybe that PP&E of yours is worth something after all," James laughed.

At home, James relayed this conversation to Katrina, who was not surprised and said that it had happened before during the depression of the 30s when the copper mines all had had problems. World War II had changed that, but as far as she knew, there were no world wars in the offing to save the copper industry if the prices dropped dramatically. Still, for the time being, all was well, and they should enjoy the prosperity that the high prices brought.

Katrina had planned an outing for Saturday afternoon and Sunday. She told James that she wanted to visit the Blue Lagoon National Park, which was west of Lusaka. The park had recently become part of the national park system when it was obtained from the Critchleys, who had created the reserve. It was more of a birders' paradise than an animal viewing park, but would be interesting as it was so different to the Luangwa parks, as it was in the flood plain of the Kafue river and was generally flooded over most of its area during the rains. In the dry season, it was part of the area known as the Kafue Flats, for obvious reasons, home to mosquitoes, flies and lechwe, an antelope particularly endemic to the flat marshlands of Zambia.

The drive to Lusaka was uneventful, and then they turned off onto the Great West Road; such a grandiloquent term for such a small road. The Great North Road, off which they lived, had its problems, but it was well-travelled and took a lot of the traffic to and from Dar es Salaam. The Great West Road was, even in Zambia, a relatively minor road that ran west from Lusaka to Mumbwa and then to Mongu in the extreme western part of the country. Only a few miles along the road, they turned off onto a gravel road that led to the park. The road had obviously been well-travelled and even maintained, something that surprised both James and Katrina.

They arrived at the park gate an hour before dark, but the gate was not manned by game guards but soldiers of the Zambia army.

"You cannot enter!" one of the soldiers announced. "Where have you come from?"

"We've driven from Mkushi today. I thought this was a national park," James protested.

"It is in use by the Zambian Army," the soldier continued. "We are conducting exercises and entry is forbidden!" he added and then picked up his rifle.

"But, we just want to stay one night and then return home tomorrow," James pleaded.

"No! Entry is forbidden," the soldier reiterated. "You must turn around and go back!" He was reinforced by two other members of the squad who were also armed with rifles. James and Katrina turned around and had just started to drive back up the road when they saw a Zambian Army Land Rover going towards the park. It was driven by a sergeant and had several officers of high rank on board, judging by their badges of rank and epaulettes.

"So, what do you think, *Suikerbossie*?" James asked.

"I think that exercise is a great excuse for a private weekend of shooting," she replied.

"Do you think it's just this weekend or do you think they've taken over the park completely?" he asked.

"Probably we hit a bad weekend, but I'll bet that before long there'll be no public access to Blue Lagoon at all and it'll become the private playground of senior army officers," she thought.

"I'm afraid you're right," he agreed. "So now what?"

"We need to find a place to stay overnight," she thought.

"What about Mumbwa?" he asked. "Can we make it before dark?"

"I doubt it, it's about fifty miles from here," Katrina thought. "And it'll be dark in about half an hour."

"Should we just retrace our steps a little and find a place to stop overnight?" he asked.

"Let's just take the road north towards Mumbwa and see what we can find?" she suggested.

They drove north and, after about twenty minutes, came upon a side track that seemed to lead to a group of derelict buildings. James turned off the main track and approached the buildings. They were deserted, and there were no people in evidence at all.

"This looks like an old mine," he commented.

"Weren't there all kinds of little mines in this area from the turn of the century?" Katrina asked.

"You're right, I remember now Rita saying something about the Big Concession and mines like Sable Antelope and Hippo," James recalled.

"Are there any still running?" she asked.

"I'm not sure," he admitted. "I heard something about the last one, the Hippo mine, finally shutting down this year, so probably not."

"Which one was this?" she asked.

"No idea," he admitted. "Let's set up camp and get something to eat."

In the shelter of a building with no roof, they parked the Land Rover and James quickly had a fire going and started on dinner. Katrina, meanwhile, had cleared an area and had laid out the groundsheet and strung the mosquito net. They had noticed that there were many more mosquitoes and other flies around than there were at Mtuga. It was not surprising, really. The whole area to the south of them was the Kafue flood plain and must be the perfect breeding ground for bugs of all kinds. As the sun was setting, they had noticed a large number of bats around, obviously drawn by the insects, and now they could hear the bats as they did their echolocation. After the sun had gone down, many of the insects disappeared for the night, but would surely be back with a vengeance with the dawn. James warned Katrina not to stray too far in the dark, even with a torch. He was sure that there were old shafts associated with the mine that had to be close at hand and did not want her to fall into one.

After dinner, James filled their pots with water and heated enough to wash with. He reminded Katrina of a trip they had taken almost three years earlier, when they had camped on the banks of the Kafue, near its confluence with the Luswishi. Then he had taken great delight in washing her down as she stood on a groundsheet in the firelight. He told her how the light had reflected off her, where she was wet and what a thrill it was for him. She, in turn, reminded him that he had been panicked by a porcupine that came snuffling around their camp.

"So, are you going to wash me again?" she asked.

"Of course," he promised. "Let's get under the mosquito net and let me help you out of those clothes."

"There's no need," she said. With that, she undid her shirt and took it off, revealing that she had had no bra on underneath, and then she undid her shorts and dropped them to the ground and then pulled the side strings on the bathing suit she had on underneath, exposing herself to him completely.

"I never noticed that you had no bra on," he commented. "Did you not have one on all day?"

"I slipped it off a while ago while you were getting wood for the fire," she explained.

"And is that a new bathing suit?" he asked.

"*Ja*," she said. "I picked it up in Kitwe the last time I was there."

"Does the top also come undone at the pull of a string?" he asked.

"I'll let you try later," she promised. "Have you looked enough, or are you going to stare at me all night?"

"I could stare at you forever," he sighed wistfully. "You've got this wonderful shape, with curves, convex and concave, and I love the way the fire light plays onto you, creating shadows that hide and suggest at the same time."

"That's all very well with the technical stuff about curves," she complained. "But I'm waiting!"

With a little sigh of wonder that he always felt when he and Katrina made love, he set about the pleasurable task of washing her in preparation. He had enough water to do the job thoroughly, so he took his time and enjoyed her curves and the feel of her. Somehow during this process, Katrina had managed to undress him and was now cleaning the day's dirt and grime off him. That eventually led to kissing and caressing and then to lovemaking. Their first encounter was kneeling on the damp groundsheet facing one another, and later on, she

257

lay back on the dry groundsheet and bedding she had laid out earlier, opened her legs wide to him and welcomed him in. Once in, she locked her legs around his back and moved with him until they both came again.

Unlike Mtuga, it was warm enough overnight to forego coverings, so they slept nude on top of the bedding under the mosquito net until the morning. The dawn chorus of birds awoke them, and James had to untangle himself from Katrina before he could get up. However, Katrina had other ideas; she reached for him and pulled him back down to her and stimulated him to a full erection that she then put to good use. Then she showed him her new bathing suit and let him experiment with undoing the top and the bottom, allowing both parts to fall away. He tried a couple of times and then could contain himself no longer and sat back and gently pulled her down into his lap. She guided him into her and then rode him to a climax, after which they clung to each other for a while, both immensely happy and content with life.

When he was allowed to get up and dress, James lit a fire and prepared tea and heated some water for washing. He also made some breakfast, and while Katrina was washing and dressing, he took a quick look around the group of derelict buildings. He had been right. It was an old mine. There was a small shaft, and the remains of what would have been the winding house and some buildings that probably housed a crusher of sorts and some kind of mill. He found quite a bit of malachite scattered around and a nice lump of native copper. Taking that home would be a challenge because it was too heavy for him to lift into the back of his Land Rover. He decided to have breakfast first and then come back to the problem.

Back from his explorations, James heard some men's voices. At their campsite site he found Katrina in conversation with two elderly men. They had been travelling towards Mumbwa, had seen the smoke from the campfire fire and had stopped in hopes of a lift. James wondered just how long they had been hovering around, but he got no indication from them as to whether or not they had seen any of the earlier activities. While Katrina gave them tea and bread rolls, James took his

Land Rover to the place where the lump of native copper was and rigged up a ramp to get it into the back. With his Tirfor winch, he pulled it into the back and then worried a little as the rear springs flattened significantly. The stuff was heavy!

Packed up and on their way, Katrina asked the *madalas* where they were from, and they told her that their village, Myooye, was very close. In fact, they were surprised that James and Katrina had missed it. They confirmed that they often saw Zambian Army officers at the park and heard them shooting. They also pointed out that the new Zambian Air Force base was close to Mumbwa and that the senior officers from the base were often at the park on shooting trips. The two *madalas* showed them the turn off to the air base and warned them against getting too close to it. The Zambian Air Force was very sensitive about people driving near or around their air base.

They then explained that the place that Katrina and James had camped at the night before had been the Red Rose mine. They went on to list all kinds of old mines that had been in the area, most of them north and west of Mumbwa. There was the Sable Antelope and Hippo that Rita had talked of, but there were many others, including those with such exotic names as Silver King, Blue Jacket and True Blue. James wondered how they got their names. He supposed that Sable Antelope suggested that someone had either seen or shot a sable at the site, and the *madalas* told him that Hippo was so called because an employee had been killed by a hippo. They also mentioned some of the landmarks in the area and named hills and villages.

As they approached Mumbwa, they told James where the petrol station was and how to find the road that went back to Landless Corner, bypassing Lusaka. James and Katrina dropped the *madalas* in the centre of the town, and as they pulled away, James saw the old men grinning away and making hand signals to him. Clearly, they had witnessed at least some of the activities earlier on. He waved back to them and grinned in turn. That set them off into gales of laughter.
"What were the *madalas* laughing at, James?" Katrina asked.
"They saw us earlier," he explained.

"Oh," she said, blushing. "No wonder there was a lot of coughing before they showed their faces!"

"I got the impression that they thought I was quite the man," James bragged.

"Hah!" she exclaimed. "It's only because I taught you all you needed to know that I let you do these things."

"What things?" he asked innocently.

"Well, if you don't know, then I may have to refresh your memory and give you some extra training sessions," she laughed.

"I don't know if I could stand the pace," he complained a little half-heartedly.

"Yes, you can," she said. "You're the one who's the randy old goat, and I have to put up with your incessant demands!" she added, turning things around.

"Are you complaining?" he asked.

"No, *ou man*, just wait till we get home and I'll give you something to remember this trip by!"

On their way out of Mumbwa, James asked Katrina if she remembered any of the villages and landmarks that the *madalas* had mentioned. She had and started to list them.

"That's it, that's the one," James said, stopping her.

"What do you mean?" she asked.

"Sitanda's," he replied.

"Yes, they mentioned that and Mount Sitanda and Mariba-Sitanda, why?" she wanted to know.

"King Solomon's Mines," he explained grandly.

"What about King Solomon's Mines?" she asked.

"Sitanda's *Kraal* is where they left their ox teams and wagon and then went on foot into the desert," he explained. "Mind you, looking at it, it can't have been this Sitanda's *Kraal*, because there's no desert around here and no mountains either, except that little range of hills over there."

"I always thought that it was likely to be Botswana," thought Katrina. "At least there, there is desert even if there aren't snow-capped mountains."

"I've often wondered just where the 'Suliman Berg' were supposed to be," James commented. "There're mountains in South Africa that get snow, then I imagine you have to go a long way north to Kenya or Rwanda to get mountains high enough to get snow."

"Yes, but Rider Haggard also talks about the Lukanga River," added Katrina. "And we were there not long ago when we went to the Lukanga Swamp."

"He must have been really confused," commented James. "Or he really just did invent a place and used names that he had heard. Let's face it, in 1885, not many whites had been here."

The seventy-mile journey from Mumbwa to Landless Corner was time-consuming. First of all, they had to be sure they were on the right road, and then they had to avoid another turn off to the air base. The road was not a major route by any stretch of the imagination and was deeply rutted in parts. Any vehicle low to the ground would have had problems, and even in a few places, James wondered just how much clearance he had for the axles. At Landless Corner, they joined the main road and followed it north to Kabwe and then Kapiri Mposhi. It was good to get home to Mtuga, and they both agreed that even if their original plan for the weekend had been spoiled that they had still had a good trip out.

It's been one year already

When the Chinese arrived on Monday to collect stone for ballast, it was with a different fleet of trucks. Whereas before they had used green, ancient-looking Chinese-made trucks, they now arrived in Scania trucks that looked new. James learned from the Italians that the episode of dropping the full load of stone that went right through the floor of the truck had precipitated this change. The new trucks looked much heavier and more capable of withstanding the loads they would receive. It only took an hour or so to load up the fleet that arrived, and then they were on their way.

James then took his walk through of the concentrator and was pleased to see that George had cleaned the place up nicely. It was a pleasure to see the place running so well. He had to give George credit. Although he was not impressed when he first met him, he had come to like George and have a regard for his capabilities. They were wringing the most out of the ore that they could, and it would take a breakthrough in technology to get a much better recovery.

In the pit, things had also improved. The pile of goolies was gone, and the new blasted faces looked good. It certainly looked as if the change in the blasting pattern to give them greater fragmentation was helping the front-end loaders. They had seen a slight improvement in availability, and they had also noticed a reduction in the time it took to load a truck with either ore or waste. This week, it was Hippo and Pete on days, so James went and found each in turn and got their stories. Pete had adapted very quickly to the change from an underground section to the open pit and was making suggestions as to traffic patterns and working area layouts. James told him to make sure that he met with all the other shift bosses before changing any traffic pattern. There had been accidents at other mines when shift bosses had changed the traffic pattern without making sure everyone knew and agreed, and head-on collisions had occurred, with fatal consequences.

Henry, his other new shift boss, had aspirations of grandeur and was vying with Hippo to see who would be the next General Manager of the company. They both had degrees and were both very bright and ambitious. It struck James that it would be entertaining to skip ten years into the future and see where each of them was on their road to fame and fortune. If John Wells was right in his predictions, then he, James, would not be in Zambia. Quite where he might be, he had no idea. Still, for now, there was a high copper price and plenty to do on the mine.

Wednesday brought a new visitor. He was with the Mines Department and was an industrial inspector, which meant that he looked at workshops, the concentrator and other surface facilities. He did not deal with the mine itself or with the magazine, just the support services. James assigned him to Angus and George and sent them off on their tour. They were back several hours later with recommendations and comments, and one item of concern. They had a number of large stationary compressors to provide air for the workshops and the mill, and apparently, the air receivers for these compressors required an annual internal inspection. James had thought that he had covered most things, but he had missed this item completely. The inspector explained that the law required them to remove the access covers once a year and do a visual inspection of the interior of the receivers, and a pressure check was also required. They had to pressurise the tanks and then look for a pressure drop over time, indicating leakage. Neither of the two items had been done. So, a fine was payable. As James was the responsible official, he would have to pay the fine. Fortunately, it was not outrageous, fifty Kwacha. What James did note was that if the company paid the fine on his behalf, then the amount multiplied considerably, so they had no desire or incentive to pay it. It truly was a personal fine.

James confessed to Katrina later that he was now a felon and had paid his fine. She thought about it for a while and then announced that she could think of innumerable items that she could fine him for and amass a fortune for herself.

"Like what, for instance?" James demanded to know.

"All sorts of sins of commission and omission," she accused him of.

"What?" he asked.

"Well, when you disagree with me, ten Kwacha, when you forget to kiss me goodbye, ten Kwacha, failing to listen, twenty Kwacha," she elaborated. "I should be rich by now!"

"*Suikerbossie*, all that I have is yours anyway, how can I pay you more?" he asked, laughing.

"It's no laughing matter," she said. "You owe me enough to be in debt and enslaved for life!"

"I am," he agreed. "What is your wish and desire, mistress?"

"Come with me tomorrow to Mkushi River?" she asked.

"Okay," he promised.

"And," she began.

"And what?" he asked.

"Come with me and start paying off the debt you owe me," she suggested.

"How?" he asked.

"By doing this," she whispered in his ear as she explained what she had in mind, then he picked her up and whisked her off to bed to pay his debts.

On the road to Mkushi River the next day, Katrina asked him how he had explained his absence to the rest of the staff. He told her that he had put it down to a visit with the District Officer and Colonel Mulanga. That comment turned out to be prophetic because they met the colonel at the Mkushi River diggings.

"Mr Martin, Mrs Martin, how nice to see you both," he started.

"Colonel," James greeted him.

"I'm sorry you were not able to camp at the Blue Lagoon this weekend," the colonel replied.

"Oh, you know that we went?" James asked.

"Yes, I had a report from the guard detail. They took the number of your Land Rover and reported it to Lusaka, and then it was fairly easy to match it to you, and then I was informed," he explained.

"I don't understand," James admitted. "I thought that Blue Lagoon was now a national park?"

"It is, but unfortunately, it is close to the air force base and Lusaka, you understand," the colonel commented. "I don't know that I hold with military activities in national parks, but apparently there are officers senior to me who do."

"Rather like army officers and government officials taking seats on commercial airline flights?" James suggested.

"Yes, unfortunately, without understanding that paying passengers come first, because even the government airline must buy fuel, parts and maintenance," the colonel agreed. "It will be a problem for us, my friend."

"What brings you here?" James asked.

"We have another camp close to here and I'm just passing," the colonel commented. James did not believe that for a minute. The colonel never seemed to do or say anything without a reason. Still, it was good to know that he had at least a talking relationship with the colonel and might get some help if ever he ran afoul of the army.

Katrina finished her business with the operation and came away confident that the deliveries she had promised would be met. She had continued to make sales to the toothpaste, paint and tyre factories and was hoping to sell some more clay to the pottery in Lusaka. She had recruited Rita to run some tests for her to see how the clay fired and was pleased with the results. The question was, would the pottery be pleased? They made general use pottery, not fine china, so the quality of the clay did not have to be perfect, but it did have to meet a minimum standard.

On Saturday, the Somali traders came. The lorry was not accompanied by its usual cloud of blue smoke, and the mine staff learned that a new engine had been acquired and installed since their last trip. Each camp member placed their next order, and the newer residents were introduced to the traders and their abilities to procure the unobtainable. The Somalis warned the mine that the ZIPRA people were becoming more active in the area east of Piccadilly Circus and that some shootings of Zambians had occurred when farmers innocently strayed across a firing line or into a training zone. The Somalis were well known to the ZIPRA people and provided them with much in the way of odd luxuries that the Zambian government would not provide. Where ZIPRA got its money from to pay for these items, they did not ask.

"Do you realise that it's almost been a year since we went on leave?" Katrina asked later that evening.

"I know," James replied. "It's amazing how fast time flies by, isn't it?"

"Such a lot has happened this last year," she added. "What did you enjoy the most?"

"That's a hard question," he admitted. "There have been so many things that have happened. It would be easier to say what I didn't like."

"*Ja*, like the shootings at the farms," she thought.

"I think that was the worst," he agreed. "Then the time you were stopped by those people. I was really afraid then."

"*Ja*, that was no fun. But I did enjoy my trip to the UK," she said.

"Really?" he asked.

"*Ja*, I know your mom was a pain, but I enjoyed visiting. I'm not sure I would want to live there, but I'd like to visit again," she confirmed.

"I think the trip to the Luangwa was one of my favourite things," he thought.

"Even though you stalled in the river and I had to pull you out?" she laughed.

"Even that," he agreed. "It was fun and I'd go again."

"What about the job?" she asked him.

"It's fun most of the time," he commented. "But, dealing with the politics of the office in Kitwe, I could do without."

"What about us?" she asked.

"Life with you is magical," he said. "I used to think I really loved you, but as time has gone on, I think I love you more, if that's possible. There's always something that comes up that makes me wonder why I should be so lucky."

"I knew the first time I saw you that you were the one," she commented. "There was a connection, or chemistry, that I couldn't resist. A lot of my friends told me I was crazy for going with a *rooinek*, but you're my *rooinek* now and I wouldn't trade you for anything."

The following week, James was kept busy with production issues in the pit and liberation issues in the mill. He quite enjoyed the technical challenges that the job had, but wished sometimes that there would be a little less paperwork. He supposed that it was a characteristic of large companies that they ran on reports and meetings, and neither was possible without paper. He had decided that, as John had predicted, a drop in copper prices in 1975 meant that the mine would likely then go on to care and maintenance or be shut down. So he might as well change his operating mode and start looking for the best grades of ore and high-grade the operation. Because of the nature of the orebody, that was easier said than done, but there were lenses that he decided he could leave until a later date, and overburden that need not be removed just yet. That would change the economics slowly and improve the overall situation. Of course, if John were completely wrong and the price stayed high throughout 1975 and beyond, then he, or his successor, would have the problem of high stripping ratios and low-grade ore lenses. Still, he would cross that bridge if and when it came to be.

Rita came to James on Thursday morning and asked for Friday and Saturday off. She was very mysterious about why, so James left it to a later date to get more information. He had his own regular review to attend, so was going to Kitwe himself, and Katrina went with him to visit her customers. They were unable to stay with the Watsons as they were away, so booked in at the Edinburgh. It was their first visit, and it was quickly disrupted when a large delegation of government officials arrived and co-opted the top three floors of the hotel. James was treated to the sight of an irate British couple and an equally irate German berating the front desk manager about the disruption. They wanted to know why they had been turfed out of the Edinburgh and what the desk manager planned to do about finding them alternate lodgings. James was amused but also sympathetic. In the countries those guests came from, this kind of thing simply did not happen, but in Zambia, anything was possible.

James and Katrina quickly went to the Nkana Hotel. While not quite the Edinburgh and certainly not the standard of the Ridgeway or the InterContinental in Lusaka, it was better than the street. They were fortunate to get a room there as there was soon a line of others that had been displaced from the Edinburgh, including the British couple and the German, all still bemoaning their fate and promising to write to their ambassadors and their favourite newspaper editors about the treatment of tourists.

James reported to the office the next day to deliver his usual report. The schedule, however, was changed when Colin Beauchamp came in with George McIntosh and all the general and underground managers from the mines in the group. James remembered Beauchamp from before and knew that he represented the interests of head office in London. His own regular meeting was delayed until later that day, and instead, Beauchamp started to talk about the company's performance as a whole. It seemed that all was not well with the world, and they were looking for better returns from all the operating units. As copper prices were high, there was an expectation that the Zambian company would deliver better earnings than it had been doing. So, the message was, improve. Some less-than-bright sparks actually asked if he meant high-grade the mines. They were told to cut operating expenses but not to jeopardise the future of the mine, and James suspected that they would get a dressing down from McIntosh or their own general managers later.

James had never before thought in terms of the company as part of a traded company on the Stock Exchange, but that was where the pressure was coming from. The stock traders were selling off the company because the performance was not as high as had been expected, and the management in London wanted that to stop. James reasoned that their current cushy numbers might actually be at risk, so they were beginning to panic. He wondered if John Wells's father had sold any of his holdings, but decided after a little reflection that that was unlikely, or John would have given him some warning before this meeting.

The managers were also told that all capital spending that was not going to return in less than a year was to be stopped, unless it was to correct an unsafe condition that could not be corrected in any other way. In which case, the justification had to go to London with a complete explanation of why it had become an issue in the first place. That sounded to James very much like a do not do it instruction, but with enough wiggle room that if anything went wrong, they could always blame the local manager and deflect blame from the head office. Of all the operations, he was possibly in the best position. All his capital spending had been done either in the previous year or earlier that year, and his production economics were improving by the month. His guess was that attention would be focused on the major underground operations, and he would be unlikely to see a *Bwana Mkubwa* for a while. Well, that was fine with him!

His afternoon review confirmed his guesses. McIntosh was not present. He was still in meetings with Beauchamp. The rest were really not that interested, except for Winter, who had taken a strong personal interest in the project and who had on more than one occasion stuck his neck out in support of the project. James, for his part, was delivering concentrate at an increasing rate, and overall expenses per tonne were edging down, whereas other operations had ever-increasing costs and declining yields. He was told to keep up the good work.

James left the office and found Katrina waiting for him in the car park. She had concluded her business and was now anxious to go home. James had to explain what had taken so long, most of which she had guessed. After he had not put in an appearance at lunch time, she had inquired of the secretaries what the delay was and had learned that things had been changed around to accommodate the pep talks from Beauchamp. She had been a little concerned at first that it was a closure notice for the Mtuga project, but had learned that it was, in fact, a plea for higher production all around.

As they were leaving the main offices, they saw McIntosh in company with Beauchamp walking towards some cars parked nearby. James waved, and he was beckoned over by McIntosh.
"Colin, I don't know if you remember James Martin, he's the one running the Mtuga open pit?" McIntosh said by way of introduction.
"Ah, yes, I remember," Beauchamp confirmed. "You're the one who came asking for all the extra money to complete the project, aren't you?"
"Yes, that's me," James confessed. "But things are going well now."

"So I understand," Beauchamp said. "That's the project that's just off the Great North Road, isn't it?"

"It is indeed," James confirmed.

"I suppose you're on your way back there now?" Beauchamp asked.

"Yes, we are," James replied.

"Well, say hello to John Wells for me, will you?" Beauchamp requested.

"I'd be happy to," James agreed.

"I have a plane to catch, so must dash, but good to see you and keep up the good work," Beauchamp finished.

On the drive home, Katrina told James about her visits and the orders for clays, sands, feldspars and other minerals she had received. For the moment, at least, the economy was doing well, and it was not only the major copper mining companies that were faring well, it was all the support businesses and industries.

It was almost dark when they turned onto the Great North Road at Kapiri Mposhi, and almost immediately they were held up by a convoy of Chinese trucks. It seemed that the lead truck had broken down and they were now trying to either restart it or organise a tow for it to return to their camp near Serenje. It was not possible to go around the convoy because they had trucks in both lanes, and the shoulders were deeply rutted from trucks that had obviously been parked there overnight. The Chinese finally got back underway and cleared the road, allowing James and Katrina to complete their journey home.

On Saturday morning, James gave his staff a quick version of the meetings held in Kitwe and answered the questions that he could. After the meeting, John Wells stayed behind and gave his view of the situation. It was as well that the others had left because he repeated his prediction to James that the market would change by 1975, so they had just over a year to produce as much as they could. Well, a market change in copper price was a bridge that James would cross when the time came, for the moment, there was a mine to run and concentrate to produce!

Monday morning, Rita explained where she had been the previous Friday. She had been at the *Boma* in Kitwe getting married. She and Attie had decided that they did not want a big ceremony, and they had sent telegrams to their respective sets of parents announcing the *fait accompli*. James asked the obvious question: was Attie coming to the mine to live, or was she going to try and commute or what? She told them that Attie would be moving to the mine and that he would be travelling to his assignments as and where they arose. His current project was some work for Zambia Railways near Kapiri Mposhi, so he could actually commute from Mtuga each day. Rita joked about the question the District Officer had asked Attie: how much *lobola* did he pay for her? Attie apparently had made a number up, and the District Officer had been impressed. She then commented that Zambia must still be using up its old paper stock because her marriage certificate was a Northern Rhodesian certificate with Northern Rhodesia blacked out and Republic of Zambia stamped over the top. She was concerned because, although she was a British citizen, she doubted that Attie could get citizenship through her. Her fear was that the rules applied to wives but not husbands. It was something she was going to check, and she wanted the following Friday off so that she and Attie could go to Lusaka and see the High Commission. She had no plans to return to England in the near future, but she liked the idea of being prepared for whatever eventuality might arise.

The following morning, James had time to reflect in his office and wondered what the coming year might hold for them all. Production was going well, and he was likely to be left alone for a while, which was really good news. He hoped that there would be no more incidents with ZIPRA, but still would have liked more official confirmation of their responsibility for the deaths in the area. It was unsettling to have a government that put politics above the safety and well-being of the local farmers. He did wonder where he might be when his contract expired and whether or not he would renew it. But that was for the future; the present was exciting enough in their mine just off the Great North Road.

Glossary

Note: ChiKabanga was the adapted language used on the mines in Zambia. It is a very contextual language: words will have varying meanings depending on the context in which they are used. ChiKabanga was derived from Fanagalo, the language developed in the South African mines. Many words in ChiKabanga remain the same as those in Fanagalo. Other words used are from various origins, including Afrikaans, Zulu and Bemba. Many of the words listed below are slang derogatory terms and would be better not used. However, in the period of this work, they were used commonly.

Aikôna	Afrikaans	no
Azi	ChiKabanga	will, know
Babelas	Afrikaans	hangover
Baie	Afrikaans	very
Bakkie	Afrikaans	light delivery vehicle, bowl
Bamba	Zulu	take, fetch, bring
Bichana	ChiKabanga	little
Bobbejane	Afrikaans	baboons
Boma	Swahili	enclosure, administrative centre
Braai	Afrikaans	grill, barbecue
Bundu	ChiKabanga	bush
Bwana	Swahili	boss
Chitenge	Bemba	thatched umbrella-like structure
Dambo	Ci-Cewa	semi-arid water hole
Dankie	Afrikaans	thank you
Donsa	ChiKabanga	tow
Drolletjies	Afrikaans	droppings
Faka	Zulu	put in
Feeks	Afrikaans	vixen, shrew, virago
Gemors	Afrikaans	mess
Goed	Afrikaans	good
Goolies	English	large boulder left from poor blasting
Hamba	Zulu	go
Howzit	South African	greeting: contraction of "How is it?"
Inindaba	ChiKabanga	why
Kaia	ChiKabanga	house (Shangaan: kaya)
Kaffir	Arabic	unbeliever
Kaffir	South African	derogatory term for African Bantu

Kanjani	Zulu	how, how are you
Katundu	Bemba	luggage, equipment
Kêrel	Afrikaans	chap, fellow
Kona	ChiKabanga	there, have (Zulu: khona)
Koud	Afrikaans	cold
Kudala	Zulu	long time
Lekker	Afrikaans	sweet
Lightie	English	diminutive term for child
Lobola	Bemba	bride price
Maak	Afrikaans	make
Madala	ChiKabanga	old man
Magwakwa	ChiKabanga	road
Maningi	ChiKabanga	much, many
Manje	Zulu	now
Manzi	Zulu	water
Mealie	English	Maize
Meisie	Afrikaans	girl
Meneer	Afrikaans	Mr
Mevrou	Afrikaans	Mrs
Mfazi	ChiKabanga	Wife, woman
Mkubwa	Swahili	big, important
Mkulu	ChiKabanga	big, important
Moenie	Afrikaans	do not
Mugodi	ChiKabanga	mine
Mushle	ChiKabanga	good, well
Muti	ChiKabanga	medicine (Bemba: úmúti, tree)
Muzungu	Swahili	white man
Oom	Afrikaans	uncle, Mr
Oppas	Afrikaans	careful
Ou	Afrikaans	chap, fellow
Oukie	Afrikaans	diminutive form of ou, ouk
Ouma	Afrikaans	grandmother
Reg	Afrikaans	right
Regtig	Afrikaans	real, true
Skati	ChiKabanga	time, occasion
Skopu	ChiKabanga	head
Slim	Afrikaans	crafty, sly, cunning
Soek	Afrikaans	look for
South West	English	outdated term for Namibia
Sterek	ChiKabanga	very (also heard as stelek)

Stoep	Afrikaans	porch
Suikerbossie	Afrikaans	diminutive of suikerbos, sugarbush
Tailings	English	concentrator waste discharge
Teef	Afrikaans	bitch
Tekkies	Afrikaans	Anglicised to takkies, sneakers
Tina	ChiKabanga	we
Tot siens	Afrikaans	goodbye
Umfazi	Zulu	wife, woman
Verkrampte	Afrikaans	unenlightened
Wanker	English	slang, one who masturbates
Wena	Zulu	you
Zonke	Zulu	all, all of them

References:
1. Nuwe Praktiese Woordeboek: H. J. Terblanche, Afrikaanse Pers-Boekhandel, Johannesburg, 1966.
2. Bemba Pocket Dictionary: Rev. E. Hoch W.F., The Society of the Missionary for Africa (White Fathers), Ndola, 1960.
3. Fanagalo: J. D. Bold, J. L. van Schaik, Pretoria, 1995.
4. Scholars Zulu Dictionary: G. R. Dent & C. L. S. Nyembezi, Shuter & Shooter, Pietermaritzburg, 1993.

Equipment & Mining Companies

<u>Equipment Companies</u>

1. Atlas Copco – founded in 1905, acquired the Ingersoll-Rand drill business in 2004.
2. Belaz – Belarussian Autoworks, founded in 1948 in Minsk, manufacturer of off-highway trucks.
3. Bucyrus-Erie – founded in 1880 in Bucyrus, Ohio and through a series of acquisitions and mergers became a major force in the mining and construction machinery businesses. The Company is now doing business as Bucyrus International.
4. Caterpillar – founded in 1890 by Benjamin Holt and Daniel Best, now a worldwide corporation dealing in earthmoving machinery.
5. Euclid – originally operating as Euclid Crane & Hoist, started to build off-highway trucks in 1934. Acquired by General Motors in 1953, subsequently sold to White Motor in 1968, Volvo Construction Machinery in 1985 and Hitachi Corporation in 1998.
6. Gardner-Denver – founded in 1829 by Robert Gardner, merged with Denver Drill in 1927, acquired by Cooper Industries in 1979 and divested by Cooper in 1994. The blast hole drill business was sold to P&H in 1991.
7. GAZ – Gorkovsky Avtomobilny Zavod (Gorky Automobile Plant), founded in 1929 as a joint venture between the Ford Motor Company and the Soviet Union.
8. Hausherr – HAUSHERR System – Bohrtechnik GmbH & Co. A German company specializing in drills.
9. Holman – founded in 1801 and merged with Broomwade in 1968 to form CompAir.
10. Ingersoll-Rand – founded in 1871 as the Ingersoll Company, merged with Rand Drill Co in 1905, sold the drill division to Atlas Copco in 2004.
11. P&H – Pauling & Harnischfeger founded in 1884 and in the latter part of the 1990s acquired Page Engineering, the Gardner-Denver blast hole drill line and Joy Mining. Now doing business as Harnischfeger Industries Inc.
12. Ruston-Bucyrus – the English subsidiary of Bucyrus-Erie.
13. Terex – founded as a division of General Motors (GM) in 1953, sold to IBH Holdings in 1980, reverted to GM in 1983 and sold to

Northwest Engineering in 1986 with a name change back to Terex in 1988.

Mining Companies

1. Bwana Mkubwa – an open pit operation of NCCM, mined variously underground and from the surface between 1903 and present.
2. Chambishi Mine – an open pit operation of RST, mined from 1961 to 1987.
3. Chingola Division – a division of NCCM. Chingola operated an underground mine and the Nchanga, River Lode, Upper, Chingola, Mimbula and Fitula open pits mined from 1955 until present.
4. Kalengwa – an open pit operation of RST, mined from 1969 to 1977.
5. Kansanshi – an open pit operation of NCCM mined variously and intermittently underground and from the surface between 1906 and present.
6. Maamba Collieries – incorporated as a limited company in 1971 under the ownership of the Zambian Government through the Zambian Industrial and Mining Corporation (ZIMCO).
7. Mkushi Copper Mines – partner with Miniera di Fragne Chialamberto in the Munshimwemba open pit operation. The mine was operated in the 1920s by Goldfields Rhodesia and the in 1950s by Falcon Mines and from 1968 to 1975 by Mkushi Copper Mines.
8. Nchanga Consolidated Copper Mines (NCCM) – originally the operating company for the Chingola mines, later the holding company for all the operations of the Anglo American Company in Zambia in partnership with the Zambian Government.
9. Roan Selection Trust Ltd (RST) – the holding company for the Selection Trust and AMAX operations in Zambia in partnership with the Zambian Government.
10. Rokana Division – a division of NCCM. Rokana operated an underground mine and open pits at Mindola and Area "E" from 1965 to 1984.

Select Bibliography

1. Alexander, Jocelyn, McGregor, JoAnn, 2004, *War Stories: Guerrilla Narratives of Zimbabwe's Liberation War*, History Workshop Journal
2. Anon, 1965, *The Leviathans*, The Zambian Review, January 1965
3. Anon, 1966, *Great North Road*, Horizon magazine
4. Anon, 2000, *Zambia: Investment Opportunities in the Mining Industry*, Ministry of Mines and Mineral Development, Republic of Zambia
5. Anon, 2003, *Placing of up to 24,330,733 New Ordinary Shares at 6p per Share: Admission to trading on the Alternative Investment Market*, African Eagle Resources, PLC
6. Anon, *Grapevines: Climate, soils and cultivation*, www.prospectwines.com
7. Anon, June 1963, *Excavation begins at Chambishi*, Horizon, The Magazine of the Selection Trust Group of Companies
8. Bailey, Martin, 1976, *Freedom Railway: China and the Tanzania – Zambia Link*, Rex Collins
9. Bancroft, J. A., 1961, *Mining in Northern Rhodesia*, The British South Africa Company
10. Beckett, Ian F. W., 1979, *The Rhodesian Army: Counter-Insurgency, 1972 – 1979*
11. Berger, Elena L., 1974, *Labour, Race and Colonial Rule: The Copperbelt from 1924 to Independence*, Clarendon Press
12. Broughton-Edge, A. B., Laby, T. H., 1931, *Principles and Practice of Geophysical Prospecting*, Cambridge University Press
13. Carr, Norman, 1962, *Return to the wild*, Collins
14. Caterpillar Tractor Company, 1972, *Caterpillar Performance Handbook*
15. Charlton, Michael, 1990, *The Last Colony in Africa*, Basil Blackwell,
16. Cole, Barbara, 1984, *The Elite: The story of the Rhodesian Special Air Service*, Three Knights
17. Cunningham, Simon, 1981, *The Copper Industry in Zambia: Foreign Mining Companies in a Developing Country*, Praeger Publishing
18. Daly, Lt. Col. Ron Reid with Peter Stiff, 1982, *Selous Scouts: Top Secret War*, Galago
19. De Waele 2004, *The Proterozoic geological history of the Irumide Belt, Zambia*, PhD Thesis, Curtin University of Technology
20. Financial Times Correspondents, 28 February 2006, *China Winning Resources and Loyalties in Africa*, The Financial Times

21. Francis, Samuel T., 1979, *The Front Line States: The Realities in Southern Africa*, The Heritage Foundation
22. Fuller, Alexandra, 2001, *Don't Let's Go to the Dogs Tonight*, Random House
23. Hall, Richard & Hugh Peyman, 1976, *The Great Uhuru Railway: China's Showpiece in Africa*, Victor Gollancz
24. Johnson, R. W., 2001, *How Mugabe Came to Power*, London Review of Books, Vol. 23 No. 4 dated 22 February 2001.
25. Jordan, E. Knowles, 1961, *Old Mkushi in 1912*, Northern Rhodesian Journal, Vol iv, No. 5
26. Lohman, Major Charles, USMC, MacPherson, Major Robert I., USMC, 1983, *Rhodesia: Tactical Victory, Strategic Defeat*, Marine Corps Command and Staff College
27. Maczka L., Cap. M., 1972, *The Mkushi River Clays*, Geological Survey Department, Ministry of Mines and Mining Development, Republic of Zambia
28. Martin, David, 1972, *As the Tension Mount: an interview with Zambian Prime Minister, Kenneth Kaunda*, New Internationalist
29. McIntyre, Chris, 2004, *Zambia: The Bradt Travel Guide*, Bradt Travel Guides
30. Miller, Denis, 1978, *Rebel People*, Africana Publishing
31. Monson, Jamie, 2007, *Freedom Railway to Ordinary Railway*, Heinemann
32. Mulenga, Maidstone, *Simon Mwansa Kapwepwe*, Famous Zambians.
33. Palmer, Robin, 1977, *Land & Racial Domination in Rhodesia*, University of California Press
34. Pearce, Edward Holroyd, 1972, *Rhodesia; Report of the Commission on Rhodesian Opinion under the chairmanship of the right honourable Lord Pearce*, Institute of Commonwealth Studies
35. Perrings, Charles, 1980, *A Moment in the 'proletarianization' of the new middle class: Race, value and the division of labour in the Copperbelt, 1946-1966*, Journal of Southern African Studies, Vol. 6, No. 2 (Apr. 1980).
36. Prain, Ronald, 1975, *Copper: The Anatomy of an Industry*, Mining Journal Books
37. Reader's Digest, 1988, *Reader's Digest Illustrated History of South Africa*, Readers Digest
38. Reader's Digest, 1990, *Reader's Digest Illustrated Guide to the Game Parks & Nature Reserves of Southern Africa*, Reader's Digest

278

39. Roan Consolidated Mines, 1978, *Zambia's Mining Industry: The first 50 years*

40. Roberts, A. D., 1982, *Notes towards a Financial History of Copper Mining in Northern Rhodesia*, Canadian Journal of African Studies, Vol. 16, No. 2 (1982).

41. Schreiner, Olive, 1983, *The Story of an African Farm*, Penguin Classics (First published in 1883 under the pseudonym Ralph Iron).

42. Sibeko, Archie (Zola Zembe) with Joyce Lesson, 1996, *Freedom in our Lifetime*, Indicator Press, University of Natal

43. Skinner, Walter R., 1972, *Mining Year Book: 1972*, Mining Year Book Limited

44. Smith, Pauline, 1990, *The Little Karoo*, St. Martin's Press

45. Strack, Don, 1984, *Railroads of Central and Southern Africa*, Historical Geography of the Railroads of Central Africa, Geography 591, University of Utah

46. Tabor, Georgem 2003, *The Cape to Cairo Railway & River Routes*, Genta Publications

47. van Lingen, A, 1960, *A Century of Transport 1860 – 1960*, Da Gama Publications

48. Varian, H. F., 1953, *Some African Milestones*, George Ronald

49. Walker, Clive, 1981, *Signs of the Wild*, Natural History Publications

50. Wilkinson, Anthony R., *Insurgency in Rhodesia 1957-1973*, The International Institute for Strategic Studies, Adelphi Paper no. 100

51. Zimmermann, Karl R., 1979, *Paradise Regained: A South African Steam Diary*, Delford Press

www.ingramcontent.com/pod-product-compliance
Lightning Source LLC
Chambersburg PA
CBHW070318260626
47160CB00003B/877